DAMAGED GOODS

STEPHEN SOLOMITA

SCRIBNER

NEW YORK   LONDON   TORONTO   SYDNEY   TOKYO   SINGAPORE

SCRIBNER
1230 Avenue of the Americas
New York, NY 10020

SCRIBNER and design are trademarks of Simon & Schuster Inc.

Manufactured in the United States of America
1 3 5 7 9 10 8 6 4 2

Library of Congress Cataloging-in-Publication Data
Solomita, Stephen.
Damaged goods / Stephen Solomita
p.   cm.
1. Moodrow, Stanley (Fictitious character)—Fiction. 2. Police—
New York (N.Y.)—Fiction. I. Title.
PS3569.0587D36 1996
813'.54—dc20   95-33277
CIP
ISBN 0-684-81584-2

For Wally and Tina,
who will never grow old

This is a work of fiction, despite well-documented examples of witness-protected psychopaths violating the civil rights of unsuspecting neighbors. For instance, the address 671 East Tenth Street is not between Second and Third Avenues. It is actually in the East River. A word to the wiseguy.

DAMAGED GOODS

PART ONE

ONE

Gildo (Jilly) Sappone wanted to see himself. That's all. Just to look into a mirror on his day of liberation. He wasn't asking for the moon. Wasn't demanding a comb, a brush, or even a throwaway razor. He knew why the screws wouldn't give him anything he could make into a weapon. That was natural; if he was in their place, it was exactly what he'd do. But the mirror wasn't even glass; it was metal, and it was cemented to a recess in the wall, and you couldn't get at it, nobody ever had. So why take it away?

Jilly ran his fingers through his beard, let his eyes take inventory. A steel bunk, a steel sink, a steel toilet; no desk, no books, no commissary. He had to brush his teeth with cold water, comb his hair with his fingers; he hadn't made a phone call in months, or received a letter, or spoken to anyone but Deputy Warden James Cooney. And you couldn't really call the dep's visit a conversation.

Cooney had opened the slot in the door, announced the parole board's reversal of its decision to keep Jilly Sappone in prison, added, "If it was up to me, you piece of shit, I would'a voted to put your ass up against a wall and shoot you. I would'a done it for the good of society. Now, I gotta let you go, but I'm telling you this, Sappone, give me any excuse, I'm gonna have an extraction team beat you into the hospital. That'll give me a couple extra weeks to change the board's mind."

Jilly, struck dumb by the unexpected news, hadn't registered the threat until after Cooney left. Which was just as well, because Jilly

Sappone didn't take to threats; threats usually made him go off right then and there. And he wasn't afraid of a beating, either. That was why the system had finally shipped him off to Southport, New York's only maxi-maxi prison. The COs had used fists in Attica, batons in Greenhaven, ax handles in Clinton; they'd locked him away in the hole for months at a time, but whenever he came out, somebody said something or did something or just looked at him out of the corner of an eye and . . .

But not this time. Cooney had turned on his heel and marched off down the catwalk; Jilly had paced (four steps to the rear, four steps to the front) the length of his cell while pondering the meaning of the dep's visit. Thinking that maybe it was a joke. Thinking Southport was created for cons who couldn't be controlled anywhere else in the system. If the New York State Department of Corrections had transferred Jilly Sappone's miserable ass to a prison where they locked you in a cell for twenty-three hours a day, then systematically had withdrawn every privilege, including his blanket and mattress, there was no legit way the board could've voted to cut him loose.

No *legit* way.

The obvious answer was that Carmine Stettecase, who maybe had the juice, had somehow been persuaded to reach into the system, pluck him out. But that didn't make sense because Carmine had dumped Jilly Sappone years before he got sent up. Never mind the fact that Carmine's son was married to Aunt Josie's daughter, Mary. Or that Aunt Josie had raised Jilly Sappone after his father got whacked. Blood didn't mean shit to Carmine Stettecase.

Twenty years later, Jilly could still remember Carmine's dismissal speech, word for word.

"What you are, Jilly, is a bug." Delivering it deadpan, voice as calm as the lead in a bullet before you pull the trigger. "Maybe it ain't ya fault—I wouldn't know about that—but a bug is what you are. I can't send you out for coffee without ya goin' off on the jerk behind the counter. Tell me, do I look like the fuckin' janitor? Huh? You think I oughta be pushin' a broom?"

Carmine had paused there, expecting an answer, but Jilly kept his eyes on the floor, figuring if he opened his mouth anything might come out. Knowing what would happen to him if he disrespected Carmine Stettecase.

"So, why the fuck," Carmine had finally asked, "am I spendin' all my time cleanin' up ya goddamned messes? If I'm not a janitor?" Another pause, this one a lot shorter. "I don't care what ya do with ya life, Jilly, but don't do it on my turf. Ya fuck around down here, I'm gonna kill ya."

Which, in a way, was exactly what he eventually did.

Jilly let his head and shoulders settle against the cool steel of his bunk. "Carmine," he said out loud, "if you could only see me now."

The joke was that he'd gotten worse, that he was barely in control from moment to moment, that his one hour a day out of the cell was an adventure for all concerned. The joke was that Jilly Sappone wasn't going to make it on the outside and he knew it. He'd be lucky to last a month.

The doc had said it straight out. Doctor Bannerman. The bullet (not even a bullet, just a little piece of lead, a dozen milligrams at most) as it punched its way through his temple and down into the back of his brain, had left a trail of scar tissue behind. It had all happened a long, long time ago, but the memory lingered on.

"Think of it," the doctor, standing on the far side of an inch-thick plastic partition, had explained, "as if someone had punched a hole in a pressure cooker. When the pressure builds up . . ."

He did think of it, of course. Had been seeing it in his dreams for more than thirty years. The shards of bloody glass sparkling in his lap, on his shoulders, in his hair. Daddy's brains on the windshield, pink and wet. It wasn't something you could forget about.

But it didn't mean that he heard voices; it didn't mean he saw monsters. No, the problem was that some little piece of bullshit a normal person would just find annoying set off bolts of lightning in Jilly Sappone's mind. Shitstorm was the word he used to describe it to himself.

"It's better if it ain't Carmine," he told the ceiling over his bunk. "Because, if it was Carmine, I couldn't do what I gotta do." He sat up on the bunk, shook his head, tapped his foot on the floor. "Aunt Josie," he finally said. "You really gone and done it now."

Because Josie Rizzo was the only person in the world who gave two shits about Jilly Sappone and Josie Rizzo *didn't* have the juice.

No, if Josie Rizzo wanted her nephew out of jail, she'd have to make a deal. She'd have to trade something for her Jilly's freedom and Josie Rizzo only had one thing to trade.

Jackson-Davis Wescott searched his face in the vanity mirror of Carlo Sappone's 1984 Buick Regal as if trying to remember something. As if his features (if he could only assemble them, make a single image out of the puzzle) would reveal some obvious truth he'd once known, but had long forgotten. Though he'd never told anyone (not Aunt Josie and definitely not Jilly Sappone), he did this whenever he was alone. If there was no mirror handy, he'd find a chunk of chrome, a darkened window, a polished tabletop.

On this particular occasion, the day of Jilly Sappone's liberation, Jackson-Davis raised the forefinger of his right hand and touched the individual parts of his face as if taking inventory. Assuring himself that it (or, he) was all there. First, he ran his finger from left to right across his ultrafine platinum hair and said, as he usually did, "Damn near to an albino."

That was what his daddy had said whenever he'd taken young Jackson-Davis on his knee. His ole ma had called it "angel hair," which was what Jackson-Davis said when he didn't say "Damn near to an albino."

From the part in his hair, he let his finger drop along his right cheek, down to a soft, flat jaw, then up to lips so thin they looked more like raised scar tissue than a real mouth.

"Maybe the reason," he said, "the boy don't talk much is that he ain't got no mouth to speak with."

Jackson-Davis couldn't remember who'd first said that. Could've been his ole ma *or* his daddy. Or maybe even Reverend Lucas Barr down at the Gethsemane Pentecostal Church. Jackson's ole ma had been real keen for the Pentecostal message, had called on Reverend Luke for all kinds of advice.

"Don't rightly know what's the matter with the boy," she'd say. "Seems awful slow to me. Don't rightly know what to do."

Reverend Luke would rub Jackson's head, say, "Trust in the Lord, Martha. Trust in the Lord."

Then one day Jackson's daddy had caught Martha trusting in the Lord's messenger. Jackson-Davis had been with his daddy on that afternoon, had seen his mother try to run, seen her panties catch at her ankles, seen his daddy's boots come down on his old ma's back while Reverend Luke's white moon of a butt flew out the window.

It was the last anybody in Ocobla, Mississippi, ever saw of Reverend Luke. Jackson's daddy, on the other hand, became a local hero for killing his wife. That's the way Sheriff Powell saw it, the way Judge Buford Addison saw it, the way the jury saw it, the way the entire damn county saw it.

"Hell's bells," his father said whenever he was drunk (which was every Friday night and all through the weekend), "if I would'a had me a pistol, I would'a got that preacher sunabitch, too."

Jackson-Davis ran his finger over a tiny, insignificant nose, muttered, "Cute as a button," then touched each of the twenty-two freckles sprinkled below his soft, pale cheekbones. The count completed, he dropped his hand to the steering wheel and stared into his own eyes.

"The eyes are the windows of the soul."

He couldn't remember who said that. Not his daddy, that was for sure. And not his ole ma, either. Maybe Miss Carson, his first grade teacher. Jackson-Davis had stayed with Miss Carson for three years before it became obvious that he was too slow to learn. Three years was a long time and Miss Carson must have said a lot of things.

Jackson-Davis searched for his soul. Tried to find it in his dark blue eyes. He'd been told that his eyes were sad. "Hurt-like" was the way Betty Ann, his first and only girlfriend, had put it. And hurt-like was what he'd put on Betty Ann one sweltering August night when she said she didn't love him any more. Enough hurt-like to put her in the hospital for a month.

Not that Jackson-Davis had waited for the doctors to count Betty Ann's broken bones. Betty Ann Strothers had enough brothers, uncles, and cousins living around Ocobla to field both sides of a football team. And they *all* kept shotguns in the back windows of rusting Chevy pickup trucks.

"I might be slow," Jackson-Davis said to his reflection, "but I wasn't dumb enough to stick around."

He'd hitched a ride all the way to Augusta, Georgia, then stolen a car and headed north, just stopping long enough to commit the odd burglary in the odd little town. Somewhere along the line—somewhere in Maryland, if he remembered right—he'd come through a farmhouse window to find a woman napping on the sofa.

The hurt-like he'd put on her was a lot more satisfying than rolling around on a blanket with Betty Ann. In fact, it pleased him so much, he decided to repeat the experience four days later in the town of Cobleskill, New York. That mistake had cost Jackson-Davis fifteen years of his life, because the stupid woman had picked up a knife and he'd gone and killed her, and the cops had gotten him an hour later on the Interstate. He was never sure how they picked him out, but the bloodstains on his white T-shirt had left no room for a claim of mistaken identity.

"Ole Jilly, he saved me from a life of shame," Jackson-Davis said. "Without ole Jilly, them niggers down to Clinton would'a tore me a new asshole for sure. Reckon for a fact I owe Jilly a big one."

As Jackson-Davis turned his attention back to the windows of his soul, the steel gate at the entranceway to the Southport Correctional Facility slid off to one side and a tall, bearded figure stepped through. The man stopped for a moment, let his head swivel from side to side, then began to walk toward the parking lot.

Jackson-Davis didn't recognize the man at first. It'd been a few years, of course, and Jackson's memory wasn't all that good under the best of circumstances. Plus ole Jilly had a thick, bushy beard, which he'd never had in Clinton, and his hair—what he had left—stuck out in a curly brown halo that only called attention to the prison-gray skin on the top of his head.

"Move it over, Jackson," Jilly Sappone called through the open window. "We gotta get outta here before I go off."

Wescott slid over without a word, waited patiently while Jilly drove aimlessly through the New York countryside. For the better part of ten years, he'd survived by following Jilly Sappone's advice. Jilly had taught him how to make a shank, where to hide it, when to use it. In the course of his instruction, Jackson-Davis had learned patience; he'd learned that, being slow, it didn't pay to rush into things like he'd rushed into that woman's house when he knew she'd seen him through the window. No, what it paid to do was hold his tongue, try not to think until Jilly told him what was what.

"Jeez," Jilly finally said, "I almost lost it back there." He pulled the car off the road, slid the transmission into park. "The god-damned screw was suckin' a piece of hard candy. Slurp, slurp, slurp. Like a baby suckin' a tit. It got on my nerves, Jackson. But I'm better, now." He rolled down the window, breathed the spring air, stared at the forest across the road. How long had it been since he'd seen a tree? Three years? Four? In Southport, you never saw the sun. That was part of the punishment.

"Real pretty, ain't it, Jilly? Real homey like. Kinda reminds me of Ocobla." Jackson's thin lips moved apart to reveal a set of tiny, yellow teeth. "Nice weather for gittin' out."

Jilly grunted, turned back to face his partner. "You done what I told you, Jackson?"

Jackson-Davis took a few seconds to get the sequence right before he spoke. "Sure I did, Jilly. Went direct to Aunt Josie after I got out. Took the subway and, boy, that was weird. Never did see a train go under the ground like that. More people on that subway than *lived* in Ocobla."

"Get to the fuckin' point, Jackson."

Jackson-Davis listen to the rumble in Jilly's voice, heard it as thunder before a storm. Thunder before a shitstorm.

"Well, Aunt Josie was real good to me. Sent me off to Cousin Carlo on Long Island. Carlo was real good to me, too. Had me doin' deliveries and things. And he give me a little *house*, first place I ever had all to myself."

"This house in your name, Jackson?"

"Pardon?" Jackson-Davis stalled for time. He had no idea what Jilly meant by "in your name."

"Did you sign anything? When you got the house?"

"Uh-uh. Just moved in."

"That's real good, Jackson. You get me that address?"

"Address?"

"The bitch, the fuckin' bitch," Jilly roared. "What the fuck is the matter with you?"

Jackson-Davis felt his mind slide into a familiar whirl. Thoughts flew by like dry leaves in a twister. He usually handled this particular situation by striking out at the closest breathing object, but when the closest breathing object was Jilly Sappone . . .

"Awright, Jackson," Jilly continued. "Slow it down. My wife, Annunziata. If you recall, I told you to get her address before you came up. I admit that was a long time ago. Anybody could forget a thing they got told that long ago."

Jackson's face suddenly lightened. "Well I guess you just pegged me wrong, Jilly, because I sure did get your wife's address. Aunt Josie wrote down a whole bunch of addresses and give 'em to me. Guess I jus' forgot for a minute."

Jackson-Davis handed over a carefully folded sheet of paper, and Jilly read it slowly, trying to absorb the facts without going off. His wife, Annunziata, who now called herself Ann, had divorced him (which he knew), then remarried a Con Edison worker named Paul Kalkadonis (which he didn't know), and had a kid, Theresa-Marie, now four years old. Six months ago, Paul Kalkadonis had been electrocuted on East Twenty-Fifth Street when a thoroughly stoned coworker with a known history of drug abuse failed to throw a switch. Ann was now suing and, according to Aunt Josie, the only relevant legal question was exactly how many millions Ann Kalkadonis was going to get.

So you take care of her, Josie had concluded, *and the rest of them except for Carmine. Carmine's not for you.*

"I brung ya these here, Jilly. Aunt Josie said they might help."

Jilly Sappone looked down at the small, pink tablets in Jackson Wescott's palm and knew exactly what they were. Dilaudid was what the docs called them; pink dope is what they were called on the street. Jilly had never injected himself with heroin, because he was afraid of needles, but somewhere in early adolescence he'd learned that opiates relieved the pressure. Not that dope made him a nice guy. No, the shitstorm was always there, but when Jilly Sappone was stoned, he could sometimes decide when the winds would blow. Sometimes.

He took the Dilaudid, popped one in his mouth, dry-swallowed, put the rest in his pocket. Drugs being as common behind the walls as out on the street, Jilly had used whatever was available whenever he had the money throughout most of his prison years. That had ended when they transferred him over to Southport. Cons in Southport didn't mix with other cons and there was no such thing as a contact visit, so he'd learned to do without. Or, he'd *tried* to learn. What had actually happened was that he lost control almost every time they opened the door of his cell.

"What else, Jackson? What else ya bring me?"

Jackson-Davis popped the glove compartment, removed two pistols, a nine-millimeter automatic and a .38-caliber revolver, held them up for Jilly's inspection.

"See? I didn't forget a damn thing."

Jilly took the automatic, checked the slide and the clip, then stuck it in his belt. The weight of the nine-millimeter Colt felt good, as did the touch of cool metal against his skin.

"Ya did great, Jackson." Jilly rubbed the top of Jackson-Wescott's head for luck, then put the Buick in gear and pulled back onto the road. "Aunt Josie didn't give ya no money, did she?"

"Nossir. Aunt Josie said you was gonna ask. She said I should tell you to get your *own* damn money."

By the time Jilly Sappone pulled Carlo's Buick to the curb, some five hours later, he was, in his own judgment, ready for anything. He'd dropped another tab of Dilaudid somewhere east of Scranton, Pennsylvania, and the drug, as it washed gently through his body, had taken him all the way down. Down to the point where he could look at the other cars on the road and not feel like an alien. Fourteen years in a world where progress meant slopping a fresh coat of institutional green paint on cinder-block walls had left him without any real sense of time and place. Sure, he was down on the Lower East Side of Manhattan again. No doubt about it, he'd driven from Southport to Ludlow Street without hesitation, knowing exactly where he was going and what he intended to do when he got there. But that didn't mean that Jilly thought he was going home. No, home was where he'd be a month from now, when the pigs caught up with him. Home was the four walls of a prison cell, or the four sides of a coffin.

"Hey, Jackson. Wake up, boy."

Jackson-Davis came out of his nap ready to fight. That was because he was confused. He raised his fists, blinked twice, then recognized his prison partner's face. No shitstorm; Jilly's brown eyes were dead lumps of wet brown paint. That was enough to calm Jackson down, though it had zero effect on his state of confusion.

"This ain't home," he said. "I mean this ain't where Cousin Carlo put me. This ain't where I thought we were goin'."

"I know that, Jackson. We're just makin' a little stop to pick up some money. Plus, I gotta visit my wife, show the bitch how much I love her. You see that plumbing supply store across the street."

"Plumbing?"

"Yeah, as in pipes and faucets." Jilly looked at his partner, shook his head affectionately. He knew, from long experience, that Jackson-Davis had to be brought around slowly. If you took him through it one step at time, he'd do whatever he was told.

"Well, I don't see no pipes, Jilly. Them windows is so dirty, I can't see nothin' a'tall."

"How 'bout the *sign*, Jackson. Can't ya see the goddamned sign?"

Jackson-Davis turned his hurt-like eyes on Jilly Sappone. "And I 'spose you ain't heard that I cain't read. Like it's some damn mystery."

"If you can't read, how'd ya get a driver's license?"

"Hell's bells, Jilly, what kinda license? I started into drivin' my daddy's plow when I was nine years old. That's my license." He dropped his eyes to the floor, folded his arms across his chest. He would have pouted, but his lips were much too thin to bring it off.

Jilly reached out, squeezed Jackson's knee. "Hey, Jackson, I didn't mean nothin'. I knew ya couldn't read; I just forgot for a second." He paused, bit at his lower lip. "Things was pretty bad in Southport. I'm lucky I could remember my own name."

Jackson-Davis raised his eyes to meet Jilly Sappone's. "I heard about that, Jilly. Heard Southport was a real bad joint."

"Ya got that right, Jackson. When you're alone by yourself from morning to night, there's always somethin' gets to ya. For me it was the faucet in my cell. It leaked a little bit, ya know what I mean? Like drip, drip, drip. Only sometimes, instead'a drippin', the fuckin' thing boomed. Like giant footsteps bouncin' off the walls: boom, boom, boooooom." He put both hands on the steering wheel, pushed himself back against the seat, cocked his head to one side. "The thing about it, Jackson, was the screws wouldn't fix the drip. Like they fuckin' *knew* what it was doin' to me. Like it was part of the package. So I had'a find some way to keep the noise from gettin' inside of me and what I did was I thought about what I had to do if I got out. Ya followin' me so far?"

Jackson-Davis nodded solemnly. Jilly, he knew, loved to go on about things. Like Reverend Luke preachin' hellfire and damnation to his Ocobla flock. What Jackson Wescott had to do was what he'd done then, sitting beside his ole ma on a folding chair. He had to wait it out. Wait for ole Jilly to get to the point.

"Tell me something," Jilly finally said, "ya still go out lookin' for women?"

"No, I ain't. I ain't done nothin' like that." Jackson-Davis tried to look indignant, like he was insulted or something. But the truth was that except for one lousy month fifteen years ago, he'd never been out on his own. Yeah, maybe he did look at women on the street and think about what he done with Betty-Ann, but then he ran back to his house and waited for Jilly. Waited for Jilly Sappone to come out of jail and tell him what was what.

"Ya remember when I used to talk about plannin' what I was gonna do when I got out?" Jilly slid an arm across his partner's shoulder.

Jackson-Davis nodded solemnly.

"What I figured was that some of the people I used to run with owed me a little payback. Like I don't know how much time I got on the outside, but whatever it is, I'm gonna make it so nobody forgets me. You catchin' my drift?"

Jackson-Davis nodded again, stared up at Jilly Sappone's bushy beard, thought, Jilly sure does look like one of my ole ma's prophets. Cept for the hair. Ain't none of them prophets was bald. Maybe they was Pentecostal prophets; maybe you can't be no Pentecostal prophet unless you got hair on your head. Course, my daddy was bald. But my daddy didn't go for the Pentecostals. . . .

"Jackson?"

"Yeah, Jilly?"

"Are you with me?"

"Damn, Jilly, you know as well as me that I *gotta* be with you. Bein' as how you helped me out when I first come up to Clinton, I can't see as I have no choice. Fact is, all that's happenin' here is I'm waitin' on y'all to tell me what to do."

TWO

Jim Tilley stood beside the Roberto Clemente Boxing Gym's single ring and half watched his adopted son, Lee, shadowbox along the ropes. A part of him evaluated his son's quick hands and smooth, practiced footwork, deciding that, no doubt about it, Lee Tilley, at thirteen years old, had all the tools. The only question was whether or not he had real desire and that particular question wouldn't be answered for several years. That was when the street kids who were stepping into gyms all over New York for the first time would have enough experience to get into the ring with Lee Tilley. In the meantime, Lee was the king of the juniors, a 115-pound. YMCA badass, "Tilley the Terrible" in PAL tournaments.

There was no way to accelerate the process and truth be told, Jim Tilley (at least the piece of him that didn't daydream about his son winning a world title) hoped that Lee would fail the ultimate test of boxing fitness. That one night, while he was still an amateur and young enough to find something else, Lee Tilley would meet an opponent with equal skill, that the contest would be reduced to a battle of wills, to the pure ability to endure pain and keep coming. He hoped his son would lose.

In the meantime, Jim was free to indulge an earlier, more primitive passion—a long-term love affair with the gym itself. He could listen to the squeak of his son's shoes on resin-sprinkled canvas, smell the sharp, funky odor of sweat-soaked leather, submerge himself in the voices calling back and forth, in the gangsta-rap tones of the street, the raspy, half-bored instructions of thoroughly disillusioned trainers. In Tilley's mind, the gym was its own place, as exclusive as a country club. Millions of people watched boxing regularly—big fights drew worldwide audiences of a half billion—but very few of those viewers had ever stepped into a ring. Boxing wasn't tennis or basketball; you didn't run out to box after watching a fight the way you snatched up your racket and headed for the courts after the Wimbledon finals.

Tilley closed his eyes for a moment, let himself drift back to a time when he'd been dubbed the hottest prospect on the amateur scene, when he'd been courted by the sharks who swim in the waters of professional boxing. Those were his glory years, before an injury ended a long amateur and very short pro career, before he'd joined the cops, become a detective. It wasn't that he hated wallowing in the endless misery of New York City crime, just that sometimes he needed a quick vacation. He needed to inhale the odor of liniment, listen to the snap of a speed bag, watch the prospects and the opponents dance their peculiar dance.

"Hey, Pop. Better check this out."

"Huh?" Tilley opened his eyes to find his son leaning out over the ropes.

"Uncle Stanley, Pop. Somebody busted him up."

Tilley looked to his left, watched his old partner make his way across the gym. Moodrow looked pretty much the same, an enormous square body topped by an enormous, square skull, the skull dotted with tiny, expressionless features. Even the blood running along the back of his neck, from his scalp to his already soaked collar, seemed, given Moodrow's determined stride and composed expression, reasonably appropriate.

"What happened, Stanley," Tilley said, trying to suppress a smile. "You get mugged?"

"Ambushed is more like it." Moodrow looked around the gym. "You seen Doc Almeda?" Jose Almeda, though he'd never seen the inside of a medical school, was the gym's unofficial doctor. "Betty's leaving for Los Angeles tomorrow and I don't want her to see me like this."

"Yeah, Doc's around somewhere, maybe in the office." Tilley stepped forward as his partner turned away, examined the cut more closely. "You positive you don't wanna go to the emergency room, get it sewn up by a professional?"

"Almeda knows how to keep the scar tissue down. That's his job." Moodrow turned, began to walk away. "You wanna hear the story, Jim, you gotta keep up with me. Betty made a farewell dinner and I'm late already."

Resigned, Tilley trotted along behind, waited patiently until Moodrow was seated on the trainer's table, a lump of greasy coagulant stuck to the wound in his scalp.

"This was really stupid, Jim. I feel like a complete jerk."

"There's a first time for everything."

Moodrow looked at his ex-partner, wondered exactly how he was going to explain his bloody shirt and bandaged head to Betty. He did have faith in Doc Almeda's skills, had seen Almeda work dozens of times, but a big part of his reason for coming to the gym for help had to do with Jim Tilley. He wanted to run the story by his best friend, see how it played before taking it home.

"The thing about it was it happened too fast. I didn't . . ."

"Just the facts, Stanley. Save the excuses for later."

Moodrow flinched as Doc Almeda pressed a square of gauze soaked with antiseptic into the wound. The reaction was pure reflex, gone almost as soon as it appeared, though the pain continued.

"There's not all that much to tell. I was going into the liquor store, the one on Avenue B just off Fourteenth Street, to pick up a bottle of wine for dinner when this kid bumps into me. *Crashes* into me is more like it. A real punk, Jim, with a shaved head and four earrings in his nose, swastika tattoos on both arms.

"I think he expected me to fall down or something, because he looked surprised when he bounced off my chest. 'Hey, pops,' he says, 'why don't ya watch where the fuck ya goin'?'

"Jim, I should've stopped it right then and there, just backed off and forgotten about it. But what I actually did was slap him in the face. That's when his buddy sandbagged me from behind with a wire trash basket."

"Did you go out?" Tilley asked.

"Go out?"

"Out cold, Stanley. Unconscious."

Moodrow blinked as he tried to absorb Tilley's question. When he finally got it, he shook his head in contempt. "Are you crazy, Jim? I already told you these guys were punks." He stopped as if expecting a reply, then continued. "What I did was stuff the second prick *into* the trash can. It was a tight fit, which is why I'm so late."

"What happened to the first kid? The one with the earrings?"

"When I slapped him, he took off like a rabbit. Left his partner to face the heat alone. A real punk, Jim, and what bothers me is that two years ago, he would've been able to look at me and know enough to back off without gettin' his face slapped. And, me, I would've never let a jerk like that get under my skin. Hell, two years ago I would've seen them coming."

Tilley didn't say anything for a moment. Moodrow was a couple of weeks short of his sixtieth birthday, the mention of which had been entirely forbidden. As was the fact that, two months before, a prostate infection had put a catheterized Moodrow in the hospital for several days.

"Ya know, Stanley," he finally said, "you gotta stop being so hard on yourself. Last week I got sucker punched by a mutt as I went to put on the cuffs. The asshole turned and hit me before I could react. You know what I did? I beat the living shit out of him. You know what I didn't do? I didn't see it as the end of my youth, the loss of my manhood."

It was a complete lie and Tilley knew it. He'd gotten drunk after coming off duty, pissed and moaned to his wife, Rose, for days. It was a complete lie, but James Tilley couldn't think of anything better to say and the sight of Doc Almeda's needle sliding in and out of Moodrow's torn flesh was making him queasy. "Stanley," he asked, glad to change the subject, "don't you feel that?"

It was Jose Almeda who responded. "Jus' a pinch," he said. "An' after, you look beautiful again. Like a young girl." Almeda, short to begin with and shrunken further by a painfully curved spine, was standing on a milk crate. He continued to sew as he spoke. "You tole me you was a fighter, Jim, so you must'a been sewed up once or twice."

Tilley took a stick of gum from his shirt pocket, began to unwrap it. "I admit it looks a lot worse than it feels," he said. He popped the gum into his mouth, began to chew thoughtfully.

"*Mira*, Señor Stanley," Almeda said. "I think you are a crybaby. I would give my sight to jus' one time put a *pendejo* li' that in a garbage can."

Moodrow snorted. "I never said things couldn't get worse." What he didn't add was that they were *already* worse, but that given Jim Tilley's reception to his first story, he'd decided to save the second for Betty and dinner. "You almost finished, Doc?"

"I'm gonna bandage it now. Then you go home, take the penicillin I gave you, an' stay quiet. You gotta watch out you don't have a concussion."

"Don't make the bandage too thick, Doc. My girlfriend's gonna flip as it is."

Moodrow watched Lee Tilley, now wrapped in a terry-cloth robe, walk into the trainer's room. "Christ," he muttered, "this is gonna be worse than facing Betty."

For the better part of two years, he'd been lecturing the boy about fighting on the street. "Sure," he'd explained, "somebody starts up with you, it feels good to punch him out. I'm even willing to admit that, for the most part, it's easy, too. Only you can't live that way, Lee. Self-defense is one thing, but you can't solve your problems with violence. People who solve their problems with violence never get anywhere in life. It's like an anchor."

"Uncle Stanley, what happened?"

Moodrow glanced at Tilley, noted the smirk on his friend's face, knew he'd find no help from that quarter.

"Would you believe," he said, "I was attacked by the entire New York chapter of the Hell's Angels Motorcycle Club?"

THREE

"What I had to do was tell Lee the truth, Betty. Which is what I'd already told Jim. I swear, I felt like a complete schmuck." Moodrow was sitting at a small table in his Fourth Street apartment, toying with the remains of a thoroughly overcooked leg of lamb, a bowl of pearl onions in a muddy cream sauce, and a wrinkled baked potato the size of a boiled egg.

"How did he take it?" Betty, even as she asked the question, was trying to decide how *she* was taking it. She was scheduled to depart La Guardia Airport at ten the following morning, her destination Los Angeles and her cousin, Marilyn, badly injured in a freeway accident. What she needed, in her own estimation, was a farewell dinner with her lover of the last six years, quiet (or maybe not so quiet, depending on how many drinks they had before they got down to business) sex, and a decent night's sleep. Marilyn was her only living relative; the trip would be painful, perhaps devastating.

"He let me finish without saying anything," Moodrow responded. "Then he gave me a lecture, told me these weren't the 'good old days,' that everybody's got a gun and I was lucky to get slammed with a puny trash basket."

"Lee's a smart kid," Betty observed. "You could have been killed."

Moodrow began to clear the table. He and Betty had a firm rule: One cooked, the other did the dishes. As a result, they ate dinner out more often than not. "It wasn't like I planned it." The excuse sounded lame, even to him.

"How many bodies did you see in thirty-five years on the job? How many homicides because somebody had to be *macho?*"

"Dozens," Moodrow called over his shoulder. Having retreated to the sink, he began to scrape the remains of their dinner into the garbage pail. "Maybe hundreds. But that doesn't mean I'm gonna be afraid every time I step out of my apartment. I can't live that way."

"Why not, Stanley? I do. And so do several million other New Yorkers. What makes you special?"

Moodrow stacked the plates in the sink, turned on the hot water, then calmly walked to the table where Betty was standing. He retrieved the leg of the lamb, strode back to the sink, wrapped the meat in aluminum foil, and dropped the platter into the sink.

"Fear or no fear," he finally said, "the reason I reacted the way I did this afternoon was because of something that happened at ten o'clock in the morning. That's when Jean Ressler fired me."

Betty leaned back against the refrigerator. Her sharp black eyes bored into the bandages covering the shaved area of Moodrow's head. "You're telling me this came as a surprise? It's been three weeks with no hint of progress. How long did you expect her to fork over two hundred a day plus expenses?"

Moodrow shrugged. Four months ago, Jean Ressler's husband, Paul, had emptied the bank accounts, redeemed the certificates of deposit, looted the mutual funds, then taken off for parts unknown. Though Jean Ressler had no wish to see her husband again, she did want a piece of the roughly three hundred thousand he'd snatched. Moodrow had put in the hours, talked to friends, relatives, coworkers, waiters, bartenders, barbers. The results had been less than negligible.

"Getting fired was exactly what I expected," Moodrow admitted. "The surprise came two hours later when she called to say the new firm she hired, Landis Security, managed to find her old man in thirty minutes."

Betty, instead of yielding to impulse and putting her arms around Moodrow's waist (they wouldn't reach around his chest), simply asked, "How?"

"They did it with a computer." Moodrow turned to face his lover.

"According to Jean, they put his social security number into some program and a half hour later they had him. Seems he got tired of dragging a suitcase full of cash everywhere he went and opened a checking account at the Greater Bank of Birmingham. The bank ran his social security number through a credit agency and that's where the computer found it. Along with his address and telephone number. Now, Jean wants a refund."

"Are you going to give it to her?" Betty stepped up to the sink, took a wet dish from his hand, and put it in the drain basket. Then she began to unbutton his shirt.

"Never. Jean Ressler's an accountant. She makes more money in a week than I do in a month." He dried his hands on a towel, hung the towel on a hook, ran his fingers through his lover's hair. "May I ask what you're doing?"

"I want to lick your nipples." She pulled his shirt open, let her tongue wander through the mat of hair on his chest. "You can talk about this depressing crap later. After I finish using you and fall asleep."

Slowly, with extreme deliberation, she undressed him, following her progress with mouth and fingertips. After six years, she knew exactly what excited him. She also knew that Stanley Moodrow, when he was really hot, liked to draw the whole process out. To conserve his excitement like a miser hoarding a stack of shiny-bright Krugerrands.

They made love for the next forty minutes, worked their way from room to room, left a trail of clothing to mark their passage. Betty was on the bed, Moodrow kneeling on the floor beside her, when he finally hooked his fingers beneath the elastic band on her panties and began to slide them down. He caressed her exposed flesh with his lips and the tip of his tongue, didn't relent until she called for him, until she half dragged him onto the bed, until their bodies were locked.

Then he lay still for a moment, supporting his bulk with his knees and elbows, content to feel the impossible hot-wet sensation of her flesh surrounding his. He lay there until she began to move under him, drawing him deeper and deeper. He wanted her to reach out for her own orgasm, to snatch the prize like a thief reaching into a jewelry display case.

Betty, who'd been through this before, let her fingers trail over his ribs, her tongue trail over his throat; she waited until he began to tire, then reached beneath her right thigh, took his testicles in her hand, and squeezed hard enough to flip him onto his back.

The games were over, the foreplay done; they'd been with each other long enough to know it. Sweat dripped from Betty's breasts onto Moodrow's chest as she began to move faster, as Moodrow, eager now, rose up to meet her plunging hips. Eventually, their breathing joined as tightly as their bodies, they found a space without separation, when thought itself had drawn down to a small knot of sensation, and they exploded together.

For the next several minutes, neither spoke; they simply lay beside each other, hands clasped, and allowed the sweat coating their bodies to evaporate while they waited for the practical realities to force them into action. Betty moved first. She turned onto her side, ran the backs of her fingers over Moodrow's cheek, then headed off to the bathroom.

When Moodrow heard the water running in the shower, he leaned back and tried to relax. He was grateful for what they'd just done, happy that he'd been able to give her what the occasion demanded. Each of them knew this separation could last for weeks, even months. The cousins, Betty and Marilyn, had been very close as children, had actually lived together for a brief time. It didn't take a computer genius to conclude that Betty wouldn't return as long as Marilyn needed her.

Meanwhile, the intense, throbbing pain in the back of his skull kept reminding him that no matter how good the night, he'd had a very bad day. And the worst of it was that he could easily have done what Landis Security eventually did. There were several computer companies in New York that specialized in providing information to private detectives; he'd known about them, even had a rough idea of their capabilities. But he'd stuck to the paths he'd always walked, burnt that shoe leather, just like he'd been taught by the NYPD sergeant who'd broken him in. Forty years ago.

Maybe, he thought, I should stop taking cases from people who have money. People who disappear and then open bank accounts.

Bank accounts had never been a factor when the job had him chasing down Lower East Side mutts. The mutts didn't use credit cards, either. At least, not their *own* credit cards. Street criminals left trails of blood, not paper. You ran them down by grabbing their friends, relatives, and coconspirators. By getting information any way you could. By pleading, by trading, or by outright extortion.

Moodrow sat up, let his feet drop over the side of the bed, tried to ignore a sudden burst of pain. Computers are just machines, he told himself, and if I don't intend to retire, I have to get with the program. It probably won't be that hard, won't be like that VCR, which I still can't program. Or the clock on the microwave, which I still can't set.

But the problem, he knew, was more basic than his failure to adjust to household technology. He simple couldn't imagine his six-foot-six-inch frame sitting behind a desk in some adult-education course. Couldn't imagine himself, at age sixty, raising his hand to answer a question.

"Teacher, teacher, teacher."

He shoved himself erect, put on a light robe, and headed for the bathroom. The water in the shower had stopped running. Betty would be combing out her hair, dusting herself with powder, squeezing a line of toothpaste onto a worn, red brush. He stopped for a moment, his hand on the doorknob, and let himself think about how much he was going to miss her. They'd been together long enough to know each other's most obnoxious habits, yet neither—at least, he *hoped* neither—had become bored, much less turned off.

The door opened abruptly and Betty, wrapped in a towel, stood in front of him. He put his arms on her shoulders, looked into her eyes, wanted to tell her to come back soon, not to go at all. But there was no point to it, nothing to be gained. She had to go; it was what he'd do in her place. Besides, on some level he knew that he, with his last relative some fifteen years dead, was actually jealous.

"You get in trouble out there," he finally said, "you let me know. I'll be on the next plane."

Her broad mouth widened into an impish grin. "*You*, Stanley? In Tinseltown?"

"Hey." He put a finger to her lips. "The kid knows how to adjust. I'll just grab a pair of Day-Glo, spandex bicycle shorts and be on my way."

Moodrow was in the shower, trying to keep his bandaged head above the water, when Betty knocked on the door ten minutes later.

"You decent?" she called.

"Never!"

"Praise the Lord." She pushed the door open, stepped inside. "Leonora called."

Leonora Higgins, a former FBI agent who'd left the bureau to become an assistant district attorney in Manhattan, was an old friend of Moodrow's. Not that he was in the habit of associating with FBI agents. Like most career cops, Moodrow both disliked and distrusted the Bureau. But he and Leonora Higgins had once shared a great adventure, an adventure that'd ended with her shooting him.

"She been elected mayor yet?" It was a standing joke among the three of them. Leonora had political ambitions and wasn't afraid to admit it.

"She's coming over, Stanley."

"Now?" Moodrow stepped out of the shower, accepted a towel from Betty, began to dry himself. "I think we should spend the night by ourselves."

Betty, after checking to make sure the lid was down, sat on the edge of the toilet. She liked to watch her lover perform small, mundane tasks, to observe the daily rituals. Except for a few brief weeks, they'd never lived together, but at the same time, they were rarely apart for more than a day. Neither of them could have explained the why of it; neither cared to. Both had been through enough failures to accept whatever worked.

"Leonora has a job for you."

"A job that couldn't wait until tomorrow afternoon?"

"What could I say, Stanley? You know the drill. She was in the neighborhood, she has to be in court all day tomorrow, it won't take more than half an hour. I couldn't refuse to give her thirty minutes. Besides, you need the money."

"The money?" Moodrow snorted. "Betty, if this job isn't pro bono, I'll kiss your ass in Macy's showroom window at high noon on Christmas Eve."

Betty got up, checked her reflection in the mirror. "Damn, Stanley," she said as she turned back to him, "for that kind of thrill, I'll pay you myself."

FOUR

Any residual annoyance Moodrow might have been nursing vanished the minute he opened the door. Leonora Higgins was absolutely resplendent in a gold double-breasted jacket with jet-black panels on either side, a black skirt that fell to mid calf, and a scoop-necked silk blouse. Understated gold earrings complemented the amber beads worked into her long jheri curls, while a string of polished black stones—onyx, Moodrow guessed—gleamed quietly against her deep brown throat. If she hadn't been carrying a briefcase, Moodrow would have taken her for an uptown matron come to the slums in search of a cheap thrill.

"Very nice, Leonora," Moodrow said as she passed. "But you better dump the curls if you wanna be District Attorney. Unless you plan to campaign by scaring the ethnics. Which strategy would be a big mistake."

All three understood the comment. It was impossible to win borough-wide office in Manhattan with the support of a single block of voters. Black candidates needed white liberals and a decent piece of the Jewish vote; white candidates had to hold their own in line while appealing to conservative Latinos, to Cubans and South Americans.

"Doesn't matter," Leonora said. "Morgenthau's gonna run again." Robert Morgenthau was the Manhattan district attorney and would continue to be until he quit or died. "But I'm only forty. I can wait."

"Forty?" Betty stared at Leonora's unlined face and shook her head. "It doesn't seem possible."

"Is that a compliment?"

Betty, to their mutual surprise, took the question seriously. "It's more than the beauty, Leonora, though I admit I'd kill for those eyes. It's the energy, the optimism. I don't think I've ever seen you down."

Leonora eyed Betty speculatively. "Something's bothering you, Ms. Haluka. And, being a former FBI agent and an experienced trial lawyer, I think you want to tell me about it."

Moodrow spent the next twenty minutes pretending to watch the Yankees pound the crap out of their ancient enemies, the Boston Red Sox, while he listened to Betty unburden herself in the kitchen. There was nothing, Moodrow knew, Leonora could say to make it better. Betty had to go through it, accept the pain, and come out the other side. He'd done it often enough in his own life, most recently eight years before when Greta Bloom, who'd been his friend and mentor for almost fifty years, had taken nine months to die of a stroke.

For Betty, of course, the process was just beginning and Moodrow knew she was now more frightened than sorrowful, that she was still hoping for a miracle, hoping some steely-eyed surgeon with the hands of a concert pianist would put Marilyn back together.

"Mr. Moodrow?" Betty was standing in the doorway. Her eyes were moist, her mascara smeared. "The doctor will see you now."

Moodrow let her pass without saying a word. He waited until the door to their bedroom closed behind her, then entered the kitchen and sat down.

"I know I came at a bad time," Leonora began.

"This is true."

Leonora flashed a dazzling smile; a shake of her head rattled the beads worked into her braided hair. "Stanley, you're a prick."

"This is also true," Moodrow conceded. He spun on the chair, took a bottle of Wild Turkey from the cabinet behind him, poured three fingers of bourbon into a glass. "Actually, I gotta thank you. Betty needed to talk about her troubles and what I am, I guess, is good for other things."

"That's not true."

Moodrow waved her off. "For now, it's true." He sipped at his drink, let the smoky liquid sit in his mouth for a moment before swallowing. "I don't wanna be abrupt, Leonora, but as you can see, I got other things on my mind. So, as they say in the hood, whassup?"

"Maybe I ought to come back tomorrow. This is fairly complicated."

"Leonora, you wouldn't be sitting here if I was the one who picked up the phone. Meanwhile, Betty invited you, so I can't very well kick you out." He spun the glass on the table, looked down at his hands. "Maybe your timing wasn't so bad, after all. Right now, I'm lookin' for work."

"Don't jump to conclusions. You might change your mind before I'm finished." Higgins took a folder out of her briefcase, laid it on the table. "As you know, for the last several years I've been working as an unofficial liaison between the shelters for battered women and the Manhattan DA's office. I help get orders of protection, push the cops to look for the husbands, talk to sentencing judges. It's strictly voluntary, of course. I do it on my own time."

"For the brownie points?" Moodrow couldn't help interrupting.

"That's part of it," Higgins admitted, "but it's also something I believe in. Most of the women I see have been in abusive relationships for years. They really don't believe that law enforcement is on their side. Maybe that's because they all have stories about cops looking the other way." She paused for a moment to stare into Moodrow's eyes.

"There's two sides to that story," Moodrow responded evenly. "The other side starts with assaulted women who swear out complaints, then don't show up to testify. I've had women attack me when I went to arrest their husbands. Women beaten so bad they should be in a hospital coming off a couch to jump on my back. Most cops, male or female, become cynical after a while. Just like the victims."

Leonora put her briefcase on the floor. "I didn't come here to argue, Stanley. Let's say my job is to confront that cynicism, to encourage both sides."

"I'll drink to that." He raised his glass, drained it, waited a moment for the alcohol to wash through his body before continuing. "And I thank you for not asking what happened to my head."

"If you're referring to that bandage on the back of your skull, I was hoping you'd tell me on your own."

"No chance. I've been to confession three times in the last four hours and my sins, as they say, have been forgiven. Let's get down to business."

Higgins picked up the file, glanced at it briefly. "Two days ago, the Department of Corrections released a prisoner serving fifteen to life for murder. Seven or eight hours later, this prisoner turned up on the Lower East Side with a partner. They held up a plumbing supply store on Ludlow Street, then went to the apartment of the prisoner's ex-wife where they assaulted the wife, sexually and physically, then kidnapped the wife's four-year-old daughter. The wife is in Kings County Hospital. She's conscious and she wants her child back."

"Is that where I come in? You want me to find the kid?" Moodrow's head had finally stopped hurting.

"I don't think that's the question you want to ask."

"You're right." Moodrow read Leonora's expression as a mix of determination and curiosity, her gaze as the gaze of a born prosecutor. The political wanna-be had vanished. "The question I want to ask is real simple. Why *me*? Why not the cops? Why not your old buddies at the Federal Bureau of Incompetence?"

Leonora leaned over the table. "I came to you, Stanley, because, with one exception, you know all the parties. You know the wife, the child, and the perp. You know all their friends and all their associates."

"Spill it."

"The wife's name is Ann Kalkadonis, the daughter's name is Theresa-Marie, the ex-husband's name is . . ."

"Jilly Sappone." Moodrow noted Leonora's quick grin. Her large, even teeth reminded him of a closed trap. "How long was he in prison?"

"Fourteen years."

"I can't believe they let him out."

"That's part of the puzzle, Stanley, because the parole board turned him down last September, then reversed itself. He was paroled directly out of the Southport Correctional Facility."

"Southport? That's the maxi-maxi prison, right? The new one?"

"It is."

"I thought they only put you there if you were too crazy to be anywhere else."

"You thought right, Stanley. According to the Department of Corrections, Jilly Sappone committed more than a hundred acts of violence before they shipped him off to Southport."

Moodrow poured himself a second drink, took a moment to sift through his cop's memory, to let the bits and pieces rise to the surface. "Jilly Sappone, best case, leads to Carmine Stettecase through his aunt, Josephine Rizzo. Her daughter, Mary, is married to Carmine's son, Tommaso. Carmine is pretty big on the Lower East Side, but not big enough to fix the parole board. Maybe he reached up the ladder, called in some markers. But it still doesn't make sense, because . . ."

"Look, Stanley, whatever happened up in Southport is dead and done. It's irrelevant, because Jilly Sappone will never see the outside world again."

"Aren't you getting ahead of yourself? You haven't got him yet."

Higgins smiled, flipped her right hand, palm up, into the space between them. "Well, that's why I'm here, isn't it? The child, Theresa, isn't related to Jilly Sappone. Jilly hasn't demanded ransom, either. So, why did he take her?"

"Three reasons." Moodrow took Leonora's glass, refilled it from a bottle of chardonnay in the refrigerator. As he closed the refrigerator door, he recalled a time, before he met Betty, when the only thing in his refrigerator was ice. "First, he's crazy. Second, he's stupid. Third, he hates his wife. Jilly has what the shrinks like to call 'poor impulse control.' Most likely, he didn't plan on taking the kid. It just happened."

"And how long will he keep her?"

Moodrow shook his head. "Save the guilt for a jury, Leonora. I know what the stakes are." He stared down into his glass, tried to reconcile the contradictions. The last really dangerous animal he'd hunted was Davis Craddock, the cult leader. How long ago had that been? Four years? Five? It seemed like a hundred.

"Jilly Sappone," he finally said, "will try to kill you, me, or anyone else who comes after him. How can I ask Betty to carry that baggage? It's gonna be hard enough out in Los Angeles."

"I'm not asking you to capture Sappone. Just to help find him."

"And suppose I get close. Suppose I get close and he's still got the kid. You want me to drop a dime, call the cops, hope they don't fuck it up?" He stopped abruptly, waited for some kind of a response. When he realized that Leonora had nothing to say, he continued. "A little history lesson. Carmine Stettecase went into business just about the same time I went into the cops. Which was just about the time the Italians started moving out of the city. By the time Jilly Sappone came along, Carmine and his partner, Dominick Favara, now dead, were running the rackets on the Lower East Side. I mean *all* the loan sharks, pimps, bookies, and heroin dealers paid him tribute. Jilly, meanwhile, had a rep for being the wildest kid in a very tough neighborhood. By age sixteen, he'd been up in Spofford twice, the last time for a year."

Moodrow paused again. He was going on too long, dragging it out because he didn't want to see her leave. Because he didn't want his "no" to become final. "What I'm getting at is this—Dominick and Carmine were Jilly's role models. Without them, he was just another terminal psychopath and he knew it. So when Carmine's son married Jilly's cousin, Jilly asked him for a job. It was only natural, right? And it was only natural that Carmine, who has a sentimental attachment to the old neighborhood, set his new relative up to collect the vig for a connected loan shark named Paulie Marrano. Now, it's a funny thing about collecting money from deadbeats with dope or gambling habits. You gotta be strong, but you can't forget that dead men don't pay you back. Likewise if you get 'em so shit-scared they figure the cops are their only hope. Unfortunately, Jilly was unable to grasp the subtleties. Maybe he figured that being in the family, he was immune to discipline. Or maybe he tried, but he just couldn't control himself. Whatever way it went down, Jilly Sappone became a royal pain in the ass. He fought with everybody, killed at least three people, though. . . ."

Moodrow, as he picked up his glass, saw Betty out of the corner of his eye. She was standing in the doorway, her face a closed, neutral mask. He started to get up, thought better of it, suddenly realized that this is what he'd been waiting for all along. That Betty Haluka, unlike himself, wasn't obliged to say, "No."

FIVE

Moodrow, as he waited for Betty to find a glass, to fill it with wine, to take a seat at the table, to absorb the story Leonora Higgins patiently repeated, cursed himself for the manipulative cop bastard he actually was. He knew that Betty, who'd risked her own life to save a child, then stayed in that child's life through the intervening years, would, at the very least, refuse to decide for him. He knew that if he kept his own expression close to indifference, let the mask announce that it was no big deal, that he'd heard it all before, she'd eventually confuse the fate of Theresa-Marie Kalkadonis with the fate of her cousin, Marilyn. As if preserving the life of the child would save the adult.

It went exactly as Moodrow expected. Betty, confronted with the utterly irrational, asked herself an obvious question: Why had Jilly Sappone kidnapped an innocent child? That question led to a second and a third. Why did Marilyn, at age fifty-three, run head-on into a drunk speeding in the wrong direction on the Santa Monica Freeway? Marilyn who'd kept all those appointments with the gynecologist, taken the yearly mammograms, quit smoking, switched to a low-fat diet, jogged every other day through the southern California smog.

Unbidden, a line from an old Neil Young song floated up into her mind: "Helpless, helpless, helpless." Just like a child in the hands of Jilly Sappone.

"What do *you* want to do, Stanley?"

Moodrow, already prepared, took a deep breath, then lied through his teeth. "There's not much I *can* do." He turned slightly, addressed himself to Leonora Higgins. "You say I know all the players and you're right. I actually went to school with Carmine Stettecase. But the local cops know the players, too. Ditto for the feds who must've been called in on the kidnapping. The problem, for everybody, is that the players are bad guys. Why would they talk to me?"

Higgins toyed with a silver ring on the forefinger of her right hand. She was pretty sure that Moodrow wanted the job, that they were going through some kind of ritual. Her role, as she understood it, was to play along, make the capture of Jilly Sappone little more than handing out a traffic summons. She looked across the table at Betty, then cursed Moodrow, then cursed herself.

"The Department of Corrections was supposed to notify Ann Kalkadonis before releasing Jilly Sappone. They didn't and now Ann doesn't trust law enforcement. Its really that simple."

"Did she happen to mention why Jilly Sappone went to her apartment, what Sappone was after?"

"No."

"Did she tell you she ratted him out fifteen years ago? That she passed over his bloodstained clothing?"

"No."

Moodrow looked down at his empty glass, decided against a refill. "Let's back up. Make it, say, five or six years before Sappone went up for the murder. Carmine Stettecase, who'd been protecting Jilly, finally decided that enough was enough, that Jilly Sappone was out of control, bad for business. Standard mob procedure demanded that Carmine eliminate his problem, but Jilly was half-assed related. I mean, how can Carmine live in the same house with his son's mother-in-law if he whacks the nephew she raised from five years old? No, what Carmine did was tell Jilly to get out of New York, that he was fired. And what Jilly did was get drunk and beat the crap out of a cabdriver who wouldn't take him to Brooklyn. The cabdriver, a Russian immigrant who didn't know enough about the Land of Opportunity to fear Jilly Sappone, said he was willing to testify.

"Now, what I'm telling you here is a story I got in bits and pieces from my snitches, but this part of it rings true. If Carmine Stettecase wanted to save Jilly Sappone, who couldn't make bail, he would've had somebody pay the cabdriver a visit. That's what every-body in the DA's office expected. Only Carmine never made a move and Jilly went upstate, did two years of a six-year bit, settled down in Philadelphia when he got out. The way I heard it, Carmine broke out the champagne the day of the sentencing.

"Now, move forward a few years, to maybe nine months before Jilly got popped for the murder. Suddenly, he turns up on the Lower East Side with a wife—her name, back then, was Annunziata—and a kid. Both of them, the wife and the kid, are beaten so bad they look like cockroaches just before the shoe comes down. Not that either one of them complains. No, what they do is take it, try to hide the bruises, stay inside most of the time. They give us—meaning, the cops *and* the social workers—an excuse to look the other way.

"Jilly, of course, was as crazy as ever, the kind of mutt citizens cross the street to avoid. What I figured, at the time, was that he'd self-destruct before long and that's exactly what happened. One day, a stiff—later identified as Alfonse Chavez, convicted hijacker—turned up in an alley near Grand and Ludlow, dead from a single .22-caliber round. We naturally made it for an execution, pure and simple, the kind of homicide where you do the scutwork for a few days, then pass it off to a task force. In this case, Organized Crime.

"But then, miracle of miracle, a witness comes forward. One Harold 'Buster' Levy, owner of Levy Plumbing Supply, known to be a loan shark and connected to Carmine Stettecase, swears that he saw Jilly Sappone kill Alfonse Chavez. Buster claims that he was in his shop, located fifty feet from the crime scene, having sex with a housewife named Carol Pierce when he heard loud voices outside. Being that it was after hours, he naturally took a peek.

"Three hours later, Annunziata Sappone comes into the Seven with a set of bloody clothes—shirt, jacket, pants, underwear—says her husband asked her to wash the blood out, but she couldn't do it. Plus, she'll testify in open court.

"A gift from God, right? Up to and including Carol Pierce, who re-members the incident without any encouragement, and a third wit-ness who wanders into the precinct two days later. Even Jilly eventually saw the light. He took a plea, fifteen to life instead of twenty-five, and justice was done."

Moodrow stopped abruptly. His head was starting to throb again, a matter, he decided, of pure conscience. And the funny part was the guilt he felt at that moment had nothing to do with his sympathy for Betty. No, his feelings were genuine; he was determined to support her through the bad times, wanted to protect her, though he knew that was impossible. Unfortunately, another side of him needed to track Jilly Sappone, to pursue him, bring him down, hold his bloody head aloft. And that particular desire, despite his pounding head, was closer to lust than anything else he could name.

"Do you think Jilly was framed?" Not surprisingly, the question came from Betty, who'd spent most of her working life defending criminals.

"Not by us. I said it was a gift *from* God." Moodrow, on impulse, splashed another inch of bourbon into his glass. "I didn't say we *played* God."

"What about Carmine Stettecase?" Leonora asked. "Could he have set it up?"

Moodrow waved the question away. "He didn't try to stop it, which amounts to the same thing. Don't forget, Buster Levy worked for Carmine. Still does, for that matter. Leonora, you didn't mention any homicides. I take it Buster Levy is still among the living."

"They worked him over, Stanley, but he's alive."

"Why?"

"Why?"

"Yeah, why didn't Jilly kill Buster Levy? You think he didn't know how? Or maybe he couldn't bring himself to pull the trigger?" The questions were purely rhetorical and Moodrow continued without a pause. "Jilly wants Carmine to know what's coming. He left Buster alive to spread the news. It's that simple."

"What about Ann?" Leonora leaned over the table. After twenty years in law enforcement, she loved to talk up a case. It was one of the few pure pleasures the job afforded. "Sappone didn't kill her, either."

"He did worse. He took her child." Moodrow, tired of staring down into his glass, raised it to his mouth and drank. "Did you get anything on his partner? It has to be someone he knew in prison."

"Not yet. But what I can do, if you want to come in on this, is have the robbery and the assaults transferred over to Jim Tilley. That would give you access."

Moodrow stifled the urge to smile. Leonora had set it up nicely. "That brings me back to the original question. What, exactly, am I supposed to do about Jilly Sappone that the locals, the feds, and Carmine Stettecase *can't* do?"

Betty Haluka supplied the answer Moodrow expected. Somehow, it didn't please him all that much.

"Maybe Ann just needs to know that somebody's on her side, committed to her and only her."

"That's a good part of it," Leonora said. "But she's also convinced that Jilly's coming back to get her and the daughter they had together. Myself, I don't see any way that can happen. Ann will remain under police guard while she's in the hospital and be transferred to a safe house on Long Island when she's discharged."

"How many daughters are we talking about here?" Betty asked. "How can Sappone come back for a daughter he's already kidnapped?"

"Theresa-Marie, the child Sappone took, is the daughter of Ann and her second husband, Paul Kalkadonis. Theresa, of course, was born long after Sappone went to jail. Sappone's own child, Patricia, is eighteen years old. She was away at Boston University when Jilly showed up."

Betty organized the information in her memory, then pushed her chair away from the table. "I've still got some packing to do." She stood up, reached across the table to embrace Leonora, turned back to Moodrow. "Are you going to take the job, Stanley? It doesn't sound like it'll amount to much."

Moodrow managed an insincere frown. "I assume this is your basic pro bono situation?" he asked Leonora Higgins.

"Not at all," she replied evenly. "The Haven Foundation funds the shelter and they've got deep pockets. They expect to be billed a hundred dollars a day, plus expenses."

"That's half what I've been askin', but go ahead, abuse me. I'm used to it."

Betty reached out, started to cuff Moodrow on the back of the head, saw the bandage as if for the first time. "Just be careful,

Stanley," she said. "I've got enough to worry about in California."

Moodrow watched Betty leave, waiting until the bedroom door closed before turning back to Leonora Higgins.

"The victim, Ann Kalkadonis, when can I talk to her?"

"Tomorrow, Stanley. She's at St. Vincent's on the west side. I'll meet you there at two o'clock."

"Good, I'll speak to . . ."

Moodrow stopped suddenly, then giggled. Though she'd heard it many times before, the odd sound made Leonora Higgins squirm in her seat.

"You wouldn't consider sharing, would you?"

"I was just thinking about Sappone's aunt, Josefina. Carmine's gotta believe, true or not, that Josie knows where Jilly's hiding—we're talkin' about his son's mother-in-law, don't forget—and it's gotta be makin' him crazy that she won't tell him."

"Why is that funny? Won't he *make* her tell?"

Moodrow shook his head. "If you knew Josie Rizzo, you wouldn't ask that question. Carmine might kill her, but he'll never make her talk."

"You're saying this aunt let her daughter marry . . .? I don't believe it."

"Well, Aunt Josie was trying to get her nephew a job with the only major employer in need of his particular talents. What else *could* she do?" He stood up. "After I take Betty to the airport, I'll stop in at the house, talk to Jim before I meet you in front of St. Vincent's. Meanwhile, I wanna spend the rest of the night with Betty."

"Sit down, Stanley." A wicked grin split Leonora's face. "There's something else you have to know." She waited until he was sitting, until his expression had passed from surprised to sullen. "The Haven Foundation is funded by a small group of very wealthy women. For a number of reasons, they were reluctant to hire a male investigator."

"And you talked them into it?"

"Actually, it's worse than that. They retained someone before I had a chance to talk to them, a licensed investigator named Ginny Gadd. The cops won't give her the time of day, Stanley. And she's not having much luck on the street, either. Speed is everything here."

"So that's when you suggested me?"

Leonora nodded. "After I outlined your relationship with Jim Tilley and your knowledge of the neighborhood, they decided to make you an offer."

"And what's-her-name . . . Gadd? What did she have to say about it?"

"She said she'll try to work with you."

"Yeah, right."

Leonora slung her purse over her shoulder and stood up. Sometimes, it seemed as if she spent most of her working life babying grown men and women into doing what they wanted to do in the first place. "It's not like she has nothing to contribute, Stanley. Ginny Gadd specializes in computer investigation. I hear she's one of the best."

SIX

Jim Tilley, as he made his way along Tenth Street toward Third Avenue, told himself to stay calm. Sure, Captain Armando Ruiz, Commander of the mighty Seventh Precinct, had called him at nine o'clock in the morning, a single, pitiful hour after he'd come off duty, to drop another case into his lap. And, yes, Captain Ruiz had decreed that Detective Jim Tilley give this case "four-star priority" while still clearing every other case on his desk. All that could be shrugged off, the ways of the job being inscrutable, if not downright arbitrary. The real problem was that he was heading for the apartment of Ann Kalkadonis and a rendezvous with the FBI agents manning her telephone on the off chance that Jilly Sappone would decide to give his ex a call.

In theory, the meeting was to be a mutual briefing, a sharing of information. In fact, he would spend fifteen minutes enduring smug grins, questions that bordered on cross-examination, perfectly pressed suits, freshly laundered shirts, polished Florsheim wingtips.

Tilley, secure in the knowledge that after ten hours of bouncing from crime scene to crime scene, his own suit hung on his body like cold, wet spaghetti, ran the palm of his right hand over the stubble on his cheeks. He didn't bother to look at his shoes, Rose having declared them eligible for disaster relief weeks before.

What's happening, he told himself, is that I'm getting closer and closer to becoming another Moodrow. To becoming a grizzled, seen-it-all, burned-up and burned-out veteran with no time for anything but the job.

Burned up and burned out? It was a concept the silks, the chiefs and their deputies, couldn't understand. They'd been stiffing the detectives for ten years, relegating investigation to the back burner while they assembled super squads to blitz drug-infested neighborhoods. All to no end, as far as Tilley could see, unless the end was publicity and an ever-expanding budget. Now, with the shift to community policing, the emphasis was on stopping crime before it happened, not investigating afterward. Too bad crime went on forever, too bad the actual result of an increased police presence was fewer and fewer cleared cases, desktops covered with dusty files, burned-up and burned-out detectives.

Tilley, as he rode the elevator up to Ann Kalkadonis's fourteenth-floor apartment, resolved not to feel sorry for himself, that self-pity stoked the fires of terminal burnout. Outside her door, he managed a smirk to match the anticipated smirks of the agents inside, then, despite the ripped-out lock, knocked softly.

The smirk, along with his resolution, vanished the minute he entered the apartment. Not only were the two agents wearing their jackets, the jackets were actually buttoned. It was disgusting.

"Agent Ewing." The younger of the two men offered his hand and Tilley grasped it briefly.

"Jim Tilley." He slipped out of his own jacket, tossed it onto the couch. "You don't mind, do ya?"

The two agents exchanged a smile before the older agent introduced himself.

"Agent Holtzmann. With two *ns*."

Tilley took the man's hand, received a not unexpected crusher grip. Holtzmann appeared to be in his early fifties, a little too old for a field agent. Still, his thick, silver-gray hair and matching mustache, his military posture and flat gut, his sharp, blue eyes and firm, thrusting jaw all proclaimed his fitness-to-serve. Despite the advancing years, he fairly dripped testosterone.

"Where's the coffee?" Tilley glanced around the room. It was as neat as a pin. If a pair of New York cops had been assigned to the same duty, the apartment, he knew, would look like his shoes.

"Actually," Ewing said, "I don't think it'll take that long."

"You mean the coffee isn't made?" Tilley started for the kitchen. "Just point me toward the old percolator and I'll fix . . ."

"He said it won't take that long." Holtzmann stepped in front of Jim Tilley. "Why don't you sit down. You seem a bit anxious."

Tilley stopped a yard from the agent. "Tell you the truth, grandpa, if it's gonna be short and sweet, I'd rather stand." No question about it, he was beginning to feel better.

"Hey, guys." Agent Ewing quick-stepped across the room, put his hands on both their shoulders. He was taller than Jim Tilley, and clearly in shape, but his grip was relaxed, as was his wide smile. "Isn't it a little early for a tussle?"

A tussle? Tilley grimaced, guessed that Agent Ewing said bullpucky instead of bullshit. Screwed instead of fucked.

"Tell ya what, Ewing . . ."

The phone sounded before Tilley could finish his sentence, an old-fashioned ring, harsh and demanding, that cut through his resentment. He took out his notebook and the stub of a pencil, followed the agents to the monitoring equipment stacked on a small Formica table in the dining alcove.

"Cellular phone," Holtzmann said. "Could be coming from anywhere." He picked up the two headsets lying on the table, handed one to Jim Tilley, put the other on, motioned for Ewing to answer the phone.

"Hello."

"Hello, Marvin?"

"Pardon me?"

"This ain't Marvin. Don't kid me, pal. I know Marvin's voice when I hear it. It ain't right that you should pretend you're Marvin."

"I think you have the wrong number."

"The wrong number?"

"Look, I've got to clear this line. . . ."

" 'I've got to clear this line.' Ya sound like some kinda fuckin' faggot. A real man would'a just hung up the goddamned phone by now."

Ewing dropped the phone, turned to his partner with a shrug. Before he could speak, the phone rang again.

"Hello?"

"This is Marvin, did anybody call for me?"

Ewing's head snapped back as if he'd been punched. "Who is this?"

"I think I got a credibility problem here. Didn't I just say my name was Marvin?"

Holtzmann put his hands out, palms down. He mouthed the word, *slow*, then adjusted the volume on the already spinning tape recorder.

"All right, Marvin. Let's play. Who do you want to speak to?"

"Speak to? I don't wanna speak to nobody. All I wanna know is if anyone called for me."

Ewing hung up the phone, but didn't let go of the receiver. Twenty seconds later, when the phone rang, he nodded to his partner before picking it up.

"Hello?"

"So, what kinda pig do I got here? Do I got a regular New York pig? Or do I got a genuine federal FBI pig?"

"If you don't identify yourself, I'm going to hang up again. I really don't have time . . ."

"Yeah? Suppose I cut off the little cunt's right ear and let ya listen to her scream. Would ya have time for me then?"

"Jilly Sappone."

"Yeah. So tell me, right now, are you an Officer Pig or an Agent Pig?"

Ewing covered the mouthpiece, looked over at his partner. "Try to bond him up," Holtzmann said. "Give him your office number and your beeper number. Let him know you're available to negotiate."

"My name is Bob Ewing, Jilly. I'm an FBI agent."

"How did I know?" Sappone paused briefly. "My dear sweet wife isn't there, is she?"

"No, Jilly, she's not here. Ann's in the hospital."

"Yeah, well, you know how it is, Bob. I went fourteen years without kickin' her fat guinea ass and I got carried away. Next time I'll try to be more gentle." His laughter was harsh and mocking. "Why don't ya tell me what hospital she's in. So's I can send some flowers."

"Why don't we talk about Theresa-Marie, instead. Is she with you?"

"What's the matter, Bob, ya gettin' tired of my company?"

"Not at all. In fact, I'm going to give you my beeper number. That way, you can reach me any time you want." He paused, smiled slightly. "I already have *your* number. The cellular phone was a nice touch, by the way. We're running into that more and more often these days." He paused, glanced at his partner. "Jilly, are you there?"

"C'mon, talk ya little bitch. Talk to the fuckin' man, or I'll slap the shit out of ya."

"Hey, Jilly, it's okay." Ewing's voice was dead calm. "If she doesn't want to talk . . ."

"Don't fuckin' tell me what's okay." Sappone was shouting, now. "If I want the bitch to talk, she'll talk."

"Don't hurt her, Jilly. She's not part of this."

"Ya wanna keep tellin' me what to do? Huh? I swear to God, I'll rip her fuckin' heart out. I'll mail her back in pieces. Ya tell that to my sweet, innocent wife. Tell her if she ain't back in that apartment next time I call, I'm gonna get myself a long knife and play butcher. Tell her I'm gonna give the kid to my partner. He likes little girls."

"Damn, Jilly, that weren't right." Jackson-Davis Wescott peered over Jilly Sappone's right shoulder, tried to catch a glimpse of his own face in the rearview mirror. The angle was wrong, but he just knew his hurt-like eyes were even more hurt-like after what Jilly told those cops. "I never had nothin' for no little girls. That was a damned lie."

Jilly Sappone didn't bother to respond. He was too busy trying to get his head back together. They were traveling south on the Harlem River Drive, down toward the Lower East Side of Manhattan, the heart of Carmine Stettecase's territory. If one of Carmine's boys spotted Jilly Sappone, he'd know exactly what to do. And if Jilly wasn't ready . . .

Of course, he looked a lot different now. He'd trimmed his beard, cut his hair to within two inches of his scalp, dyed both—his beard and his hair—a dull gray-white. Fourteen years ago, the last time any of the boys had laid eyes on Jilly Sappone, he'd had a full head of dark, curly hair and no beard. He'd been fourteen years younger, too, twenty-six instead of forty. A kid instead of the man he'd become.

He glanced back over his shoulder, saw Jackson-Davis with his arm around the kid, trying to comfort her. The sight irritated him, but he wasn't about to say anything. When Jackson wasn't around, the kid cried all the time. That was a lot worse than irritating. It threatened to produce a serious shitstorm, the kind of shitstorm that blew whiny kids out the window, smashed them up against walls. Which was probably what would happen in the long run but, for right now, he needed the kid alive. He needed the kind of reaction the fed pig had when he thought about getting chunks of Theresa Kalkadonis in the mail.

"Jackson?"

"Yeah, Jilly?"

"Wrap the bitch up. We got work to do."

"Hell's bells, Jilly, Theresa really hates that."

Sappone took a deep breath, told himself to hold on, that one day old Jackson-Davis would smash up against walls of his own.

"Jackson?"

"Yeah, Jilly?"

"We can't leave her alone, can we? Can't have her screaming out the window. Suppose a cop sees her? Ya know the pigs are lookin', don't ya?"

Jackson-Davis didn't bother to reply. Jilly was right, he was always right, even when he was wrong he was right. Sometimes it made Jackson-Davis mad, but when he thought about goin' out on his own, without Jilly to tell him what to do, he flipped right over, from mad to near scared to death.

He looked at Theresa huddled next to him. She was shaking like a leaf.

"Now, c'mon, sugar, it ain't gonna be so bad." He began to wrap her in the blanket, making sure to cover her feet and her hands the way Jilly had told him. "I fixed the trunk up real nice and soft with foam rubber. Why, it'll be just like goin' to beddy-bye. Ceptin' for the story, a'course. I can't tell you no story in the trunk, but if you're a good little girl, tomorrow I'll run down to the Toys "R" Us store and buy you the biggest ol' teddy bear in the whole wide world. That way, next time Jilly says you gotta go in the trunk, you could have some company."

•   •   •

It was a little before eleven when Jilly parked the car on Fifteenth Street, a half block from the highway, and switched places with Jackson-Davis. This was the part he hated. The part about trusting a retarded hillbilly rapo with a man's job. The part about Jackson-Davis fucking it up and Jilly Sappone going out of business. Too bad he didn't have any choice. There was just no place to park a car in Manhattan and not risk having it towed away. Not unless he wanted to leave it in a parking lot and walk eight or nine blocks.

"You know what you gotta do, Jackson-Davis?"

"I sure do know."

"Which is what?"

Wescott felt the blood rush up into his face. Sometimes Jilly treated him like a little kid, like Jilly treated Theresa, like Jackson-Davis Wescott was some kind of a dog.

"We been through this, Jilly," he muttered. "Been through it a whole lotta times."

"Then one more time ain't gonna hurt. Bein' as it's *my* ass on the line."

"There you go again, Jilly. Actin' like I'm some kinda he-she. I swear to the good Lord above. . . ."

Sappone reached out, grabbed his partner's earlobe, twisted sharply. "Ya wanna mouth me? Huh? Ya wanna mouth me?"

"No, Jilly. No way." Jackson-Davis tried to pull back, which made his punishment hurt even more. But maybe that was good, too. Maybe he needed to remember about Jilly's shitstorms. That they came out of nowhere, that when ol' Jilly got mad, he drooled like a pit bull chained in the sun. "I'm gonna park the car by a fire hydrant and stay there until I seen you done the deed. Then I'm gonna pick you up and drive off real slow. I'm gonna drive straight down the avenue till you tell me to turn. And I'm not gonna panic, no matter what happens."

The deed didn't take all that long to get done. They parked on the west side of Avenue C, next to the enormous complex of redbrick high-rise buildings collectively known as Stuyvesant Town. Jackson-Davis started to shut down the engine, then remembered that he was supposed to leave it running. He raised a defensive hand to his ear just in case Jilly had seen him, but Jilly was already opening the door, stepping out onto the sidewalk.

"Get ya shit together, Jackson." Jilly leaned over, put his face in the open window. His hand snaked down into his jacket, came up clutching his nine-millimeter Colt. "The prick is comin' right for us."

Jackson looked down the avenue. The middle-aged fat man carrying the Bloomingdale's shopping bag sure didn't seem like no Mafia guy. No, what he looked like was the ol' pudge who ran the feed store in Ocobla, Tommy-Lee. Hell, Tommy-Lee didn't even hunt. . . .

"Hey, Jackson-Davis, don't stare at the fuckin' guy. Look at me."

"Sure, Jilly." Jackson-Davis did as he was told, though he didn't much like the expression on Jilly Sappone's face. It wasn't exactly Jilly's shitstorm expression. More like Jilly was gettin' ready to jump one of them he-she bitches up at Clinton prison. Jackson had seen that look a time or two, and he remembered what came next. That's why he wasn't surprised when Jilly spun around as the fat man passed the car, took a step forward, and splattered the man's brains all over the sidewalk.

No, what surprised Jackson-Davis was the echo of nine millimeter bouncing off city walls. It was real, *real* loud. Loud enough to bring people running out of the garage down the block, running out to get a good look. So why was Jilly bending over to snatch the fat man's shopping bag off the sidewalk? Why was he fishing in the fat man's pocket?

Suddenly Jackson-Davis felt like he just had to get away before the whole world fell down on him. All he could think about was jammin' that car into gear, layin' him a line of rubber from Avenue C to the Mississippi border. He squeezed his eyes down, grabbed onto the wheel, remembered that it would've been Jackson-Davis's butt gettin' jumped in Clinton if Jilly hadn't helped him out.

"You *owe* Jilly Sappone," he screamed. "Don't you be no fraidy-cat. There ain't no such thing as a Wescott fraidy-cat." His daddy had told him that.

The door opened and Jilly slid in next to him. "Get it goin', Jackson. Nice and slow."

Jackson-Davis responded by throwing the transmission into low. He was about to mash the gas pedal into the floorboard when Jilly put a restraining hand on his knee. Jackson, his breath coming in short heaves, turned to look into his partner's eyes. He was expect-

ing to find a hurricane, but Jilly's eyes were calm, brown pools. Like
the eyes of the Pentecostal saints in his ole ma's picture books.

"Nice and slow," Jilly repeated. "Remember what we got in the
trunk. You wouldn't wanna give our insurance policy a bumpy ride."

They drove down Avenue C to Third Street, stopping twice for
red lights, then made a right turn.

"Awright, pull it over here, Jackson. Over against the curb."

"But, Jilly, they could be comin' after us." Jackson-Davis obeyed
even as he protested.

"Who, Jackson? Who's comin' after us?"

"The cops, the . . . the damned ol' *posse.*"

Jilly reached under the seat and pulled up a set of license plates
and a screwdriver. He opened his door, started to get out, then
leaned back to remove the keys from the ignition. "One thing, pal. If
ya should hear horsey-hooves in the distance, be sure to let me
know."

Thirty seconds later, Jilly tossed a pair of stolen New Jersey license
plates into the storm drain on the corner. The New York plates he'd
replaced them with had been stolen in upstate Sullivan County and
wouldn't appear on a city hot sheet. The car itself, a faded-blue 1990
Taurus stolen out of a parking lot near the Sunrise Mall, was so non-
descript as to be actually invisible.

"I done it good, Jackson." Jilly opened the driver's door, waited a
moment for Jackson-Davis to slide over. "It was a lotta work, but I
took care of the details." He pronounced it "*dee*-tails." "That's what
makes it work. Lookin' out for the details."

He put the car in gear and began to drive west on Third Street.
"Jackson-Davis, you remember what comes next? What you gotta
do?"

"Yeah, Jilly. I remember every damn bit." Jackson-Davis felt his
whole attitude change. Now that he wasn't scared anymore, now
that he knew they'd gotten away, he felt . . . well, he felt proud, like
he'd really accomplished something. After all, how many Ocobla
boys got to make a real, live, Mafia hit? Probably not a single one.
He'd bet on it.

"Tell me."

"Okay, first thing is I take the keys."

Jilly held up two house keys and a set of car keys on a key ring. "Which is which?" he asked.

Jackson touched the house keys. "The big one is for the front door on the building. The little one is for the apartment."

"Keep goin'."

"I take the elevator up to the sixth floor and I find Apartment 6C. Then I use the key all quiet-like and get inside. Then I find the bitch and show her my gun. Then I tape her mouth and I tape her hands. Then I do whatever I want real fast and come back to the car." He turned to Jilly and smiled. "Don't worry, Jilly. I didn't forget a damned thing. Before I do whatever I want, I tell her, 'Jilly Sappone says, Hello.' "

SEVEN

It'd been a perfectly miserable morning, but it was over, now, and Stanley Moodrow was determined to put it behind him. He and Betty had arrived at La Guardia Airport's Delta Terminal forty-five minutes before her plane's scheduled takeoff only to face the usual indefinite delay. For the next two hours, he'd perched on a hard plastic chair, balancing a coffee container and a glazed doughnut on one knee while he listened to her talk about Michael Alamare, the five-year-old boy she'd risked her own life to save. The usual airport mix of scruffy college kids, briefcase-toting executives, and immigrant families lugging taped boxes and young children had swirled about them, coming and going in response to the public-address system. Yet, despite the buzz of conversation, a buzz that at times threatened to become a roar, they'd somehow created a space that was entirely their own, a space into which nothing could intrude.

Except, of course, Moodrow's guilty conscience. And it wasn't just the half-truth he'd pushed on her the night before. No, far worse, even as he'd listened to her, as he'd sympathized, nodded at the right moments, taken her hand, kissed her good-bye, a part of him was lining up a strategy that led from Leonora's unexpected appearance to the apprehension of Jilly Sappone.

What it is, he told himself as he walked through the doors of the Seventh Precinct, is that I'm just not what you call a sensitive type. After forty years in the crime business, I'm a hardened urban warrior. My psychic armor is . . .

"Hey, Moodrow, you turn fuckin' senile or what?"

Moodrow stopped short, realized that he'd giggled out loud. He looked over at the desk sergeant, a twenty-year veteran named Martin O'Dowd, and shrugged.

"I wouldn't deny it. What's doin', O'Dowd?"

"Ya mean, since the last time you were in here bustin' balls?" He laughed shortly. "What's doin', Moodrow, is crime and punishment. The same doin' that was doin' when you were doin'. If ya get what I'm aimin' at."

Moodrow nodded, took a deep breath, remembered that when he was still a cop he'd despised the house, avoiding it for weeks at a time. Now, he sucked at the mingled odors of anger and despair, disinfectant and mold, sweat-soaked crack addicts and homeless men who hadn't seen a shower in months. He lapped them up like a sick junkie looking for his get-well fix.

"Jim Tilley around?"

O'Dowd shook his head. "Tilley caught a multiple up in Stuyvesant Town."

"That's out of the precinct."

"Hey, you wanna listen or you wanna tell me the fuckin' sky is blue?" O'Dowd paused briefly to drive his point home. "*Detective* Tilley said you should get your ass up there, said it could be related. The scene is on Avenue C, near Sixteenth Street."

Moodrow took a last sniff, then stepped back into the sunlight. He looked around for a cab, but the yellows had their off-duty signs lit and there wasn't a gypsy to be seen. In an earlier time, of course, he'd have simply hitched a ride in the first patrol car to come along. Now he'd have to hoof it.

He walked north, under the Williamsburg Bridge and up Pitt Street toward Houston. Pitt Street was a notorious drug center, even by the standards of the Lower East Side. The junkies called it a twenty-four/seven spot, meaning it was open twenty-four hours a day, seven days a week. No matter what, no matter when—if you had the bank, you could always get well on Pitt Street.

"Yo, coke, crack, dope, smoke."

"Jums, baby. The sweetes' the bes'."

"Got the baaaad shit, here, bro. Take the worl' offen yo chest. Give you a positive mutha-fuckin' *attitude*."

Moodrow ignored the offers, avoiding eye contact without looking away, demanding his space, but offering no disrespect. It was a trick everybody in the neighborhood, male or female, young or old, tried to learn. To be neither predator, nor prey, a true noncombatant. For the very young, the disabled, the elderly, for anyone who couldn't maintain the fiction, it was, of course, pure hell.

Everybody blamed the cops, and not without reason. After all, if the dealers would hawk their wares to a sixty-year-old white man in a business suit, they wouldn't shrink from an undercover cop in a sweatshirt. So if mutts weren't arrested, if they weren't punished, it was because the cops were corrupt, or lazy, or . . .

The truth was a lot sadder. The NYPD made nearly twenty thousand felony drug arrests every year, busting users and dealers alike, while the prosecutors and judges did their level best to send them to jail. None of it had more than a temporary effect on the drug business, the number of dealers and addicts remaining virtually constant from year to year despite the billions spent on law enforcement. Coping with that reality, if you were unfortunate enough to live in a drug-saturated neighborhood, was a simple fact of life.

But where, Moodrow wondered, did that leave *him*? He had the money to move out. If he chose to stay on the Lower East Side because he'd lived there all his life, there was no way he could whine about it. Besides, it wasn't Stanley Moodrow who'd been stuffed into a trash basket.

He was crossing Thirteenth Street when he caught his first glimpse of the Avenue C crime scene—just the flashing lights of a cruiser dyeing the brick a deep, rich crimson. It was enough to push every other consideration into the background. He picked up the pace, drank in the scene as he closed the distance.

The crowd was small, a few pedestrians, a knot of Con Ed workers in blue hard hats, several print reporters trying to edge close enough for a shot of the bloodstained sidewalk. A half dozen patrol cars—their lights flashing, radios screaming, doors open—were nosed up against the yellow crime-scene tape. Behind them, four black Dodge sedans formed a protective half circle, effectively blocking southbound traffic while forcing the curious to the east side of the avenue.

For Moodrow, the scene had a timeless quality. He evaluated the chaos as he approached, found it to be controlled, the uniforms and the detectives standing outside the tape while a forensic team gathered evidence.

"Hey, pop, you goin' somewhere?"

Moodrow pulled up, remembered that he wasn't a cop anymore, that the miniature badge and the ID card declaring him RETIRED wouldn't mean squat to the young patrolman holding the small spiral notebook.

"You the recorder?" The job of the first patrolman to reach any crime scene was to seal it off, then record the name of anyone, from the sergeant to the commissioner, who entered.

"Yeah. You a cop?" His face registered open disbelief, one blond eyebrow rising into the shadow of his cap.

"Retired. I'm lookin' for a suit named Jim Tilley. You register him on the scene?"

The patrolman ran down the list of names on his sheet.

"Yeah, came in thirty minutes ago."

"You wouldn't know where he is now?"

"He didn't leave me his schedule but I hear they got a second stiff inside the complex. Found her dead when they went to notify this one's next-of-kin. Maybe your man dropped in to have a look. The ME's still up there."

Five minutes later, Moodrow stepped out of an elevator at 1277 Avenue C, to confront still another patrolman. This one had dark red hair and a thin mustache but, to Moodrow, he looked exactly like his brother. He looked like a baby.

"I'm trying to locate Detective Jim Tilley. He inside?"

The cop glanced at his book. "Yeah, I'll get him." He leaned back through the open doorway, yelled, "Detective Tilley. You got a visitor."

Jim Tilley appeared a moment later. He smiled apologetically as he explained why he couldn't get his friend inside. "It's not my squeal, Stanley. I'm a beggar here, myself."

Moodrow nodded thoughtfully, just as if the smell of blood drifting through the open door wasn't calling to him like the sirens called Ulysses. "I understand. What's the connection with Sappone?"

"The victim inside is Carol Pierce. She was a witness in the case that put Sappone away."

"No shit. And the one outside?"

"Her boyfriend. Guy named Patsy Gullo."

"Gullo works for Carmine Stettecase."

Tilley leaned back against the wall. He pulled a stick of chewing gum from his shirt pocket, took his time getting it into his mouth. "What can I say, Stanley? I'm impressed. Is there anybody you *don't* know?"

Moodrow shrugged. "Look, Betty's plane was delayed and I have to meet Leonora at the hospital in a half hour. Why don't we get down to business. Do you have a witness who can make Sappone?"

"Are you kidding? We got a balding white male between twenty-five and forty-five years of age. Five-six to six feet tall. Hair gray or blonde or brown. Driving or being driven in a white, blue, or light green Toyota, Chevy, Nissan . . ."

"Okay, Jim. I heard enough. What about Carol Pierce? I can smell the blood from out here."

Tilley looked serious for the first time. He spoke through pinched lips. "The prick took her apart with a can opener. He taped her mouth and hands, then dragged her into the bathroom. There was no sign of a struggle."

"That's not Jilly's style."

"Maybe not. Gullo was taken out with a single shot to the head. A pure mob hit."

Moodrow touched the bandage on the back of his head. The wound was healing, the stitches pulling tight. "Sappone had a partner when he took Buster Levy. It's gotta be someone he knew in the joint. Anybody working on that?"

"Yeah, me. I got a call in to the warden's office in Attica. Prisoners don't mingle with each other at Southport." Tilley pushed himself away from the wall. "Look, I got no reason to hang around here. Give me a second to say good-bye and I'll drive you over to the hospital."

•   •   •

"I got a question," Moodrow said, "that keeps coming back to me." He was sitting next to Jim Tilley, staring down at a prison photo of Jilly Sappone. Taken five years ago, it revealed a clean-shaven, balding man with a sharp, bent nose and a thick, prominent chin. "How did Sappone get out of prison? Leonora told me the board turned him down, then reversed itself. How often does that happen?"

Tilley pulled the Dodge out in front of a taxi, endured the blaring response. "Don't know, Stanley. I just get 'em *into* prison. Letting 'em out isn't up to me."

"Yeah, fine." Moodrow continued to stare down at the photograph. He traced the lines on Sappone's brow, from the edge of his forehead to the sharp delta between his eyes. "Look, I've got a bad feeling about the parole board."

"You think somebody reached them?"

Moodrow shook his head. "The problem is I can't see who or how. Carmine wouldn't do it, even if he had the muscle. And if Jilly ratted to get himself an early parole, why hasn't anyone been arrested? Where's the Grand Jury investigation?" He paused for a moment, shook his head again. "I wanna play it safe. Don't tell anybody at the house where Ann Kalkadonis is staying. The hospital or where she goes later. Nobody."

"Might be too late for that." Tilley passed on the details of Sappone's phone call to the two agents, Ewing and Holtzmann. He made no attempt to convey the quality of the experience, mentioning Sappone's Jekyll-and-Hyde mood swing in the same matter-of-fact tone he used to state the man's final demand. "The fibbies decided they had to tell her. They want to cover their asses, let the victim make the final decision." He glanced at his watch. It was nearly two o'clock. "They've most likely been and gone by now."

EIGHT

Moodrow stood in the entranceway of St. Vincent's Hospital's cafeteria and watched the four women seated around Styrofoam coffee containers at a far table. Leonora Higgins was there, of course, as sharp as ever in a no-nonsense charcoal business suit. He didn't recognize any of the others, but he knew they were from the Haven Foundation, a committee met to evaluate his personal worth. It wasn't the first time he'd been through the process. Having done just enough corporate work to be familiar with the politics of selection, he fully understood that his task was to reduce their choices to Stanley Moodrow or Stanley Moodrow.

Time for the show, he said to himself as he crossed the cafeteria floor. Time for the game face.

"Stanley." Leonora stood up. She extended her hand, but refused to meet his eyes. "There are some people here you need to know. Margaret Cohen, Patricia Burke, and Toni Alicea. They're from the Haven Foundation."

Moodrow nodded to each in turn, wished, not for the first time, that he knew his client's room number. He snatched a chair from a nearby table and sat down.

"Did you see Jim Tilley?" Leonora continued.

"I just left him." He glanced at the women, saw no question marks on their faces, and assumed they'd been well briefed.

"What's your take on the police effort?" Leonora was playing to

65

his strengths. The way any good prosecutor would display a friendly witness.

"Except for Ann's personal protection, they dropped the whole thing in Jim's lap. No help and he's expected to continue working his caseload while he looks for Jilly. Jim'll put the word out to the patrol cops in the Seven, supply them with mug shots and a history, tell 'em to be on the lookout. Given the crime rate on the Lower East Side, that's the best he can do."

"That's it?" Toni Alicea's dark eyes flashed an obvious anger, just as Moodrow had hoped. She, like the other women, appeared to be in her mid-thirties. And, like the others, she was dressed for business.

"What could I say? The cops are running it as two assaults and a robbery. They're leaving the kidnapping to the FBI, which is par for the course." He didn't mention Carol Pierce, figuring to pick his spots, leave it for later.

Alicea glanced at the other women before turning back to Moodrow. "That's just not good enough," she said.

"Look, Ms. Alicea." He leaned toward her. "Theresa Kalkadonis has a better chance if the cops stay out of it. You have to understand something here. Jilly Sappone is a dead man and he knows it." Moodrow went on to describe the Stuyvesant Town crime scenes, including the relationship between Carmine Stettecase, the two victims, and Jilly Sappone. "Carmine's going to kill Jilly," he concluded. "If he doesn't catch Jilly on the outside, he'll have him hit in prison. It's just a matter of time."

"Then why did Sappone do it? Is he suicidal? Is he crazy?"

Moodrow took a moment to consider the question. As far as he was concerned, Jilly Sappone had ceased to be human; something or someone had reduced him to the status of a natural disaster. In fact, Sappone reminded Moodrow of a crack-crazed psychotic named Levander Greenwood who'd once terrorized the Lower East Side. At the time, Moodrow recalled, he and Jim Tilley had thought of Greenwood as a force of nature. To be dealt with, but not hated.

"That's the wrong question," he finally announced. "Jilly Sappone's gonna keep on killing. Like I just explained, the man has no reason to stop, no way out." He leaned back, swept the table with his eyes. "The question you need to ask is this: What would Jilly Sappone do to Theresa Kalkadonis if, for instance, Jilly woke up from his afternoon nap to find ten or twenty well-armed cops massed outside his door?" He laid his palms on the table, paused for a moment. "I'm not trying to be dramatic here. Do what any cop would do. Run through the possibilities."

"Excuse me."

Moodrow turned to meet Patricia Burke's sharp green eyes. He noted the clenched jaw, the slight underbite, the flaming cheeks. She was pissed, too, and that was just fine with him. That was why the bait had been cast in the first place.

"You seem to be telling us to give up."

"Not at all."

"No? Didn't you just infer that Jilly Sappone will . . ." She hesitated for a moment, took a deep breath. "You said that he'll kill Theresa before he'll surrender."

"Look." Moodrow tightened his voice down, forcing Patricia Burke to lean into him in order to hear. "The odds are stacked against Theresa Kalkadonis. That's the truth of it. But poor odds are no reason to give up. You have to accept your hand and find the best way to play the cards. One or two people have a better chance of surprising Jilly Sappone and his partner, of taking them down before they can hurt the child, than an army of by-the-book cops or FBI agents. Cops and FBI agents have to give suspects a chance to surrender." He waited until Patricia Burke's eyes told him she'd digested the information, then continued. "Besides," he said, "I have an ace in the hole. I went to grammar school with Carmine Stettecase. I know he's a man who can be persuaded to act in his own self-interest."

Moodrow hesitated outside the door to Room 436. He knew what he was going to find inside, had stood at the hospital bedsides of hundreds of beating victims in the course of his career. Ann Kalkadonis's face would be so badly swollen as to actually appear featureless, a dimpled balloon stretched to the point of bursting. By turns, the color of her skin would range from purple to red to green to a faded, sickly yellow. As if her face had been tie-dyed by Jilly Sappone's fists.

"Stanley?"

Leonora Higgins was standing beside him. He'd wanted to interview Ann Kalkadonis by himself, but wasn't surprised when the entire committee had insisted on coming along. Leonora had been the compromise.

"Gimme a second to get ready," he said. The trick was not to let ordinary human pity stop you from asking the questions that had to be asked. Maybe all you wanted to do was mumble your condolences and get the fuck out, but the man paid you to be a detective and you couldn't detect without information, therefore . . .

"All right," he said, "let's go."

He nodded to the bored cop sitting beside the door, stepped inside, found no surprises. Ann Kalkadonis was awake, though probably drugged. Her face, as she slowly turned toward him, was every bit as grotesque as he'd expected. At least, the parts that weren't bandaged.

"You got older," she mumbled.

"Say that again?" He crossed the room, sat on the plastic chair beside her bed.

"You got older," she repeated.

"I guess that means you remember me." Moodrow crossed his legs, settled back in the chair. "Tell ya the truth, Mrs. Kalkadonis, I'm flattered."

"I remember you from the fight."

"That was a long time ago." He looked up at Leonora and motioned for her to take the other chair, before explaining. "Once upon a time, Jilly and I had what cops like to call an altercation. It happened in a bar on Houston Street. Jilly was loud, as usual, sounding off about all cops being scumbag thieves. Me, I was off duty and too close to drunk to walk out. You could say I won the fight, being as how I was standing up when it ended. But the truth is that nobody wins a fight like that. I hurt for a week."

Leonora nodded thoughtfully. She'd been setting up Moodrow's punch lines for two days because she really believed that he was Theresa's best chance. That didn't mean she enjoyed being used. "Did he come after you? Later on?"

Moodrow shook his head. "Back then, you didn't kill a cop." He turned to Ann Kalkadonis. "I know you're hurting, Ann, so I'll try to keep it brief. After I finish, we'll talk about what we're gonna do."

Slowly, with many pauses, they established a list of Jilly Sappone's friends and relatives. The list, of course, was fifteen years old, the last time Ann Kalkadonis had had any contact with the family, but it was a place to begin. When they were finished, Moodrow leaned back in his chair and crossed his legs.

"Have the feds told you about Jilly's call?" He waited for a nod, then continued. "Jilly wants you in the apartment. He wants you to answer the telephone next time he calls. I need to know if you're gonna go, if you're gonna give Jilly a target?" The questions were purely rhetorical, Ann Kalkadonis having no choice in the matter. Moodrow received a nod, then continued. "If your other daughter, Patricia, is still in Boston, bring her back. There's at least a chance that Jilly could find her. Just like he found Carol Pierce. Just like he found *you*."

Leonora started to say something, but Moodrow motioned her into silence. "From what I hear, Ann, you want me to be your bodyguard. We both know that won't work. I have to locate Jilly and I have to do it fast. The FBI has your apartment wired. They'll stay with you twenty-four hours a day. The same goes for the New York cops."

Ann Kalkadonis mumbled something that Moodrow didn't catch. He leaned closer, asked her to repeat herself, then came up laughing.

"What did she say?" Leonora asked.

"She said, 'I'm Sicilian. I don't trust cops.' " He turned back to his client. "In this case, you've got the cops and the FBI agents to watch each other. Just make sure Patricia doesn't decide to stroll through the neighborhood. If we're careful, Sappone will never know she came back."

Outside, in the hallway, Moodrow tried to think of a nice way to break the bad news. He'd gotten what he wanted, access to Ann Kalkadonis, and now the committee had to go. It was really that simple, but simplicity didn't make it easier. Leonora was sure to be pissed off and he didn't need that. Nevertheless, as the committee was waiting in the cafeteria, he plunged on.

"Hold up a minute, Leonora," he said to her retreating back, "I'm not going down there with you."

"Now what, Stanley?" She spun around, faced him with her shoulders squared. "What's the game?"

"I've decided to take the case pro bono. That means the foundation is out. I'm not reporting to anybody but my client." He folded his arms across his chest, absorbed the full force of Leonora's glare.

"You know, you're really a prick. I've been playing your game for the last two days."

"And now it's my turn to play yours?" He hesitated, searched for an inoffensive way to phrase what had to be said. "Look, those people have nothing to contribute. *Nothing*. I'm not putting them down, Leonora. They offered Ann refuge and that's all to the good, but they can't find Jilly Sappone. I just don't have time for them."

"That's great, Stanley. I can see your reasoning. If you don't want their money, they have no hold over you. But somebody's got to tell them and if that somebody is me, I'm going to smack you so hard, you'll forget about what happened to the *back* of your head." She stared up at him through narrowed eyes. "It's really that simple."

It went better than Moodrow expected. He began by thanking the Haven Foundation for all they'd done on behalf of Ann Kalkadonis, then carefully explained that client confidentiality obliged him to report directly (and only) to Ann Kalkadonis. Even the cops had no real claim, though he fully intended to use them whenever necessary.

"Time is what it's all about," he concluded. "Days, maybe a week at the outside. I don't wanna insult anybody, but I can't be running off to meetings every afternoon." He glanced down at his ancient windup Timex, a watch he'd dubbed "Old Reliable" because it stopped every morning and afternoon at 3:22. "In fact, if I hurry, I can still find Carmine at the Gemini Lounge. That's where he spends his afternoons."

Moodrow stood up before the protests could begin. "Leonora, you wanna walk me out? There's something I need to ask you."

Leonora, now more bemused than angry, told the other women to wait for her, that she'd be back, then quickly joined Moodrow as he made his way between the tables. "You did that very nicely," she said. "Short and sweet."

"Don't worry, Leonora, you've still got them by the balls."

"The balls?"

Moodrow pulled up short, stifled a giggle. "I'm gonna ask Jim Tilley to keep civilians out of Ann's apartment. That means you're the foundation's only source of information. You oughta be able to work with that." He took her by the arm. "You mentioned a private eye last night, said she worked with computers."

"Ginny Gadd. I assume she's out, too."

"No, I need her. And I need you to do me a favor. I want you to give her a call, tell her I'll be in touch later this afternoon."

"First you insult me, then you ask a favor. Stanley, if I didn't love you, I'd hate your guts."

"Bullshit. You may be playing two games here, but you want Jilly Sappone as much as I do. That's why you came to me in the first place." He gave her a chance to deny it. When she didn't, he continued. "I need a second favor, Leonora. Somebody has to go over to Ann's apartment and check it for security."

"She's fourteen floors off the ground and there's no fire escape. Unless Jilly learned to fly in prison . . ."

"Check the lock, make sure it's shielded. The frame, too. I don't want that lock punched out; I don't want the door jimmied. The shades have to cover the windows completely and the lamps have to be up against the windows. No shadows, no silhouettes. I'd do it myself, but I have to catch Carmine before he goes home. Jilly's aunt lives there and I'd bet my left testicle that she's in touch with him."

NINE

"Take me away, Moodrow. Take me the fuck away." Carmine Stettecase held out a pair of small, pudgy hands. "The shit that's happenin' to me now, I'd rather be in the joint."

They were sitting at a back table in the Gemini Lounge, Carmine's supper club, located at the intersection of Wooster and Prince Streets on the western edge of what had once been Little Italy. The Italians, who'd occupied the neighborhood for more than eighty years, had begun to move out in the early 1950s, with Latinos, mainly Puerto Ricans, coming in to replace them. The process continued for the better part of two decades, until trendy New Yorkers in search of affordable housing "discovered" the neighborhood in the late Seventies. The ten years that followed saw the manufacturing lofts remodeled, the ancient tenements refurbished, and the neighborhood renamed, emerging as the Soho district.

The new settlers brought something Little Italy had never had; they brought money, and Carmine Stettecase had gone with the flow. He'd traded his candleholder Chianti bottles for halogen wall sconces, purged his jukebox, dumping Frank Sinatra and Vic Damone in favor of Thelonius Monk and the Kinks. His menu no longer featured calamari *fra diavolo*, but the marinated asparagus (or so Moodrow had heard) was to die for.

When the lounge (much to Carmine's surprise) began to catch on, he'd added strings of white Christmas lights to the ceiling trellis, a matched pair of platinum-blond bartenders (one male, one female), and a performance artist with a tattooed skull. His own operation was moved to a back table and confined to the afternoon when the restaurant and bar were closed.

"I'm not a cop anymore, Carmine. Haven't been for almost five years. Not that I wouldn't like to do the world a favor and oblige you." Moodrow, his face a dead mask, stared into a pair of eyes so light they were nearly invisible, eyes the color of an ice cube in a glass of vodka.

"Forget it. If you ain't busted me by now, you'll never bust me. I did some time with the feds, but punk cops like you never got close."

"Life isn't over, Carmine. Unless you retired and forgot to hold the party." In spite of the defiant words, Moodrow knew the man was right. Unless they were bent, precinct detectives like Stanley Moodrow stayed clear of big-time mobsters like Carmine Stettecase. Sure, if you stumbled on them, caught them in the proverbial act, you'd make the bust. Long-term investigations, on the other hand, were the province of whatever federal-local task force happened to be operating at the moment.

"Never happen, Moodrow. Ya wanna retire, ya gotta have someone to step into your shoes. Me, I got a kid that can't even control his mother-in-law. I swear to Christ, if Tommaso wasn't my own flesh and blood, I'd shoot him." Stettecase opened a Veniero's cake box, plucked out a miniature cannoli, popped it into his mouth. "So, whatta ya want, Stanley? Bein' as I know you always hated my guts and this ain't a social call."

"After I left the cops, I went into business for myself. Right now, I represent Ann Kalkadonis." Moodrow stared across the table, tried to gauge Stettecase's reaction. As a kid, Carmine had built his reputation on a hot temper and a squat, fireplug physique. Now, at sixty-two, his temper had gone the way of his body. At least a hundred pounds overweight, Carmine Stettecase seemed about as volatile as the pastries he stuffed into his mouth. Not that he wouldn't kill Jilly Sappone or Stanley Moodrow or anybody else who got in his way. "I assume you know what happened to her."

Carmine shrugged. "Guess I'm gonna solve both of our problems at the same time. Lucky me." He stared at Moodrow for a moment. "How the fuck did you jerks let that maniac outta jail? I don't care if he's been inside fourteen years. You gotta be crazy to put a maniac like Jilly on the street."

"Gee, and all this time I thought you were the one pulling the strings. Life sure can surprise you."

"It ain't funny, Moodrow." Carmine ran a soft palm over what was left of his hair. "What I shoulda done is listen to Dominick." Dominick Favara had been Carmine's boss for thirty years, right up until cancer did what a dozen would-be assassins had failed to do. "Dominick told me to make Jilly disappear. He said, 'Fuck ya son, fuck ya daughter-in-law, and fuck ya daughter-in-law's mother. Fuck Josie Rizzo.' He told me I should put Josie in the same hole with her nephew."

Moodrow nodded solemnly. Just as if they weren't talking about murder, about an execution. As if Carmine's bodyguards weren't scattered about the restaurant. "Why didn't you?" he asked.

Carmine looked at his lap for a moment, then sighed before consoling himself with a cream puff. "In case ya haven't heard, we don't kill women. We ain't like them fuckin' spics, them Cubans and Colombians. Women don't get hit unless they're gonna rat."

"I wasn't talking about Josie, Carmine. Why didn't you kill Jilly Sappone?"

He shrugged, managed a laugh that rippled through his jowls. "The first mistake I made was lettin' my kid marry into that family. I knew better at the time, but I figured I was such a hot shit I could take care of anything. My second mistake was doin' the Godfather bit and givin' crazy Jilly Sappone a job. Then I let Josie Rizzo move into the family building and I was fuckin' history. Hey, three strikes you're out, right? I figured for sure somebody would kill Jilly in prison."

Moodrow reached into his jacket pocket, noted the alarm on Carmine's face, and grinned broadly. "Hey, Carmine," he said softly, "you already searched me, remember? Your gorilla's holding my piece." He gestured to the three-hundred-pound giant sitting at the bar. The three-hundred-pound giant in the two-thousand-dollar suit.

"Habit, Moodrow. When ya live this long in my business, ya pick up habits." Stettecase shifted inside his own two-thousand-dollar suit. He played with the diamond ring on his finger, twisting it back and forth. "So, whatta ya got in there?"

Moodrow took out a sheet of folded paper, laid it on the table in front of him. "Tell me something, Carmine. Whatta ya think's gonna happen to Ann's kid, Theresa, if your boys start blasting away at Jilly Sappone?"

"Yeah, I heard about the kid. Bad break for Annunziata." He stared at the paper for a moment, then looked up at Moodrow. "Bad break for both of 'em."

"So what you're saying is the kid doesn't matter. Just another casualty of war."

Carmine laughed. "Hey, bad things happen to good people, right?" When Moodrow didn't respond, he raised his hand, palms up, and said, "Nobody wants to hurt the kid. Like I already said, we're not fuckin' spics here. But it ain't like I could show myself soft. If it wasn't for soft, I wouldn't be in this mess." He popped another cannoli into his mouth. "Jilly's gotta be an example. You heard what he done to Carol Pierce?"

"Yeah, I heard. I was up there an hour after it happened."

"Well, I'm gonna do the same thing to Jilly. I don't care if I have to do it after he's dead. And I'm gonna leave what's left of him on a street corner in the neighborhood. And . . ."

"Enough." Moodrow waved him off. "You don't have to impress me. I know what you are." He ignored the fat man's frown. "Look, I want you to lay off for a week of so. Give me a chance to find Jilly on my own."

"In ya fuckin' dreams, Moodrow." Carmine's voice had lost its jovial tone. "And if ya insult me again, ya dreams are gonna take place under a coffin lid. You ain't a cop no more."

"Somehow I didn't expect you to cooperate out of the goodness of your heart." He raised the sheet of paper. "When was the last time you—or anybody you know—laid eyes on Jilly Sappone? Fourteen, fifteen years ago?"

"Yeah, about that."

"What makes you think your boys'll recognize him? What makes you think he won't walk right by them when he comes after *you*?" Moodrow tapped a forefinger on the table. "In fact, I'll bet most of the creeps in this room never knew him."

Carmine pointed to the sheet of paper. "I take it you got a photograph?"

"One for you, Carmine." Moodrow didn't bother to mention that the undated mug shot was five years old.

"And you wanna make a deal."

"Right, again."

"And ya got some way to stop me from reachin' out and snatchin' it away."

"You're too fat to reach across the table, but I'm willing to admit that you could *have* it snatched. Only then you wouldn't get to phase two."

Carmine shook his head, muttered, "Christ, Moodrow, you always had balls. Elephant balls. So, what's 'phase two'?"

"Jilly didn't do Carol Pierce. Ann Kalkadonis, either. No, Jilly's running with a partner, as you already heard from Buster Levy. It's gotta be somebody he met in the joint, somebody whose picture's on file. I'll have a list of Jilly's prison buddies within a few days. After Ann makes an identification, I'll pass you a photo."

"And all you want is I should lay off for a week?"

Moodrow smiled, knowing a promise extracted from Carmine Stettecase would carry all the sincerity of a kiss from a Delancey Street prostitute. "Yeah, Carmine, I want you lay off for a week, give the kid a chance. But I want something else, too. I want you to call Buster Levy, tell him to speak to me. I want you to ask him not to lie."

"Whatta ya want from Buster?" Stettecase's mouth narrowed suspiciously. "What's Buster got to do with *you*?"

"I'm sure he'll tell you after I finish with him." Moodrow pushed the photo across the table, watched Carmine pick it up, unfold it, stare down at Jilly Sappone. "Jilly got a lot older, right?"

"Yeah, just like the rest of us."

"Ya know what I think, Carmine? I think for the most part Jilly's laying low. I think he sends his buddy out to run errands, to set things up. Jilly may be crazy, but he was never stupid." Moodrow paused briefly, then continued. "I know you already put a bounty on Jilly's head, that you've got every crew within a hundred miles looking for him. What good is it gonna do you if Jilly's not on the street? If the key to finding Jilly Sappone is finding his partner?" Moodrow stopped again, gave the idea a moment to sink in, then broke into a giggle. "Carmine," he said, "listen up. I'm making you an offer you can't refuse."

Moodrow stepped out of the Gemini Lounge and into a slow, steady rain. He stopped under the restaurant's canopy, watched the raindrops splash onto the gray pavement, and smiled to himself. Somehow he'd missed the gathering clouds, the weather forecasts, the prepared and practical citizens with their furled umbrellas. It was a familiar story. All through his NYPD career, important cases (important by his standards, anyway) had devoured his concentration, demanding his full attention, leaving no room for day-to-day considerations, for the merely mundane.

He wanted to grin madly, shout, "I'm baaaaack," like the kid in the ghost movie, but held himself in check. Remembering that the world had its ways—like a cold, steady rain or a phone call from the west coast—of asserting its own claims. He was standing on the corner of West Broadway and Prince. The offices of Ginny Gadd, private investigator, were on Sixth Avenue, near Twenty-eighth Street, a good three miles away. There was always the Sixth Avenue subway, but if he had to walk over, he'd ruin his suit, the package he carried under his arm, and the first impression he hoped to make. On the other hand, with virtually no hope of finding a taxi in the rain, he wasn't about to hang around with his hand in the air.

After a minute or two, he accepted his fate, took the only course open to him. He turned and knocked at the door of the Gemini Lounge.

"Whatta ya want?"

The gorilla in the two-grand suit glared down as if he'd never seen him before, and Moodrow, his first impulse tempered by need, carefully repressed the urge to drive a fist into the man's hanging ribs. Instead, he worked up a thin, apologetic smile.

"Hey," he said, "ya think Carmine could lend me the use of an umbrella?"

TEN

Moodrow, his borrowed umbrella having surrendered to a sudden gust of wind on Twenty-fourth Street, dripped steadily onto the clean tile floor of Gadd Computer Investigations, Inc. He was sitting on a preformed plastic chair, sliding, really, on the wet seat while he tried to maintain a reasonably dignified equilibrium. He needn't have bothered. Ginny Gadd, having passed her few years in the NYPD behind the wheel of a Harlem-based patrol car, had seen far worse.

"Cream and sugar?" She turned to the enormous man perched on the small chair, a pot of coffee in one hand, and watched him watching her. Knowing his penetrating stare was standard cop procedure, something this old dinosaur had mastered so long ago it'd passed into pure habit. While still on the job, she'd hated that look, feeling (often correctly) that the evaluation was already tainted by the simple fact of her gender.

"Both, please. Light and sweet."

"Does that mean two, or three sugars?"

"Two."

She'd been right about Moodrow's stare. It *was* pure habit, his evaluation as automatic as strapping on his shoulder rig before leaving his apartment in the morning. Even as he accepted her coffee, he notched her appearance in typical cop fashion: somewhere between twenty-five and thirty; five feet, two inches tall, 115 pounds; thick dark hair cut short and swept across the sides of her head; features small and neat except for a pair of large, slightly jugged, ears. He ignored the merely transient, the blood-red blouse and the charcoal skirt, the ankle-high boots and the hoop earrings.

"Thanks. The wind cuts right through you when you're wet."

He watched her walk back to her desk, noted the muscular, bouncy gait and suspected an underlying confidence that matched it.

You gotta be careful, he told himself. Because she can be insulted real easy and you need her.

"So what's up, Moodrow?" She sat in the leather chair, laid her palms on the armrests, and crossed her legs. "What can I do for you?"

He reached into his jacket pocket, produced a second copy of Jilly Sappone's mug shot. "I thought you could use this. It's five years old, but it's better than nothing."

Gadd unfolded the wet paper carefully, laid it down on the desk blotter. "You look at a mug shot," she observed, "and sometimes you think you can draw the man right through the paper. That's how bad you want him." She glanced up at Moodrow, gave him a chunk of her own cop stare. "But you didn't come up here to give me a picture."

"True." He drained half the coffee. "I knew Jilly Sappone," he said, "back before he got sent up. He was always crazy, always liable to go off without notice, but he wasn't stupid. What I'm gettin' at is this: I think Jilly planned it out. And I think he started long before the parole board cut him loose."

"There's nothing I hate worse than a party pooper," Gadd interrupted. Her dark eyebrows curled up into little tents. "But I have to tell ya, Moodrow, your opinion doesn't exactly come as a revelation. How else could Jilly find Ann Kalkadonis seven hours after his release?"

"Okay, so we agree: Jilly had somebody on the outside collecting information. What I'm saying here is we have to assume that particular someone—maybe his aunt, Josie Rizzo, or maybe his new partner—also found him a hideout."

Moodrow went on to detail the relationship between Jilly, his aunt, and Carmine Stettecase. "Time is everything here. I don't know Jilly's plans for Theresa Kalkadonis, but I guarantee they

aren't long term. Plus, there's a good chance he'll lose control somewhere along the way. In which case, the *plan* is gonna go out the
window."

Ginny Gadd waited patiently for Moodrow to finish, to get to the
point. When he simply stopped talking, she nodded thoughtfully,
leaned back in her chair, rocked slowly from side to side. The man
obviously wanted something. Something she could give him. The
only real question was what *she* wanted, what *he* had to give.

"You ready for more coffee?"

"I really gotta get moving."

"No, Moodrow, what you *really* have to do is get to the point."

Moodrow shrugged. "When you're right, you're right." He leaned
forward, almost slid off the wet seat.

"Sorry about the chair. Someday I'll have a full set of leather arm-
chairs." She smiled, a gesture that involved her entire face. "In fact,
someday I hope to have an office that isn't over a porno shop. But,
for now . . ."

"No matter." Moodrow returned her smile. On the way up, he'd
run a gauntlet of neighborhood demonstrators carrying picket signs:
FILTH OUT/FAMILIES IN. "See, the thing about it is that me and Ann
Kalkadonis put together a list of Jilly's friends and relatives. That's
the logical place to begin, right? My problem is that the list is fifteen
years old and most of the people on it have moved away to parts unknown. I need to run them down, but if I have to do it by knockin'
on doors, the game'll be done before I'm half started."

"And you want me to find them with the computer."

It was a statement, not a question, and Moodrow simply nodded.

"I take it you don't have social security numbers to go with the
names?"

"No, but I might be able to get something even better. Did you
hear about Buster Levy? The guy Jilly attacked before he went to
Ann's apartment?" He waited for her nod before continuing.
"Buster's a loan shark, been operating on the Lower East Side for
twenty-five years. The word on the street is that he branched out
into the credit-card business a few years ago. He gets active card
numbers from clerks at the big department stores and makes his
own plastic. What I'm hoping is that Jilly got his hands on some of

those cards and used 'em. If I can match the place he used them with somebody from Ann's list, I'll know where to start looking."

Gadd tugged at the gold hoop in her right ear. The earring, brand new, was supposed to be .18-carat gold, but the nagging itch told a different story. "Are you saying you can get this man—Buster Levy— to actually supply you with a list of forged credit-card numbers?"

"Yeah, that's exactly what I'm saying." Moodrow had no desire to reveal the bargain he'd made with Carmine Stettecase to a virtual stranger, but if she wanted to believe he was a miracle worker, that was just fine. "Not that I'm sure Jilly actually took any credit cards. Right now, it's just a possibility. I'll be going over to see Buster right after I leave here. Then I'll know for sure."

Ginny Gadd looked at the brand-new (and still unpaid-for) IBM sitting on a desk against the south wall of her office. Her ability to maximize its capacities (at least as they pertained to the field of private investigation) had given direction to her post-cop life, but the sad truth was that she was already bored. Computer investigation was purely mechanical, a series of searches proceeding from the most to the least likely to produce results. Moodrow's list of Jilly's relatives was a perfect example of the process. She would begin with New York motor-vehicle records, then move out to New Jersey and Connecticut. If the individuals in question had ever been licensed to drive a car, she'd have their social security numbers and an address, current or not. A search through credit, bank, and property records would confirm or update the addresses. It was that simple and that mindless.

"Tell me if I heard right, Moodrow. This afternoon you kissed off the Haven Foundation, told them to take their money and put it where the sun don't shine. You . . ."

"Save the lecture, Gadd." Moodrow stood up, began to move toward the door. "What I heard was that you used to be a cop. And what I was *hoping* was that you were a cop long enough to know that you can't let civilians direct an investigation." He stopped in the middle of the small room, went back into his jacket pocket for another sheet of wet paper. "You want the names, Gadd? Or do I have to find someone else?"

Ginny smiled again, raising two huge dimples. "Well, being as I haven't had the foresight to dump my clients, I'll definitely take the names. But I want something for the time I spend on the computer."

"Like what?"

"Like maybe you could describe, in great detail, exactly what happened to the back of your head."

ELEVEN

It was nearly midnight when Moodrow finally stepped out of a cab in front of his Fourth Street apartment building. His head began to swivel even before he shut the door. The action was pure reflex, like a pigeon checking the sky for the silhouette of a hawk before leaving the refuge of a shaded branch. Moodrow's gaze jumped from shadow to shadow, resting momentarily on the few pedestrians, evaluating potential threats before moving on. He remained where he was, one foot in the gutter, one on the curb, until he'd achieved what he'd often described to Jim Tilley as "the illusion of safety." Then he walked quickly forward.

The rain had stopped an hour earlier, leaving an eerie stillness and a soft, blurry mist in its wake. Amber street lamps threw pale, self-contained spheres of light that seemed to absorb passing cars, only to spit them out on the far side. In the distance, lighted windows glowed dimly, as if suspended in the empty air.

The net effect, beautiful and threatening at the same time, like the haunted forest in a fairy tale, was lost on Stanley Moodrow. His attention, divided between his conversation with Buster Levy, the phone calls he had to make before he got to bed, and the key in his hand, couldn't be commanded by atmosphere. He needed something stronger and he got it as he thrust his key into the lock.

The first shot, muffled by the heavy mist, could have come from anywhere. It might have been a backfiring truck on an adjoining block, or an M80 firecracker tossed off a roof. But the second, third, fourth, and fifth left no room for doubt. Moodrow dropped to the pavement, dug for his .38, tried and failed to locate the shooter. Meanwhile, the shots continued, adding quickly to ten, then twenty, before he stopped counting. They came one after another, a relentless fusillade softened by the fog, reflected by the brick and stone of the city, seeming an irreducible part of the city itself.

When the last echo died (only to be replaced in his ears by the rapid-fire drumming of his own heart) Moodrow sat up and took inventory. There were no bodies on the street, no cries for help. There'd been no ricochets, either, nothing to indicate that he'd been the target. Nothing to indicate there'd been *any* target. He knew the gangbangers, as feral as wolves howling at the moon, like to go up on the roofs to empty their AK47s, their Tech 9s, their Uzis. Perhaps it had been no more than that.

Moodrow's judgment was confirmed ten minutes later when the authorities failed to show up. If someone had been hit, the cops and paramedics would have come racing to the scene, their revolving roof lights slashing through the fog. As it was, the gloom had simply resettled on the heads and shoulders of the few passing civilians, the hoods and roofs of the cars moving down Fourth Street.

As he turned away, a dozen confused thoughts and images ran through his consciousness. He envisioned the Lower East Side of fifty years ago, filled the streets with the rowdy companions of his youth. The rough-and-ready kids of 1945, including Stanley Moodrow, had been ready to fight at the drop of a hat. The more daring, like Carmine Stettecase, had carried switchblades and zip guns. They'd seen themselves as tough guys, worthy of their idols—John Wayne, Humphrey Bogart, and James Cagney—but, compared to the children of the Nineties, they'd been closer to Fay Wray in the hands of King Kong.

By the time he entered his apartment, Moodrow had already thrown off the incident. It was after midnight and he was very tired. There'd been a time when he could go for two or three days, when the occasional fifteen-minute nap was enough. That time was long passed and he knew it. He knew he'd need a decent night's sleep if he was going to find Jilly Sappone.

He went to the phone, picked it off the desk, dialed a familiar number, then sat on a high-backed wooden chair. After a moment or two, he was patched through the Seven's switchboard to Lieutenant Quentin McWhirter, the precinct whip, a man he knew well enough to address by his first name.

"Quentin, it's Stanley Moodrow."

"If you're lookin' for your buddy, you could forget about it. He's out and I don't expect him back until the end of his tour. A pair of mutts got into an NYU dormitory room, raped the four girls living there. It's gonna be an all-nighter."

"I thought you had Jim doing homicides?"

"A uniform on the scene reported that one of the girls ain't gonna make it." McWhirter cleared his throat. "Look, Moodrow, I got a drive-by on Orchard Street and no suits to cover it, so if you'll pardon me, I'll write Tilley a note and have him call you when he gets in."

Moodrow hung up, walked into the kitchen, took a beer out of the refrigerator, then trudged back to the phone. Two calls to go, two calls before he slept. He dialed Ginny Gadd's office number, was amazed to hear her answer on the second ring.

"It's Moodrow. I thought you'd be gone by now."

"I sacked out for an hour; I feel fine. How'd it go with Buster Levy?"

"The prick kept me sitting in his living room for two hours, but he gave me what I wanted."

"Why'd he do that, Moodrow?" Gadd jammed the phone between her right shoulder and her ear, fiddled with the paperwork on her desk. Having decided what she wanted from Stanley Moodrow, it was now a matter of convincing him that their interests were mutual. "Why'd he talk to you at all?"

"He did it because Carmine told him to." Moodrow's expression soured. He didn't care to be cross-examined, but he didn't see any way out of it, either. "And don't ask me about Carmine. Believe me, Gadd, you don't wanna know how I convinced Carmine."

"All right, Moodrow," Gadd said after a pause, "have it your way. Do I take it Jilly Sappone lifted some credit cards when he hit Levy's business?"

"Yeah, four. I don't know squat about computers. Is that a lot to check out?"

"What it is, Moodrow, under both New York State and federal law, is a felony. Four felonies, actually. One for each card."

"You serious?" Moodrow held the phone away from his head, told himself not to lose his temper. If she was going to back out, she would have done it while he was in her office.

"Absolutely. You have to have a legitimate interest—or represent somebody with a legitimate interest—in the financial affairs of an individual before you're legally entitled to credit-card transactions." Gadd stopped, allowed herself a gleeful grin, the one her last boyfriend had termed goofy. She could feel Moodrow's discomfort, feel it ooze through the phone she held to her ear. "On the other hand," she finally continued, "you could pass the numbers on to the cops or the feds, let *them* get the records."

"First of all, there are no *cops* to give it to." Moodrow again reminded himself to hold his temper in check. "The assault on Ann Kalkadonis and the robbery at Buster Levy's business were turned over to a single cop. His name is Jim Tilley. As for Carol Pierce and her boyfriend, there's no real proof that Jilly Sappone was involved."

"So Tilley's working all by himself?"

"All by himself while clearing every other case on his desk. Jim's a good friend of mine and he'll get every scrap of information that comes my way. He's also a good detective, but he can't move fast enough to save the kid. As for the feds . . . well, I'd rather cut off my dick than go to the feds."

"Nicely put."

"Thank you, Gadd." He hesitated briefly, decided to change the subject. "Lemme ask you this, did you have any luck with the list of names I gave you?"

"Out of the ten, I ran down four who live close enough. Two in Jersey, one in Connecticut, one on Long Island. Two of the others are in jail, two are dead, and two I couldn't locate."

"Good enough. Lemme get a pencil and a piece of paper." He put down the phone, took a spiral notebook and a Bic out of his pocket, laid them on his desk, then watched the second hand circle his wall clock twice before retrieving the phone. "Okay, I'm ready. Fire away."

The dinosaur being a lot sharper than she expected, it was Ginny Gadd's turn to hesitate. If she gave him the information, he could simply walk away from her. On the other hand, if she had the credit-card numbers, their roles would reverse in a New York minute.

"What about the credit cards?"

Moodrow registered the sharpened tone. He allowed himself a smile before responding. "I can't ask you to commit a crime. No matter what kind of risks I'm willing to take."

"Look, Moodrow, it's not like you could actually get caught. Or like anybody in law enforcement gives a damn. Didn't you tell me you had experience in this business?" She ran on before he could respond. "There's a lot of illegal information out there and it's all for sale. The problems kick in when you try to use the information, but in this case the target isn't likely to complain. After all, it's not like we're cops."

Moodrow scratched his head, smiled ruefully. "No, it's not like that," he said. "Not like we were cops."

"So, you wanna give me the card numbers?"

"If I do that, I'll have nothing. No names, no addresses." He stood up and started to walk away. When the phone dropped to the floor, he stopped short. "Shit, you still there? I knocked the phone off the desk."

"I'm still here." She kept her tone sharp, but felt no insult what-ever. "Why don't we stop playing games? I was a cop long enough to know the rule: nothing for nothing. Give me the card numbers and tomorrow I'll tell you if they were used. Favor for favor. Just like the good old days."

Moodrow took a moment to think it over. He could always take the names Ann Kalkadonis had given him and hire another com-puter expert to run down the addresses. But that didn't help him with the credit-card numbers.

"You wouldn't consider billing me at the regular rate? Maybe if I paid cash?"

"Sorry, pal, your money's no good here."

Moodrow read off the card numbers, made an appointment for the following morning at nine, then hung up. He was pretty certain she was going to ask to go along with him, to become a partner. What else did he have to offer? And the truth was that he could use her, as long as she was willing to commit a few more felonies along the way.

He got up, crossed to the window at the far side of the room, and started out. The gloom failed to hide the expected flash of a propane lighter on the rooftop across the street, though it successfully hid the faces of the huddled crack junkies who gathered there nightly. Not that they cared one way or the other about anonymity. The entire building, though officially unoccupied and actually owned by the city, was given over to the sale of one drug or another. The cops, at the behest of the Fourth Street Block Association, had been through a dozen times, making nearly a hundred arrests, but the trade continued, the sellers and buyers seemingly as uniform and interchangeable as lightbulbs.

All right, enough with the local color, Moodrow told himself. Do what you have to do.

The words failed to move him, though fatigue continued to wash through his body. The call he had to make, the last detail of a day filled with details, was to Betty in California. In the course of their conversation, she was going to ask him how the investigation was progressing and he was going to lie and he didn't want to lie. No, what he wanted, at that moment, was to have her close to him, to take her in his arms and into his bed, to wake up in the morning and listen to the soft hiss of her breath against the pillow.

The ringing phone jerked him away from his small fantasy. The mountain, he thought, coming to Muhammad. He picked up the receiver on the second ring, muttered, "Hello."

"Stanley, I thought you were going to call me."

"I just got in." The first lie of the evening. "How's Marilyn doing?"

He listened to the sharply indrawn breath, knew she was holding back tears. "Marilyn's broken, Stanley. Her body is gone, smashed. The doctor tried to prepare me, but it didn't help. I wanted to run out of the room, out of the hospital. I can't believe she's still alive." Another quick breath. "We're just waiting, now. Waiting and hoping."

Hoping Marilyn would die. Moodrow heard the words without Betty saying them.

"Is she conscious?"

"Her eyes were open; I think she was there, but she can't talk. Not with the tubes. And she can't move, either. Not enough to let me know for sure."

Bad things happen to good people. The cliché popped into his mind, though he managed to keep himself from actually saying it. "What about Artie?" Artie was Marilyn's husband.

"Artie's out of it." Her voice was edged with anger. "He spent his whole life making money. Everything else was up to Marilyn. Now he acts like an infant who needs his diaper changed. I didn't come out here to take care of him, Stanley, but that's apparently what he expects."

"It sounds like he's lost." Moodrow tried to imagine life without Betty, how he'd feel if she was suddenly gone. *Lost* didn't begin to describe it. "They've been together a long time."

"Does that mean I should make his bed for him?"

"Not unless you slept in it."

A momentary silence followed by a deep chuckle. "Only you, Stanley." She sighed, then rushed on. "It's much worse than Artie led me to believe. I thought I was coming to help Marilyn, but it's actually a death watch. The doctor told me her liver's barely functioning. They're not sure about her brain, how badly damaged it is."

"Look, I'll fly out there if you need me." The second lie. Moodrow couldn't have been pulled off the case with a crowbar and he knew it.

"Did you find the girl?" Betty's surprise at the offer was evident, exactly as Moodrow had expected.

"No, but there's a lot of other people looking."

"Stay where you are, Stanley." She sounded weary now, weary and resigned. "Stay where you are and do what you have to do."

TWELVE

It was bad, all right, as bad as it got for old Jilly Sappone. Even Jackson-Davis could see *that*. And for once it really wasn't Jilly's fault. No, the way it was, dark as a bandit with the rain pouring down so you couldn't see the street names, even old Reverend Luke would've lost his temper. Hell, they must've gone over this one bridge six times. Back and forth across some kinda river Jackson couldn't see, until finally Jilly made him get out to ask somebody where they were.

"That's Harvard."

The tall, bearded man pointed to these old buildings, then hurried on through the downpour. That seemed kind of strange because the man had on a slicker *and* an umbrella, while Jackson-Davis was standing out there in a little-bitty jacket with the cold rain pounding his hair into his skull.

"That's Hazzard," he told Jilly Sappone once he was back inside the car.

"Hazzard?"

"Yeah, like in the *Dukes* and . . . and stuff." He'd started to say *shit*, but caught himself in time. Little Theresa was sitting next to him in the back and it didn't seem right-like to curse around Little Theresa. Not no more it didn't.

"What the fuck does that mean? 'Like in the *Dukes*'?"

Jackson-Davis Wescott's mouth curled into a tiny circle. He'd complained to old Jilly about cursing in front of Theresa. ("Little

pitchers have big ears, Jilly. Can't say you never heard *that* one.")
But Jilly had just laughed at him.

"*The Dukes of Hazzard,* Jilly. The TV show?" He wrinkled his
nose, not once, but twice. That was by way of explaining to Jilly how
he felt about the cursing. Course, it was too dark for old Jilly to actually *see* his nose, but it made Jackson-Davis feel much better.

"I thought I told you to find out where we are." Jilly pulled away from
the curb. His head was pounding and the oncoming headlights carried
a familiar halo. He wanted to tell Jackson-Davis to drive, but with a shitstorm on the immediate horizon, he didn't trust himself near the kid.

"I did find out, Jilly. Them buildings back there? Them's *Hazzard.*" He hesitated momentarily as an idea began to form. "Say,
what if it's the *real* Hazzard?"

Jilly didn't bother to respond. He was having a hard enough time
driving the car. The lights pierced his eyes like knives, even though
he'd already flipped up the rearview mirror, even though he tried to
keep his eyes glued to the side of the road. The lights and the
pounding (which didn't really hurt, more like somebody put his
heart where his brain should be) were always the first sign that he
was about to lose it altogether. Unless he did something real quick,
the buzzing would sound, the lightning flash, the world narrow
down to a thin, angry slit.

> "*Fiiiiive bottles of beer on the wall.*
> *Fiiiiive bottles of beeeeeeeer.*
> *If one of those bottles should happen to fall,*
> *Foooooour bottles of beer on the wall.*
> *Foooooour bottles of beer on the wall.*
> *Foooooour bottle of beeeeeeeer.*"

"Shut the fuck up." Jilly spat the words through clenched teeth.

"But, Jilly, you told me to make sure little Theresa didn't do no
whinin'."

"I didn't tell you to fuckin' *sing.*"

"You didn't tell me nothin' about *no* singin'." Jackson-Davis
folded his arms across his chest. He knew he had a good point, a
damn good point.

"I'm tellin ya now."

"Why are you whisperin', Jilly? You sick or somethin'?"

"I'm fine." But he wasn't fine; he was lost. And somehow the little streets all seemed to come back on each other so no matter what direction he took, he ended up back at Hazzard. Instead of on the bridge he shouldn't have crossed in the first place.

He turned onto a wide street, saw a sign and an arrow: DOWN-TOWN BOSTON. Great, maybe the nightmare would finally come to an end. The way he saw it, he had two major problems and both of them were cops. With no paper for the car, no registration, and no license, he couldn't very well stop and ask a cop for directions. And he couldn't pull over at every corner to check the names of the streets, either, because a cop on patrol might decide to help out. Jilly had already made up his mind: He was going to kill any cop who approached, kill him quick, *before* he got suspicious.

> *"Patty-cake, patty-cake,*
> *Baker's man.*
> *Bake me a cake*
> *As fast as you can.*
> *Patty-cake, patty-cake,*
> *Baker's man.*
> *Bake me a cake*
> *As fast as you can.*
> *Patty-cake, patty-cake . . ."*

Jilly groaned, his anguish spilling out despite all efforts to hold it in, then pulled to the curb. Pushing his cop fears firmly to the side, he fished a small glassine envelope out of his shirt pocket and sucked the contents up into his nostrils. His hands twisted the steering wheel, tried to rip it apart, while he waited for the heroin to take effect. As it did, as it slowly filtered down into his bloodstream, the pounding in his head withdrew, moving from his ears into the center of his skull where it panted like a sullen Doberman.

"Jackson-Davis?"

"Yeah, Jilly?"

"What'd I say about singin'?"

"We ain't singin', Jilly."

"Then what were ya doin'?"

"We was playin', Jilly. We was playin' patty-cakes. You know, like when you pat your hands together?" He cocked his head and smiled. "See, your hands are the cakes. Paaaaty-*cake*. Theresa loves it."

Jilly took a deep breath. He was in control, now, though he couldn't be sure how long it would last. The main thing, a thought he clung to as his eyelids sagged, was that he was too stoned to drive.

"Jackson-Davis?"

"Yeah, Jilly?"

"I want you to come up front and drive." He turned slowly, looked down at Theresa-Marie. She was already beginning to whimper. "I'll sit in the back and try to read the map."

Jackson-Davis tried to think of some way to refuse without refusing. That was because old Jilly didn't like people saying no to him. Unfortunately, refusing without refusing was beyond his abilities.

"Jilly?"

"Yeah?"

"You ain't gonna hurt Theresa, right? You ain't gonna have one of your shitstorms if we get lost again?"

"Look at it this way, Jackson. If we stay here, the cops are gonna stop and ask what the fuck we're doin' pulled over to the curb in the rain. If that happens, I'll have to blow the cop away; I won't have no choice." He waited for Jackson-Davis to nod agreement. "You know me, Jackson. Once I get started, I got a real hard time stoppin' again." Another nod. "So maybe you better get up in front. Right now."

"Yeah, but Jilly?"

"What, Jackson?"

"You promised me you wouldn't hurt Theresa no more."

"I ain't gonna hurt her, Jackson." Jilly was still drifting down, still perfectly calm. He could stare at his partner's eyes, dream of the day when he'd empty a clip into those eyes, when they'd disappear, along with the back of Jackson-Davis's head. "But if ya worried about it, we could put her in the trunk."

Now Theresa was really sobbing. Jackson-Davis pulled her close, glared at Jilly Sappone.

"C'mon, Jilly. You know how Theresa hates the trunk. You promised you wouldn't put her in the trunk unless it was darn sure necessary."

"What's necessary, Jackson, is for you to get up here and drive the fuckin' car. Before any of that other shit happens."

Jilly dropped into the backseat like a sack of potatoes. He was vaguely aware of the car pulling away from the curb, but he couldn't bring himself to care about its destination. The dope was cutting its own path through his mind.

"I should'na come up here," he mumbled.

"You say somethin'?" Jackson-Davis was hoping Jilly had gone into one of his dope nods. Dope nods made Jilly real quiet-like, maybe so quiet that Jackson-Davis could flip down the vanity mirror behind the visor and take inventory.

"Things were too good." Jilly's voice, like his thoughts, seemed to come from a great distance. "Just about ready to go and I had to take a goddamned detour."

"Go where, Jilly?"

"Away," Jilly whispered. "Away from Carlo."

"From *Cousin* Carlo? Fits and conniptions, Jilly, why're we goin' away from Cousin Carlo when he's been treatin' us real good-like?"

Jilly was in too deep to explain. (Not that he would have bothered even when he was straight. Explaining things to Jackson-Davis was a losing proposition, like teaching algebra to a hamster.) But the truth was that Carlo Sappone was a weak link in every sense of the word, a drug dealer who snorted, shot, and smoked his profits. If the cops put the heat on Carlo, he'd give Jilly up. It was that simple.

Coming out of prison after fourteen years with no money in his pocket, Jilly hadn't had a lot of choices. It was Carlo Sappone or sleep on the streets. That had all changed when the package he'd retrieved from the puddle of blood surrounding Patsy Gullo's body turned out to contain four ounces of reasonably pure heroin. Carlo's small, dark eyes had flashed pure greed when Jilly broke the bags open; he'd been more than willing to part with every dime he admitted to having.

Seven grand wasn't half what the dope was worth, but it was enough to buy some independence. His Aunt Josie, now that he had the money to pay for it, had found him an apartment in Manhattan. All he had to do was pack up his few belongings and move in. But then he'd gotten this great idea: drive up to Boston, snatch his daughter, Patricia, then come back to New York and throw it in his wife's face.

It hadn't seemed like any big deal at the time. Josie had gotten the address from a letter Patricia had written to her mother, had taken it right out of the mailbox as one piece of the revenge she and Jilly were determined to take. If it was going to happen sooner or later, why not sooner? Four hours of driving, a quick grab (or a quick kill, depending on whether Patricia decided to resist), then four hours back. No muss, no fuss.

That was almost nine hours ago. Nine hours of heavy rain, of one construction project after another. A bad accident had forced him off the interstate and onto the mean streets of Hartford, Connecticut, at five o'clock in the afternoon. Another accident on the Massachusetts Turnpike had pushed four lanes of traffic onto the shoulder. Finally, there was Boston itself, a nightmare of dark and narrow streets that curled back on themselves like snakes swallowing their own tails.

"Jilly, you awake?" Jackson-Davis slid the mirror down, stole a quick look at his reflection. "Huh, Jilly?"

No answer, not even a glance. Jilly Sappone was in a place beyond thought.

"How 'bout you, Theresa? You with old Jackson-Davis?"

"Yes."

Jackson-Davis took another look in the mirror. His "damn near to an albino" hair was plastered so tight against his head he seemed almost as bald as his old daddy. He ran his fingers over his skull, tried to fluff his hair up.

"You wanna get a burger or somethin'?" he asked.

"I wanna go home to my mother."

"Don't say that." Jackson-Davis glanced at Jilly Sappone. "If old Jilly hears you say that he'll get himself into a terrible snit. We don't want that, do we?"

Theresa didn't answer. She sat back with her head against the door in an attitude of utter resignation. Events, beginning with the sudden death of her father, had swallowed her whole.

"I tell you what, Theresa." Jackson-Davis stole another glance in the mirror, this time at his narrow mouth. He liked to watch his lips move when he talked. "Let's go find that place old Jilly's lookin' for. That'll put him in a good mood when he wakes up."

Jackson's problem was that he couldn't remember the name of the street, only that it was on some kind of a hill.

"I bet," he said to his reflection, "if I find that hill, the name'll just come right back to me."

For once, Jackson-Davis Wescott was right. He found a steep hill after twenty minutes of random driving, paused at the bottom, and remembered the name of the street.

"Myrtle. Ain't that right, Theresa?"

Theresa didn't answer, the word having absolutely no meaning to her, but Jackson-Davis, preoccupied with another problem, didn't seem to mind.

"Dang and darn," he said after a moment's reflection. "Guess the joke's on me. I couldn't read them old signs even if I could see 'em, which I cain't."

He drove up and around the hill for the next twenty minutes, trying to think of a solution to his problem, even though he knew he wasn't good at solutions. In the meantime, Jilly began to awaken. Thoughts came first, thoughts devoid of any emotional content, then awareness slowly crept through his thoroughly stoned brain. He noted Theresa cringing against the door, the back of his partner's head, the rain still falling, the windshield wipers slapping back and forth. A few minutes more and he began to place the various images in a particular time and place, remembering that he was in the city of Boston, looking for his only child.

"Jackson-Davis?"

"I done found that old hill, Jilly." Jackson-Davis turned and grinned at his partner. "But I ain't found the street on account of I cain't read the signs."

Jilly, after a serious effort, managed to raise his slumped body to a sitting position and look out the window. What he saw brought him fully awake. Knots of druggies, dealers and buyers, milled about on all four corners of the intersection, while prostitutes, barely dressed despite the cold rain, strolled beneath wide umbrellas on the avenues. The whores beckoned to the passing car and the two white men inside, one girl even lifting the edge of her mini to give them a good look at the available merchandise.

"Holy fucking shit," Jilly moaned. "Where have you got us to?"

"You said a hill, Jilly." This wasn't going the way Jackson-Davis had expected. "I remember you sayin' about Patricia livin' on a hill."

"Are you kidding me? This is fucking niggertown. Would my daughter live in fucking niggertown?"

Jackson-Davis swallowed. "Guess not, Jilly."

"Make a left turn, get down the goddamned hill and find a main street."

"But, Jilly . . ."

"One more word, Jackson, and I'm gonna kill ya."

Jackson-Davis made the turn, remembering that sometimes when Jilly Sappone talked real soft it was worse than when he shouted. He glanced into the mirror, watched his partner unfold a map, then turn on the overhead light.

"Real good, Jilly. Real . . ."

"I told you to shut the fuck up." Jilly studied the map carefully, thinking that, in some ways, this was the best part of being high on dope. Though he was mightily pissed off, he was in complete control. Or, at least, he *felt* like he was in complete control, which was all he could hope for in life.

They found Columbus Avenue at the bottom of the hill. According to Jilly's map, Columbus led directly into central Boston and Beacon Hill, which was where Patricia lived. All he had to do was make a left on Charles Street, a right on Revere, and another right on Myrtle, three simple turns and the deal was done.

They found the turn on Charles Street easily enough, the road was large and well marked, but then, without any warning, Charles turned one-way against them, forcing Jackson-Davis into a left on Beacon which led away from . . .

"Make the first right," Jilly commanded. He didn't know the name of the street, didn't care. With the river on one side and a steep hill on the other, he figured they'd *eventually* stumble across Myrtle Street. As long as they didn't cross that fucking river again.

Eventually turned out to be thirty minutes of pure torture during which he passed Revere three times without being able to turn into it, until he finally happened upon Myrtle from Anderson Street.

"Which way, Jilly?"

"No way, just park the goddamned car by that hydrant. I'll walk from here." He took inventory while Jackson-Davis maneuvered the car into the only open space on the block. The neighborhood was much fancier than he'd expected, but that might actually work in his favor. Between his neatly trimmed gray hair and beard, his black, London Fog trench coat, and the private security badge pinned to a billfold in his pocket, he'd most likely be able to pass himself off as a cop. As long as nobody got close enough to see the fire in his eyes.

"You sure you don't want me to come along?"

Jilly yanked Theresa down on the seat, covered her with a blanket, ignored her sobbing. "The bitch is still gonna be under this blanket when I come back, right?"

"Yeah, Jilly. The blanket'll make her nice and comfy-like."

"And you're gonna keep her quiet, right?"

"Not a peep."

Jilly opened the door, stepped onto the sidewalk, listened to the muted buzzing in his ears. Shitstorm on the horizon? His brain had begun to pulse softly again, the streetlights to flare ominously. He told himself to hold on, to get it done, that he'd have plenty of time to relax, then walked off in search of his daughter.

He found her building on the next block, a four-story town house with a shielded lock on the front entrance. Patricia's apartment was on the top floor, but Jilly rang Apartment 1A, announced, "Police," into the intercom, then waited patiently while an old man shuffled down the hallway to check him out.

"Police," he repeated, holding up the phony badge.

The man peered at the badge for a moment, then up at Jilly, then back at the badge. Finally, he stepped back to let Jilly into the hallway. "What's this about?"

"I'm looking for a young woman named Patricia Sappone, a college student."

"There's a couple of girls up on the fourth floor. Four B, I think, but I don't know their names." He squinted up at Jilly through watery eyes. "What'd they do, Officer?"

Jilly threw the old man a reassuring smile. "Sorry to disappoint you, sir, but they didn't *do* anything. Patricia Sappone witnessed an assault a few months ago and I need to go over her testimony." He leaned forward. "Just between you and me, the cops who interviewed her the first time around screwed it up real bad. Took her address, but didn't get her apartment or her phone number. It's the new *element* on the force. The affirmative-action bullshit crew. That's what I like to call 'em."

He winked, turned his back, started up the stairs. Thinking that maybe the old man would call the real cops, but he'd be out before they responded. One way or the other.

As he climbed the winding staircase, he switched the nine millimeter from his belt to his coat pocket. There was always the chance that Patricia, though she hadn't seen him in fourteen years, would recognize him through the peephole. In that case he fully intended to forgo the pleasure of her company, to empty a clip through the door.

He needn't have worried because there was no peephole on the door to Apartment 4B, no way for anyone inside to see his face without opening the door first. And once that door opened, even if they had the safety chain attached, he'd be inside.

His knock was answered after a minute by a soft, "Who is it?"

"Police." Jilly held up the badge with his left hand, kept his right in his pocket.

The door opened a few inches and a face appeared in the crack. Jilly, who'd been worried about his own ability to recognize his daughter, knew the Asian girl peering out at him definitely wasn't Patricia.

"What's it about?"

"I'm looking for a woman named Patricia Sappone."

"Patty? She's not home."

"Will she be coming home soon?"

"I don't think so, but I'm not really sure. Patty went back to New York to be with her mother. She left an hour before you got here."

The shitstorm ripped into Jilly's brain with the sudden fury of a cyclone descending to earth. The first lightning bolt jerked him upright, the second ran down through his arms to yank at his fingers.

All his fingers, including the one wrapped around the trigger of his nine-millimeter Colt. At first, Jilly thought the resulting explosion was just part of the show, but when the girl in the doorway let out a scream, then slammed the door in his face, he realized that something was seriously wrong. Unfortunately, he didn't fully understand what it was until his attempt to rip the gun out produced a spent shell which bounced off the side of his coat to land in a small puddle of blood next to his right foot.

THIRTEEN

Stanley Moodrow swung his legs over the edge of the bed and pulled himself into a sitting position. The box spring squealed in protest, echoing the complaints of his own body. According to the battered wind-up alarm clock on the night table, it was 5:47, much too early, he decided, for a sixty-year-old. . . . He stopped, automatically corrected himself: for a *nearly* sixty-year-old man to be up and about.

BZZZZZZZZZZZZZZZ

"I'm comin'."

He looked back to see if the buzzer had awakened Betty, then remembered that she wasn't there, that she was in California with Marilyn, that a man named Jilly Sappone lay in his immediate future, that he had a dozen things to do.

"I'm comin'," he repeated.

He lurched to his feet, threw on a robe, padded off down the hall to open the door for his former partner. "What happened, Jim? You finish early?"

Tilley stepped into the apartment, held out a copy of the *Daily News*.

"Finish?" he said. "No such thing. I still have to generate tonight's paperwork. The whip tells me I haven't met this week's quota. Check out the headline."

Moodrow unfolded the newspaper, read the block letters below the paper's logo. NO REFUGE. His eyes dropped to the two photos, one of Jim Tilley and several other detectives outside the NYU dormitory, one of a gurney sliding into an EMS ambulance. He studied them for a moment, then read the caption at the bottom of the page: "State-of-the-art security system fails to prevent tragedy. Four girls attacked in NYU dorm. Story on page 3."

"The *Post* go with it, too?" he asked.

"The *Post* and *Newsday*. It's 'life in the fishbowl' time." Tilley set a paper bag on the table, removed two coffee containers and a half dozen frosted crullers. "How many days you think I have? Before they start screaming?"

Moodrow grunted. *They* meant Tilley's NYPD bosses; all politicians, in and out of power; the entire media, from the *New York Times* editorial page to the fulminating Rush Limbaugh; a thoroughly cowed (and cowering) public.

"I'd say you got maybe fifteen *minutes*."

"Wanna hear the kicker?" Tilley popped the lid on one of the Styrofoam cups, added a packet of sugar.

"Shoot."

"Two of the girls were white, one was Asian, one was black. The black girl's name is . . . no, *was* Keesha Montgomery, daughter of City Councilman John Montgomery. Keesha was beaten to death with a table leg. A weapon, as they say, of convenience."

Moodrow nodded sympathetically, then took off for the bathroom. Knowing that despite Tilley's pro forma cop protest, the investigation was a no-lose proposition for a precinct detective. If Jim found the mutts before the case was transferred out to the Sex Crimes Unit, a matter of forty-eight hours at the outside, and if he played it smart by allowing the lieutenant and the precinct commander to steal the collar, he'd most likely be promoted to Detective, First Grade. On the other hand, if he failed to pull the perps out of the proverbial hat, the job would move away, become somebody else's responsibility. By the time the cops were ready to give up, he'd be too far removed to take the blame.

That's not the way it was going to be with Jilly Sappone, of course. There was no out for Stanley Moodrow, no way to shift responsibility. The simple fact that the media wasn't looking over his shoulder meant less than nothing to him. Moodrow looked over his *own* shoulder.

His teeth brushed and bladder emptied, Moodrow went back into the kitchen and sat down at the table. He yanked the lid off the second Styrofoam coffee container, added two sugars, took a long satisfying drink.

"So, what's up, Jim?"

Tilley opened his briefcase. "We got some possibles on Sappone's partner." He took out several sheets of paper and laid them on the table. "Plus, something real interesting on Jilly himself. I got a medical report here says that Sappone is brain damaged. Something about . . ." He picked up a single sheet, scanned it quickly. "According to this report, Jilly is some kind of an epileptic. Seizures in the temporal lobes. The doc says that unless he has brain surgery, Jilly is a hundred percent guaranteed to reoffend upon release."

Moodrow broke a piece off one of the crullers, popped it into his mouth, took a moment to let the glaze dissolve on his tongue. "I must be missing something here. Does this help us in some way? Maybe we should get him on Prozac."

"Can't you see what's happening?" Tilley stared at Moodrow through bleary eyes. "The fucking doc set up a perfect insanity defense. Correction: *temporary* insanity defense. Jilly could have the surgery and claim he's cured. His lawyer can use the goddamned *state* to prove his case. I don't . . ."

"Jim, this time the doc ain't lyin'. Jilly Sappone is strictly damaged goods." Moodrow raised a hand, saw that it held the rest of the cruller. "Damn, but I'm hungry." He took his time finishing it off, chewing slowly, licking his fingertips clean. There was something he had to tell his ex-partner, but he didn't quite know how to put it. How to break through Tilley's evident paranoia. "Sappone was just a little kid, five, six, seven, when his old man got blown away. They were in the car together, parked at the curb after a trip to grandma's, when two shooters opened up from close range. They weren't trying for Jilly, but a slug fragmented on his father's skull and Jilly caught a piece of it. From what I understand, it's still sitting there."

Moodrow paused, then, when Tilley didn't respond, took another tack. "Look, Jilly's gonna get brain surgery, all right, but it's more likely to be done with an ice pick than a scalpel. You understanding me here? The cops are the least of Jilly Sappone's problems. That's what makes him so dangerous."

Tilley's white-on-white complexion reddened. He looked down at his hands, then back at his ex-partner. "Yeah, you're right. When I saw the report, I got carried away. It seems like every mope on the street has some kind of an excuse." His voice dropped to a guttural whisper. " 'See, ya fuckin' Honor, the reason I butchered that old bitch was because my stepdaddy used to fuck me in the ass.' After a while you can't hear it anymore."

Moodrow held his partner's gaze, deliberately refused to let him off the hook. "If you don't slow down, Jim, the job is gonna eat your whole life. Rose, the kids, your whole fucking life." He gave Tilley a chance to respond, though what he expected and received was an angry stare. "You gotta back up. You gotta back up or get out altogether. Every time I see you, lately, you sound off like one of those PBA jerks." He pitched his voice up, ran the next words in a mocking singsong. "They're back out on the streets before I finish the paperwork. The jails are country clubs and nobody goes there anyway. The liberal judges, the liberal media, the sleazy lawyers, the technicalities." He slapped his palm on the table. "If there's anything in life more disgusting than a whining criminal, it's a whining cop."

Again, Moodrow stopped. He could feel Tilley's anger now, feel it rise up like the stink off a week-old corpse. Nevertheless, he plunged forward.

"You have to forget about the stats, man. You have to pick and choose your cases, what you're gonna pursue and what you're gonna let go. If the silks don't like it, let them go fuck themselves. Better the job should bury you, than you should bury yourself." He flicked a contemptuous hand in Tilley's direction. "How many pounds you lost in the last year? Fifteen? Twenty? That suit hangs on you like a wet blanket."

Tilley froze halfway out of the chair. He leaned forward, palms on the table. "Who are you to tell me how to live? You spent your whole life buried in the job."

"That's true." Moodrow bit into another cruller. "But in thirty-five years, Jim—thirty-five *years*—I never once lost weight. Think about it." He chased the cruller with the rest of his coffee. "Meanwhile, let's get back to business."

"Just like that?"

Moodrow shrugged. "There's no point in me running my mouth if you can't hear what I'm saying. I know the feeling because I've been there. It's like being surrounded in a dark alley, fists and feet coming from all directions. You get to punching back so fast, there's no time for strategy. You've been in the ring, so you know what I'm talkin' about. If you wanna survive, you gotta force the enemy to fight *your* fight."

"Are you saying that the job is an enemy?"

"What I'm saying is what you already know. The silks at One Police Plaza don't give a shit about you. No more than Don King with his fighters. One goes down, another comes up, like pushpins in a cork board."

Tilley let himself drop back onto the chair. He knew there was no disputing the truth of what his friend had told him. It was a reality every veteran lived with. The bosses would sacrifice you in a heartbeat, claiming it was for the good of the department when it was really for the good of their own precious careers. It had been that way for a hundred and fifty years and it wasn't going to change.

"Stanley, you're right," he said. "It's time to get back to business."

"Sounds good to me." Moodrow began to shovel ground coffee into an ancient percolator. "You ready for another cup, Jim?"

"Desperate is more like it."

Moodrow added water, set the percolator on the stove, turned on the burner. "So what about Jilly's partner? What have you got?"

"First things first." Tilley managed a weak smile. "It seems like maybe Jilly took a little side trip last night. Up to Boston. Looking for his daughter, Patricia."

The information brought Moodrow up short. "*Maybe?* What does that mean?"

"That means a Boston cop faxed a report to the Seven last night. According to said report, one Mary Ling was confronted in the apartment she shares with Patricia Sappone by a man claiming to be a cop. When said cop asked to speak with her roommate, Mary Ling informed him that Patricia had left to be with her mother in New York. Whereupon said cop shot himself in the foot."

Several thoughts rumbled through Moodrow's brain, the strongest (and worst) of which concerned itself with how much he wanted Jilly Sappone for himself.

"They get him?"

"No. And they didn't get a positive ID either. What they did get was a spent nine-millimeter casing and a blood trail."

Moodrow scratched the side of his face, remembering the advice he'd given Ann Kalkadonis. He told himself not to let it go to his head, that he could win every battle and still lose the war.

"Why didn't you tell me this when you came in?" he asked.

"It was supposed to be a surprise." This time Jim Tilley's grin was genuine. Moodrow was his mentor and his friend, a pair of roles that held any number of contradictions. "But I think your lecture threw off my timing."

Moodrow sat down. "I'm worried about you. You haven't been looking good." It was that simple.

"That's fine, Stanley, but your solutions are out of date. There's no 'pick and choose' anymore. The bodies come too fast. You remember the forty-eight-hour rule? The one that says if you don't clear a homicide in the first forty-eight hours, you'll never clear it?" He waited for Moodrow to nod. "Well, Stanley, the forty-eight hours you worked with is now down to forty-eight minutes. In ten years, it'll be forty-eight seconds."

Moodrow started to respond, but Tilley waved him off. "Down to business, right?" He spread six photographs across the table. "I spoke to four deputy wardens yesterday and got three responses. From Attica, Clinton, and Greenhaven. The way I hear it, Jilly didn't have a lot of friends."

FOURTEEN

By the time Stanley Moodrow passed the photo of Jackson-Davis Wescott to Ann Kalkadonis, he was absolutely sure that Wescott was Jilly Sappone's partner. So sure, that he intended to assume the fact, even if Ann failed to make a positive ID. He needn't have worried. Ann Kalkadonis, with Patricia looking over her shoulder, took a single glance, then handed the photo back to Moodrow.

"That's him," she said.

It was eight o'clock in the morning, a little too early to be ringing doorbells, but as long as Moodrow could bring himself to wait. He'd been staring at Wescott's blank, open face since Jim Tilley had left for the precinct. The other photos had gone back into a manila envelope, so far off the description given by Ann Kalkadonis and Buster Levy as to be unworthy of consideration. Meanwhile, Jackson-Davis, an innocent smile plastered to his face, had beckoned like the scent of game to a hungry fox.

"His record fits," Moodrow answered. He was hoping to leave it at that. The details, the borderline retardation, the attacks on women, the violent sexual fantasies lovingly detailed by a prison psychologist who'd recommended against parole, were far too grim for the mother of a kidnapped child.

"How does it help you?"

Moodrow looked up at Patricia Kalkadonis, noted the dark, piercing eyes and sharp, straight nose. Under other circumstances, he realized, he might tell her how much she favored her old man.

"This guy," he gestured at the photo, "Wescott, knew your father in prison. He came out fourteen months ago, made three visits to a parole officer in lower Manhattan, then disappeared. I have to assume he set things up, got the apartment, the guns, the car. Hopefully, the local merchants will recognize his face where they might never have seen your father's."

The last part was true enough, the part about the merchants. But with an IQ in the mildly retarded range, Wescott hadn't set anything up. No, that task must have fallen to somebody else, to the *only* somebody else available, Josephine Rizzo.

"Jilly Sappone is not my father," Patricia said after a moment. She crossed her legs, let her hands drop down to rest on her knee. "No more than he's my mother's husband."

Moodrow, not knowing what to say, looked over at Ann Kalkadonis who managed a weak smile and a shrug.

"It doesn't matter what you think." Moodrow met Patricia's eyes, held them tight. "Not as long as Jilly Sappone is walking around." He stood up, touched the back of his head. "Look, I cut myself a couple of days ago and it seems to be . . ." He hesitated momentarily, then giggled. "It seems to be *oozing*. Nice word, right? Meanwhile, being as the cut's on the back of my head and I can't see it, I gotta make a trip to the emergency room."

"I'll check it out." Patricia Sappone was on her feet before she remembered that Moodrow was more than a foot taller, that her head barely came up to his chest. "I'm pre-med, worked in emergency rooms since I was sixteen. There's something I want to ask you, anyway."

Moodrow, old-fashioned enough to equate a trip to the hospital with a near-death experience, allowed himself to be led past two disgusted FBI agents (the same pair who'd disputed his right to an unsupervised visit with his client) and into the bathroom. He sat on the commode, let Patricia tear off the bandage while he considered what, if anything, he owed the agents. After all, they were covering the actual kidnapping and Wescott's photo might be invaluable, assuming they didn't already have it. On the other hand, like all city cops, active or retired, he hated everything about them, from their casual arrogance to the conservative cut of their vested suits.

"Who sewed this up?" Patricia dumped the old bandage in the trash can beneath the sink.

"A friend of mine."

"What'd he use, rope?" She probed the edges of the wound with her fingertips. "I'm just kidding. Actually, he did a decent job, who-ever he is. Once it heals, it won't reopen. Leave a hell of a scar, though." She wrapped a towel around his neck, then opened a pack-age of sterile gauze pads and held them under the hot water in the sink. "You've got a little infection going here. No surprise on a ragged tear like this. Are you taking antibiotics?"

Moodrow remembered the penicillin in his sock drawer for the first time since putting it there. "I had some penicillin, but I been so caught up in things, I forgot all about it."

Patricia rummaged through the medicine chest for a moment, then turned to him with a small brown vial. "Take a couple now, then one every four hours or so. It'll hold you over until you get home again." She waited for Moodrow to chase the two white tablets with a cup of water, then began to clean his wound. Her fin-gers moved swiftly and confidently as she washed the jagged gash. "You don't wanna let this get ahead of you," she said.

Moodrow shrugged, what was done was done. "Didn't you have a question you wanted to ask me?"

"My mother said you were the one who told her to bring me back to New York. Before that, we'd both assumed I'd be safer out of the city. Even the FBI thought so."

"Well, you could say I had a big advantage, being as how I knew Jilly and his Aunt Josie. You were still pretty young when your mother took you away from all that. As for the Federal Bureau of In-competence, they don't know the first thing about the streets. It's not their fault, really, but that's the way it is."

Patricia continued to work, first covering the wound with thick bandage, then taping it down. When she was finished, she backed away to lean against the door.

"That wasn't the question I wanted to ask," she said.

Moodrow turned to face her. "I didn't think it was."

"I want to know why they let him out. I want to know why they didn't kill him in the first place." Her mouth narrowed as her anger came to surface; her hand rose in a fist. "He killed before and now he kills again. How can that be?"

Moodrow took a deep breath. He started to speak, but she cut him off with a wave of her hand.

"The parole board sent my mother a letter. *Parole denied* is what it said. That was two months ago. Does it make any sense to you? I need to know why he's out. I need to understand the kind of justice that allows a killer to kill again."

Moodrow was still considering the question as he made his way to a fenced parking lot on Thirteenth Street near Avenue A. The gloom of the previous night, driven by sharp northwesterly winds, had vanished; the sky above him was a deep, pure blue, the air he breathed clean and cool. Even the ancient tenements and store-fronts gleamed. The city's peculiar geometry, the brick and lime-stone, windows and doors, sidewalk squares and long narrow streets, jumped out as if its sharp edges had been deliberately etched by the intense May sunlight.

Despite his preoccupation, the effect wasn't lost on Stanley Moodrow. No, he recognized the beauty, all right, and he recognized the irony as well. Spring renewal in a city that had given up on itself? That had separated out into ethnic and racial enclaves? It seemed almost sacrilegious, as if the cold wet New York winters had no right to end.

"Hey, Moodrow, wha'chu doin'? You need the car?"

"Yeah, I'll be gone all day."

Moodrow watched Walberto Quintera slouch over to the tiny shack in search of his keys. Still half boy (in Moodrow's eyes, any-way) at age eighteen, Walberto wore his X-cap with the bill turned defiantly to the back. The crotch of his oversize coveralls dropped al-most to his knees, his sneaker laces were untied, and the tails of his plaid shirt hung fore and aft like the flaps of an urban loincloth. He seemed every inch the ghetto warrior, the kind of macho Latino who made the old ladies of the Upper East Side cross the street to avoid his shadow.

The macho part was true enough. Walberto, like most of the

Puerto Ricans Moodrow knew, would fight at the drop of an insult. The rest of it, however, was pure fiction. Walberto worked in the parking lot from six in the morning until six at night, shuffling cars from one space to another. Afterward, while other New Yorkers sat down to an evening of television, he rode the subway up to John Jay College on Tenth Avenue where he took courses in police science. Moodrow had come upon Walberto sitting in the shack with an open textbook on his lap any number of times.

"See, how I figure," he'd explained to Moodrow, "is the cops do real good. Forty grand a year and the benefits and the pension? Shit, man, ain't no way a Loisaida Puerto Rican is gonna find no better job. Alls I gotta do is pass the exam and stay outta trouble."

Then why did he dress like a gangbanger, a knucklehead? Why did he listen to gangsta rap on his little boom box? Why did he roll and dip his shoulder when he walked? Why did he want to look like what he wasn't?

Moodrow had never asked the questions and never would. At best, Walberto would see them as an old man's complaint. At worst, he'd find them purely insulting.

"Man, she don' wanna run today, Moodrow. She complainin' like she got her curse." Walberto eased Moodrow's 1988 Chevrolet Caprice up to the gate, threw the car into park, and stepped out. "All them horses under the hood, man, I think they must'a went lame or somethin'."

Moodrow eased his body behind the wheel, slid the bench seat all the way back, and put the car in gear. He'd bought the Chevy two years ago from a body shop in Astoria that specialized in adapting used police vehicles for the New York taxi trade. Moodrow's car had come all the way from Alabama; it sported a huge eight-cylinder engine and an ignition system that hated rainy nights.

"Save me a space, Walberto. In case I get back after you close up."

The car bucked its way up to the light on Avenue A, then stalled when Moodrow took his foot off the gas. Moodrow responded the way he'd responded to thirty years of driving balky police vehicles. He flipped on the radio and patiently restarted the engine.

By the time Moodrow pulled to the curb in front of the Academy Gun Shop on 19th Street, the car, as expected, was running smoothly. He switched off the ignition, shoved a police restricted parking permit in the front window, and got out. The series of actions had an easy familiarity, even if the reason for his visit was so far outside the normal as to carry an actual sense of betrayal.

"Hey, Moodrow, how's it hangin'?" David Mushnick had a box of Winchester .38 Special ammo off the shelf and on the countertop before Moodrow closed the door. "What else can I do for ya?"

Moodrow took a deep breath. He felt like a schoolboy facing the principal as he pushed the cartridges away. "Forget the .38, Dave," he said. "I'm here to buy a gun."

"Are you sure you don't wanna think about this? You and that .38 have been married for a long time."

Moodrow shook his head. "I'm not dumping my .38. What I'm after is a .25-caliber automatic."

"Twenty-five automatics are for women and hit men." Mushnick shook his head in amazement. "I don't think you can pass for a woman."

"In that case, Dave," Moodrow said without smiling, "I guess I'll have to pass for a hit man."

FIFTEEN

The first thing Ginny Gadd shouted when Moodrow came through her door was, "You're late." Followed quickly by, "What happened, you run out of rumpled suits?"

"That's just it," Moodrow shouted back, "I'm late because I had to go home and change."

They were shouting for two reasons. First, a baritone sax, accompanied by piano, bass, and drums, was blasting its way through an extended solo. The music was coming from a back room and, presumably, could be turned down. That wasn't true of the jackhammer ripping up the Sixth Avenue asphalt.

"Lemme shut off the stereo."

Moodrow watched Gadd disappear into the back room, noted the way her butt pushed against the seat of her jeans, and decided to mention her the next time he spoke to Betty. This despite Betty's never having a jealous moment. Despite his own unthinking fidelity.

"That was Gerry Mulligan." She was standing in the doorway, looking impossibly youthful in an oversize black cable-knit sweater. "With Thelonius Monk. Would you believe it? Mulligan sounds like he's just going through the motions. Maybe he couldn't keep up."

Moodrow nodded, gestured to the room behind Gadd. "You live back there?"

The question drew a blush that ran up into her jugged ears. "You want to hear the sad story?"

"Sure."

Gadd crossed the room, held up a blue coffee mug. "You want?"

"Yeah."

She filled the mug, added milk and two spoons of sugar, then turned back to him. "You ever had a lover who moved away from you? I'm not talking about physically here." She waited for his, "Yeah, I guess so," then continued. "Buddy and I were college students, at Columbia, when we met. I suppose we shared the same ambitions, but that was nine years ago and I can't remember well enough to be sure we actually spoke about it. After graduation, I went into the cops and he went on to get his MBA."

"A match made in hell," Moodrow observed, taking the mug.

"It's funny you should look at it that way." Gadd went back to her desk and sat down. "Because there was never any real violence, physical or psychological. Buddy went to work for Price, Waterhouse; I bounced from tour to tour. He spent his days behind a desk on the fortieth floor; I spent mine with the mutts and the mopes. I can look back now, look back and know there was never any real hope for us, but I must have fooled myself at the time because I didn't make any preparations for living by myself. Two months after I left the job, Buddy moved to Greenwich, Connecticut. That wouldn't have been so bad if he hadn't taken the furniture—*his* furniture—with him. Or if I could have afforded the uptown apartment we shared."

"So you ended up here?"

She shrugged. "I'm just getting started and I can't pay two rents."

The jackhammer stopped abruptly, leaving her words to echo in the unexpected quiet. It was a silence neither was tempted to break and Moodrow took advantage of the moment to examine her more closely. Or, better yet, to examine his own growing attraction, an attraction he carefully termed *fatherly*.

Her face was small and symmetrical, her features, taken one by one, unremarkable. Only her eyebrows, thick, dark crescents that swept down to frame the corners of her eyes, held any hint of character. She might have chosen to pluck them (or shave or wax them, Moodrow wasn't sure of the process), but she'd clearly decided to let her face speak for itself. That was why, he decided, she wore so little makeup, why she projected so much confidence, despite the crappy office and the bed in the back room.

"So what happened with the suits?" she finally said. "I figured you were the kind of detective who picked a fresh suit off the closet floor every morning."

"And dumped orange juice on the lapels before venturing out to face the public?"

"Tomato juice seems more appropriate."

"Nice." He stood up, spread his arms wide. "This is my undercover outfit. Whatta ya think?"

He was wearing a navy blue, Members Only jacket over a gray polyester shirt, charcoal slacks, and a pair of foam-soled Rockport Walkers.

"Well, I have to admit you don't look like a working cop."

"What'd I tell ya."

"No, what you look like is a *retired* cop who's about to take his grandson to a baseball game." Her mouth jumped into a mischievous grin. "The white socks give you away."

Moodrow sat back down. "Damn, and I was trying for sporty sophisticate."

The jackhammer started up again, slamming into their conversation. Moodrow sipped at his coffee, reminded himself that the city—*his* city—was literally falling apart. Construction sites were a permanent feature on every bridge and highway; water mains spouted like blowing whales. In the early 1980s, when the work had begun, orange signs at every site had announced the Koch administration's good intentions: WE'RE REBUILDING NEW YORK. The signs were gone, now, but the work continued. The FDR Drive along the East River had been under repair for more than fifteen years.

Gadd started to speak, then shook her head and got up to shut the windows. Back in her seat, the jackhammer reduced to a muffled roar, she shuffled the paperwork on her desk for a moment, then looked up at Moodrow.

"Maybe we oughta get to work," she said. "Being as the city isn't gonna let us play."

Moodrow crossed his legs, leaned slightly forward, and let his hands drop into his lap. A narrow smile pulled at the edge of his lips as he realized just how much he'd been looking forward to this next step. As if there was no possibility that Santa would leave coal instead of presents under his tree. "Your move, Gadd."

She nodded, accepting the obvious. "Well," she said, "it looks like we've got a hit. One of the credit cards was used."

"Where?"

"Long Island."

"That would be Carlo Sappone, right?"

"How did you know that?" Gadd waved off his response. "And how did you know they were going to use the card?"

"Carlo Sappone was a guess. He's Jilly's first cousin, Josephine Rizzo's nephew. I didn't know he was on Long Island, but I was pretty sure he was still close to the family. As for using the card . . ."

Moodrow jerked to a halt when the pounding outside the window stopped again. An angry voice drifted up, almost a whisper after the roar of the jackhammer.

"Ya stupid cocksucker. Ya cut the fuckin' cable. Now we'll be here all morning."

Gadd scratched her chin. "I *love* New York." She waited for Moodrow's smile. "You were saying about the cards?"

"Right." Moodrow tapped the bandage on the back of his head. The wound had begin to itch, but he was afraid to dig in, afraid of opening it again. "You asked me how I knew Jilly was going to use the cards, correct?"

"Correct." Her eyes were somewhere between quizzical and amused.

"Well, ask yourself this: If Jilly wasn't gonna use 'em, why would he steal 'em in the first place?"

The obvious struck Gadd like a fastball slamming into a catcher's mitt. "But using them was such a risk." It was all she could manage.

"If the criminals weren't stupid, where would *we* be?" The cop cliché rose to Moodrow's lips unbidden. "Besides, it wasn't all that much of a risk. The cards were forgeries, so that leaves the cops out of it. How could Jilly Sappone know that Stanley Moodrow would get next to Buster Levy? How could he know what Ginny Gadd can do with a computer? If you look at it from Jilly's point of view, he's been having a run of very shitty luck."

Gadd cocked her head to one side and shrugged. "Your reasoning," she admitted, "is beyond dispute. As for Carlo Sappone, I have an address, a phone number, and a piece of his rap sheet."

"His rap sheet? How'd you get that?"

"I'm tied into a system called Lexis. They've got conviction records for forty-seven states in their database. Convictions, mind you, not arrests. Carlo Sappone's a coke dealer, been convicted three times, in 1982, 1986, and 1990. Altogether, he's done six years and four months, county and state time. He's on parole, even as we speak."

"Are you telling me that *anybody* can get this information?"

"Don't get pissed, Moodrow. It's a matter of public record."

Pissed? Moodrow's emotion was closer to despair. He'd been going to Jim Tilley with his hat in his hand, a beggar, pure and simple, whenever he needed a rap sheet. Meanwhile, every other private investigator had the information at his fingertips. Correction: *her* fingertips. He looked over at Gadd's computer, successfully resisted an urge to empty his .38 into the screen, then turned back.

"Last night," he said, "we talked about a trade. Favor for favor. You put Jilly with Carlo and Carlo with an address and a phone number. That's your favor. My favor is a mug shot of Jilly's partner. His name, by the way, is Jackson-Davis Wescott."

Gadd leaned back and put her feet up on the desk. "You know, Moodrow, you've got a way of springing nasty surprises on people. I've always associated that particular ability with being a prick."

"Sticks and stones, Gadd." He got up, crossed the room, and filled his coffee mug without asking permission. When he was seated again, he pulled a folded copy of Wescott's photo out of his jacket pocket and laid it on the desk. "You might as well take this, being as I can get Carlo Sappone's address on my own."

Ginny Gadd watched Moodrow's larynx bob as he drained the mug. Somehow, the motion was more obscene than an upraised finger. "You keep sucking on that, you're gonna dissolve the glaze."

Moodrow cupped the mug in his palm. "So, what's your next move?"

"Me?" She smiled her nastiest smile. "What I'm gonna do is go directly to Carlo Sappone's domicile and ask him if he knows where his cousin Jilly is hiding. In fact, I might not even bother driving.

Maybe I'll just give him a call the minute you walk out the god-damned door."

Moodrow sat up straight. He was trying for righteous indignation, but an obscene giggle betrayed his true inner state. "Yeah," he admitted, "that's exactly what I'd do if I was in your shoes." He took a deep breath and started over. "The problem, Gadd, is that when I put the big question to Carlo, he's most likely gonna lie to me. Now, the way I see it, Theresa Kalkadonis doesn't have time for bullshit; if someone doesn't get to her soon, she's gonna be dead. That's if she's not *already* dead. To be honest, I didn't think she had much of a shot when I caught the squeal, but now that I'm close, I can't afford to let Carlo Sappone tell me fibs." He tapped the desktop with one finger. "It sets up like this: If you wanna come along, I could use your help. But you can't draw any lines. I don't know what's gonna happen when I catch up with Jilly Sappone, but you can take one thing to the bank. If I have to shoot him down like a dog, if it comes to that, I'll do it without thinking twice. Being as you're still young and still ambitious, you might not wanna deal with the consequences."

SIXTEEN

"This is a definite opportunity for me. I'm not trying to be dramatic here—not saying it's my big break or anything like that—but the women who run the foundation are all corporate types and they as much as told me I'd get some work out of the deal." Gadd smiled ruefully. "Assuming I'm . . . assuming *we're* successful."

Moodrow nodded thoughtfully. He could remember a time when he was ambitious, when he'd been determined to ride the tail of that particular comet. Fortunately, the price of a ticket had been too high.

They were on the FDR Drive, crawling north behind a long line of cars and taxis. (This after two hours of begging an amused lieutenant for a copy of Carlo Sappone's mug shot.) The delay came as no surprise to either of them. As cops, they'd become hardened to frustration, only occasionally blasting holes in the traffic with the lights and the siren. But that didn't mean the lure of Carlo Sappone wasn't yanking at their adrenals like a milking machine at the udders of a cow. For Moodrow, the sensations, the elevated heart rate, the flushed face, were very familiar. He handled them by focusing his attention on a Suffolk County street map. Ginny Gadd, on the other hand, though she'd made the patrol officer's jump from utter boredom to full, heart-pounding terror often enough, had no experience with the steady pace of an investigation. She was sure the prickle at the back of her neck was an allergic reaction, one she could subdue with the edges of her short fingernails.

"Plus," Gadd tapped the wheel with the palm of her hand, "I need the exercise."

Moodrow continued to flip the pages. Even with the aid of his drugstore reading glasses and a pocket magnifier, he was having trouble finding the location of Carlo Sappone's home on Winston Drive in the village of Mastic. The problem was that Suffolk County, encompassing the eastern two-thirds of Long Island, was divided into a dozen large townships, each of which contained a number of smaller villages, while Moodrow's Hagstrom map, a vintage 1980 edition, listed street names under particular townships only.

"It makes you long for Brooklyn," he finally said. "Or for a better map."

"What does?"

Moodrow rubbed his eyes. "Long Island, New Jersey, Westchester. It doesn't matter. Every time I leave New York City, I feel like Dr. Livingstone." He replaced his glasses, reopened the map. "You grow up in New York?"

"Ridgewood."

"Then you know what I mean."

"I know that attitude is why people hate New Yorkers." Gadd edged the car slightly to the left and peered around the line of traffic. Several hundred yards ahead, a construction worker in a blue hard hat waved a red flag. The motion was oddly graceful, as if the worker was standing in a tank of water. "I think the traffic's gonna break up in a minute." When Moodrow didn't respond, she added, "That's in case you have any particular route in mind."

"What I have in mind is a village called Mastic. You wouldn't happen to know where that is?"

"Afraid not. But if it's in Suffolk County, doesn't it have to be on the map?"

"Yeah, unless it's in *Nassau* County. Or fucking Iceland." He laid the map on his knees. "Snatching Carlo isn't the only problem. We have to find a place we can take him, a quiet place where he can be convinced that giving up cousin Jilly is in his immediate self-interest. The funny part is that I was out on Long Island last summer—me and my girlfriend, Betty Haluka—and we went to a place that'd be perfect. If I could only find it."

Gadd slid by the flagman (who turned out to be a flag *woman*), merged into the far right lane, then accelerated along with the rest of the traffic.

"I think what I'll do," she announced, "is head east and hope for the best."

One rubber duckie!

Jilly Sappone rolled onto his back and groaned softly. He was dreaming his happiest dream and did not want to awaken. Not before he finished with his wife.

Twoooooo rubber duckies!

Jilly's dream was unfolding in the kitchen of a Lower East Side apartment he'd once shared with his wife and daughter. Little Patricia was nowhere to be seen, though her muffled sobs could definitely be heard. She was in her bedroom, hiding under the covers the way she always did when he went off. That was all right, because he had other things to consider. Ann was on the floor, crouching in a corner beneath the kitchen cabinets. The side of her face was nicely puffed and her nose was bleeding steadily.

Threeeeee rubber duckies!

The plan, now that Jilly had his wife totally cowed, was sexual humiliation. And not because Jilly had any particular interest in her body. He might or might not take her, depending on how the mood struck him, but, either way, he'd decided to leave her kneeling on the kitchen table while he watched the baseball game. Leave her kneeling there like a trussed turkey while he watched all nine innings.

Foooooooooour rubber duckies!

Slowly, with a deeply felt regret that threatened to explode into instant, uncontrollable rage, Jilly raised himself to a sitting position and rubbed at his eyes. What he saw, when he was awake enough to focus, did little to elevate his mood. Beyond the two silhouettes seated in front of the glowing television, a caped puppet sporting a monocle and a wide mustache counted a flock of rubber ducks floating in a white, claw-foot bathtub.

Fiiiiiiiiive rubber duckies!

Jilly tried to say "Jackson-Davis," but his mouth was so dry his tongue stuck to his palette. He tried again, this time managing a hoarse croak before exhausting his patience.

Siiiiiiix rubber duckies!

That did it, that was the final straw, the one that was going to break the back of a camel named Jackson-Davis Wescott. Jilly threw his legs over the side of the bed, leaped to his feet, and collapsed.

The television shut off with a soft pop.

"You might wanna stay off that leg, Jilly. Truth to tell, I don't believe it's ready to carry no real weight."

The events of the previous night flooded Jilly Sappone's consciousness with the force of one of his own shitstorms. He groaned softly, looked down at his leg, knew he'd been very, very lucky. The bullet had grazed the outside of his right calf. If it had gone through his foot, he'd be crippled.

But that didn't mean it hadn't hurt like hell. Or that he hadn't left a trail of blood from his daughter's apartment to the car where Jackson-Davis played patty-cake with Theresa Kalkadonis.

"Where are we, Jackson?" Try as he might, Jilly couldn't remember.

"We're in a motel, Jilly."

"I know that, you fucking jerk." Lying on the floor was making Jilly nervous. He'd spent most of his life staring down at his enemy-of-the-moment and this new position was thoroughly unfamiliar to him. "Help me up."

"Sure, Jilly."

Back on his feet again, Jilly fumbled in his pants for the medicine he knew he'd need if he was going to get through the day, then hobbled off to the bathroom. Ten minutes later, as he washed the shaving cream off his face, he remembered that he was in a motel room outside the city of Worcester, Massachusetts, and that he had a long way to go. His leg still hurt, but two bags of dope had driven the pain so far away that it seemed to belong to someone else.

He limped out of the bathroom and watched Jackson-Davis and the kid spoon cereal into their mouths. The scene struck him as funny. Jackson really liked the little bitch, that was obvious, but, sure as shit, the minute Theresa grew up, Jackson would kill her. He'd kill her because he needed to kill women; she was alive because he didn't need to kill children. Figure that one out.

"Jackson?"

"Yeah, Jilly."

"Where'd ya get the cereal?"

"At the 7-Eleven right down the street." Jackson-Davis grinned his proudest grin. "Little children need a good breakfast. I seen that on *Sesame Street* this mornin'." He pointed at the battered television set. "Right there on that TV."

Jilly took a deep breath. "And what'd ya do with the kid while you were gone?" Though he knew better, he was hoping Jackson had locked the brat in the bathroom. Or tied her to the bed. Or beat her into unconsciousness.

"Why, I took her with me, Jilly. And she was such a *good* girl." He rubbed the top of Theresa's head. "She didn't make nary a goldarn peep."

"I'm really glad to hear that, Jackson, but there's somethin' I just gotta say, somethin' I think you should keep in mind. It goes like this: If you take that little cunt outside again without my permission, I'm gonna get myself a big ol' butcher knife and cut her into a hundred pieces. Then I'm gonna make you count the pieces. Before I make you *eat* them." He gave Jackson-Davis a minute to absorb the information before continuing. "Now pack up your shit and put it in the car. It's moving day and we got a lot to do."

Stanley Moodrow knew exactly what he wanted from his marriage of convenience to Guinevere Gadd. He wanted her to drive the car while he discussed reality with Carlo Sappone. Once this simple objective had been realized, he fully intended to sue for an immediate and unconditional divorce.

That didn't mean he disliked her. Or that he resented her intrusion into a case he considered his own. Or even that he didn't honestly admire her determination. Moodrow had spent virtually all his thirty years in the detectives working by himself. The joys of partnership, as much a part of cop mythology as chasing down the bad guys or hating the politicians, were almost unknown to him.

Perhaps if he'd had just a bit more experience, Moodrow might have understood the nature of the bonding process a little better. He might have known, for instance, that far from taking place while standing shoulder to shoulder in a tenement hallway, true partnerships are formed in the void created by long hours of boredom, hours that can only be filled with words.

They were parked in the back of an Exxon station at the intersection of William Floyd Parkway and Winston Drive, staring out across a manicured lawn at the front entrance to a small, split-level house that might have been the clone of a half dozen others lining both sides of the street. It was a perfect spot for a surveillance. Stuffed between a battered delivery truck and a fenderless Volvo station wagon, Moodrow's dirty black Caprice was about as conspicuous as a cockroach in a welfare hotel. Moodrow had secured the space by flashing his PI license and a twenty-dollar bill at the station's manager.

"A divorce thing, you know." He'd followed the explanation with a shrug and a leer. The station manager had responded with a wink and a snatch at the double sawbuck.

Gadd had handled the rest of it by calling the house from the Exxon station's pay phone. She'd gotten as far as "Valente's Vinyl Siding" before Sappone had cut loose with a string of curses and hung up. That put him in the house, but it didn't tell them who, if anybody, was in there with him.

"What we gotta figure," Moodrow had explained, "is that Carlo, like any other drug dealer, is livin' in a fortress. Which translates into us not goin' in after him. We gotta wait for him to come out, no matter how long it takes."

Gadd had nodded wisely, then handed Moodrow a napkin. "You've got jelly on your chin. And on the tip of your nose."

"What, no powdered sugar?"

"The powdered sugar's on your lap."

The next two hours had passed fairly quickly. They'd stared at the door as if their mere arrival on the scene would draw Sappone into the open. Moodrow, though he knew better, was no more able to control the reaction than his partner of the moment. That was how much he wanted Carlo Sappone.

"You know," Gadd finally broke the spell, "considering our boy's occupation, we have to figure he's probably not coming out before dark." She glanced at her watch. "And it's only four o'clock."

"So whatta ya think we should do, break for dinner?"

"Actually, I was thinking more along the lines of a trip to the lady's room."

Moodrow shook his head. "I don't know, Gadd. That's not in the true cop tradition. Mostly, we just use an empty coffee container."

Gadd responded by opening the door. "If you're not here when I come out," she said, "I'll catch a cab."

She returned with two cans of Pepsi and a small bag of potato chips. Moodrow grunted his thanks, popped the tab, grabbed a handful of chips.

"Now I can add the crumbs to the powdered sugar." He waved the can in a small circle. "Like a mixed message for my dry cleaner."

"Don't forget to grind it in."

Moodrow chewed on the potato chips until they reached the consistency of wet plaster, then washed the lump down with a few ounces of soda. "So, tell me, Gadd, how long were you on the job?"

Gadd straightened. "Four years. What about you?"

"Thirty plus. It makes for a nice pension." He finished the Pepsi, tossed the can into the scavenged Volvo. "So why'd you quit?"

The back door of Carlo Sappone's house opened, freezing the question. Then a tiger-striped cat stepped onto the tiny porch, gave a soft meow, and leaped into the shrubbery.

"Think we should pick him up?"

Gadd's question was meant to change the subject. At least, that's the way Moodrow read it. He thought about letting her off the hook, finally decided that he liked her enough to want the answer.

"Nah, looks too tough for us. Probably ask for a lawyer." He opened the glove compartment, then closed it again without taking anything out. "I was in the detectives for twenty-eight years. Right up until the bosses decided to make me a Community Affairs Officer. It wasn't a deal I could refuse, so I put in my papers."

Gadd knew he was prodding her and she resented it. She wanted to tell him to mind his own business, that they were using each other and he knew it, that their temporary partnership didn't call for shared intimacies. But she couldn't imagine sitting next to him for the next several hours wrapped in a bad attitude. That would be worse than allowing herself to be manipulated.

"It's not that simple," she finally said.

"Pardon?"

"Why I left the job." She paused, tempted to leave it like that, then realized that once she'd opened the subject, she couldn't close it off again. A second realization followed quickly: She'd explained it to herself a thousand times, tried to share it with her husband and her friends, but never with another cop. Despite the fact that only another cop could possibly understand it.

"It wasn't something I really decided to do," she said. "I went out on vacation and never came back."

"Just like that?" Moodrow resisted an urge to turn and face her. "On impulse?"

"It'd been coming for a long time." Gadd took a moment to put her thoughts together, to decide just how much she wanted to let out. "What you can't know," she finally said, "is what it's like to be a cop and a woman. You understand about *us* and *them*, right?"

Moodrow nodded. *Us* was any cop below the rank of lieutenant who happened to be sitting next to you. *Them* was every other human being on the face of the Earth.

"*Us* and *them* is what makes it work for cops. That sense of being surrounded by enemies." She waited for another nod. "The first time I found a dildo in my locker, I shrugged it off. I figured I had to take it, rookie hazing, boys'll be boys, all the bullshit. Same for the spread-eagled centerfolds pushed through the vent slots. I'm not saying I liked it, mind you, or even that I thought it was okay. See, I'd heard that black cops sometimes find bananas or toy gorillas or even watermelons in their patrol cars, and they don't quit." She stopped, took a sip of her Pepsi, set the can between her feet. When she resumed speaking, her voice was tinged with anger. "The truth is that I expected it to end. You get the point, Moodrow? Like, sooner or later, I'd be in their club and the bullshit would stop. Only it didn't happen. And the joke is that I was three years into the job before I got the point. That was the night my partner, Harry O'Neill, asked me to toss a car we'd pulled over on a routine stop while he kept an eye on the two bad boys spread over the hood.

"I went through the interior first, between the seats, the glove compartment, like that. Then I popped the trunk and walked around to have a look. What they'd done was stuff a blow-up doll in there, with the head jammed under the spare tire and the legs spread out, and me, when I looked inside, I thought I saw the gaping genitals of a spread-eagled DOA. I was going for my service revolver when the laughter finally got through to me."

"It was your partner set that up?" Moodrow, unwilling to face the woman sitting next to him, kept his eyes glued to Carlo Sappone's front door.

Gadd shrugged, her anger fading. "Harry was a drunk with seventeen years on the job. I think he felt bad, but it wasn't something he could admit." She finally turned to face Moodrow. "Anyway, that's not the point."

Moodrow, facing the inevitable, let his head swivel until he was looking into her eyes. "The point," he said, remembering his own problems with the job, "is that you could never be *us*. As opposed to *them*."

"Yeah, but that didn't mean I didn't have options." She put her hands between her knees. "I knew women on the job who cultivated a 'don't fuck with me' attitude, who'd file a sexual harassment grievance if a male cop looked at them cross-eyed."

"Did they get what they wanted?"

"That's a good question. I mean they still found porno in their lockers, but nobody, not even the lieutenant, got in their faces." She rolled down her window, took a deep breath. "*Us* and *them* is what makes spending a third of your life wallowing in other people's misery halfway bearable. Without it . . ."

Moodrow nodded sympathetically. Just as if he hadn't spent most of his NYPD life nurturing an outsider self-image. But, of course, he realized, the label hadn't been forced on him. It's one thing to refuse an invitation to the prom, another to be blackballed just because you don't have a dick.

"What I finally decided," Gadd resumed, "is that I'd be better off on my own." Her eyes returned to Carlo Sappone's front door even as her shoulders dropped into their natural set. "And now I have to deal with the boredom."

SEVENTEEN

Theresa Kalkadonis wasn't going to cry anymore. She was sure of that, sure the crying time was past. That was partly because she wasn't thinking about her mother, about wanting to go home, and partly because Uncle Jilly had changed. Now, he mostly sat next to her with his chin on his chest, eyes all droopy, like Mackie, her stuffed dog.

Theresa wondered if Mackie was lying between the pillows on her bed. That was his place. She hoped mommy would take good care of him, now that she couldn't do it herself. Now that she had put her old life behind her.

"Good-bye, Mackie."

She didn't mean to say it out loud, but she must have, because Uncle Jilly was suddenly looking down at her.

"Didn't I tell you about cryin'? Didn't I?"

The words came slowly, bubbling out like the water in Theresa's bathroom sink when the toilet was filling up. Theresa wondered if she was supposed to answer. When Uncle Jilly was real angry, it was better not to say anything. Saying things didn't help. Only she couldn't hear any anger now, so maybe he really wanted to know, maybe he forgot what he said before about crying.

"She ain't cryin', Jilly."

Theresa looked up. Uncle Jackson was staring at her through the rearview mirror. He tossed her a big wink.

"Then what's she doin', Jackson-Davis, fartin' through her mouth?" Jilly laughed at his own joke, a rough snort that quickly worked its way from his nose down to his chest where it ended in a phlegmy cough. Theresa watched him roll down the window and spit, then dropped her eyes to her lap when he turned back. "So what were ya doin', Theresa? Fartin' through ya mouth?"

She could feel him looking down at her, though she didn't move her head. When Uncle Jilly took his medicine, his eyes were like the eyes of Mr. Cambesi's pet snake. You couldn't tell what they were seeing. She guessed that was better than before, when Uncle Jilly didn't have any medicine, but his snake eyes still frightened her.

"Doggone, Jilly, she's just a little kid. She probly ain't even *heard* of fartin'. I swear to the good Lord above, Jilly, you shouldn't be usin' that language."

"Swear to *who*, Jackson?"

"To the good Lord."

Theresa raised her eyes, knowing, somehow, that Uncle Jackson was drawing Uncle Jilly's attention away from her and toward himself. That's what he always did when Uncle Jilly got mad at her, and this time it was working. Uncle Jilly's mouth was right next to Uncle Jackson's ear and he was scratching the back of Uncle Jackson's neck with his middle finger.

"Tell me something, Jackson."

"Sure, Jilly."

"Do you remember when you were in the room with Carol Pierce?"

Theresa could see Uncle Jackson's face in the mirror. He had that pouty look he got when Uncle Jilly was making fun of him. The one mommy said would stay there all the time if Theresa put it on too often. Like he was gonna cry.

"Yeah, I remember."

"You remember what you did to her?"

"That was different."

"Different than what?"

Uncle Jackson shook his head—as if Uncle Jilly's finger was a bug he wanted to make fly away—but he didn't answer.

"What I wanna know, Jackson," Uncle Jilly whispered, "is if the good Lord above was watchin' you when you worked on Carol Pierce?"

Theresa couldn't put any images together with Uncle Jilly's words, but she knew he was saying something important, something her new life required her to learn. So she concentrated real hard—just like she did when she was reciting her ABCs—and tried to picture Uncle Jackson at work.

"Ain't gonna do that no more." Uncle Jackson shook his head from side to side.

"That right?"

"It's the God's truth, Jilly."

"Too bad, cause I had somethin' real nice all set up for ya. Guess I'll have to handle it myself."

Theresa was still thinking about Uncle Jackson's job when Uncle Jilly dropped back onto the seat next to her. She wanted to look up at him, but her head seemed frozen, like a Popsicle on a stick. It just wouldn't move.

Moodrow drained his fourth Pepsi of the afternoon, belched softly, rubbed his swollen gut by way of apology. It was nearly seven-thirty and a blazing orange sun hung just above the flat roofline of a Pathmark drugstore on the other side of William Floyd Parkway. Time, Moodrow thought, for the vampire to rise from his grave.

"Whatta ya think, Moodrow? Think I should give Carlo another call? Make sure he's still in there?"

Moodrow tossed the empty can into the Volvo, then rolled up the window and started the engine. The temperature was dropping fast. They'd need some heat before too long.

"We going somewhere?"

Moodrow looked over, noted the crumbs on Gadd's sweater, wondered if there was something about surveillance that wilted investigators. Maybe the boredom, or the cramped quarters. "Just warming it up," he said. "Carlo'll be coming out soon. We'd better switch seats."

"If you knew when he was coming out, why'd we get here so early? We could've gone to a movie. Read a book. Enriched our miserable lives."

"Just a feeling." Moodrow stepped out of the car without acknowledging the joke. He walked around to the other side, opened the door, then simply stood there, shifting his weight from one foot to the other. All irrelevant considerations—Betty, the foundation, Jim Tilley, the FBI, even Theresa Kalkadonis—had vanished without a trace, like gangsters in a New Jersey swamp. Carlo Sappone himself had been reduced to something less than human, to a resting moth awaiting the appetite of a mother robin.

"Hey, Moodrow, either get inside or close the damn door."

"What?" He squatted down, stared at Gadd as if trying to place her.

"First, it's getting dark and the overhead light's on." She pointed to the glowing dome light. "But even if it wasn't, you're much too big to be inconspicuous. If Carlo should happen to look out the window and see you hopping around, he's not gonna think you're the Easter bunny on a trial run."

Moodrow nodded agreement, slid inside, closed the door. "If Sappone makes the tail," he said without preamble, "if he flies, I want you to come right up on his bumper. This Chevy used to work for the Alabama State Police and it's got enough horses to run with almost anything on the road. Carlo's sure to think we're narcs. He'll pull over, eventually, try to bluff us."

Gadd let her eyes follow Moodrow's back to the house. The wall closest to them, part of the garage, had no windows, which was good and bad. Good because they couldn't be spotted from inside; bad because there were no cars parked in the driveway and Carlo would appear without warning. If he went right, away from William Floyd Parkway, they'd have a hell of a time catching up before he vanished into the suburban night.

"Hey, tell me something, Moodrow. It's almost dark and the street lamp's on the other side of the road. If somebody backs out of that garage, how are we gonna know who it is? How are we gonna know it's not Sappone's grandmother on a laxative run?"

"Whoever it is, they're gonna have to get out and close the garage door."

"What makes you think the door's not automatic?"

Moodrow answered without turning to face her. "Because I checked it when we drove by."

Gadd closed her eyes for a moment, thinking, It's not bad enough that I have to obey this old bastard's commands like a trained puppy, I also have to come off looking like a complete jerk. What I should've done is drive out here by myself. Then I could have come off like a jerk without anybody noticing.

"Game time."

She looked over at Moodrow, then at the house. The garage door was opening up and out, pushed by an invisible hand from inside. A moment later, a heavily customized van backed onto the driveway and stopped. Carlo Sappone emerged, strode up to the garage door, and closed it with a single, smooth motion.

"He's wasted, look at him." Moodrow licked his lips and rubbed his hands together, both gestures totally unconscious. "The mutt's doin' his own product."

Gadd watched Carlo Sappone walk back to the van. Skinny, verging on gaunt, his obviously expensive clothes hung on his narrow frame like hand-me-downs from an older brother. She couldn't see his face, but she could easily imagine the red-rimmed eyes, the runny nose, the tight, nervous jaw.

"Don't you ever get tired of being right?"

She threw the car into reverse, turned around without flipping on the headlights, then inched up to the edge of the road.

Theresa endured the long, boring ride from Worcester, Massachusetts, to the northern outskirts of the Bronx by pretending she was Mackie, her stuffed dog. You could leave Mackie any place you wanted and he was always waiting in exactly that same place when you came back. It didn't matter how long you were away or where you went. One time, her mommy and daddy had taken her all the way to Disney World, in Florida, and they stayed so long that she nearly forgot Mackie. But there he was, flopped on her pillow, his black button eyes and round white nose tilted up. As if he was expecting her any minute.

Of course, Mackie was part of her old world, not her new one. In her old world, she made the grown-ups happy by doing things. Things like brushing her teeth without being reminded or reciting the alphabet without making a mistake. Her new world was a lot more complicated. Uncle Jilly hated it when she did something. He didn't want her to eat or talk or wash her hands before dinner; he didn't even want her to go to the bathroom. And he could be very mean, like when he put her in the trunk.

Uncle Jackson was different. He liked it when she played his baby games and sang his baby songs, but when she recited the alphabet, he got very angry and called her a "highfalutin darn show-off." She didn't know exactly what that meant except that she shouldn't recite the alphabet, a fact she dutifully added to a growing "do and don't" list—her Book of Rules.

It was her daddy who first told her about the Book of Rules. "It's in the book," he'd say whenever she asked why she had to do something like go to bed at eight o'clock. "It's in the Book of Rules."

She'd almost forgotten about the Book—like she'd almost forgotten about the monster under the bed—but the Book was very important in her new world. That was because the monster had come out and was sitting right next to her.

"Jackson?"

"Yeah, Jilly."

"Gimme the phone. I gotta make a call. And slow it down. We're gonna be makin' a stop pretty soon."

Theresa wanted to watch Uncle Jilly use the special phone, because she'd never seen one like it in her old world. But she knew better. Looking directly at Uncle Jilly was a definite don't.

"It's Jilly. We on?"

She could hear a tinny voice coming from the phone, but she couldn't understand the words.

"Yeah, yeah. Twenty minutes." He stopped again. "Don't give me no fuckin' bullshit about you gotta go and pick up the package. Not when ya chargin' me twice what the shit is worth. Wait, wait, wait. Don't say nothin'. I'm gonna be over your way in about twenty minutes, maybe a half hour at the fuckin' most." He was yelling now, the roar of his voice filling the small car. "You ain't there to meet me, I'm gonna come lookin' for ya."

Theresa heard him click the little button that shut the phone off, then take a deep breath.

"Hey," he said, "you wanna talk to ya mommy? Huh?"

At first, Theresa didn't realize that Uncle Jilly was speaking to her. Uncle Jilly hardly ever spoke to her now that she had stopped crying.

"What's the matter with this fuckin' kid, Jackson? She sits there like a fuckin' doll and when you talk, she don't answer. I swear, it's gettin' me pissed off."

"Theresa?" Uncle Jackson was grinning at her in the mirror. "Didn't you hear what ol' Jilly just said? About gettin' to speak with your mommy? You wanna speak with your mommy, don't ya?"

What was she supposed to say? What response did her new world require? Theresa wasn't sure and when she turned slightly to find Uncle Jilly's black snake eyes fixed on her own, she became even more confused.

"My mommy's gone," she finally whispered. "You . . . she got hurt."

Jilly's nasty laugh echoed in the small space. "Fuckin' kid's smarter than she looks." He grabbed her left earlobe and twisted sharply. "I'm gonna call ya mommy and talk to her for a minute. Then I'm gonna put you on the phone. Ya better not clam up on me, kid, 'cause if ya do, I'm gonna rip this ear right off ya fuckin' head."

He held her close to him while he dialed the telephone, close enough for her to understand the man's voice on the other end of the line.

"Hello."

"Which little piggy stayed home?"

"That you, Jilly?"

"Hey, that's answerin' a question with a question. I'm surprised the nuns didn't teach ya better."

"I'm not a Roman Catholic. I'm a Lutheran."

"That ain't what I asked ya. I asked ya which little piggy stayed home. As in, who am I fuckin' talkin' to?"

"This is Agent Ewing. I spoke to you last time you called."

"Did you do what I told ya to do?"

"What's that, Jilly?"

Theresa watched Uncle Jilly closely, hoping for some hint of what was expected from her. He was breathing real fast through his mouth, which he always did when he got mad. What she didn't know was who he was mad at, her or the man on the phone. She wanted to wriggle away, to slide across to the other side of the car, but the arm wrapped around her waist was rock-hard.

"You wanna play fuckin' games?" Jilly's eyes were blazing. "Cause I got games you never dreamed about."

"No, Jilly." The man's voice was very calm, as if he was trying to soothe a frightened puppy. "She's here, just as you asked."

"Good. Now put the bitch on the phone."

"Hello, Jilly?"

"Is that my ever-lovin' wifeykins? Is that my sweet honey-girl?"

Even though her crying time was past, Theresa felt like she wanted to sob. Mommy was part of her old life and she couldn't think about her old life without becoming very, very sad. That was *why* she didn't think about her old life.

"Please, Jilly . . . Theresa . . ."

"Fit as a fiddle. Except for when her right hand got crushed with the pliers." Uncle Jilly's laugh boomed out. "But she's a southpaw, right? So it ain't no big deal."

Theresa held her right hand up to her eyes. What was Uncle Jilly talking about?

"I'm okay, mommy. My hand's okay, too." Theresa shouted the words into the telephone, then squeezed her eyes shut. She was sure Uncle Jilly would kill her for talking before he said to, but Uncle Jilly just kept on laughing.

"Theresa? Theresa?"

Uncle Jilly jammed his fingers over her mouth before she could answer.

"Listen up," he said, his voice suddenly cold enough to send a shiver up the back of Theresa's neck. "Because I ain't got a whole lotta time here. See, I got no reason to hurt the little brat. *Theresa* ain't done nothin' to me, if ya catch my drift. But that don't mean I won't go into one of my shitstorms. Ya with me on this?"

"I'm listening, Jilly."

"Okay, so what ya gotta do is gimme some kinda reason to hand her over. Like *before* I go off. Y'understand?"

"Tell me what you want."

"What I want is my fourteen fucking *years* back."

"I can't give you that."

"Well then, we got something in common, bitch." He paused, wiped his wet mouth with the back of his hand. "Because I got somethin' *you* want. Somethin' I can't give back."

When Uncle Jilly finally shut off the phone and loosened his grip, Theresa slid over to the opposite side of the car. Before she could make any sense of what had happened, Uncle Jilly leaned forward and tapped Uncle Jackson's shoulder. "A little ways up," he said, "you're gonna see a sign for the Cross Bronx Expressway. Take the exit for the east Bronx. We're goin' to the zoo."

"The zoo?" Uncle Jackson seemed very excited. "That's just great, Jilly, but you better keep a sharp eye out. Bein' as you know I cain't read no signs."

"Would you mind telling me exactly what you're waiting for?" Gadd put the Caprice in gear and pulled out onto Montauk Highway. She was careful to keep two vehicles between their car and Sappone's van, as instructed, but she had the definite feeling she could ride on Sappone's bumper without his noticing. "Because if this goes on much longer, the mope's gonna overdose and we'll end up taking him to the hospital."

They'd been following Sappone for more than an hour, trailing him as he bounced from one bar to another along a seemingly endless series of commercially zoned roads that crisscrossed Suffolk County's southern shore like varicose veins on the back of a dowager's thigh. Privately owned businesses lined both sides of the road, sharing strip-mall space with the inevitable fast-food operations and the company-owned gas stations. McDonald's, Pizza Hut, Wendy's, Taco Bell, Citgo, Exxon, Gulf, Texaco . . . the list went on and on and on.

The terrain itself was table-flat, the buildings no more than two stories high. As if the county planners had conspired with nature to create a world so lacking in definition as to be without any character at all.

"What it is," Gadd said, once she realized that Moodrow wasn't going to respond, "is that I'm used to vertical. Horizontal makes me seasick."

What it is, Moodrow said to himself, is that your nerves are showing.

Still, she was right about Sappone. He was distributing powder (most likely to bartenders running a little coke business on the side) and clearly sampling the product as he made his rounds. With each ten-minute stop, he looked a little more like a mature gobbler on the weekend before Thanksgiving. Getting him off the street would be no problem. Getting him off the street without being seen by some misguided citizen was something else again.

Moodrow forced his attention back to the detailed map spread across his knees. Even if the abduction—there was no other word for what he planned to do—went smoothly, they still had to transport Carlo to some private place. Transport him without getting lost on the way. Once Sappone was in the car, of course, both he and Gadd would have enough to do without reading a map.

Sappone's van made a right turn onto Route 110, a road marked Broadway on Moodrow's Hagstrom map. Gadd dutifully followed, stopping directly behind him at a traffic light. Even with her window rolled up, she could hear the heavy thud of a bass drum pounding inside the van.

"I got a bad feeling here, Moodrow. I got a feeling our boy's on his way home. It sounds like he's celebrating."

Moodrow shook her off, his finger tracing Route 110 as it wandered north through the town of Amityville, past the Southern State Parkway and Republic Airport to the Long Island Expressway. Satisfied, he carefully folded the map and laid it on the seat.

"Carlo's got at least one more stop to make. We'll take him there. You all right?"

"Me? What could go wrong? I step on the gas; I step on the brake; I turn the wheel. It's not exactly particle physics." The light changed to green and she allowed Sappone to put some distance between himself and the Caprice before following. "You hear that music? How loud it is? It's hard to believe he's riding around in a bloodred van with smoked windows and ear-splitting music if he's still carrying drugs. It's goddamned suicidal."

Sappone's van pulled to the curb before Moodrow could respond. The street was dark, every store closed with the exception of the Landmark Tavern in the middle of the block.

"Circle around, then pull in next to the pump in front of his van. We've got him now." Moodrow pressed his palms into his thighs, took a deep breath, told himself to calm down. Sappone would have to walk right past him to get back to his van.

"Do you know you're grinning from ear to ear?"

Moodrow touched his mouth, was surprised to feel teeth instead of lips. "We're gettin' close, Gadd. I can tell because I always twitch when I get close."

Gadd kept her eyes glued to the rearview mirror. When Sappone turned into the club, she spun the car into a U-turn, came back down the road, made a second U-turn, and parked. Moodrow was out of the car and leaning back through the open window before she could shut off the headlights.

"This street runs all the way up to the Long Island Expressway. According to the map, it wanders a little bit, so be careful; if we make a wrong turn, we'll be weaving through these developments for the next two weeks. Take the Expressway east to exit 70, then your first right. It's a long way out, at least an hour from here, but that's to our advantage because he'll be coming down by then."

Gadd nodded thoughtfully. Hoping her partner wasn't as crazy as he looked at that moment.

"I could put the question to Sappone in the car," Moodrow continued. "That'd save a lot of time. Only I'm afraid he'll lie and I have no way to get back to him if he does. I figure an hour in the backseat with me for company . . ." Moodrow snuck a look at the door to the Landmark Tavern, willing it to open. When it remained closed, defying his psychic abilities, he turned back to Gadd. "What I'm gonna do here is convince Sappone that I've been sent by Carmine Stettecase. You can see the point, right? Carlo might lie to the cops, but he can't bullshit Carmine. Not unless he plans to leave town."

"That sounds great, Moodrow, but where do I fit in?"

"You remember that movie? The one with Angelica Huston and whats-his-face?"

"Jack Nicholson." Gadd smiled. "I think it was called *Prizzi's Honor.*"

"That's the one. You're gonna be a hit lady."

"Does that make you a hit *gentleman?*" Gadd's head jerked up before Moodrow could answer. "Enough with the small talk," she said. "Our boy's on his way."

Moodrow didn't move a muscle. "Lemme know when he draws even with the car."

Gadd watched Sappone hesitate in the doorway, take a deep breath, rub his nose with the back of his hand. Drops of sweat ran down the side of his neck and into his collar. She'd seen it all before, of course, seen it on the mean streets of New York. The man was halfway to an overdose.

"What's he doing?"

"I think he's waiting for the sweat to dry." She glanced at Moodrow. His eyes were tightly focused, though on what she couldn't say. "Look, this guy's heart is probably close to exploding." She slid over a bit, put her hand on Moodrow's cheek and kissed him. "I don't know what you have in mind, but if you hit the bastard too hard, you're liable to put him in the morgue." She drew back a few inches and smiled. "He's moving. Twenty feet away . . . fifteen . . . ten . . . five . . . now."

Moodrow spun, took a single gigantic stride. He was expecting some kind of resistance, but Sappone simply continued walking until Moodrow wrapped a hand around his throat, then slammed a fist into his right kidney. The pain buckled Sappone's knees, but he didn't fall. Instead, his body rose momentarily, then flew across the space between himself and the Caprice. The resulting collision would have been devastating if Gadd hadn't already opened the back door. As it was, Sappone's momentum carried him across the seat and against the far door. Moodrow's body followed, pinning the much smaller man.

"Do me a favor, Carlo," Moodrow said as the Caprice pulled away from the curb, "and don't make me kill you in the car. The last time I killed somebody in a car, they crapped their pants and I had to ride with the stink for weeks."

Jilly Sappone did everything he had to do without once losing his temper. That, Theresa realized, was because the first thing he did (the first thing he *had* to do) was take his medicine. Theresa watched him open the folded paper, raise it to his nostrils, suck in the white powder, toss the paper out the window. She watched him sit there holding his breath until his eyes closed and he sank down into the seat.

When he opened his eyes again, he caught her by surprise, caught her looking directly at him, but he didn't get angry as she expected. Instead, he smiled at her.

"Wrap that blanket around yourself, kid."

"C'mon, Jilly," Uncle Jackson said, "you promised there wouldn't be no more goin' in that darn trunk."

"I said no more *unless* it was necessary, Jackson." Uncle Jilly looked at her, but she was careful not to raise her head. "Whatta ya think, kid, is it necessary?"

Theresa didn't answer, because she didn't know what Uncle Jilly wanted her to say.

"Hey, I'm talkin' to ya." He reached out and turned her head to face him. "Do ya think it's necessary?"

"There's a sign up ahead, Jilly. Better see what it is or I'll miss my turn."

Uncle Jilly let her go with a final instruction: "Wrap yourself in the fuckin' blanket and do it now." He looked out through the windshield for a moment. "Okay, Jackson, this is it. You wanna keep all the way to the right here. If we make a wrong turn, we're gonna end up in New Jersey."

Uncle Jackson must have done everything the way Uncle Jilly told him, because when they were on the new highway, Uncle Jilly leaned back, saw that she had the blanket around her, and smiled again.

"Where we gettin' off, Jilly?" Uncle Jackson asked. "I don't see a zoo no place around here."

"We're gettin' off at the Bronx River Parkway. Make sure ya don't miss the sign."

"But I cain't read no sign."

"Then why don't ya shut ya fuckin' mouth and keep drivin' till I tell ya what to do?" Uncle Jilly waited a minute, then turned to face Theresa. "I ain't gonna put ya in the trunk. That's because ya been a good girl and ya done everything I asked. But I don't want anybody to see ya when we get to the zoo. That's why ya gotta wrap yourself in the blanket and lay down on the seat. Understand?"

Theresa nodded, but Uncle Jilly had already forgotten about her. He was leaning forward, speaking into Uncle Jackson's ear. "Ya know what we're gonna do?"

Uncle Jackson shook his head. "Uh-uh."

"Ya don't remember I told ya this morning that we're gonna pick up some weapons?"

"Yeah, I remember now." Uncle Jackson was looking at Uncle Jilly in the mirror. His head was bouncing up and down. "Guess that means we ain't goin' to the zoo, right?"

"Just to the parking lot. That's where we gotta meet a guy named Espinoza. He's gonna sell us the guns." Uncle Jilly was being very patient, pausing between every sentence until Uncle Jackson nodded to show he understood. "Now the thing is, Jackson, if a dude sells guns, he has guns. And a dude that has guns might use guns to rip his customers off. You gettin' this?"

"Sure."

Uncle Jilly shook his head. "It's fuckin' hopeless." He tapped Uncle Jackson's shoulder. "Take this exit comin' up. Go to the light, make a left, then another left, then get on the parkway."

They rode in silence for a few minutes. Theresa, wrapped tightly in the blanket, looked out the window, but it was already dark and there wasn't much to see except for the other cars. She was getting very tired, but she didn't want to fall asleep, not with Uncle Jilly talking about guns.

"Lemme give this one more try, Jackson. Ya remember when ya were back in Clinton?"

"Yeah."

"And ya remember some of the boys in the joint, they wanted to hurt ya real bad?"

"You mean like the niggers, Jilly? Like the niggers wanted to tear me a new . . . ?" He looked at Theresa in the mirror. "Like what they wanted to do?"

"Now ya got it." Uncle Jilly put his hand on Uncle Jackson's shoulder. "And do ya remember the look they had, the look in their eyes just before they came after ya?" He waited for Uncle Jackson to say, "I sure do," then continued. "Well, if ya see that look tonight, it means we got big trouble. It means we gotta be prepared to defend our *sacred* honor."

By the time they rolled into the Buffalo parking lot of the Bronx zoo and parked next to the red car, Uncle Jilly had forgotten all about her. He must have, because he didn't ask her to lie down on the seat like he said he would. Instead, he and Uncle Jackson got out of the car, walked up to a short fat man, and shook hands. They spoke for a minute before Uncle Jilly took a roll of bills out of his pocket and handed it to the fat man, who counted it really fast, then opened the red car's trunk.

Theresa couldn't see what Uncle Jilly was seeing, but it must have made him happy, because when he turned around with the box in his hand and started walking toward her, he was grinning. The grin stayed on his face while he opened the trunk of their car and put the box inside and closed the trunk again, but it disappeared when Uncle Jackson started shooting.

"I seen it, I seen it," he screamed. "You ain't tearin' me no motherfuckin' new asshole."

Uncle Jackson's gun went off six times before Uncle Jilly got to him. Theresa counted the shots, then counted the clicks. One click, two clicks, three clicks, four clicks. Then Uncle Jilly and Uncle Jackson were running back to the car and the car was flying out of the parking lot.

"I seen it, Jilly," Uncle Jackson said. "That damned look. I seen it real, real clear."

At first, Theresa thought Uncle Jilly was going to use his *own* gun. Use it to kill Uncle Jackson. But then he started laughing. He laughed for a long time, his chest bouncing up and down like he just couldn't stop, like he'd just seen the funniest thing in the world.

Moodrow had planned to ride in utter silence, had actually encouraged this twice in the first few miles by slamming his elbow into the side of Carlo Sappone's head. Unfortunately, the shots, though well delivered, had the opposite of the intended effect. They stimulated Carlo's already pumping adrenal glands to even greater efforts, the hormone then chasing the cocaine through his brain and into his tongue.

"What? It's money, right? It's money you want and, baby, I got it. Down in my basement I got a safe it's *packed* with cash. That's cause I got a buy comin' up tomorrow. Sixty-five large, man. It's a score, a fuckin' score, all ya gotta do is jump off the Expressway at William Floyd Parkway. Take ten minutes at the most and ya walk away splittin' sixty-five large. Hey, it couldn't hurt, ya know what I mean?"

Moodrow slowly turned his head, letting it swivel like a tank turret until his eyes were inches away from Sappone's.

"You're really getting me pissed off, Carlo," he said. "I mean *really* pissed off." He took out the .25 automatic, laid it on his lap, watched Sappone's eyes widen. Hoping it would shut the man up.

"This ain't right. I mean it just ain't right. I haven't done nothin' to nobody. Like I never step on nobody's toes, like I don't owe nobody, like I don't mess with nobody's old lady. I'm a fuckin' *good* guy."

Moodrow glanced from the side of Gadd's face to her reflection in the rearview mirror. Was she repressing a grin? A smirk? He couldn't be sure. But she was definitely holding the car's speed down. Old ladies in Hyundais were passing them like they were standing still.

"Okay," Sappone said, "I think I got this figured out. Somebody's got a grudge against me for somethin' I don't even know nothin' about, right?" He paused, tried to pull his head back far enough to focus on Moodrow's eyes. "Hey, somebody else wants my territory, that's fine with me. I'm already gettin' tired of the life, plus my woman's bustin' my balls I should take a test for the Post Office. Hell, man, I got a kid, she's not even a year old. Ya wanna see a picture?" He stopped again, rubbed his nose with the back of his hand. "Kids need their fathers, right? Ain't that what's fuckin' wrong with America these days? Kids growin' up without no fathers? You don't want that on ya conscience, do ya?"

"You can't have something on your conscience," Moodrow observed, "unless you *have* a conscience."

"Yeah, I could definitely see that. But think about this. . . ."

Moodrow put his left forefinger to his lips, then raised the automatic and laid it against Sappone's temple.

"If you don't shut the fuck up," he whispered, his mouth inches away from Sappone's ear, "I'm gonna open the door, pull the trigger, push you out, see how far you roll before somebody runs you over."

"All right, all right. I won't say another word. But just think about what I been tellin' ya, because I'm willin' to do whatever it takes to walk away from this." He made a cross on his left breast. "Sacred word of honor."

Moodrow was tempted to put the question to Sappone right then and there. The man was ripe, that was obvious enough, but making Sappone talk (assuming he really did know where Jilly was living) would lead to another problem. What was to stop Carlo, once he was released, from warning Jilly? There was fear, of course, but who Carlo would be most afraid of was anybody's guess. Handcuffing the man to a tree in a place where he wouldn't be found until the following morning—that was the kind of guarantee Moodrow needed. He wasn't about to settle for anything less, even if it put another hour between himself and Jilly Sappone.

They rode in merciful silence, the traffic thinning out as they pierced the heart of the Long Island pine barrens. The headlights of oncoming cars revealed a dense, seemingly impenetrable curtain of scrub pine and dwarf hardwoods that turned solid black as the cars rushed by. Carlo Sappone's hopes seemed to darken as well. Moodrow could smell the pungent mixture of cocaine sweat and pure terror rising off the man's body like fog off the surface of a swamp.

Carlo only stirred once. As they came up on the exit for William Floyd Parkway, a mile from his home, he turned to gaze at the off ramp. When it slid by, he looked up at Moodrow.

"This is really gonna happen, right?" His voice was soft, wistful, surprised.

Moodrow didn't answer and fifteen minutes later, at Exit 70, Gadd turned off into a landscape so dead black they might as well be driving down into a cave. She made the first right, as instructed, onto a two-lane road, and gradually eased the Caprice up to sixty miles per hour.

"Ya think I could have one last snort? Like for old times' sake?"

Moodrow, having other things on his mind, carefully maintained his great-stone-face impression. His eyes were riveted to the cone of illumination thrown by the car's headlights. When they swept past a white, red-roofed house with the single word GRACE'S painted on its siding, he breathed a sigh of relief. The place was a glorified hot-dog stand, the only restaurant within miles. He and Betty had stopped there on their visit to eastern Long Island the previous summer. Which meant the Shrine wasn't more than a couple of miles down the road.

"Rrrrrrrrrroar, rrrrrrrrroar." Jackson-Davis bounced his plastic dinosaur along the top of the front seat. He'd found the tyrannosaurus in his McDonald's Happy Meal and now he was pretending to entertain little Theresa. What he was really doing was entertaining himself. Wishing that someone had given *him* a plastic dinosaur when *he* was growing up. Thinking his life would've turned out a lot different if his old ma had given him a plastic dinosaur instead of sinnin' with Reverend Luke.

He looked over at Jilly, wondering if maybe he should say what he was thinking, but old Jilly was spooning the last of his third ice-cream sundae into his mouth. Bitter experience had taught Jackson that Jilly didn't like to be interrupted when he was eating.

Jackson-Davis shifted his focus to little Theresa. She looked so cute with a napkin spread across her lap, nibbling at the edges of her little hamburger like she was eating an ear of corn.

"How is it?" he asked. "Ain't that a deeeeee-licious hamburger." His old ma us to say it like that: "deeeeee-licious."

Theresa looked at Jilly, then back at him. "It's fine, thank you." Then she looked over at Jilly, again, ready for an explosion.

But Jilly didn't explode. Instead, he tossed the remains of his sundae out the window, leaned against the seat, and closed his eyes. They were a few blocks off the Long Island Expressway in the town of Little Neck. Their small house was still an hour away and he was very tired.

If he'd kept to his original plan—his *game* plan—he'd already be moved out of that house. But, of course, his game plan hadn't included shooting himself in the leg or staying overnight in Worcester,

Massachusetts. That didn't mean he *couldn't* move. After all, there was no furniture, no dishes, no silverware to pack. How long could it take him to throw his small wardrobe into a plastic trash bag? Only he was tired after all the driving and his leg was starting to throb.

"Hey, Jackson."

"Yeah, Jilly."

"You remember what I said about movin' today."

"Sure do, Jilly. Only it ain't today no more. It's tonight."

Jilly resisted the urge to slap his partner, knowing that if he indulged that urge every time it rose into his brain, Jackson's ugly face would be swollen to the size of a pumpkin.

"Now, listen up, Jackson. This is important." Jilly waited for Jackson-Davis to face him. "Whatta ya think about movin' tonight? Because, what it is, I'm worried about that punk, Carlo. Sooner or later, somebody's gonna figure they can find *us* by findin' *him*. I mean let's face the truth, Carlo's a fuckin' coke junkie and he'll give us up in a hot second. You with me here?"

Jilly watched Jackson's face work as he considered the question, watched his eyes roll, his nose twitch, his mouth scrunch up. The performance was so disgusting that Jilly was instantly sorry he'd brought the subject up.

"Darn it all to heck, Jilly, I just can't, for the life of me, see why you gotta use that language around little Theresa. Ain't you got no respect for innocence?"

Moodrow had almost given up when he saw the small metal sign in the grass by the side of the road. There wasn't much to it, just an arrow and the single word SHRINE.

"Take the right," he told Gadd.

The Caprice swerved onto an even narrower side road without slowing down. A few seconds later, the lanes separated and the car's headlights swept over a full-size, intensely white replica of Michelangelo's *Pietà*. It was gone in a moment, seeming to Moodrow almost an afterimage, a dream memory, yet it had the desired effect on Carlo Sappone.

"What kind of fuckin' place is this?" he asked.

"It's where people come to pay for their sins," Moodrow replied. He pressed the .25 into Sappone's ribs. "Slow it down," he said to Gadd. "I don't wanna miss the trail." A few seconds later, a small wooden sign mounted on metal strips swam up in the headlights. "This is it. Right here." The car slowed further, then came to a stop with the lights illuminating a single word, "CALVARY."

Moodrow reached across Sappone's body, pushed the door open. "Last stop, Carlo. Everybody out."

Slowly, as if nursing an injury, Sappone slid his right leg over the edge of the seat. His foot grazed the asphalt, then came back into the car. He turned to Moodrow, a half smile on his sweating face.

"I don't wanna hear no sad stories," Moodrow said. "I'm in a hurry."

He shoved Carlo out, followed quickly, breathed in the cool, country air. A steady breeze whistled through the pines, forming a base for the repetitive, metallic cry of some animal. Moodrow, his left hand gripping Sappone's right bicep, listened for a moment.

"What is that?" he asked.

"What's what?" Gadd, four-cell flashlight in hand, was standing behind him. Her voice was chipper, actually cheery.

"That noise. What is it, some kinda bug?"

"Tree frogs," Sappone said. "Spring peepers. It's like a mating call."

Gadd ran the flashlight beam through the scrub for a moment. "Must be *invisible* tree frogs. Invisible *alien* tree frogs from outer space."

Moodrow grunted, then dragged Sappone onto a narrow path leading up through the trees. He could feel Carlo tremble, feel the man's fear through his fingertips as they followed the narrow beam of light. Moodrow was expecting some kind of resistance, a last stand, but Sappone stumbled along in silence until he caught sight of the first statue, a kneeling Roman soldier leaning on a shield. The soldier was looking up, one hand in front of his face, as if to ward off a blinding light.

"Oh, Lord," Carlo moaned. "Lord, Lord, Lord."

His knees buckled, but his forward progress continued because Moodrow simply dragged him along, refusing to allow the smaller man to fall. Then the second statue, a soldier on one knee holding a spear, jumped into focus as if the flashlight beam was a theatrical spotlight exploding onto a darkened stage.

Sappone began to cry, then actually wail as Gadd's flashlight swept relentlessly forward to reveal a white-robed Christ standing with upraised hand and face, then a flat, gray building with a square of stone pushed off to one side of an open doorway.

Moodrow half carried Sappone through the door, pushed him down into the long, rectangular sarcophagus inside, then stepped back. He took the flashlight from Gadd and shoved it to within a foot of Sappone's face.

"You like game shows?" he asked.

Sappone shook his head, nodded, shook it again. He couldn't stop crying long enough to form a sentence until Gadd slapped his face. Then he took a sharp breath, whispered. "I don't know."

Moodrow cocked the little automatic, producing a sharp click that sent Carlo back to blubbering. Gadd slapped him again, this time much harder.

"Yeah, yeah, yeah," Sappone almost shouted. "I like game shows."

"Good," Moodrow said, "because I'm gonna ask you some questions. If you get them right, you win a nice prize. On the other hand . . ." He let his voice trail away, let the silence surround them for a moment. "First question: Who sent us?"

Sappone finally managed an expression beyond pure terror. While it wasn't exactly hope, it did show interest in the possibility of a life beyond the grave.

"What's the matter," Gadd said, "cat got your tongue?"

"I'm tryin' to think."

"That's all well and good, Carlo," she continued, "but letting the buzzer go off without giving an answer may not be in your self-interest."

As he waited, the silence as enveloping as the darkness outside Sappone's illuminated face, Moodrow felt his heart pounding in his chest. He'd been moving from point to point with perfect confidence. As if he was certain that Carlo Sappone knew where his cousin was hiding. Now that the moment of truth had finally arrived, his own doubts threatened to overwhelm him.

He told himself that, no matter how it came out, he'd made all the right moves, that he'd been forced by circumstance to race headlong into the investigation, to keep his face forward, that even if his assumptions were correct, even if this miserable coke junkie led them directly to Jilly Sappone, Theresa might be already beyond help.

"Carmine sent ya," Carlo finally whispered. "Carmine Stettecase."

Moodrow's breath whooshed out. He started to ask the next question, realized he was panting and his knees were shaking.

"Why?" he finally said. "Why did Carmine send us?"

"I didn't mean nothin' bad for Carmine," Carlo whined. He was looking directly into the flashlight beam, as if into Moodrow's eyes. "I swear to God, man. When Josie called me last year, told me Jilly was gonna get out, when she sent the *retard* over? Swear to Christ, man, I didn't *know* Jilly was gonna go crazy. What was I, fifteen years old when he got sent upstate?"

Moodrow dropped to one knee, pushed the flashlight closer to Sappone's face, watched a bead of sweat roll the length of his nose to hang from the fleshy tip like a drop of snot.

"Where is he, Carlo?"

"Are you gonna kill me if I tell ya?" The question was innocently put, the query of a child.

"No, I'm not. I can't kill you, because you might be lying to me and if you're dead I can't ask you again." He tapped Sappone's forehead with the edge of the flashlight. "See, what I plan to do is handcuff you with your arms around one of those trees outside. If you're tellin' me the truth, I won't have to come back and somebody'll find you in the morning. Me, I'll be too busy with Jilly to worry about you." He dropped the beam of light onto Carlo's face and waited.

"Jilly's got a house."

"Where?"

"On Middle Island Road. Six-twelve Middle Island Road. In Medford."

Moodrow started to rise, then remembered the most important part. "What *township*, Carlo. If you don't tell me the goddamned township, I'll never find it on the map."

• • •

"The place is called the Shrine of Our Lady of Long Island," Moodrow said, "and the reason I remember is because of the vans and the kids." Having surrendered the map to his partner, he was driving with a heavy foot, steering the Caprice back toward the Long Island Expressway and not giving much of a damn for the speed limit. He was more than eager now, and the car seemed to echo his haste, jumping forward with every tap on the gas pedal. "What somebody did—or some group, I don't know which—was buy up a big parcel, fifteen, twenty acres at least, and cut a path through the woods. Then they carved out niches between the trees and set up the Stations of the Cross. Were you raised Catholic?"

Gadd shook her head, kept her eyes glued to the map. "My father hated organized religion, used to rave about it. My mother didn't give a damn one way or the other." She held the flashlight close to the map, found herself squinting nevertheless. "Go west on the Expressway, to Exit 64. I'll figure out what to do next while we're riding."

"Got it." He eased the Caprice onto the Long Island Expressway, then accelerated up to seventy-five. "What I was saying about the vans. Me and Betty, we visited the Shrine last summer. Betty called it a 'functioning artifact,' something like that, which was why she wanted to see it. For me it was mostly boring, because I was raised Catholic, so the Stations weren't exotic. Besides, this was in August and it was blazing hot. By the time we came out the far end of the trail I was soaked with sweat."

Moodrow stopped abruptly. His mind kept pushing ahead to Jilly Sappone's house in Medford, running through the possibilities. A direct assault was clearly impossible. They couldn't walk up and knock on the door, demand entry. Jilly would kill them, even if he thought they were cops. But that didn't necessarily mean they had to sit in the car and wait for Jilly to come out. They might find the house unoccupied, try a little b&e, prepare a nice surprise for Jilly when he eventually came home. That would depend on how close the neighbors were, how much shrubbery surrounded the house. Or he could get Jim Tilley on the horn, let the NYPD notify the Suffolk County cops and the FBI.

"What happened with the vans?" Gadd was looking over at him, the map lying across her thighs.

"Yeah, the vans." Moodrow glanced down at the speedometer, eased off the gas slightly. "All I could think about, when we finally got back to the parking lot, was the air conditioner in the car. I'd parked it under a tree so I figured it wouldn't be too heated up. Then I noticed these vans, there must have been six or seven of them, unloading kids at the entrance to the Stations. Some of these kids had no hair, like it'd fallen out from chemotherapy. And all of them had that kind of gray complexion people get when they're terminally ill.

"It was something you definitely couldn't ignore. Pitiful, right? Like they were making their own march to the cross. But what caught my attention was that the parents were missing. There were maybe twenty or thirty kids and only six adults, three of them nuns, to herd everybody up onto the trail. Hot as it was, I walked over to one of the vans, spoke to the driver, asked him what was going on. He told me they take the kids to the different Stations and pray for a group miracle. Like the miracle could hit one kid or be shared by all of them. I don't know why, but it got to me. 'Shotgun salvation,' that's what Betty called it."

"I see what you mean." Gadd rolled down the window, took a breath of fresh air. "I guess Theresa Kalkadonis could use a little piece of a miracle right now. Like maybe there won't be anybody home when we get to Jilly's house. Better yet, she'll be there by herself."

Moodrow, with nothing to add, kept his eyes glued to the road. The darkness seemed to be sucking the car forward, the headlights merely illuminating a path into the whirlwind. Jilly Sappone's house stood at the calm center of that storm. It was as if there was nothing between the the two of them but time.

"I don't know what Exit 64 is called," Gadd said. "I can't tell from the map. Could be Route 112, Medford Avenue, Patchogue Road— it seems like the name of the streets change from town to town. What you have to do is go north, then take the right-hand fork when you get past Horse Block Road. That'll be Middle Island Road."

The first sign, EXIT 64/2 MILES, flashed by and Moodrow dutifully moved to the right lane and eased off the gas pedal. Out of the corner of his eye, he watched Gadd take an S&W Airweight from her purse, open the cylinder, slide a bullet into an open chamber. Like many cops, she kept the hammer of her .38 on an empty chamber, accepting the loss of firepower in the name of safety. This despite the manufacturer insisting that the weapon cannot discharge with the hammer down.

"When was the last time you fired that piece?" he asked.

Gadd answered without looking at him. "Three days ago," she said. Then, after a pause, "I used to shoot in department competitions. Best I ever got was a third place, but I met a lot of ranking officers. For all the good it did me." She hesitated again. "Don't worry, Moodrow. I'll hit what I'm aiming at. Assuming I'm not paralyzed with terror."

"All right, all right." Moodrow braked sharply as he slid onto the off-ramp. "I'm sorry I brought it up. You can't blame me for wanting to know."

Gadd said nothing for a moment, waiting until the car came to a full stop at the end of the ramp. "Take a right. The fork should be at the next intersection."

They drove the block in silence, pulling up as the light turned red.

"How 'bout you, Moodrow? You fire the gun on the job?"

Gadd was turned to him now, her .38 lying in her lap. As he watched, she emptied her bag onto the floor, then put the revolver inside the bag. She did it, he noted, with her hands, not her eyes, snuggling the weapon into a place where she could get to it fast.

"When I came on the job," Moodrow said, "if some jerk ran away, all you had to do was fire a single warning shot. After that, assuming he didn't take the hint, you could kill him and the job would back you up. Didn't matter if he was unarmed."

Gadd was about to say, "That's not what I asked you," when the light changed and Moodrow accelerated onto Middle Island Road. Two narrow lanes wide and devoid of any on-street lighting, the road curved through the woods with only an occasional house on either side. The first house they came to, set back forty feet, bore the number 238 under a porch light. The second was completely dark, as was the third. The fourth and fifth were set close to the sidewalk. Gadd called out the numbers 446 and 490 as they passed, added, "We're closing in."

They drove the next several hundred yards in total darkness, until Middle Island Road took a sharp bend to the right and they passed a dark house, then a house numbered 636. A hundred yards farther on, Gadd announced the number 772.

"We passed it," she said, "two houses back."

Moodrow nodded, allowed himself a moment to visualize Jilly Sappone's home. He pulled up the image of a small, single-story house served by a long, straight driveway. There were no lights of any kind, not even over the tiny porch, the building just a darker shadow against the trees behind it.

"There was nothing close by, right?" he finally asked. "No neighbors?"

"None." Gadd was smiling, her eyes sparkling despite the car's dark interior. "Christ," she said, "it's a gift."

"Yeah," Moodrow agreed, "but we still have to find a place to park and we still have to hike back to the house. You see a way to circle around, come past again?"

"Take a right at the next intersection. Granny Road."

"*Granny*? You gotta be kidding."

Gadd turned to Moodrow, started to respond, thought better of it. She put her handbag on her lap, finding the revolver's weight somehow reassuring. Her heart was pounding in her chest, but as she'd bought her own ticket, she couldn't bring herself to start complaining now that the roller coaster was cresting the hill.

Even with no traffic, it took Moodrow almost ten minutes to get back to the intersection of Route 112 and the Long Island Expressway. Roads that seemed relatively short on the map stretched out into the darkness for what seemed like miles. By the time he pulled up to the red light, he was cursing himself for not using someone's driveway to make a simple U-turn.

There were three cars driving north on Route 112 and Moodrow scanned them impatiently, anxious to make a right turn against the light. The first two carried no passengers and took an immediate left onto the Expressway service road, but the third caught his attention. He could see two men in the vehicle, one in front and one in back. The setup would have been unusual, even in a large sedan, a Cadillac or a town car, but the men were riding in a Ford Taurus. Maybe they were running with the front seat pushed all the way up, but, even so, the man riding behind had to be squeezed in.

As the car slid past Moodrow's Caprice, the man in back turned to glance out the window. Despite the fourteen years and the tight gray beard, Moodrow recognized Jilly Sappone without hesitation. It might have been the large, sharp nose, Sappone's most prominent feature, or the way his narrow, probing eyes swept over the Caprice to lock onto Moodrow's. Either way, the shock charged Moodrow down to his toes. He barely had time to register the Ford's sudden acceleration when he was seized by a single idea: If I lose Sappone now, I'll never get him back.

He made the turn, jammed the gas pedal against the floorboard, was almost on Sappone's trunk before he even considered the near certainty that Theresa Kalkadonis was in the car. By then it was much too late. Even as Moodrow began to fall behind, the sunroof on the Taurus slid back and the flapping edges of a white blanket appeared in the opening. Slowly, inch by inch, the blanket, and the object it so obviously concealed, rose above the retreating automobile. Then, all at once, Jilly Sappone tossed the package into the night air and the blanket flew open, framing the small, frightened child like the wings of an angel.

EIGHTEEN

Despite Betty Haluka's prevailing mood, a mix of anxiety and self-righteous anger such as a parent might feel for a wandering child lost at the beach, the view got to her. The American 757 out of Los Angeles, after a nearly interminable cross-country voyage, was on its final approach to La Guardia Airport, running straight up the East River with Manhattan spread out beside and beneath. The aircraft was moving very slowly, seeming almost at stall speed, a mere thousand feet above the taller buildings, offering a perspective that reduced the city to a scale model (like the one in a Flushing Meadow Park museum) while at the same time forcing Betty to acknowledge its overwhelming mass. Below her, on First Avenue, a pair of EMS ambulances tore north, their revolving lights drawing her face to the window as she automatically strained to hear the sirens.

"Beautiful, isn't it? I fly at least once a month and I always hope the plane will take this approach on the return."

Betty turned to the middle-aged woman (who'd been mercifully silent up to this point) sitting next to her. "Awesome is more like it." She paused, reconsidered. "Or awe*ful*. I can't decide. Maybe both."

She looked down at the lights strung along the cables of the Triboro Bridge, then north across Harlem to the George Washington Bridge on the far side of the Island. Street lamps lined every block, throwing patches of orangey light, their softly defined perimeters contrasting with the sharp, harsh rectangles offered by thousands upon thousands of lit windows.

The plane took a leisurely turn to the east, descending rapidly, and Betty tightened her seat belt. She'd never been afraid of flying, never had to fortify herself with a few quick belts in an airport bar. That was Stanley's act, one of several, or so it seemed. Like his failing to call her, like Jim Tilley having to call her instead.

"He's taking it real hard," Tilley had said after a long, detailed preamble. "The job's sending me out to Chicago, to pick up a mutt we've been after for a long time. I'll probably be gone a couple of days."

The message had been clear enough and Betty, with her cousin now in what the doctors called "an irreversible coma," had abandoned Arthur and jumped on the next plane out. Not before calling, however. She'd called several times from the house, several times again from an LAX passenger terminal, her mood flipping from worry to anger with every unanswered ring.

She was angry because she was convinced that *he* should have called her. They'd been lovers and best friends for almost six years. If he couldn't (or wouldn't, or didn't) reach out to her . . . well, the consequences were obvious enough. The whole relationship would have to be redefined. Hell, the relationship would redefine itself.

But the worry was just as real, a nagging fear she didn't want to acknowledge. Moodrow's failure to call was beyond any response she could have predicted. Thinking about it, she finally understood why he'd always insisted that he absolutely *hated* mysteries.

"Stanley blames himself for the kid," Tilley had said. "And the funeral's two days from now."

"He told you that?"

"About the funeral?"

"About blaming himself."

"He didn't have to, because I've been there myself a few times." Tilley had hesitated, as if determining exactly how much he wanted to say. "My first year, on foot patrol, I ended up on a roof with a jumper, a woman holding a baby. I didn't know what to do, what to say, had no training whatever. Meanwhile, I was the only one there, so I had to make a choice: try to talk her down or wait for the sergeant to show up with a department expert. Being young, stupid, and pitifully ambitious, I decided to be a hero. I took a step toward her and over she went. It's ten years later and I still dream about it."

The plane was up against the ramp, the other passengers standing, when Betty finally pulled herself together. There were practical things to be done, a taxi to catch, luggage to retrieve, a mystery to be confronted. Best not to get obsessed, she told herself, until you know what to be obsessed *about*.

Forty minutes later, her taxi rolled off a Brooklyn-Queens Expressway ramp and up onto the Williamsburg Bridge. A subway J Train clanked and screeched a few feet to her left, coming out of its hole to pace the cab for a moment, then falling behind as Betty's driver accelerated away.

"Too loud, too loud." The driver waved a hand in dismissal. "Make me nervous. One day bridge falls down from that damn train. You see."

Betty nodded, but didn't answer. Suddenly, the simple fact that she was going to arrive on Stanley's doorstep unannounced jumped into the forefront of her consciousness. What would he say? What would *she* say? It would be easy enough to use Marilyn's condition as an excuse for suddenly coming back, to keep her own counsel until she had a better grip on events. On the other hand, if Stanley was sitting there, nursing a bottle of Wild Turkey and a wounded ego, she might not be able to control her response.

Her dilemma was resolved a few minutes later when she opened Moodrow's door to find him seated at the kitchen table, a bottle of bourbon and a half-full glass within easy reach. His back was to her and he clearly hadn't heard her make her entrance. That, most likely, was because he was talking to himself.

"There's things in your life that just can't happen. There's mistakes you just can't make, because when you do make them, they run you straight into hell. I mean if you decide to swallow the gun, and flinch when you pull the trigger, there's a certain price to be paid, right?" He reached out for the glass, but instead of drinking, held it against the side of his unshaven face. "I should've checked up. When I asked Gadd to find a way to come around again. If I'd just looked at the map for a minute, I would've known how long it was gonna take to get back to the Expressway." He waved the glass like a baton, slopping the drink onto his shirt and trousers. "I tell ya, Betty, I don't know why I didn't make that goddamned U-turn. I mean who was gonna see? Some jerk in a house two miles away from Jilly's? And what was he gonna do, call the fucking cops? By the time the cops arrived, if they even bothered to respond, we would've been inside that house, waiting."

Betty flinched at the sound of her name. Did he know she was there, standing in front of the door? Probably not, she decided. And that was because he was *definitely* drunk.

The anger she'd been nursing cut through her initial confusion, providing just enough focus to get her moving. She dropped her bag onto the carpet, strode across the room, wheeled to face him.

"Stanley . . ." Her first impression, that he was crying, passed almost immediately. His collar and hair were soaked; beads of moisture covered his scalp and forehead. Unless teardrops had somehow learned to defy gravity and run upward, something else was happening.

"I mean what was it?" He was staring directly into her eyes now, as if she'd been there all along. "An ego trip, nothing else. Hotshit Stanley Moodrow riding to the rescue. I should've paid a price for that, Betty, and maybe I really have, because I can't get Theresa's face out of my mind."

Betty took a step forward, brought her palm and fingers to rest on her lover's cheek. Even as she spoke, she felt the tears spring into her own eyes.

"Christ, Stanley," she whispered, "you're on fire."

PART TWO

PART TWO

ONE

Stanley Moodrow spent the first thirty-six hours after his admission to Beth Israel Medical Center on First Avenue and Sixteenth Street drifting in and out of consciousness. On the bottom end, when the fever burned throughout his body (when rivulets of sweat ran through the white hospital sheets to lie in small insistent puddles on the plastic-covered mattress) his mind was filled with shifting images. He met friends, enemies, rivals, the living and the dead, as if reviewing his memories without first ordering the internal chaos. Sometimes these images stayed in his mind long enough to offer some piece of advice, to remind him of some forgotten obligation, but just as often they were no more than profiles at the outer edges of his vision, disappearing before he could turn his head.

The landscape shifted as well, from Moodrow's Lower East Side apartment to a Long Island shrine, to an interrogation room in the old Seventh Precinct on Pitt Street. At one point, he watched himself, at age thirty, questioning a man suspected of rape. (This at a time when confession by way of torture stood up in court.) The young Moodrow had danced around the issue. Bouncing from one foot to another like an enraged gorilla, he smashed the side of his fist into the desk, screamed until his own throat was raw, but never actually touched the man in front of him.

The scene, though it lasted no more than a minute, had nearly perfect clarity, as if the sixty-year-old Moodrow had actually been present, a neutral observer, when it happened. Still, despite this (and despite the histrionics), he continued to maintain a neutrality that bordered on outright indifference. Even when the fever pushed his body temperature above 103 degrees, he watched the unfolding kaleidoscope with equanimity, feeling no emotion greater than mild curiosity.

On the other end, however, when the fever dropped off toward morning and he rose to a vague, exhausted consciousness, Moodrow was overwhelmed by what he saw. A chrome IV pole, framed by a recessed fluorescent light in the ceiling, stood just to his left, its arms extending outward to form an abbreviated cross. In the center of the cross, as if deliberately placed and kept there, a transparent plastic bag filled with a clear fluid slowly emptied into a narrow tube.

Moodrow, lacking both the will and the energy to focus his eyes, saw it all, the light, the bag, the relentless dripping, as a single unit, as the crushed torso of a young child surrounded by an illuminated white blanket. He wasn't ready for it, not even close, and he jammed his eyes closed, squeezing the lids down as if resisting some misguided physician determined to pry them open.

A few minutes later, he fell into a dreamless sleep, from there back into fever and delirium. Another fourteen hours passed before the antibiotics pouring into his bloodstream overcame the infection. At times he was conscious, or at least awake, but if he recognized Betty as she moved around the bed, soaking towels in cool water, wringing them out, laying them across his forehead, he gave no indication. Instead, he kept his face turned to the right and pressed down into the pillow, tried to pull his tethered hands up to further shield himself.

Inevitably (the only other option being actual death), Moodrow returned to a ragged consciousness, a consciousness predicated on the belief that an IV pole and a bag of saline solution laced with antibiotics and glucose are neither more nor less than they appear to be. He opened his eyes to find Betty standing at the foot of the bed, instinctively tried to reach out to her, only to discover that his hands were tied to the bed rails.

"They were afraid you'd pull out the intravenous line." Betty's round face was striped with tears.

"Why are you crying?" His mouth was so dry he could barely get the words out. Nevertheless, he answered his own question. "They already buried her, right?" He stared at Betty's puzzled face for a minute, then repeated himself. "Ann," he said. "Ann already buried her."

"Stanley, you might have died. Do you know that?"

A short black woman carrying a pen and a clipboard entered the room before he could reply. Her starched, white uniform crackled pleasantly as she strode to his bed and calmly took his temperature.

"Fever's down," she announced. "Are we ready to return to the land of the living?" She spoke the words in a pronounced singsong, her voice pitched a full octave above its normal range. As if talking to a child. "My name is Nurse Rashad."

Moodrow, too weak to react with anything more forceful than out-and-out submission, raised his tethered wrists. To her credit, the nurse took a pair of scissors from a voluminous front pocket and began to saw at the gauze binding his hands.

"If the fever returns, I'll have to tie you again. That IV up there?" She pointed to the nearly empty bag at the top of the pole. "Look at it like it was your life's blood coming down that tube."

For a moment, Moodrow thought she'd said, "*Her* life's blood." He started visibly, wondered if he was still hallucinating.

"Are you thirsty?" Betty was standing on his right. She held a plastic drinking cup in her hand, offering it, along with its bent, plastic straw, for his inspection.

He started to reach for the cup, but Betty was already lowering the straw to his lips. The cold water helped to clean his mouth, but hit his stomach like a rock. He let his head drop back to the pillow.

"You'll get something to eat tonight," the nurse said. "Juice, broth, like that. If everything goes well, the catheter will come out in the morning. Then we'll get you on your feet, see how strong you are. In the meantime, stay in the bed."

"What if I need to use the bathroom?"

"That's what the catheter's for. Anything else, you call me."

Moodrow watcher her execute a perfect about-face, listened to her uniform crackle as she marched through the open doorway, then took a moment to look around the room. The walls were a dull, faded orange, in deference, Moodrow suspected, to the belief that hospital rooms should be warm and cheery instead of cold and clean. Several shiny-blue plastic chairs, further proof, were scattered about his bed and the empty bed next to the window. Above and behind him, a computer monitor displayed his blood pressure, pulse, respiration, and body temperature.

"Stanley?"

He turned slowly, took her hand. In stark contrast to her normal efficiency, Betty seemed tentative, almost frightened.

"Just the facts, ma'am." He managed a weak smile, though it was the last thing he wanted to do. "How long have I been here?"

"A day and a half."

"What happened to me?"

Betty let go of his hand, offered the water again. "You had an infection. From when you got hit."

Moodrow took a minute to digest the information. "With the trash can? That's what you're talking about?" The incident seemed infinitely remote, as if it had happened in another lifetime. To somebody else.

"You let it go too long, Stanley. When they brought you in, you had a fever near 104."

Moodrow let his eyes close. His shoulders and back ached, the pain dull, but insistent. He managed to shift his weight a bit, but the effort exhausted him and he quickly fell into a dreamless sleep. Two hours later, as he began to wake up, an idea crawled into his drifting consciousness.

Maybe, he thought, I had a fever when I decided to chase Jilly Sappone. Maybe I didn't know what I was doing.

The idea beckoned to him, as sweetly seductive as his memories of Annabella Sciorio, his first love. If he could somehow make it pass through hope and belief to firm conviction, he'd be all right.

"Stanley?"

He opened his eyes to find Betty leaning over him.

"You've got visitors." She gestured to Jim Tilley and Leonora Higgins standing by the foot of the bed.

"How are you feeling, Stanley?" They said it together, then laughed nervously.

Moodrow took the water from the bedside stand and drank. "I

feel like I tried to empty the Hell's Angels' clubhouse on Third Street. By myself."

"He must be doing better," Leonora observed. "If he's making jokes."

It didn't seem like a joke to Moodrow. He tried to roll onto his side, found it difficult to balance himself.

"Do you want me to raise the bed, Stanley?" Betty pressed the button before he could answer, and the top half of the bed rumbled upward. "Better?"

Moodrow nodded, then turned to Jim Tilley. "They get him yet?"

"Not yet, Stanley. But his face is all over the tube. It's just a matter of time." Tilley paused, smiled, then realized that Moodrow wanted more detail. "I don't know shit," he finally admitted. "The job's not in the precinct. I'm out of it."

Leonora took a step forward. "The NYPD formed a task force, naturally. *After . . .*"

Higgins stopped abruptly, tried to hide her embarrassment. She and Jim had decided not to mention the child, Theresa Kalkadonis. Without hearing it from Moodrow, they'd simply assumed he'd eventually blame himself. Moodrow, for his part, recognized the assumption and drew the obvious conclusion: If Leonora had made the same decision, the decision to chase Jilly Sappone, she'd hold herself responsible for the child's death.

Maybe, he thought, maybe I was already infected. I could have been running a fever. It isn't impossible.

"Anyway," Leonora finally continued, "if the detectives on the task force have any serious leads, they're keeping it to themselves. Ditto for the feds. There's a special agent named Holtzmann who won't return my calls."

The nurse came back into the room, accompanied by a small Asian man with a stethoscope draped around his neck.

"I said a minute and a minute's up," she declared. "He'll be out of the ICU tomorrow. Visiting hours are one till eight."

Moodrow watched Tilley and Higgins wave good-bye, then march out. Tilley, predictably old-fashioned, stepped back to let Higgins go first. Suddenly, Moodrow realized that he both wanted to be alone and was terrified at the prospect. He looked over at Betty. Sooner or later, she'd go, too; sooner or later the staff would turn down the lights and leave him to himself. He decided to ask for a sleeping pill, to keep asking until he was unconscious.

"Mr. Moodrow, how are you feeling? I'm Doctor Chen."

"All right." The shorter the answers, the faster he'd be gone. Doctors, in Moodrow's experience, were always in a hurry.

Chen nodded enthusiastically, then put the metal face of the stethoscope against Moodrow's chest and listened for a moment. "Can you roll onto your side? I need to get to your back." He tugged at Moodrow's shoulder, had the stethoscope against Moodrow's ribs before he settled onto his stomach. This time Chen moved the scope around and thumped Moodrow's back several times with his fingertips before standing abruptly.

"You had a serious staphylococcus infection, Mr. Moodrow," Chen said. "We treated it with antibiotics, and your temperature's returned to near-normal. We're going to draw some blood, and culture the wound tissue again. If the test results are favorable, you'll be out of here the day after tomorrow. Assuming, of course, that your fever doesn't return." Finished, he spun on his heel, started toward the door.

"Doctor Chen." Betty, a trial lawyer for almost thirty years, addressed the doctor in tones usually reserved for hostile witnesses with extensive criminal records. She waited for the doctor to stop and turn around before continuing. "I have a few questions."

Moodrow watched Chen smile, alert enough to recognize the underlying annoyance. "Doctor," he said, interrupting Betty, who'd been about to speak. "The fever. Can you tell me when it started?"

"I don't understand." Chen ran the fingers of his right hand along the narrow tubes of the stethoscope.

"How long before I was brought into the hospital? When did the fever actually start?"

"There's no way to know. The infection probably began within forty-eight hours of your receiving the injury. The fever could have started any time after that. It would depend on the strength of your immune system, your general health. . . ." His voice trailed off as he turned to Betty. "You said you had some questions?"

"About his recovery." Betty was smiling, now that she had his attention. "What can we expect?"

"A week to a month before he's fully recovered. Remember, he had a general septicemia. His whole body was affected. If we don't expect miracles, we won't be disappointed."

"Will he have to see you again?"

This time Chen's face actually registered his annoyance. He glanced at his watch before answering. "Does he have a regular doctor?"

"Yeah," Moodrow said, "but he died two years ago. They're running a phone-sex operation out of his office now."

"Well, I'll give you a referral to our clinic. It won't hurt to have somebody take a look at the wound in a couple of weeks. Maybe run some bloods." He stepped back toward the door. "I'll be in to see you tomorrow morning, of course. In case you have any more questions." He took another step. "I'm not anticipating a problem here. These kinds of infections, once we get them under control . . ." He was gone before he completed the sentence.

"They're always in a hurry," Betty observed, turning back to Moodrow. "Stanley, is there anything I can get you?"

"How about another chance?" The words were out before he could call them back.

Betty moved closer to the bed. "Was that why you asked him when the fever started?"

"Yeah, well . . ." He took a deep breath and let his head drop onto the pillow. "I'm trying to figure out why I did what I did. Why I chased him."

"How could you know Sappone was going to do . . . *that?*

Moodrow felt his eyes begin to close. "You remember," he said, his voice reduced to a whisper, "when the FBI attacked that cult in Texas? When the compound went up in flames and all those children died? Afterward, the feds claimed the fires were deliberately set, but that was just a diversion. When you pressure a crazy man, you have to expect a crazy reaction. Jilly couldn't run away from me and he couldn't surrender, so what he did was take the only way out. The only way out for a *crazy* man. Meanwhile, he stopped me cold and got away."

"Maybe you should tell me exactly what happened. Remember, I was in Los Angeles at the time."

Moodrow looked up. Betty was smiling at him, a good sign, no doubt. Pausing occasionally to order his thoughts, he worked his way through the events leading up to his and Sappone's mutual recognition. The words came more slowly as he went on, but he was determined to get the whole story out. Knowing the longer he waited, the harder it would be.

"It was just bad luck," he concluded. "Me and Jilly coming into that intersection at the same time. But it didn't have to end the way it did. I should've let him go."

"I think you need some rest, Stanley." Betty lowered the bed down without asking permission. "But you might want to consider this. Neither Jim nor Leonora blame you; in fact, they were both amazed that you actually found Sappone."

"What about Ann? Ann Kalkadonis."

"She released a statement to the press. You weren't mentioned by name, but she said she was satisfied with the police effort. From what you just told me, the police weren't involved, so I guess she must've been talking about you and your partner."

"What she told the vultures doesn't have to be the truth. You have to give them something or they'll never leave you alone."

"Good point, Stanley. Because somebody released your name to the press and the hospital security already caught a reporter trying to get into your room."

Later that same night—it could have been any time after visiting hours, though it had the feel of early morning—Moodrow woke up to a room lit only by the monitor behind his bed and a dim, shielded bulb over the closed door leading to the nurse's station. His strength was clearly returning, enough so that rather than remain imprisoned in his own thoughts, he seriously considered the pros and cons of checking himself out of the hospital.

A tug on the heavy plastic tube jammed into his penis demonstrated the clear impossibility of that impulse. There was something holding it in place and he couldn't very well carry a bag of urine under his coat, the ultimate kinky flasher. That was assuming he had a coat, or any other clothing, in the hospital.

He pulled himself to a sitting position, found the switch that controlled his bed, kept pressing buttons until the head rose. He wanted to swing his legs over the edge of the mattress, but the rails were up on both sides and he couldn't find the release. Never a quitter, he kept trying until the pulse monitor sounded an alarm. Nurse Rashad entered a moment later.

"I thought I told you not to get out of that bed."

"Does it look like I'm out of the *fucking* bed?"

"Don't run your mouth to me. I'm your nurse, not your wife."

His anger having fled as suddenly as it had appeared, Moodrow offered a quick apology. He didn't know what had provoked his reaction, but it clearly wasn't Nurse Rashad.

"Are you hungry?"

Moodrow took the question to mean she was making an apology of her own. "No, not really."

"I've got some cold orange juice in the pantry. In case you're thirsty."

He shook his head, let himself fall back against the sheets. "What time is it?"

"It's three-thirty."

"In the morning?"

"That's right."

"How long have you been on?"

"Since four o'clock in the afternoon. I'm working a double shift, sixteen hours." She smiled, shrugged her shoulders. "What could I say? I've got two growing MasterCards and an aging grandmother to support."

Nurse Rashad was gone before Moodrow remembered to ask for a sleeping pill. He spent a minute looking for the call button, then, when he couldn't find it, resigned himself to the inevitable. Moodrow had joined the NYPD in 1953, been promoted to the rank of detective five years later. Cold factual analysis was as much a part of his ordinary life as washing his hands before lunch or brushing his teeth in the morning. He might avoid it with Betty or Nurse Rashad for company, but not at three-thirty in the morning, not alone in a darkened room.

He listened to a monitor alarm sound in one of the other rooms on the ward, heard the distant wail of sirens on First Avenue. Background music to the scene he had to reconstruct. His eyes closed briefly, then opened to stare at the blank orange wall across the room as he visualized an intersection in Suffolk County.

When he could see it clearly, the traffic lights, the cars rushing by on the Long Island Expressway, Gadd sitting next to him, he began to work with his own mood. Remembering that he was annoyed with himself because they'd taken the long way around instead of making a U-turn on . . . He couldn't recall the name of the street for a moment, but then it came back to him, Middle Island Road in the town of Medford. They were stopped there, at the intersection, and despite his annoyance, he was very excited, very pleased with himself because every decision he'd made that day had brought him a step closer to Jilly Sappone. Because he'd done everything right.

Moodrow had a prodigious memory. He wasn't sure if it came by way of a Catholic school education or if he was born with it, but either way, he truly believed his memory to be the single attribute separating him from other NYPD detectives. He remembered everyone he met, good guys, bad guys, and noncombatants, had an internal file of mug shots and brief bios to go along with them. Even after thirty-six hours of near delirium, he could see the two cars, an ancient, rusted Cadillac and a small Toyota, turn left onto the Long Island Expressway service road, see the Taurus sliding up to the intersection.

The seating arrangement, two adult males, one in front, one in back, had intrigued him and he'd examined the men closely as the car rolled by. That was when he and Sappone had recognized each other. There'd been that moment of shock, of suspended animation, then the small Ford had careened across the intersection.

There'd been no time for calculation, for any weighing of profit and loss. Moodrow was on unfamiliar territory, a few seconds and Sappone would be gone, lost in the maze of some residential development. So, what he, Moodrow, had done, before he even considered the child, was give chase. What he'd done was confirm his identity by coming up on Sappone's bumper, then slamming on the brakes.

He didn't take it any further. What was the point? Every significant event had occurred in that intersection, every important decision had been made then and there. He shook his head, took a deep breath, then returned to the scene. Again, the Taurus rolled up, again his attention was drawn to the two men in the car. Sappone had been staring straight ahead, maybe focused on home, only a few blocks away, then he'd turned and their eyes had locked.

What he, Moodrow, should have done was hide his face, maybe turn to Gadd, lower his head, whisper, "That's Sappone, don't look at him." Anything but sit there with his mouth open, dumbfounded, like the time Father O'Shea caught him masturbating in the rectory bathroom.

It didn't sound much like delirium, he finally decided. In fact, it didn't sound *anything* like delirium. Picking up on the odd seating arrangement was not the act of a deluded man, a man lost to fever. No, the simple truth was that he'd reacted too slowly. And not once, but twice. After he came up on the Taurus, he'd remembered Theresa Kalkadonis all right, remembered her in time to jam on the brakes, but not, of course, in time to actually save her life.

TWO

Carmine Stettecase liked to think of his row house on East Tenth Street, between Second and Third Avenues, as "my brownstone." In the most literal sense, he was entirely correct—located in the middle of a block of renovated town houses, the five-story building did, in fact, retain its original facing of milky brown, New Jersey quarried sandstone. That, however was its *only* resemblance to the 1861 town house constructed in the emerging Italianate style for *Braumeister* Willem Bauer and his large, extended family. Not that Carmine— who had as much respect for tradition as anybody in the organized-crime business—had been the one to butcher 671 East Tenth Street. Far from it. In his own mind, he was the one who'd restored the structure, if not to its original glory, at least to solid, middle-class respectability.

The butchery had been accomplished a year after WWII, when Martin Tighe, a small-time landlord (formerly slumlord, this being his big move up) bought the building from the heirs of Miss Octavia Shankman, an octogenarian who'd maintained herself (and her middle-class sensibilities) by cleaning and cooking for six respectable female boarders. Tighe, in the habit of predicting the postwar housing crunch to anyone who'd listen, began by dumping the tenants, none of whom had had the foresight to secure a lease. New York, at the time, was locked into a rigid system of rent control; serious landlords either built new or bought empty. Tighe, the way he figured it, had bought empty, and the courts had backed him up.

Once the old ladies were packed off to whatever fate awaited them, Martin proceeded to the building itself. The high stoop leading to the parlor floor went first, along with an elaborate cast-iron railing, the double oak doors, and the carved brackets supporting the stone hood over the entranceway. A new entrance was cut into what had formerly been the basement, while the old one was sealed with brick and faced with sheets of stone stripped from a demolition site in Fort Greene, Brooklyn.

For the next several months, Tighe made his nut by selling off architectural details to an interior decorator on East Seventy-fifth Street. Everything of value went—the sliding oak doors and the mahogany shutters, three rococo mantels carved from the purest white marble, a finely wrought chandelier dating back to 1843, seventy feet of black walnut molding, even the parquet floors. When the contractor was finished, when rooms originally running half the length of the building had been reduced to eleven-by-twenty-foot boxes, Tighe had his name put on New York University's approved list for student housing, filling his boxes at a stroke while, at the same time, avoiding cumbersome leases that would have bound him to the same rent-control laws Octavia Shankman had avoided by cooking for her tenants.

The following fifteen years were reasonably good to Martin Tighe. His properties, including 671 East Tenth Street, chugged out profits with the relentless determination of the Little Engine That Could. Enough profits to support two ex-wives, six children, and a sizable gambling habit that finally exploded in 1962 when Tighe's main bookie, Johnny Bono (with ex-wives of his own to worry about) sold Tighe's hundred-thousand-dollar debt to Carmine Stettecase.

It might have gone badly for Martin Tighe. Carmine, not especially noted for his patience, might, for instance, have sent Jilly Sappone to collect the debt. But Carmine was beset with an obsession all his own, an obsession inspired by two prominent politicians, Estes Kefauver and Robert Kennedy, and by a series of connected mobsters (mobsters formally sworn to the law of *omertà*) willing to testify in front of television cameras.

Carmine was living in a tenement on Elizabeth Street at the time, the walls of which were thin enough to let in the sounds of newly-

wed love from an adjoining apartment. As he listened to the shrieking bedsprings late at night (as he reconstructed the day-to-day con-
spiracies hatched in his own kitchen), Carmine imagined FBI
microphones in the walls, the ceilings, the light fixtures, the television set. He imagined himself surrounded by spinning reel-to-reel
tape recorders, IRS agents in glen-plaid suits, imagined a dismal future in a cold, damp cell up near the Canadian border.

A lesser man would have collapsed under the weight of his fears,
but Carmine Stettecase hadn't clawed his way up from the bottom
by refusing to meet his problems head-on. The smart move, he rea-
soned, was to insulate himself from attack in the hope that his pursuers—if pursuers there be—would veer off in search of easier
targets. The way experienced b&e artists avoided houses with big
dogs, barred windows, and burglar alarms.

One solution, already taken by many of his colleagues (and by
tens of thousands of other New Yorkers, it being the era of white
flight), was to buy a house in New Jersey or out on Long Island or up
in Westchester, a house that sat on its own lot. There were three
things wrong with that idea as far as Carmine was concerned. First,
he had a sentimental attachment to Manhattan in general, and to
his old neighborhood in particular. Second, he hated the idea of running away. Third, he was afraid of the wide-open spaces surrounding
most private homes. There were just too many potential bad guys
out there, too many cops, too many jealous rivals. It was hard
enough defending a single apartment front door, maybe the window
leading out to the fire escape. How could you protect an entire
house? They might come at you from anywhere.

Now, more than twenty years later, Carmine sat on a leather recliner in his five-hundred-square-foot living room and sipped at a
glass of freshly squeezed orange juice. As he watched his wife and his
son's mother-in-law prepare the breakfast table, he realized just how
lucky he'd been to run into Johnny Bono on that long-ago night.

"The worst thing about it, what's really bustin' my balls," Johnny
had explained after a long preamble, "is I know this scumbag could
raise the bread to pay me off. All he gotta do is sell some of that
property." They were sitting inside Carmine's restaurant, Bono
chugging down 7&7s like there was no tomorrow. "But he won't do

it, Carmine. Says the properties are mortgaged out, the real-estate market's depressed, he's got partners to worry about. I mean the prick has a different excuse every time I talk to him, which I ain't doin' too often because he's makin' himself scarce."

Carmine nodded thoughtfully, figuring Johnny was going to ask him to collect the debt, which he was willing to do, for a price.

"Meanwhile," Bono resumed after draining his glass, "I know the guy's lyin' to me. This afternoon I went down to City Hall, looked up this brownstone Tighe owns on Tenth Street. Guess what, Carmine—no partners, no mortgage. The man is a *deadbeat*."

Carmine refilled the bookie's glass, shrugged his shoulders, grunted his acceptance of Martin Tighe's infamy. "What kinda brownstone?" he asked.

"It's like apartments, now. For college kids. Between Second and Third Avenue. A nice neighborhood, Carmine. There ain't a fuckin' spic for miles around."

Carmine was proud of the way it finally went down. First, once it became clear that Johnny Bono didn't have the balls to collect on his own, Carmine bought up the debt for seventy-five cents on a dollar. Then, all by himself, he convinced Martin Tighe that his life depended on the prompt payment of this honorably assumed obligation. It wasn't all that difficult.

"What it is," Carmine explained, "is if ya don't pay me the way I wanna get paid, I'm gonna kill ya."

The trick, of course, the important thing, was that he meant what he said, a reality Martin Tighe was quick to recognize. Tighe's hand dipped into his back pocket, fished out a thick wallet.

"I need a little time," he explained, "but meanwhile I got a week's vig right here."

Carmine, his face a mask of cold determination, shook his head. "No, forget the fuckin' money. It's too *late* for money. What I want you should do is sign over that house on Tenth Street to my mother. She's sick and she needs a decent place to live." He left out the fact that his mother was, at that moment, lying in a nursing-home bed.

Once Carmine got rid of the college kids (most of them left in

June of that year, the rest vacated after a little encouragement), he went to work on his "brownstone" with all the vigor Martin Tighe had demonstrated fifteen years before. He began by installing two steel doors, one at the outer entrance to the building, the second on the inside of a little vestibule. Then he'd transformed Martin Tighe's tiny studios, dividing the building into three apartments, two duplexes with a floor-through on top. Along the way, he sound-proofed the walls, covered all the windows with heavy drapes, barred every piece of glass on the first two floors.

Satisfied at last, Carmine moved his family (he couldn't bring himself to trust an outsider, neither tenant nor servant) inside. He and his wife, Rosa, took the lower duplex, installing their son, Tommaso, Tommaso's wife, Mary, and the grandchildren to come (who never came) directly above them. Tommaso's mother-in-law, Josie Rizzo, had gotten the top floor, a condition, supposedly temporary, that had grown to be the permanent thorn in Carmine Stettecase's life. A thorn already more deeply buried in his flesh than he could possibly imagine.

"Hey, Pop?"

Carmine jumped awake, then silently cursed himself. Remembering a time when *nobody* snuck up on him, when he'd watched the world around him with the nonchalant paranoia of a homeless cat.

But that was then, he said to himself, and this is now, and there's no goin' back.

Out loud, he said, "You ready?"

"Yeah. I didn't mean to startle you."

Carmine figured his son's wet smirk was meant to be friendly. That was because the kid—the *punk*—didn't have the nerve to make fun of him.

"Just get to work, Tommy. The boys'll be here soon."

"Sorry, Pop, I guess I got up late again."

Carmine looked at his only male child and shook his head. Tommy Stettecase, at age thirty-eight, was rail-thin and as bald on top as an egg. His face was the color of a peeled cucumber (except for the black pouches beneath his eyes) and his chin merged smoothly into the wrinkled skin of his neck. He would never take over his father's business, never be the Don, which was perfectly okay with him. Tommy loved his father, but had long abandoned any hope of living up to his father's expectations. Or that his father would ever come to appreciate Tommy's own accomplishments.

But there was one accomplishment Carmine definitely *did* appreciate, an accomplishment that dovetailed nicely into Carmine's ever-blossoming paranoia. Tommy's job, performed before every business meeting, was to sweep the dining room for bugs. Never mind the fact that he'd been doing it for over a decade without finding any device more threatening than a percolator with an electrical short. Never mind the fact that Carmine hadn't been arrested in thirty-five years. Carmine had been in the courtroom when John Gotti went down, had listened to Sammy the Bull's testimony, heard the FBI tapes that sealed Gotti's fate. On the day the jury came in, he'd taken his wife aside and told her the bad news.

"Our day is done, our thing, our *cosa nostra*. The spics and the Chinks are comin' up, the niggers, too. Maybe that's the way it's supposed to be, maybe everything in life eventually gets finished with. Meanwhile, the cops and the politicians keep comin' after us, like old dogs who can't learn new tricks. Anyone who's been around long enough to pick up an FBI file's gotta figure to die in a cell. Rose, you know I backed off the drug business a long time ago, but now I got an ace in the hole. So what I'm gonna do is look for a big score."

Carmine's ace in the hole was a factory named Paradise Fashion Designs, a pure money loser whose sole attractions (for Carmine Stettecase) were its location in the village of Tangail in the country of Bangladesh, and the desperation of its owner, Sanjay Gupta. Carmine, acting through a broker, had convinced Gupta (for a price, of course) to open a Paradise Fashion bank account on Grand Cayman Island in the Bahamas. Every six weeks or so, Carmine had his son, Tommaso, fly into Grand Cayman via private jet and make a large deposit. A month later, the money, in the guise of profit distributions (and as clean as mob money could get) was wire-transferred to Carmine's personal account in Panama. From there it went to numbered accounts in Switzerland, Luxembourg, and Hong Kong.

"What would you say to a triplex in Rome?" Carmine had put his arm around his wife, looked into her still-handsome face, wondered just where the hell Tommy came from. If the kid had a little more balls, Carmine would've turned the family business over to him on the spot, let the punk take the fall.

Rosa had leaned her narrow frame into her husband's bulk. "With servants?"

"Definitely."

"And a villa in Switzerland? Just in case the summers in Rome are too hot?"

"Sure."

"And Josie Rizzo dead in her grave?"

"Without a fucking doubt."

Josefina Rizzo, née Sappone, took four Wedgwood cups and four matching saucers out of an enormous china cabinet, pausing momentarily to admire the delicate gold rims, the tiny hand-painted roses that seemed to dance across the milky porcelain. The cups and saucers were part of a service for twenty-four and much too fine, in her opinion, for Carmine Stettecase and the three *cafones* he called "my aides." But that was Carmine, that was the way he was, a fat guinea stuffing pastry into his mouth while he imagined himself a British lord. And why not? There was no one to contradict him, no one to hold up the mirror. No one to say, "Hey Carmine, putting on a tutu don't make a ballerina out of a dancing bear."

Josie set the cups and the saucers on the table, then went back to the china cabinet in search of plates and bowls. She had to move around Tommy Stettecase who was making a quick physical search of the room before beginning an electronic sweep. Josie liked Tommy, the way a soldier might be fond of a stray dog trapped inside a battle zone. In Josie's narrow world, innocence was the rarest commodity, to be wondered at, to be tossed a scrap of food now and again, but never to be taken seriously.

"Good morning, Mama-Josie."

She didn't bother to answer and he didn't pursue it. In truth, she rarely spoke to any of them, not even to her daughter. What was the point? The play had been written a long time ago, the actors chosen for each part. Besides, she had to save all her strength to nurse the spirit within her, to keep it strong. The obligation was absolute; it demanded that she conserve her energies, keep her own counsel.

Once the plates and bowls were laid out, Josie placed the sugar bowl, the creamer, and a large tureen for the fruit salad on a silver tray and went into the kitchen. There she found Carmine's wife, Rosa, dropping eggs into a steel bowl. Rosa, at her husband's instruction, was preparing *omelettes aux fine herbs*, just as if the boys in Carmine's band wouldn't prefer eggs and peppers deep-fried in olive oil. Just as if Carmine himself hadn't grown up on breakfasts of sour milk and two-day-old bread, suppers of pasta fazool and water.

Josie opened the refrigerator, took out the fruit salad and the heavy cream. Quickly, her large raw-knuckled hands driven by years of practice, she filled the tureen and the creamer, then topped off the sugar bowl before returning to the dining room. She was a strong woman, nearly six feet in height with a massive forehead and heavy, prominent cheekbones that squeezed her sharp black eyes into permanent shadow. The net effect was more than an accident of birth. Josie Rizzo didn't want anyone looking into her eyes. She went through life with her features turned defiantly down, had been doing it for so long that her neck jutted forward at an odd angle, even when she was alone.

In the neighborhood, she was, she knew, an object of pity, if not out-and-out ridicule. She shopped every day, no matter what the weather, striding along, eyes glued to the sidewalk, in the widow's weeds she'd donned more than three decades before when her brother was murdered. That was five years before her own husband died.

"Mama-Josie, would you put on the radio?"

Josie flipped the switch, turned the volume up, tried to hide her inner laughter. Tommy used the sound to activate hidden bugs before he started looking for them with his electrical gadgets. His father, Carmine, always watched this part, standing just inside the doorway with his hand on his hips. Josie had no idea what Tommy was actually doing; all she really knew was that once it was over, once Tommy pronounced the room safe, Carmine relaxed. As if that was all there was to it.

She set the tureen, the creamer, and the sugar bowl on the table, then carried the tray across the room to a large buffet. Her path took her within a few feet of Carmine, who tossed her the most ferocious glare in his repertoire. The one that said, "I'm gonna kill you and I'm gonna do it soon."

At least that's the way Josie read it. Carmine Stettecase was going to have her killed, just as her father, husband, and brother had been killed before her. The decision had already been made.

Josie Rizzo was not afraid of death. Physical fear was an emotion entirely unknown to her. She had no regrets, not for anything she'd done, or anything she was about to do. As far as she was concerned, it was all fate, anyway, the only tragedy being that you couldn't know in advance, couldn't see the blows coming. Josie hadn't been inside a Catholic church, not even for wedding or funerals, in twenty years. Not since Father Murtagh (an Irishman, naturally) preached a sermon on the doctrine of free will.

"You done yet, Tommy? The boys're here."

"Couple minutes, Pop."

As Carmine walked off, Josie returned to her chores, setting out the silverware and the linen napkins before returning the tray to its place in the china cabinet. Then she hurried off to the kitchen to find Rosa standing in front of the stove.

"The rolls," Josie said. "In the oven."

Rosa shifted over a few feet. "Croissants, Josie. They're called croissants."

Josie snatched a large warming tray off the kitchen table, carried it over to the stove, and began to arrange the steaming croissants on its smooth surface. She took her time, folding the pastries into each other, making three even rows. This was the critical point in a particularly important morning, the morning she saved her boy, Gildo, again.

"Tommy, for Christ's sake, how long is this gonna take?"

"Another minute, pop."

Josie carried the loaded tray back to the kitchen table and set it down. She opened the refrigerator, took out three small dishes, each with a ball of whipped butter in its center, and carried them into the dining room. Tommy was at the far end of the room, on his knees with his ass in the air. He was running one of his gadgets along the baseboard, looking exactly like the servant he was.

"Done, Pop."

Josie watched Tommy clamber to his feet, gather his instruments, and flee to his own apartment, the innocent civilian deserting the battlefield. Carmine stepped aside to let him pass, then entered the dining room, followed by the boys, Vinnie Trentacosta, Guido Palanzo, and Little-Dominick (*Big*-Dominick being, of course, the now deceased Dominick Favara) Guarino. All three men were in their early sixties. They'd grown up with Carmine, had served alongside him under Big-Dominick's leadership. Nevertheless, Carmine searched each of them from time to time, searched them personally and in private. After Sammy the Bull, he trusted no one outside the family.

"Get the goddamned rolls, Josie," Carmine growled. "Can't ya see I'm in a hurry here?"

"Croissants," Josie muttered as she went back to the kitchen. "They're called croissants."

By the time she picked up the warming tray and returned to the dining room, Carmine and his three flunkies were seated around one end of the table. Josie like to think of them as the three blind mice. The image fit nicely with the fate she had in store for them.

"Hey, Josie," Carmine said. His fat mouth was already twisted into a smirk. "I heard that Jilly's gonna be a fuckin' poster boy." He stopped, looked at the other men, winked broadly. "I mean, why not? Now that his mug's all over the TV and the papers, maybe they'll even make a movie of his life. Whatta ya think, Josie? You think Hollywood'll turn ya head? Ya won't forget us, will ya?"

Josie didn't bother to respond, didn't look up even when the three blind mice broke into uproarious laughter. She continued on her way across the room, set the warming tray on the buffet and plugged in the extension cord, thereby activating the microcassette recorder in the tray's false bottom.

THREE

Betty arrived just before breakfast, striding into Moodrow's room as if she'd been taking lessons from Nurse Rashad. A soft-sided green overnight bag dangled from her left hand.

"Clothing," she announced. "Just in case they decide to let you go this afternoon."

"Or in case I decide to walk out?"

"You think you can do that?"

"Not unless they take the tube out of my dick."

Nurse Rashad chose that moment to walk through the open door. "That's just what I'm here to do," she announced. "My final act of mercy before I go home and collapse." She pulled the privacy curtain around Moodrow's bed, then yanked down the sheets. "You might wanna close your eyes here. If the tube's attached to something, it could get real ugly."

Moodrow, who'd been through it earlier in the year, knew the joke was supposed to relax him. Nevertheless, he gritted his teeth, closed his eyes, held his breath until she was finished.

"From now on, you pee in the bottle." She held up a clear, flat-sided, plastic jug. "We have to measure output."

"What about that?" Moodrow pointed to the dripping IV.

"Another twenty-four hours, at least. Doctor Chen's orders. If you decide to take a walk, it rolls along with you. Believe me, if it wasn't for that bottle, you probably wouldn't be here."

Twenty minutes later, after a breakfast of cold scrambled eggs, pureed peaches, and cranberry juice, Moodrow asked Betty to let the bed rails down.

"I'm gonna take that walk now, see what I got."

It took him nearly ten minutes to make it once around the ward, his legs always a beat behind, as if they were following him. Betty walked alongside, pushing the IV stand, not saying much of anything until he stopped to lean against the wall.

"I could get a wheelchair." She was holding his arm with one hand, as if she could actually support his 265 pounds if he started to fall.

Moodrow shook his head, continued on until he was back to his room. Despite its being too small by five or six inches, he couldn't think of anything but his bed. He wanted to crawl in, to fall asleep, to forget.

A strange nurse woke him up an hour later to announce that he was being transferred out of the ICU. Betty was standing beside the bed, the overnight bag in her hand. In the hallway, just outside the door, an orderly lounged behind an empty wheelchair.

"Your limo awaits you," he announced. "Curb-to-curb service, no tipping allowed."

The trip took less than ten minutes, but Moodrow's bed, in Room 511, was still occupied when they arrived. A harried nurse explained that a discharged patient's wife had failed to arrive with his clothing. A phone call had found her still asleep, but she was definitely on her way. Meanwhile, with the IV bag now hanging from a pole attached to the chair, Moodrow would have to remain seated in the hallway.

Betty started to protest, the medical profession and its decidedly user-unfriendly attitude being one of her pet peeves, but Moodrow tapped her on the hand.

"I don't have the energy for a beef," he explained.

Betty nodded reluctant agreement. "I saw some chairs by the elevators," she said. "We can wait out there and get some privacy at the same time. I need to talk to you."

When they were alone, sitting across from each other, Betty said, "I called your partner in crime, Ginny Gadd, last night. I called her from your apartment, told her to come by this morning."

"Ginny? You two are friends now?"

He was hoping for a smile, hoping to see Betty's wide mouth expand into a quick, slashing grin. No such luck. Her lips remained slightly pursed, her jaw tight, though not clenched. Moodrow recognized the look. Betty was in her problem-solving mode.

"What you did the other night to Carlo Sappone? That's called kidnapping." She waved her hand in front of his face. "No, don't say anything. Just listen while your lawyer explains the facts of life. Gadd told me that when the Suffolk cops asked how you found Jilly Sappone, you told them you'd gotten an anonymous tip, that you put the word out and somebody dropped a dime. I don't know, maybe it'll hold up, maybe it won't. What we have to do is be prepared for the 'won't.' Just in case."

"Betty," Moodrow finally got word in, "Carlo Sappone's a coke dealer. He's not gonna go to the cops. Right now, with Carmine and Jilly both looking to catch up with him, I'd be surprised if he's still in town."

"I'm not worried about him going to the cops, Stanley." She was frowning now, her eyes slightly narrowed. "I'm worried about the cops going to *him*. Like, for instance, if the lease for Jilly's house is in Carlo's name, the Suffolk cops, not to mention the New York cops and the feds, might want to ask him where he was on the night in question. In fact, they might use his being a drug dealer to squeeze the truth out of him. Or offer to protect him from those two entities you just mentioned."

Moodrow shrugged. "Maybe I'm just too tired to focus, but I don't get the point."

The elevator doors opened before Betty could reply, disgorging a brown-uniformed orderly pushing an empty gurney. Guinevere Gadd followed, looking around until she spotted Moodrow and Betty sitting off to one side.

"What's the deal, Moodrow, you couldn't afford a bed?" Gadd's voice was chipper, cheerful, though her eyes were rimmed by dark circles. She was wearing a navy jacket over a white blouse. The jacket, a blazer, was rumpled, the blouse pulled nearly out of her skirt on one side.

"Think it's the insurance? Or should I take it personally?"

Moodrow kept his voice soft. Remembering that she'd seen it all, been right there with him, had gotten out of the car and run over to . . .

Christ, he thought, this is the last thing I need right now.

"I asked Ginny to come by this morning." Betty stood up, shook Gadd's hand, the gesture quick and formal. "Because I didn't want someone from law enforcement showing up first. There are so many jurisdictions involved in this case, somebody's bound to arrive on our doorstep. Sooner or later."

Betty sat back down, waited for Gadd to follow before speaking. She leaned forward, drawing them into a tight circle, keeping her voice low. It was a technique perfected in courtroom hallways and tested on thousands of clients.

"The first thing," she said to Gadd, "you have to understand is that I can't represent you if I'm representing Stanley."

Represent? Somehow the prospect cheered Moodrow. What would they charge him with? First-degree Fucking Up? How about Reckless Endangerment? Murder by Depraved Indifference? That one had the ring of truth.

"Nobody's after me, as far as I know." Gadd's palms were on the seat of the chair, taking enough weight to push her shoulders up around her ears. She looked like she was trying to hide. "A fed came around yesterday, Special Agent Holtzmann with two *n*s. I stuck to the story Moodrow told: We used a list of names provided by our client, got the word out to various lowlife types, somebody decided to take advantage." She paused as the elevator doors opened, waited for the young couple who got off to disappear through the swinging doors leading to the ward. "I told him that after the call, we drove straight out to Sappone's house, made a pass, then . . ." She smiled, ran the fingers of her right hand through her short hair. "Then everything happened just the way it happened."

"The agent, Holtzmann, do you think he believed you?" Betty tossed Moodrow a sidelong glance. "Because I sure as hell wouldn't. Cops use that 'anonymous informants' bullshit all the time."

"I got the feeling," Gadd said, "that he was going through the motions. The reporters are being more persistent. My office phone's ringing off the hook. I've been giving them a straight 'no comment,' claiming client confidentiality, the cops want me to keep my mouth shut. Like that."

Both women turned to Moodrow, as if expecting him to contribute, but he was too tired. The only thing he really wanted was the bed.

"Why don't you just go on, Betty? Say what you have to say. I don't have the energy for a debate."

"All right." Betty straightened up momentarily, crossed her legs, then leaned back into the circle. "The cops might ask for a list of names, everyone you spoke to about Sappone's whereabouts. What you do is tell them to go to your client, if they haven't done so already. Do what Ginny did, cite client confidentiality. If the cops want to take it further, let them get a court order." She paused, looked from Gadd to Moodrow, her voice a notch harder when she resumed speaking. "On the other hand, if they even *mention* Carlo Sappone's name, you ask for a lawyer. I mean it. Don't give them a statement of any kind, not even a denial. Right now, this particular murder, this particular investigation, is the hottest story in town. Everyone here knows what that means. If the cops find Jilly Sappone right away, they'll forget about you. But two weeks from now, if Sappone's still out there and the cops are getting their collective asses nailed to the wall by the media, the boys are gonna look for a scapegoat. Remember: You *did* kidnap Carlo Sappone; you *are* guilty."

"Enough," Moodrow said. "You're into overkill."

"Not enough." Betty waved him off. "Remember, you left Carlo handcuffed to a tree. The fact of the kidnapping is undeniable. Now, suppose Carlo Sappone testified against you. Suppose the cops found somebody at that gas station where you set up surveillance, somebody who remembers you. Do you want to pin the next five years of your life on convincing one or two jurors that Carlo is such an evil bastard it doesn't matter what you did to him?"

"Well, it worked for Lorena Bobbitt," Moodrow said.

Gadd flashed a quick smile. "Hey, Moodrow, Carlo was *intact* when I left him." She got up, took off her jacket, then sat back down. "I've got a friend, a semiboyfriend, actually, who does some criminal law. That's when he's not writing wills. What I'll do, I'll talk it over with him, make sure he's available if worse comes to absolute disaster."

Her voice trailed off, the silence holding for a moment until Betty finally stood up. "I think I'll go see what's happening with your bed, Stanley. Give the two of you a chance to talk." She took a couple of steps, then turned. "What could I do? I'm a criminal lawyer. I'm paid to be paranoid. Most likely, it won't come to anything."

When they were alone, Gadd tossed her jacket onto Betty's chair, then folded her hands, squeezing tightly. "You gonna be all right?" she asked.

"Someday."

"When your dreams all come true?" Her hand dropped onto her thighs. "No kidding, you look like hell. This bug knocked the crap out of you."

"Is that a question?" Moodrow knew where she was going. And knew there was no way to head it off short of outright fainting.

Gadd leaned forward, laid her right hand on Moodrow's forearm. "Sappone used one of the credit cards, rented a car on the Upper West Side, and bought himself breakfast the morning after it happened. I braced the rental agent and he described Sappone just the way we saw him."

"You didn't show the agent a photo?"

"I didn't wanna go that far, actually show him Sappone's picture. If he put the photo together with Jilly's face on TV, he might call the cops in."

Moodrow took a deep breath, held it for a moment. It was much to early to be thinking (much less actually talking) about Jilly Sappone's escape. Moodrow wasn't sure he still gave a shit about the man anyway. They'd gone out to rescue a child, not capture Sappone and his partner. Why should the focus change because the rescue had failed? Maybe Gadd wanted to pretend they'd been after Sappone all along, that losing the child had been a temporary setback, that the good guys would eventually triumph.

"I don't think I've got the energy for long explanations," Moodrow finally said. He looked at her for a moment, realized that she was in no way prepared for what he was going to tell her. Gadd's eyelids were dark and swollen, as if she hadn't slept in days, but her eyes, themselves, were glittery with excitement. "Why don't you just let the cops handle it, give them a chance. I could pass the car-rental info to Jim Tilley and he could pass it to the suits running the case, say it came by way of an anonymous informant. It'll be all over in a few days. No matter what we do."

Moodrow had done his level best to make his words plain, but he might as well have spoken in Swahili, a fact that became clear to him when Gadd ignored everything he said.

"I'm gonna take a ride tomorrow, up to Binghamton. After a dozen calls, I finally got an appointment with someone on the parole board. Name's Arnold Dumont. What I'm gonna do is ask him how Jilly got out, why the board turned him down, then reversed itself. Maybe you'll be feeling better by the time I get back. The Upper West Side's a big place and I could use some help."

Moodrow glanced at the doors leading to the ward, hoping Betty would come riding to the rescue. When the doors remained stubbornly closed, he turned back to meet Ginny Gadd's stare.

"I'm gonna make this as plain as I can, Gadd. I fucked up out there. Not once, but twice. Five years ago, I don't think it would've happened. It's not like being a clerk in the post office, you make a mistake and a package gets lost. The way I see it right now, I shouldn't be putting myself in situations where *human* lives are at risk. That's why, in the future, I'm gonna specialize in dognappings."

The joke seemed to such out the last of his remaining energy and he slumped visibly.

"You can't blame yourself for what happened to . . ." Gadd's tongue swept across her lower lip. "I can't say her name," she admitted. "I can't even think it."

"There's no blame." Moodrow said, his voice just above a whisper. "Look, I have to take responsibility. I know that's un-American; if I could find some way to get out of it, I would. But I've been over the whole deal, everything that happened in that intersection, and I can't find any explanation except pure fucking-up. I made choices, and they were bad choices." He hesitated for a fraction of a second. "And there was a time in my life when I wouldn't have made them."

Gadd moved to the edge of her chair. "You're sayin' you just wanna give it up? You won't help me?"

"Look . . ."

"You have to."

Moodrow, surprised by her tone, jerked his head up. Gadd's mouth was curled into an angry, petulant circle, her eyes narrowed down to slits.

"You have to," she repeated. "If you don't . . ."

Without any warning, she drew back her fist and punched him square in the face, the force of the blow jerking the wheelchair back several inches despite his weight. After a moment, Moodrow raised his hand to his cheek.

"You wanna talk about responsibility?" Gadd's mouth was screwed into a tight, contemptuous frown; her hands lay, un-clenched, on the arms of the chair. "What about your responsibility to *me?*" She crossed her legs, gathered her thoughts. "You wanna believe you were fucking Superman five years ago, that's your business. You wanna believe you fucked up, that's okay, too. But I need some help out there and you owe me. Don't forget, I saw it, too. I saw it and I can't get her out of my mind. Awake or asleep. I can't get her out." Gadd began to cry, the tears running in nearly unbroken streaks along the sides of her nose. "It was so small, Moodrow. The coffin was so fucking small."

FOUR

It wasn't fair, Abner Kirkwood decided. No way a guy makes two mistakes in his whole adult life and that's all she wrote, the whole ball game, *finito* and good-bye. A major-league baseball player could have a bad year, collect his two million, still put it together with a good season. A surgeon could slip, butcher some old guy, let his insurance company pick up the tab. Hell, a US Senator, guy like Arlen Specter, could make every goddamned woman in Pennsylvania hate his guts and still get reelected.

But not Abner Kirkwood, right? Not United States Attorney Abner Kirkwood, now, after twenty-five years in the Department of Justice, finally head of the whole goddamned Southern District and looking to go higher yet.

The funny thing was he hadn't seen the first one coming, the first mistake when he joined the Democratic Party, started hanging around the clubhouses. That was because it happened while he was still in college, in 1967, when it looked like the dems would stay in power forever. Like the New Deal was part of the Constitution.

Kirkwood leaned forward in his chair, picked up the framed 5x7 on his desk, and stared at the two smiling men in the color photograph. He and Rudolph Giuliani shaking hands at an office party ten years ago.

You'd think, Kirkwood thought, between the lisp and the haircut, the schmuck wouldn't have the balls to show his face in public, but there he was, Mayor of New York City and looking for a shot at the

Senate. Waiting for Al D'Amato to finally make the big mistake (Christ, the guy had more lives than Al Sharpton), or Moynihan to drink his way into a stroke.

The bitter truth—the part that made him want to spit—was that Rudolph Giuliani became a Republican right about the time Abner Kirkwood became a Democrat, that Giuliani leapfrogged from the DOJ under Nixon, to private practice, then back into the DOJ under Reagan. Working his way up to Assistant Attorney General, Chief of the Narcotics Section, Chief Special Prosecutor, his face on the news more often than the goddamned Attorney General.

Kirkwood put the photo down, thought, me and Giuliani, we're not that different. Both grew up tough in those lily-white New York neighborhoods, the ones everybody left when the first black family moved onto the block. (Only they didn't say "black," his parents, the neighbors, the kids in the schoolyards, they said "nigger," grinding the word beneath their heels.)

But, then, he'd pulled out, too, moved on to NYU and Brooklyn Law a month or two before his parents took off for New Jersey. Nobody would believe it, now, what it had been like to grow up in the Bronx, the only white, Anglo-Saxon Protestant for miles around, everybody else Jewish or Italian or Irish. The Lithuanians up by the zoo had more identity than he did.

Sometimes it got so bad he pretended his mother was Irish, but the sad truth was that she and dad were half-literate Alabama crackers who'd come north after the war, come to make it in the big city, only picking the wrong one, New York instead of Los Angeles, the Bronx instead of the San Fernando Valley.

The intercom sounded, a single, civilized chirp instead of a harsh buzz. Kirkwood pressed the button, said, "Mrs. English?"

"Agent Holtzmann to see you, Mister Kirkwood. Along with Ms. Rizzo." She drew the Ms. out a bit. *Mzzzzzz.* Letting him know how she felt about Italian widows who stared at the floor.

"Have them take a seat, Mrs. English. I'll buzz you when I'm ready."

Nothing in Abner Kirkwood's rolling tones revealed his inner state. If his colleagues wanted to see him as some kind of Bronx patrician (an oxymoron, he noted, if there ever was one) that was okay with him. The truth, on the other hand, was that Josie Rizzo was his second mistake and the thought of her in his office was enough to get him wheezing. He took an inhaler from the middle desk drawer, popped it into his mouth, then squeezed once, holding his breath momentarily.

When Bill Clinton got himself elected President of the United States, Kirkwood had figured that his dues were finally paid. Which was only fair, considering that he'd worked on parts of every major case to hit the Southern District in the last decade, attended five thousand Democratic fund-raisers, donated ten thousand hours of free legal work to the Democratic National Committee, the NAACP, Catholic Charities, the Association of Jewish Philanthropies. Every ethnic group in New York but the Nation of Islam.

In the end, Clinton had come through, appointed Assistant US Attorney Kirkwood to head the Southern District, his golden opportunity if he could bring the kind of cases that attracted the media. Because the bottom line was you could speak at the Elks Club, the Knights of Columbus, the Anti-Defamation League until you turned purple and it didn't mean shit. Meanwhile, put yourself next to John Gotti, Mike Milken, Ivan Boesky, Leona Helmsley and the next day three million voters knew your name.

So what he did was reach out, let it be known he was looking to get busy, and a couple of weeks later, Special Agent Holtzmann waltzed into his office, said, "I have something here, Abner. Don't know if it's worth going forward. Have to get approval from your office."

As if five or ten lunches scattered over half a decade gave Agent Holtzmann the right to call United States Attorney Kirkwood by his first name.

"Carmine Stettecase, Italian mobster, mid-level." Holtzmann had paused to run his fingertips over his lapels, a nervous tic he repeated a dozen times before he left. "An informant came forward last week. Just called the New York office and made an appointment. Claimed she had access to Stettecase's inner sanctum. Willing to deliver him up if we help her out with a small problem."

"The woman's name, Karl, if you please." Time to take over the conversation, establish the old chain of command.

"Josefina Rizzo."

"And what's her access?"

"She's the mother-in-law of Carmine Stettecase's son, Tommaso. Lives in Carmine's house, claims that Carmine does serious business over breakfast, that the room is swept beforehand by Tommaso, but she can get a recorder in and out." Holtzmann smiled for the first time, ticking the facts off on his fingers. "She had a serving tray with her, a bread warmer with a heating unit built into the bottom. Said if we could put a tape recorder inside, she'd see to changing the tapes, making delivery to a drop, even give us a free sample to prove their value."

"I assume you took advantage and the sample was satisfactory."

Holtzmann had straightened, done his lapels again. "It has the potential to be a major case."

There it was, the magic phrase. Major Case. Meanwhile, Kirkwood knew Carmine Stettecase was not the boss of all bosses, not even close. In fact the only interesting thing about Carmine was that he'd been around forever.

"The quid pro quo, Karl. Let's hear it."

"Her nephew, Gildo Sappone, been in jail for almost fifteen years. State parole board turned him down and she wants him out."

"And?"

"And?"

Abner Kirkwood had tapped his desk impatiently. "Gildo Sappone, Karl. Is he, for instance, a mass murderer? Did he, perhaps, rape and dismember a dozen nuns?"

"No, no." Holtzmann noted Kirkwood's harsh, sarcastic tone and smiled inwardly. Like many a law-enforcement officer, he found it in his interest to encourage the macho affectations common to prosecutors. They loved to play at being tough and one of the ways they did it was by cross-examining cops. "Nothing like that. Just a run-of-the-mill homicide."

"Then why did the parole board turn him down?"

"Bit of a bad actor. Prison scrapes, that kind of thing. High risk to reoffend."

Kirkwood had leaned back in his chair, tried to estimate how many vicious criminals had received light sentences or been turned loose altogether in exchange for testimony against more inviting targets. It was one of the best-kept secrets in law enforcement, all those mutts in the witness protection program going off on unsuspecting neighbors.

"Rizzo swears the nephew has changed. Just wants to get out and live his life." Holtzmann had produced a pipe, a curved meerschaum, his trademark, but didn't have the nerve to light it. "Willing to submit to whatever supervision the parole board demands."

"And."

"And?"

"Did you check him out, Karl?"

Holtzmann had looked down into the bowl of the pipe. He'd come to the Federal Bureau of Investigation by way of Princeton Law and knew all there was to know about Abner Kirkwood. Including what the US attorney wanted to hear.

"Nobody can read the future," he'd said, his voice dead even, "but Sappone's spent the last fourteen years in prison. Hard to imagine him wanting to go right back." He'd tapped the bowl of his pipe against his palm, then looked up at Kirkwood.

"Thing about it, Abner, on the tapes Rizzo brought in, the samples? Appears that Stettecase is negotiating a very large heroin deal. Very large indeed."

Abner Kirkwood picked up the newspaper lying on his desk and stared at Jilly Sappone's photo on the front page. The way he figured it, the child, Theresa, was a casualty of war. Yeah, if he had *known*, if he could read the goddamned *future*, Sappone would still be in prison. No way he would've gone ahead with the deal, no matter what he had to gain. But he hadn't known and what happened had just happened.

Meanwhile, how many lives would be lost if three tons of dope hit the streets instead of a DOJ evidence locker? How many people would Carmine Stettecase kill if he wasn't stopped?

What you did, if you'd been in law enforcement as long as Abner Kirkwood, was weigh the risk against the gain, calculate profit and loss, take the high ground whenever possible. The New York State Parole Board was stonewalling the press which was all to the good, but that wouldn't last. No, what they'd do was leak the truth to some reporter, take the heat off, put it on the FBI.

FBI FREES MURDERER. And what would Carmine Stettecase make of *that?*

The intercom chirped once. Kirkwood allowed himself a narrow smile before responding.

"Mrs. English?"

"I'm sorry to disturb you, Mr. Kirkwood, but Ms. Sappone asked me to tell you that she has another appointment and is unable to wait any longer."

Kirkwood shuddered, feeling about the way a priest might feel before an exorcism. Ordinarily, Josie Rizzo dropped the tapes into a mailbox on Grove Street. The face-to-face was her idea.

"You can send them in, Mrs. English. Ms. Rizzo and Agent Holtzmann." He stood up, legs apart, bracing himself against whatever gruesome detail Josie Rizzo had decided to add to the general nightmare.

Josie Rizzo was fully aware of her effect on other people, heard it in the voices of butchers, bakers, supermarket checkout girls. They saw her as crazy, demented, a royal pain in the ass. Josie didn't mind, didn't let it bother her. She wanted what she wanted and they were there to serve her, not really alive at all. More like badly manufactured robots.

Holtzmann and Kirkwood, though she definitely wanted something from them, fit into a different category. Josie Rizzo hated cops, the hatred coming to her along with her mother's breast milk. Ordinarily, she wouldn't stay in the same room with a cop, not even the same building. In fact, just the other day, in Joey Barabano's deli, she was fetching a half pound of prosciutto and a wedge of sharp, crumbly provolone for Carmine's antipasto when a uniformed cop, a sergeant, came in for his meatball hero. Tried to push ahead of her.

"Hey." More a grunt than an exclamation. She'd waited until he was looking at her. "You in a hurry?"

The dumb pig had smirked, started to apologize. She'd responded by spitting on his shoes and walking out, taking her sweet time about it, calling back over her shoulder. "Hey, Joey, I'll see you in an hour. Leave the door open."

So what was she doing, now, in this office with two of the biggest cops in New York? How could she humiliate herself in this way? The questions came to her unbidden.

The spirit was driving her. That was the only way she could understand it. A *jetatura*, first described by her *nonna*, her grandmother, a woman with eyes the color of the unforgiving soil of rural Sicily. If this spirit was inside your heart, you could hurt other people, send disease, poverty, ill fortune, even the death of a child. You had power, in spite of being a mere woman.

There was a price to pay, of course. A little matter Josie's *nonna* had left out of her description. The spirit fed on your rage, your impotence, the unrelenting need for revenge. It grew in you, born with the death of your father, maturing the day they slaughtered your brother in front of his own child. Slaughtered him while you watched, helpless, from a tenement window.

By the time she'd buried the last of them, her husband, some five years later, Josie Rizzo's fate was sealed. Her grandmother's *jetatura* was not to be expelled, as much a part of her as the black dress, the long determined stride, the enormous bony hands.

Josie was living in an Elizabeth Street tenement at the time, along with her infant daughter and her poor, wounded nephew, trying to get along on handouts and home relief checks. For a while, she wondered if Dominick Favara (or his shadow, Carmine Stettecase) had had a hand in the killings. The rumor on the streets of Little Italy was that Dominick's path to success was paved with the bodies of his childhood chums. But there'd been no way to find out, to know for sure, and she'd finally come to realize that it didn't matter. Dominick and Carmine had survived the great mob war that swept the country after WWII. They'd come up winners and that was enough.

Having, as she saw it, no choice in the matter, she'd cursed the both of them, only to discover that her dear, departed *nonna* had been wrong again. The spirit lived inside her, all right. She could feel it there, feel it feeding on her *own* spirit, but, unfortunately, it didn't do a damn thing to her enemies.

"Well, Josie, what's the good news? Jilly get run over by a bus?"

Josie Rizzo, her chin nearly on her chest, peered at Abner Kirkwood through bushy eyebrows. The man's face had no character, no feature too big or too small, nothing bent or twisted. His soft, grainy skin was the color of almond paste.

"I come about Gildo." She ignored his tone, knowing exactly what she had to do. "You take him in the program. Today." She spit the words out as if warding off contamination.

Kirkwood glanced at Karl Holtzmann, exchanged a knowing look, a quick smile. "The program, Josie?"

"The protection program." She pulled up a chair without being asked, dropped down into it as if she never intended to leave. "Gildo's gotta get off the street. You put him in the witness program."

"Tell me something, Josie." Kirkwood pressed the tips of his steepled fingers against his chin. "Jilly murdering that child, does it bother you at all?"

"No. Does it bother *you*?" She wasn't about to make excuses to a whore like Abner Kirkwood. It was too humiliating. No, what she had to do, if she wanted to save Gildo, was stay tough, let the pig think she was crazy.

Holtzmann jumped in before Kirkwood, his face now flushed with anger, could respond. "That's not really the point now." He looked from Josie to his boss. "What's done being actually done." He'd been playing the good cop right from the beginning.

"What'd you tell me?" Josie Rizzo answered her own question without pausing. "After I testify against Carmine, you're gonna put me in the program, because if I stay on the streets I'm a dead woman. You didn't say that?" She kept her eyes glued to the edge of Kirkwood's desk, afraid that even a quick glance would reveal the truth. Josie Rizzo did not intend to run away, hide her head in shame. Afterward, once Carmine was arrested and knew he was going to die in prison, Josie imagined herself striding through the neighborhood, her chin high in the air, letting them all have a good look at what burned in Josie Rizzo's heart. "Gildo, he comes with me. To a new life."

Kirkwood started to speak, but Karl Holtzmann interrupted him again. "Are you telling us, Josie, that you're in touch with your nephew and he's willing to be taken into custody?"

Josie Rizzo tapped the toe of her black Reeboks on the carpet beneath her chair, taking her time, as if she hadn't been expecting the question.

"Josie?" Kirkwood leaned forward. "Agent Holtzmann asked you something."

"In the program," she repeated. "No arrest, no jail. You take him to a safe place until Carmine is finished. Then me and Gildo, we go off together." Pausing briefly, she allowed herself a thin smile. If the New York cops found Gildo before she got him out of that Upper West Side apartment, the game was over. Let the feds take him to one of their hotel rooms, maybe a house in New Jersey, keep him sheltered until the heat died down. By that time, maybe she'd know what to do. "I gotta stay in touch while you got him, call every day on the telephone."

"Christ," Kirkwood muttered, "she's acting like it's a done deal."

Josie planted her legs, pressed thighs, knees, and calves firmly together. It was time to see if the pigs could stop feeding while they were still hungry. Kirkwood knew a lot about Carmine's impending deal, knew the size of it, for instance, and the money involved, but he didn't have the date or the place. That was because Carmine didn't have the information, either, which was the way his Chinese connection wanted it. On Luk Sun, trade representative for the People's Republic of China, fronted in the USA for several dozen factories on mainland China. The processed heroin might come from any of them, go to any port on the East Coast or the Gulf of Mexico. Carmine would distribute the product within a few days, had his customers already lined up, money in hand. If Kirkwood missed by even half a day it would all be for nothing.

Josie Rizzo, after any edge available, had reviewed every tape, holding onto them until she was alone with her little Walkman in her fifth-floor apartment. She knew their contents as well as either of the two men. "You don't take Gildo in the program, no more tapes. I'm takin' a big chance, here, but I'm doin' it for Gildo. If he's gone . . ." She paused to let the essential message penetrate, then continued, her eyes now locked on her folded hands. "If Gildo's gone, then it's fuck you to the feds."

FIVE

Ginny Gadd, as she pushed Stanley Moodrow's battered Chevrolet over the rolling mountains of northwestern New Jersey, tried to keep her thoughts firmly rooted in the present. It was May 10th, still early spring at this altitude, and the forest of birch and maple surrounding I–80 was fledged with tiny, translucent leaves. A bright sun, soon to be directly overhead, poured through the ineffective canopy, speckling the forest floor with delicate gray shadows. Just below the peaks, the highway had been cut through solid rock, as if the builders, having finally grown impatient, had decided to eliminate the red tape.

Gadd was on her way to visit Arnold Dumont at the local office of the New York State Division of Parole in the city of Binghamton. The fastest route (or so the AAA customer-service center had claimed) was west, through New Jersey and Pennsylvania to the city of Scranton, then north into New York again. Gadd considered herself a city girl, Central Park being as close as she wanted to get to the great outdoors. The spring light, the sun-washed rock, the carpet of buttery yellow dandelions at the highway's margins would have been little more than distractions under the best of conditions. Now, haunted by images that jumped into her mind without warning, she might as well have been driving through the Holland Tunnel.

The mile markers on the side of the road tracked her progress, diminishing, one by one, as she approached the Pennsylvania border. She'd been on the road for more than an hour, had nearly three hours to go. The drive, the time alone with her own thoughts, hadn't entered into her calculations when she'd bullied Arnold Dumont into making the appointment by declaring herself the personal representative of the victim's mother. No, as she'd waited for the receptionist to put her through, the idea of justice had coursed through her body, as real, as physical, as the blood pumped from her heart. And not the kind of simple justice that ended with Jilly Sappone dead or in custody.

The simple fact was that Jilly Sappone hadn't just appeared on the outside of the Southport Correctional Facility like he'd walked through the walls. Parole had been denied, then granted; the individuals who made the decisions had to be held responsible, even if responsibility came to no more than pulling up the bureaucratic rock under which they hid.

Of course, she hadn't told that to Mr. Dumont, hadn't given him a hint of her personal rage. That would come later, when they were face-to-face and she could look into his eyes. Instead, she'd made her case in the name of the Kalkadonis family. That was a stretch, of course, because Ann Kalkadonis was still too distraught to frame any goal beyond keeping her remaining daughter alive.

"Mrs. Kalkadonis has been through a terrible tragedy." Gadd had begun the conversation by stating the obvious. "She needs to start the healing process." Another incontrovertible truth, followed quickly by the kicker. "Surely, you can spare fifteen minutes to help her understand what happened to her daughter."

Later, she'd casually mentioned the media swarm outside Ann's apartment house, the calls from *Hard Copy* and *Inside Edition*, using the veiled threat as a clincher. Dumont would almost certainly try to stonewall her as he'd stonewalled the press, but he didn't have the balls to refuse to see her. A refusal would probably make the local news on all three major networks.

As she crossed the Delaware River and slid up to the tollbooths on the far side, Gadd's thoughts turned to Stanley Moodrow. He'd be home by now, in his Lower East Side apartment. Betty would be fending off the reporters, trying to resist the urge to rip the phone out of the wall. Journalists were like cops. They never gave up.

The clerk at the booth took her dollar, smiled, said, "Thank you."

In New York, they charged three dollars each way and the clerk begrudged you change for a twenty, looked actually put upon, as if dealing with human beings wasn't part of his job description.

The question, she asked herself as she accelerated away from the toll plaza, is why, aside from borrowing his car on occasion, I give a damn about Stanley Moodrow. If he wants to wallow in guilt, hold himself responsible, why should it matter to me?

She recalled sitting in that intersection, waiting for the light to change, Moodrow slamming the gas pedal to the floor, fishtailing into the turn. Her first reaction, grabbing the dashboard and the seat to stop herself from sliding into the door, had occupied all her attention. By the time she put it together, realized that Sappone had to be in the car ahead of them, Moodrow was slamming on the brakes and . . .

You promised not to think about the rest of it, she reminded herself. You decided to keep your mind on the job until it was over.

What she wanted from Moodrow, she finally decided, was his confidence. She wanted the Stanley Moodrow who first walked into her office, knowing exactly what *he* wanted. Her decision to punish the bad guys, that was all well and good, but Moodrow was the one who actually found Sappone. There was no doubt about who'd been using whom. Without him, she'd still be in her office, bullshitting the Foundation.

Here's what's really happening, she told herself. Right now the reporters have a better chance of getting to the truth than I do. They could use the Freedom of Information Act, demand the parole board records, write their stories a year or two down the line when the information comes through. Meanwhile, I'm gonna waste the next ten hours trying to get the truth from a bureaucrat. Like running the Iditarod Sled Race with a team of South Bronx cockroaches.

Two hours later, Ginny Gadd knew exactly how Jilly Sappone got out of jail. After introducing herself to Arnold Dumont's secretary and a very short wait (short enough to make her actually suspicious) she was shown into a large office. She noted the beige carpeting, the sturdy wooden desk in the center of the room, the two upholstered chairs in front of the desk, and decided that Dumont's assistant commissioners probably made do with tiled floors and metal furniture. That's if they had offices at all, if they weren't part-timers.

Then a door at the back of the office swung open and FBI Agent Bob Ewing stepped inside. He flashed her a welcoming smile, a grin, really, so filled with self-love as to be actually repulsive.

"Ms. Gadd." He extended a hand, crossed the room swiftly. "We meet again."

Gadd, a grin of her own spreading across her face, took his hand. She started to speak, then changed her mind, deciding to listen for a change, hear what the man had to say.

Ewing motioned her to sit, then plopped down into Arnold Dumont's leather chair. "We need to talk," he announced.

"About?" Gadd held herself still, like a child awaiting an unpleasant surprise.

Ewing's smile vanished. "About your pretending to represent Ann Kalkadonis." He laid his fingertips on the table, leaned slightly forward. "As you know, we're still protecting the Kalkadonis family, still have a presence inside their apartment. I spoke to Ann Kalkadonis this morning and she has no idea what you're doing." He tapped a forefinger against his chin, shook his head. "You know something, Gadd, I don't have any idea what you're doing, either. Maybe you can explain it to me."

Gadd ran her fingers through her hair, glanced around the room. She was still on her feet. "You recording this conversation, Agent Ewing?"

Ewing didn't turn a hair. "Why do you want to know?"

"I was hoping you'd give me a copy of the tape." Gadd recalled an incident from her years on patrol. A kid, maybe ten or eleven, had come running up to the cruiser she shared with her partner. He'd begun to babble about a mugging, the words running together like city traffic through a long tunnel. Suddenly, she'd realized that everything he said—his name, his age, where he lived, the crime—was a lie. Sure enough, the minute her partner asked for ID, the kid pivoted, tossed them a finger, sprinted off down the street.

"Clever." Ewing tossed her a grudging nod. "But somehow I don't find this situation all that funny, Ms. Gadd. Especially when I consider the net effect of your meddling to date." He paused, obviously expecting her to continue. When she didn't, when she maintained her slightly quizzical, slightly bemused expression, he shifted uneasily in his chair. "I didn't want to make this unpleasant," he finally muttered. "I wanted us to come to an understanding."

"Why don't we cut to the threats, Agent Ewing. Save some time." The smile dropped away, replaced by an inner rage that came upon her so swiftly she felt it as pure heat before she became aware of its emotional content. Her jaw tightened down as if clamped and she felt herself actually rise up as her buttocks and thighs contracted. Her hands, when she looked down at them, were balled into white-knuckled fists.

"Are you all right?"

Gadd forced herself to take a breath, say, "Perfectly." A moment later, she felt the anger drop away, like a criminal through the trap-door of a gallows. As her chest relaxed and her breathing returned to normal, she wondered when it would return. Would she welcome her anger, nourish it? It had comforted her, in a way, had relieved her of other burdens.

"What you're doing is perilously close to obstruction of justice." Ewing, apparently having taken her at her word, was sitting back in his chair. His steepled fingers lay against the collar of his white-on-white shirt.

"Bullshit," Gadd replied. Her voice, she noted, was satisfyingly flat. As intended. "One, since I haven't been fired, Ann Kalkadonis is still my client. Two, I'm under no obligation to inform my client of my every move. Three, Ann Kalkadonis is very interested in how Jilly Sappone got out of prison. If you don't believe me, ask her."

It was Gadd's turn to pause and Ewing's to hold his peace. "All right," Gadd said, acknowledging the move with a slight smile, "let's make this short and sour. If you're here to beg me, then beg me. If you're here to threaten me, then threaten me. Take it to the bank, Ewing, I got a million things to do and I don't have time for your fed bullshit."

Ewing shrugged his shoulders, a gesture Gadd interpreted as, Well, I tried, didn't I?

"You're interfering with an ongoing federal investigation." He raised a hand. "No, don't stop me. If you don't get out of the way, your investigator's license will be suspended. If that's not enough, if you continue to persist, your license will be revoked altogether." He stood abruptly. "Look at yourself, my dear. You couldn't make it as a cop. You couldn't make it as a wife. What will you do if you can't make it as a private investigator? There are things here you don't understand."

Gadd looked up at him, as she knew she was meant to do. " Well, you're thorough, I'll give you that, but the fact is that you and your bosses are responsible for letting Sappone out of jail." She stood, took a step toward the agent. "What would you do if I told you I was recording this conversation? Would you attack me, maybe rip the wire from my prostrate body?"

"You've been reading too many bad novels."

The words were defiant, but Ewing's complexion, Gadd noted, now matched his shirt. There was anger there, too, of course, but his (and, by extension, the FBI's) impotence jumped out at her.

She turned, crossed to the door, then spun around, her exit lines carefully prepared. "I've seen his prison records. Jilly Sappone's. Makes for good reading, now that I know who got him out."

Unfortunately, Ewing's preparation included a parting shot of his own. "Wasn't killing the child," he called to her retreating back, "enough for you?"

SIX

The parade began shortly after Stanley Moodrow came home to his Lower East Side apartment. Leonora Higgins arrived first, in the early afternoon, bearing a box of dark chocolate almond clusters from Le Chocolatier on Park Row. Moodrow, surprised, accepted the gift tentatively, then, suddenly ravenous, jammed one of the clusters into his mouth.

"You remember Johnny Katanos?" Leonora asked.

"I think I lost a few pounds," Moodrow mumbled. "In the hospital." He was growing stronger by the minute, could actually feel strength returning, the way a long drink of water relieved thirst after a serious workout.

"Katanos was a terrorist, right?" Betty asked. Having carefully orchestrated the afternoon's program, she wasn't about to let Moodrow's appetite prevent his receiving the essential message.

"That's right, one of the worst ever to hit this country." Leonora reached forward. "Stanley, you think I could have one of those? Before they disappear into your bloodstream."

She was wearing a dark brown dress, dark enough to complement the semisweet chocolate clusters, and a matching bolero jacket. Moodrow found the outfit a bit somber, despite the gold sunburst pinned to her breast; Leonora's tastes usually ran to the warmest end of the scale. He wondered, briefly, if this was her sick-friend outfit, then shoved another piece of candy into his mouth.

"So what about him?" Betty asked. "About Johnny Katanos?"

"He's been transferred to a mental hospital. A complete break-down, apparently."

"What does 'complete breakdown' mean? Does he hear voices?"

"It means, according to my father's sister's nephew, who works in the federal penal system, that Johnny Katanos covers himself, his cell, and any corrections officer who comes too close with his own feces."

Moodrow, his mouth too full for actual speech, nodded indifferently. Once upon a time, he'd hunted Johnny Katanos with the blind determination of a starving wolverine, had put a gun to the man's face with every intention of killing him. Leonora had prevented the murder with a bullet of her own.

"Seems like another century," he finally said.

"It was six years ago," Leonora countered. "And half the cops in New York City were looking for him. Not to mention the FBI." She snatched another piece of chocolate, nibbled at the edges before continuing. "You took him down, Stanley. All I did was follow you."

Moodrow glanced at Betty, found her looking away, embarrassed. "I don't recall issuing a denial," he finally said. "But if you're after a confession, you'll have to beat it out of me."

Leonora made her good-byes half an hour later. It was a working day and lunch was definitely over. Moodrow saw her to the door, accepted a gentle kiss on the cheek. A complex of emotions—anger, gratitude, amusement—coursed through him as he closed the door and turned back to find Betty seated at the kitchen table.

"I'm writing a shopping list, Stanley. I have to go back to Brooklyn tonight and I don't want you making an ice-cream run to the bodega. If you've got any secret cravings, better get them out in the open."

"Secret cravings?" Moodrow shook his head. "I don't know whether to kiss you or spank you."

Betty looked up, fluttered her eyelids. "Couldn't we do both?"

Moodrow nodded thoughtfully. "I *am* feeling better," he admitted. "Let's try for tomorrow morning."

Twenty minutes later, the second wave hit the beach. Two NYPD sergeants, Manny Pissaro and Paul Malone, both thirty-year men, knocked at Moodrow's door. Cops bearing gifts, they waved a quart of Wild Turkey bourbon in his surprised face.

By the time they left, half the bottle and fifty rehashed cases later, Moodrow was too tired to do more than stagger into the bedroom and fall asleep. Betty found him, fully dressed, when she returned from her shopping. She looked at him for a moment, thinking that it didn't seem fair. His face was up by the headboard, his short hair actually brushing the wood, while his feet stuck out several inches beyond the mattress. With his arms spread wide, his shoulders seemed to span the full width of the bed.

People that big, she decided, aren't allowed to be vulnerable. They're not supposed to make mistakes. If they do, if they fuck up royally, they've got to deny it, make excuses, point the finger elsewhere. Fallen heroes are a dime a dozen.

The most amazing part was that he'd actually found Sappone, that he'd done it in less than a week. How could a spur-of-the-moment decision negate the result of that carefully planned effort? Betty had been a trial lawyer for most of her adult life. She was perfectly willing to admit (to herself, naturally) that she'd blown it any number of times, put the wrong question to the wrong witness, gotten a reply that had buried her client. What you did was live with it, go to the next case, get on with the rest of your life.

But, then, she acknowledged, I wasn't there. I didn't run up to find the child's body, didn't wait, helpless, within feet of her smashed skull, for the cops and the ambulance to arrive.

The suits had grilled the both of them, Moodrow and Gadd, for nearly four hours, taking them over each detail, again and again and again.

As she started back into the kitchen, pausing to retrieve the full shopping cart, she suddenly realized that she'd never loved Stanley Moodrow more than she did at that moment.

When Jilly Sappone answered his cellular telephone, he wasn't surprised to hear Aunt Josie's voice. She was the only one who knew the number. But when he listened to her outline her plans for his immediate future, his jaw dropped open. It was ten o'clock in the morning and he'd just had his first snort of the day. That was part of the reason why he didn't hang up, the other part being that he was afraid of his Aunt Josie, had been since the day she'd come to take him out of the hospital.

"You go in the witness program," she explained. "You go tonight with the FBI. It's no good on the street. You stay on the street, they're gonna kill you." For Aunt Josie, it was a very long speech.

"This a joke?" he asked. Meanwhile, he had no memory of her laughter, couldn't remember her cracking a smile, not even when he was small enough to look up at her down-turned face.

"I got them by the balls," she replied. "You gonna be all right."

Jilly didn't ask how, just as he'd never asked her what she'd done to get him out of the joint. That was because there was only one thing she *could* have done.

"I got things I gotta get finished," Jilly muttered, knowing there was nothing he could say to change her mind, that she could give him up any time she wanted. Meanwhile, in her own way, she was gonna bury Carmine Stettecase.

What I oughta be doing, he told himself, is planning out the rest of my time on the street.

"You don't go to a jail," she declared. "They're gonna take you somewhere private, a house." When he didn't reply, she went for the jugular. "Why you gotta play the fool, huh? Always the fool. You should'a buried that kid in the ground, not throw her out in the street. I told you to kill her right away, didn't I? I said don't carry extra weight, she's gonna take you down. Meanwhile, you had'a throw it in your wife's face, had'a be a big shot, make jokes with the cops."

Not that he was going to admit it, but maybe he *had* been stupid, maybe he *should* have taken her advice. Only he'd never, not for a single moment, expected anyone to find him. Meanwhile, this old fart of an ex-cop had run him down like a stray dog after a warehouse rat.

"Aunt Josie, did you tell the feds where I'm stayin'?"

She snorted her contempt, blew it out through her nose like a racehorse after a hard workout. "Tonight, ten o'clock, when it's quiet. Broadway and Ninety-one. Stay inside till then, stay quiet. Remember who you are."

Who he was, he knew, in her mind at least, was the last male Sappone. Never mind cousin Carlo and a half dozen other male Sappones scattered throughout the metropolitan area. Meanwhile, she'd hung up and the only real question was how he was going to amuse himself for the next twelve hours.

Carmine was out of the question, of course. Aunt Josie wanted Carmine to herself. Annunziata? Now, that was a real possibility. Get up on a roof, pump fifty rounds through one of the windows, hope for the best. Unfortunately, the FBI was guarding his little honey bunch, at least according to the jerk on the six-o'clock news. They'd most likely catch a serious attitude if he blew a couple of their agents into the next universe. Make it kind of hard to surrender.

Jilly chuckled at his own joke, then tore open a bag of dope and snorted it up. He was going to have to pack the dope into a few small balloons and swallow them before he surrendered. Otherwise he wouldn't be able to spend more than a few hours in the company of the pigs without losing control.

He was going to have to do something about the car, too, the one he'd rented. Maybe put it in a garage, pay a month in advance. Odds were, he'd need the car again before he was through, the car and the weapons in its trunk.

His thoughts drifted back to the ex-cop who'd tracked him down. Now there was a man he'd like to get his hands on, take three or four hours to kill. Meanwhile, he had no idea where Stanley Moodrow lived and no time to find out.

There was still Carlo, of course. Carlo had ratted him to the ex-cop, no doubt about it. But Carlo lived a long way from the Upper West Side of Manhattan. And Carlo couldn't do any more damage.

"Nnnnnnnnnnn-twenty."

The shout tore through Jilly's high, jerked him upright in his seat. He turned toward Jackson-Davis Wescott, found him sitting at the kitchen table playing slow-motion bingo with himself.

"Hey fuckface," he snarled, then pulled up short. Talk about your basic weak link. Aunt Josie hadn't said anything about Jackson-Davis and he'd been too stunned by her message to ask.

"Beeeeeeeeee-six."

"Ya hear me talkin' to ya?"

Jackson-Davis stared down at his game card, concentrating. The tip of his tongue stuck out of the corner of his mouth and his eyes were opened so wide it looked like he'd just been punched in the stomach.

"I ain't talkin' to you," he finally said. "No sirreee. After what you done, I ain't never talkin' to you again."

"So, why don't ya just take off, Jackson? Bein' as your feet ain't nailed to the floor." He paused, then smirked. "I dare ya."

Jackson-Davis looked at the door for a moment, then turned back to his partner. "Darers go first," he muttered.

"Ya tellin' me that I should leave?" Jilly's smile dropped away. "Look here, Jackson," he explained for the twentieth time, "the pigs were comin' right up my ass. If I didn't do somethin' to slow 'em down, we'd be sittin' in a cell right this minute."

"You didn't love her," Jackson countered. "You was just *usin'* little Theresa."

Jilly got up and walked across the room. He pulled up a chair, sat down, draped his arm across Wescott's shoulders. "Maybe you're right, Jackson. Maybe I should'a thought more about how much she meant to ya, but I didn't and that's all she wrote." He paused, squeezed his partner's shoulder. "Unless maybe we go out and find you another little playmate."

SEVEN

The outside temperature was hovering just below eighty-five degrees when Jilly Sappone led his partner out of their West Ninetieth Street apartment building. Both men, as they stepped onto the sidewalk, hesitated momentarily, pulling the bills of their caps down to ward off a glaring sun. Six weeks down the line, when the brutal New York summer transformed the concrete and asphalt of Manhattan into a gigantic pizza oven, a similar day would seem downright balmy, a break in the prevailing misery. But in mid-May, when spring flowers still blossomed in Central Park, the heat was intrusive, seeming, after the long winter and brief spring, like a broken promise.

Still, the heat worked in their favor, a fact that Jilly Sappone was quick to recognize (and which went right over his partner's head). The few citizens on the residential streets of the Upper West Side moved swiftly, purposefully, eyes locked on the pavement before them. Only the inevitable panhandlers bothered to scrutinize oncomers, but their media-free horizons were limited to give or not give. They had no interest in kidnappers and murderers.

Jilly Sappone led Jackson-Davis west toward Riverside Park, a block-wide strip of grass, shrubs, and playgrounds running along the Hudson River, from the upscale white neighborhoods just above Lincoln Center to 125th Street in the heart of black Harlem. Like every other green space in New York, Riverside Park was a summertime refuge for the poor and the middle class. Cabin fever is a term usually associated with the severe winters of the far north, but to cit-

211

izens trapped in air-conditioned spaces for weeks at a time, the urge to get outside at any cost is very real. This is especially true for the wives, nannies, and weekend fathers charged with the care of small children.

"Hey, Jackson, tell me what ya think of this." Jilly Sappone's eyes, shadowed by the bill of his Mets baseball cap, swept the street, from side to side, like a metronome. He was aware of the Colt's weight pulling at the waistband of his jeans, knew exactly how long it would take to jam his hand beneath his shirt, get the show on the road. "Maybe this time we could snatch a boy instead of a girl. Variety's the spice of life, right?"

Jackson-Davis wanted to run. He wanted to tear out of there, fly across the city, race all the way back to Ocobla. He wondered, idly, if anyone he knew would still be there. Maybe his daddy or old Betty-Ann. He was sorry, now, for what he'd done to Betty-Ann, wished he could take it all back, start over again.

"It's a free country," Jackson whispered. His old pa used to say that all the time. "It's a damn free country."

"Say what?" Jilly drew a deep breath, let his eyes close momentarily. He felt exhilarated, almost buoyant, like he was stepping into a prison yard for the first time.

Hey, all you pigs out there, he thought, here I am, Gildo Sappone. Kill me if you can.

"It's a damn free country," Jackson repeated. He looked at Jilly for a moment, then said, "My ol' pa used to say that."

"Yeah, well your old man was right. At least this time. See, what we're gonna do is take what we want. Just like it was free."

As they approached West End Avenue, Jilly slowed. Two men and a middle-aged woman holding a small brown dog in her arms stood on the corner waiting to cross the street. As a matter of pure reflex, each had given Jilly and his companion a brief, sidelong glance. Jilly watched their faces, looking for any sign of recognition, but the group had apparently pronounced him safe. When the light changed, they crossed the street, then turned south.

Jilly continued west for half a block, then stopped suddenly. "Jackson, I just got a *great* idea. Why don't we take a kid and a kid's fuckin' *mother*?" He started walking again, noting that Jackson-Davis followed alongside, a whipped puppy chained to its master. "So whatta ya say? Want a mommy, too?"

At that moment, though he didn't break stride, Jackson-Davis returned to his mother's side, the scene dominating his consciousness with the force of a dream. He was standing in the doorway of Reverend Luke's bedroom, watching his old pa aim one last kick at his old ma's face. Even at age nine, slow as everybody said he was, Jackson knew his ma was already dead. That was because she'd gone and peed on the rug. There was no way his old ma would pee on the rug unless she was dead.

"I don't hear ya, Jackson." Jilly put a little edge in his tone, figuring Jackson would respond out of habit.

"I don't want no mommy."

"Ya sure?" He pulled Jackson into the shadow of a doorway, slid a folding knife out of his back pocket. "Don't ya wanna use this? Huh? Don't ya wanna do what comes natural?"

"No, I don't."

Jilly shrugged his shoulders. "Whatever suits ya, boy." Just as if he didn't know what would happen if he put Jackson-Davis in the same room with a helpless woman.

As they crossed Riverside Drive and entered the park, Jilly glanced south at the Soldiers and Sailors monument a block away. Faced with white limestone, the monument rose, a narrow cylinder, sixty feet above the intensely green lawn. Jilly stared at the circle of Corinthian columns for a moment, then let his eyes travel upward to a domed crown from which six muscular eagles, their wings outspread as if about to take flight, guarded the island of Manhattan.

"That's Grant's Tomb," he announced. "Yeah, definitely. Grant's fuckin' Tomb."

The tour officially over, Jilly turned his attention to a busy playground at the foot of a steep hill a hundred feet away. The mothers and the nannies were sitting on wooden benches (separate wooden benches, of course); they looked wilted, ready to pack it in. Meanwhile, their brats were tearing from the swings to the sliding pond to the sandbox, shrieking at the tops of their lungs.

Jackson watched the scene as closely as his partner. From this distance, the children in their bright summer clothes seemed to be playing a single game. Somehow, their joy sapped the last bit of his strength, left him feeling as if he'd been the victim of some long-ago crime. That what he knew was going to happen to him had already happened.

"Tell ya what, Jackson." Jilly nudged his partner forward. "Let's go in them bushes. Hide there till we decide who we want." As he followed Jackson into the darkness beneath the shrubbery, Jilly slid the knife out of his back pocket and thumbed the blade open. He'd never used a knife before his first bit in Sing-Sing, preferring an automatic and his bare fists. But there were no guns in the joint and no way to survive without a weapon, so he'd carried a shank, learned how to use it quickly and silently.

He recalled snuffing a con named Rolando Meara at the weekly movie for a vial of morphine tablets smuggled out of the prison hospital. Though the room had been full of prisoners, though guards stood in every corner, the act of killing had gone unnoticed until the lights went up and the prisoners filed out, leaving poor Rolando to the tender mercies of a county pathologist.

"Say, Jackson, you're a country boy. Can ya eat these little black berries?" Jilly pointed at the canopy above them. "See what I'm talkin' about?"

"You saved me, right?" Jackson-Davis spoke with his back to Jilly Sappone. He was afraid now, afraid of his partner and afraid to run. If he ran, he'd be alone again. Alone as he'd been on that first night in jail when the other prisoners, black and white, had eyeballed him like he was a midnight snack in need of cooking. "Saved me from the niggers?"

"Nah, that ain't what it was about." Jilly dropped his left hand onto Jackson's shoulder. "I was just usin' ya, buddy. To carry shit for me, get it? Dope, shanks, whatever I was too paranoid to carry myself. I never gave a shit about ya one way or the other."

Jilly let his head swivel once before driving the knife into Jackson-Davis Wescott's back with all his strength. That was the secret, of course, to killing with a knife. You had to put everything you had into the first cut.

• • •

By the time Jim and Rose Tilley, accompanied by their two children, Lee and Jeanette, showed up at five o'clock in the afternoon, Stanley Moodrow was consciously referring to his visitors as "the Ghosts of Triumphs Past." Rose had once been married to a man named Levander Greenwood, a terminal crack junkie who'd terrified the Lower East Side for several weeks before Moodrow, still an NYPD detective, brought him down. Jim Tilley had been Moodrow's partner at the time, his first partner in more than twenty years. They'd been friends ever since.

Levander's presence on the scene that night remained unspoken. He was, after all, Lee and Jeanette's biological father. But that didn't mean the essential message was lost on Stanley Moodrow. Levander had hated his wife, vowed revenge, would certainly have killed her if Moodrow hadn't taken him off the scene. In some small, but very real sense, the robust Tilley clan owed its literal existence to Moodrow's efforts.

"Uncle Stanley, I got a problem," Lee said. He bit enthusiastically into an almond cluster, chewed thoughtfully for a moment before swallowing. "A guy in the gym, Andre Carpenter. He's short, but he's got these long, thick arms. When he puts them up in front of his face, I can't get through his guard."

Moodrow drank in the cozy domestic scene. Rose and Betty were in the kitchen, chatting it up as they put drinks on a tray. Jim was perched, elbows on knees, chin in hand, on the couch next to Lee. Jeanette, off by herself, was totally absorbed in a book. Jim, Moodrow knew, was worried about his daughter, feeling she spent too much time by herself. Meanwhile, Jeanette was holding a ninety-seven average at St. Bartholomew's.

"You wanna know what I'd do?" Moodrow finally said. "Me, I'd step to the side and go to the body. Hit him in the small of the back if necessary. Anything to hurt him, make him fight." He paused, then added, "That's because I'm stupid."

Lee ignored the final comment. "It doesn't help me to know what *you'd* do. I need to know what *I'd* do."

Moodrow, though he'd slept for several hours, felt suddenly tired. The whole business of stepping into the squared circle, from the endless hours in the gym to the fat, clumsy gloves, seemed actually stupid, the ultimate expression of the worst human instincts. Nevertheless, he forced himself to speak.

"The guy can't hit you with his hands in front of his face. What you have to do is throw a lot of punches, not worry about getting through. If he doesn't respond, the judges'll have to give you the match. The important thing is not to lose your temper."

The answer, Moodrow knew, reasonable as it sounded, wouldn't solve Lee's problem. Lee dreamed of being Marvin Hagler, not Pernell Whitaker. He wanted to flatten every opponent. Fortunately, Betty and Rose picked that moment to come into the living room and the conversation turned to less macho topics.

Moodrow sat back in his chair, sipped at his bourbon, let the words run over him. An hour later, as the kids cleared the table, he tugged at Jim Tilley's sleeve and asked the question he swore he wouldn't ask.

"Anything on Sappone? Any rumors, any leads?"

"Not that I'm aware of, Stanley. I think I already told you that I'm not working the case."

"Yeah, yeah, I know." Moodrow shook his head. "I just thought you might have heard something."

"Nobody's talking to me," Tilley admitted. "But you've gotta believe Sappone's holed up somewhere. He couldn't just vanish."

Once the Tilleys were gone, Moodrow assumed the ordeal was over. He went into the kitchen, began to pile glasses in the sink.

"Stanley, you're not mad at me, are you?"

Moodrow looked up, shook his head. "That you cared enough to arrange it, that everybody showed up . . ." He turned back to the sink. "You know . . ."

Betty came up behind him, put her arms around his waist. She was about to tell him how much she loved him, to whisper it into his ear, when the doorbell sounded.

"Oh," she said, stepping away. "I forgot." She pushed a button next to the telephone, opening the lobby door.

"Forgot what?" Moodrow, on the way to his own door, drank in the expression on Betty's face, a mix of guilt and glee very familiar to him. She'd done something naughty and the joke was going to be on him.

"Forgot to tell you."

He opened the door, stepped out into the hall to find Connie Ala-mare, her grandson Michael in tow, walking toward him.

"Hey, chooch," she called merrily, "how's the head?"

"Never better, Connie."

The worst part, Moodrow knew, was that Michael would run off with Betty the instant his grandmother let go of his hand. That would leave him alone with Connie Alamare, the Ghosts of Successes Past having become the Nightmare of Failures Present.

"Good to hear." She swept past him into the apartment and re-leased her grandson. Michael, as predicted, tore into the kitchen and threw his arms around Betty.

"Connie," Moodrow said, "you want something to drink?" He smiled, waved her to a seat. "I'm thinking about hemlock for my-self."

"Michael and I will take care of the drinks," Betty announced.

"Fine." Moodrow, trapped and willing to admit it, took the arm-chair next to Connie's.

"Look at that." Connie jerked her chin at Betty and Michael in the kitchen. "It's like they shared the same foxhole, right? Like they been through a war together."

"Yes, and I saved them. It's overkill, already." The worst part, Moodrow decided, was that Connie Alamare was stunning. She'd gotten a face-lift six months before, looked thirty-five instead of fifty-five. With her dark complexion and razor-sharp features, she was every inch the exotic Mediterranean beauty, the heroine of her own novels, Melina Mercouri or Sophia Loren by way of scalpel and suture.

"Hey," Connie Alamare leaned forward, tapped Moodrow's knee, "truth is truth, right?" She ran on without waiting for an answer. "So when do you take down this *figlio di puttana*? When do you get him off the street?"

Moodrow started to tell her to mind her own business, then thought better of it. Knowing there were no words in his vocabulary strong enough to slow her down, much less stop her. "Getting Sap-pone off the street has nothing to do with me." He kept his voice strong, but matter-of-fact. "I don't have a client and I don't represent the state. The cops'll take care of Jilly. Them or Carmine Stette-case." He'd said the same thing so often in the last couple of days, the words seemed to come by rote. Like the Pledge of Allegiance or the Our Father.

"What's this about a client? Since when do you need a client?"

"Since now."

"You can say that? After you saw with your own eyes what he did to that girl?"

Moodrow sighed. The woman had all the sensitivity of a rhino with a toothache. "It's not like he's gonna get away with it. The whole city's looking for him."

Connie sat back in the chair, folded her arms across her chest. "And what do you think's gonna happen when some gung-ho *putz* of a patrolman stumbles across him?" She slapped the fingernails of her right hand against her chin. "You think Jilly Sappone's gonna hold out his hands, ask for a lawyer?"

EIGHT

It was a little after seven when Moodrow woke up the next morning to the strong aroma of brewing coffee. He looked at the clock for a moment, then remembered Betty telling him she had a court appearance at ten o'clock and needed to stop by her Park Slope apartment for a change of clothes. Though officially retired, Betty had been volunteering at a storefront legal clinic in the Fort Greene section of Brooklyn. On this particular day, she was representing a group of tenants hoping to get their crumbling apartments repaired before the building collapsed altogether, forcing them into the dreaded New York shelter system. The landlord being the city itself, Betty was expecting an especially protracted battle.

Moodrow shook himself fully awake and stepped out of bed. He swayed momentarily as he stood erect, then headed for the bathroom. Fifteen minutes later, alert if not actually refreshed, he struggled into his clothes, then headed off to the kitchen where he found Betty leaning into the refrigerator's lower shelves. She was wearing a filmy yellow slip over nothing at all.

A rush of desire washed through his body before centering itself just below his belt. He took it as a powerful indicator of his rapidly improving health.

"How much time do you have?" he asked. "Exactly."

"Do I recognize that special tone of voice?" Betty gave her butt a shake, then rose and looked into his eyes. "I've got ten minutes, Stanley. You feeling energetic this morning?"

Their quickie turned into a full thirty minutes of very slow, very tender sex, followed by a lingering breakfast. Neither wanted to separate, even for the day, reacting as if they'd survived a natural catastrophe. As if they'd already counted their losses, come to realize they had each other and that was miracle enough.

"I'll have to take a cab," Betty said as they exchanged what was supposed to be a final kiss. "If I'm going to be on time."

It was a joke, a New York joke, and both understood the punch line. The chances of finding a cabbie willing to take her to Brooklyn at the height of the morning rush being something less than zero out of a hundred, there was only one way she was going to make it to court on time.

"Why don't I drive you?" Moodrow asked. "Being as I've recovered my virility, I can't really think of a valid reason to hang around the house all day. Much as I'd like to."

By the time Moodrow reversed field and swept over the Manhattan Bridge onto the Bowery it was a little after ten o'clock and he was a step away from utter exhaustion. He managed to pilot the Chevy north to Houston Street, then east to Avenue C where he had his first break of the day, a parking space on the corner of Fourth Street. The car safely stashed (an error would mean a tow to the DMV pier on West Thirty-ninth Street and $200 in fines and charges), Moodrow walked along Fourth Street to find Ginny Gadd sitting on his stoop.

"Christ," she said as he approached, "I thought, you being sick and all, I'd find you home at nine o'clock in the morning."

Moodrow answered by plopping down next to her. "You telling me you've been sitting here for an hour?" Despite his own fatigue he noted her disheveled appearance, deciding she looked even worse than she had at the hospital. It took him a minute to recognize the emotion that followed as simple compassion.

"I wanted to tell you what happened at the parole board." She shook her head, then lit a Newport. "It was fucking unbelievable."

Moodrow pointed to the cigarette. "That something new?"

"Something old, actually." She took a drag, blew out the smoke through her nose. "We have to do this on the stoop? Because if that's the case, I'm gonna go pee in the alley."

Moodrow grabbed the railing above his head and hauled himself to his feet. He stood there a moment, considering how the fatigue came up on him without warning, admiring it almost. First he felt good, his old self, as if he'd never been in the hospital. Then, seemingly without transition, he was near collapse, 265 pounds of sausage meat jammed into a cheap suit.

"You all right?"

Moodrow turned and began to climb the stairs. "Now there's a question," he called over his shoulder, "I've really come to hate."

He felt better by the time he got into his apartment, his fatigue replaced by ravenous hunger at the sight of his refrigerator. The pattern was becoming familiar.

"You want a liverwurst sandwich? On a stale bagel?"

"I don't eat red meat." She was standing right behind him.

"Then you're in luck, Gadd. Liverwurst is gray, not red." He opened the refrigerator, began to toss jars and packages onto the kitchen table. "So, what happened with the parole board?"

"I never got to the parole board." She sat down, crossed her legs. "You know the two feds assigned to guard Ann Kalkadonis?"

Moodrow tapped a bagel against the edge of the sink. It made a soft thud instead of the expected clunk, proof, as far as he was concerned, of its fitness to enter his stomach. "Sure, Ewing and Holtzmann with two *ns*."

"You remember that? Right off the top of your head?"

"I used to think a good memory was a blessing." He cut the bagel in half, began to pile on the ingredients—liverwurst, Bermuda onion, sliced tomato, an inch of mayo, two small hot peppers. Finally satisfied, he scooped several tablespoons of coffee into the basket on his percolator, added water, then set the percolator on the stove. "Okay," he announced, his mouth already opening for the first bite. "I'm ready for the story."

"I never got to see Arnold Dumont. I announced myself to his receptionist, got shown into his office, but he wasn't there. Instead, I found Agent Bob Ewing. He told me I—*we*—were obstructing justice. Threatened to have our licenses yanked." She was lying, of course—Ewing had spoken to her as if she'd found Sappone all by herself—but Moodrow needed motivating, that was obvious. Exploiting what she assumed to be the standard cop disdain for the FBI seemed as good a place to start as any. "I mean you gotta believe they were the ones who got him out of prison. That means Holtz-mann, or somebody above him, read that report, the one that says Jilly Sappone's brain is damaged, that he can't control himself, and opened the prison doors anyway."

"And you think they have to be punished for that mistake? Pun-ished by you, personally."

Gadd sat back as if she'd been slapped. "You saw what happened." When her words had no apparent effect on Moodrow, she stumbled on. "I *know* why they did it. They traded one life for another, let Sap-pone go on a rampage so they could make a big bust somewhere down the line. That doesn't mean it's right. That doesn't mean they shouldn't have to take responsibility."

She stopped abruptly, folded her arms across her chest, watched Moodrow patiently chew, then swallow. His face, to her disgust, was dead blank, as if his features had been arranged by a child. She took it as a typical expression of paternal male arrogance.

"I've done it myself, Gadd." He took another bite, mumbled, "I've had it happen to me."

She waited for him to swallow before asking, "Done what?"

"Let snitches off the hook when I could have put them in Rikers. Most of the time it worked out all right. Sometimes it didn't." He looked at Gadd, then back at the remains of his sandwich. "I can't stop eating. Don't take it personal. I've been hungry ever since I woke up in the hospital."

"By all means, fill your face." She waved him on.

Moodrow took a small bite. "If it wasn't for my snitches, you could cut the busts I made in half. Meanwhile, sometimes they did horrible things to innocent people."

Gadd folded her hands and laid them on the table. "This isn't *sometimes*, Moodrow. They read Sappone's prison record, his med-ical records; they had to know what he was gonna do. You can't call a near certainty a calculated risk."

Moodrow looked down at his empty plate and sighed. "Add it up. Sappone was never the feds' snitch. After fourteen years in the joint, there was nothing for him to tell which means that somebody on the outside cut the deal. Now the only human being on the planet who gives a shit about Jilly Sappone is Josie Rizzo and Josie Rizzo only has one thing to trade."

"Carmine Stettecase."

"That's what Ewing was trying to say. If you expose the FBI, tell the reporters who got Sappone out and why, you let Carmine Stettecase go free." Moodrow got up, went to the cupboard, pulled two mugs off the middle shelf. "Right now, Carmine thinks the parole board fucked up. Why should he think anything else? Remember, Sappone was inside for more than fourteen years. It's not like Jilly came out in the middle of his sentence."

He filled the mugs, dropped one in front of Gadd, waited for her to respond. When she didn't, he tried again to reach her. "How does exposing the FBI for a bunch of jerks help anyone? It doesn't bring . . ." He took a deep breath, said the name for the first time. "It doesn't bring Theresa back to life. It doesn't ease her mother's suffering. What's done is done and we just have to live with it."

He turned in the chair, opened the refrigerator door, and took out a container of half-and-half. Determined not to be first to speak, he poured half-and-half into his coffee, added two spoons of sugar, stirred judiciously while he considered the part he'd left out.

Moodrow had lived with the blue wall of silence for thirty-five years, had never ratted on a fellow officer though he'd known his share of bent cops. To his credit, he took no pride in his failure to act, didn't pretend to fully understand his own motivations. But he could remember the Knapp Commission of the Seventies, the way the job had been ravaged by the media. The end result had been a thoroughly demoralized New York Police Department, not an honest one.

Of course, the essential mistake made by the FBI and the US Attorney (that was something else he'd left out, the Justice Department's near-certain involvement) had no criminal overtones. He couldn't really equate it with cops who took payoffs from drug dealers. But at the same time, he couldn't deny that springing Jilly Sappone carried a stink of pure arrogance. Nor could he deny that Ewing, Holtzmann with two *n*s, and whoever was running them deserved to be punished. For the crime of terminal stupidity if for no other reason.

Gadd, for her part, sipped at her black coffee and studied the room as she tried to form some response to Moodrow's last words.

Nothing appropriate jumped into her mind. Instead, she decided that what she wanted, right at that moment, was Moodrow's kitchen with its tilted stove, noisy refrigerator, and worn metal cabinets. She wanted busted tiles on her floor, a cheap Formica table with rickety vinyl-covered chairs, an ancient percolator that spewed steam into the air. She wanted a life.

"I'm tired, Moodrow," she announced. "I feel like I've been run over."

"I know." Moodrow lifted his mug into the air, waved it vaguely over the table. "It's hard to lose." He wanted to add *especially when you hold yourself responsible*, but decided the claim sounded too much like self-pity, an emotion he especially hated.

Gadd lit another cigarette. "Look, even if I buy what you're saying, that still leaves Jilly Sappone and his retarded partner." She blew out a stream of smoke. "Plus there's Josie Rizzo. I get the feeling she sent him out there to do what he did."

Moodrow nodded his appreciation of her insight. "Sappone went directly from his prison cell to Ann's apartment. The only way he could have known where she lived is if Josie told him. I didn't give it a lot of thought, because the only important thing was finding Sappone before . . ." He smiled, spread his hands apart. "I don't see any way to get to Josie Rizzo. The FBI's gotta be protecting her."

"Then maybe you oughta take a closer look." Gadd sat back in the chair, waved the smoke away from her face. "If you wanna punish somebody, you have to take something from them. Their money, their liberty, their lives, whatever. Ask yourself what you can take away from Josie Rizzo, what she loves more than anything else in the world." She smiled then, as she watched Moodrow nod reluctant agreement. "That's why you have to help, Moodrow. That's why you have to help me find Jilly Sappone."

"Very dramatic, Gadd, but we've been over this already. If losing her nephew is Josie Rizzo's punishment, then consider justice done. Whether *we* do anything or not."

"Does that mean you're gonna cop out?"

"No," he admitted. "But it does mean that I need my beauty sleep. Come back around five o'clock, after my nap, and we'll take a ride uptown. See what's happening on the West Side."

NINE

Tommy Stettecase took the stairs two at a time, all three flights from his father's dining room to the second floor of his own apartment. He did it without drawing a deep breath, slamming into the bedroom to find his wife, Mary, sitting on a recliner in front of the TV. The recliner's crushed-velvet upholstery was a deep blue-black, as deep as the New York sky just before the sun drops behind the Jersey bluffs. Two enormous orange poppies, connected by winding green stems, curled over the darkness, a pattern that echoed itself in the heavy drapes covering the windows, the down quilt covering the bed, and a chaise covered with Tommaso's dirty clothes. All were set against a shag rug the color of drying venous blood.

Tommy didn't notice the poppies or the carpeting. Truth to tell, he wouldn't have noticed his wife if she hadn't literally reeked of White Diamonds. The cloying odor stopped him just long enough to think the words *"poor Mary"* before plunging into the back room, the one originally meant for the children to come (who never came).

Poor Mary didn't acknowledge her husband's presence, either. She was resting, near exhaustion, from her effort to get ready. Each morning, after a cup of coffee and a glass of lemon juice in warm water, Mary began what Tommaso had come to call "the rite." She started with a steaming bubble bath, hot enough to redden her skin, into which she poured several capfuls of bath oil. While she was in the bath, letting the oil seep into her pores, she covered her face, from hairline to chin, with a facial mask, closing her eyes for the required half hour while a clock on the edge of the sink ticked off the minutes.

The bath water was inevitably cold by the time the alarm sounded, but Mary, shivering and naked, always let the tub drain completely before turning on the shower. The hot water, of course, felt pleasant, but the shower was a busy time, too busy for sensory indulgence. First, she rinsed her face, then washed and conditioned her hair (all of her beauty products came from Elizabeth Arden, all had been purchased from a catalog) before cleansing her body, inch by inch, with a hypoallergenic shower gel designed for sensitive skin.

Mary, once her shower was finished, shifted into a still higher gear, moussing, then blow-drying her coarse black hair thoroughly before tossing on a robe and heading off to her dressing room. Seated at her vanity, she barely saw her reflection as she spread astringent, then moisturizer, then a liquid foundation over her face, didn't make a single decision as she followed up with powder, eye shadow, eyeliner, mascara, eyebrow pencil, rouge, lipstick liner, and lipstick.

Her perfume came last, and that final effort seemed to exhaust her, because she never managed to open the closet, choose a dress from the two dozen that hung there. Instead, suddenly listless, she drifted into the bedroom where she sank into the recliner, raised the remote, waited for the day to finally end.

Tommy, the door firmly closed, crossed the room to his desk, plopped down in a leather chair worthy of a senior partner, jammed the earphones over his head just in time to hear his father curse the Chink. Tommy always did it this way, charging up the stairs and into his little den. Though he recorded every word, could have listened at his leisure, there was something about catching it live, as if he was in the same room, making decisions, offering opinions. . . . Well that was why he'd bugged his father's dining room, just to be there in his rightful place.

Tommy had read *The Godfather* sixteen times; he identified with every one of the brothers, even poor, treacherous Fredo. *Especially* poor treacherous Fredo. Which was not to say that he intended his father any harm. No, when it started, Tommy had just wanted to be at that breakfast table, shoveling food into his mouth, grunting in all the right places, laughing at his father's bad jokes. That was why he used the same tape, day after day, recording one meeting over another until the tape finally broke.

The fuckin' Chink says there's another delay.

Tommy nodded at the chorus of grunts and groans that followed, as predictable as Josie Rizzo's scowl.

The boat's trapped in some goddamned port in Africa. Somethin' about the niggers are killin' each other and there's nobody to unload cargo and they can't even get refueled. Meanwhile, the Chink, who says it happens all the time, won't name me the port or even the fuckin' country. He's talkin' another week, maybe ten days.

Kill him, Tommy thought, forget about the deal and kill the Chink.

What we gotta do here is forget about the fuckin' deal. Whack the Chink and write the whole thing off.

Tommy nodded. That was Guido Palanzo, who'd lost his middle son to an overdose of heroin. Guido hated the dope business, though he hadn't turned up his nose at a chance to triple his investment in forty-eight hours. None of them had.

Carmine, I ain't too sure I can hold onto the money for much longer. The boys're gettin' restless.

That would be Vinnie Trentacosta, always practical. The deal had called for three million cash dollars and Carmine simply hadn't had it, not by half. So he'd done what drug dealers have been doing for decades: He'd taken front money from potential customers. That hadn't been a problem, Carmine being who he was, but Carmine (through his boys, of course) had assured his investors that the deal would go down in a few days, maybe a week at the outside. Now it was a month later with more delay to come.

They gonna pull out?

Carmine again, his voice carrying a tinge of anger, followed by three negative grunts, then Guido Palanzo.

It ain't that bad, Carmine. I mean what the fuck are they gonna do about it? As long as we don't take off, they'll sit. But, see, what with not usin' the telephones, I'm spendin' my whole day makin' explana-

*tions to jerks I wouldn't let suck my dick. Meanwhile, my other invest-
ments are goin' in the tank.*

A brief silence, followed by Carmine's judicious tones.

*We're gonna wait and that's all there is to it. Nobody's gettin' their
money back. Much as I hate his fuckin' guts, it ain't the Chink's fault
that we gotta take front money. It ain't somethin' I could'a told him.*

That being the end of that, Carmine turned the conversation to the
purely practical. He intended to use three vans for the pickup. Two would
head off into nowhere (pure decoys in case one of the investors got
busted, decided for the witness protection program), while the third
jumped off the highway on the far side of the Midtown Tunnel, circled
through Long Island City, jumped back into the tunnel again.

Each of the vans would have to be fully staffed: a driver, a chemist,
four *very* trusted shooters armed to the teeth, one of Carmine's lieutenants to handle the money. Twenty-one psychopaths, as Tommy had
come to learn, all assembled and ready in exactly the same place at exactly the same time, made for one hell of a personnel problem. If left
to their own devices, each would play the big monkey, strut like an
aroused tomcat looking for a battle, descend into a chaos that mirrored
his inner life. Control would require a minute-to-minute effort by
Carmine and the boys.

The vans would leave from Little-Dominick Guarino's lumber
yard on East 119th Street. Assuming the deal went down as expected, the van making the actual pickup would return to a garage
on Eagle Street in Greenpoint, Brooklyn. The heroin would be divided up, then delivered, one piece at a time so as not to jeopardize
the whole load. That process would require at least two days of in-
credible tension; *everything* would have to be guarded, including the
guards themselves.

I wanna bring the money to the house. All of it.

Tommy sat up, his flagging interest suddenly revived. The money
in hand, about three-quarters of the total needed to pull off the
deal, had been stashed in several locations.

*It's botherin' me havin' it scattered. Too much risk. I mean why did I
build my brownstone like Fort Knox? Why do I gotta take a chance
when I could have it right under my nose?*

• • •

One floor above Tommaso Stettecase, in a two-bedroom apartment crammed with very old, very dusty furniture, an apartment lit
by 25-watt bulbs, an apartment without a working refrigerator, Josie
Rizzo dialed the phone number given to her by Karl Holtzmann.
She was sitting at the edge of her bed, on a gray sheet, chewing a
croissant taken from Carmine's busy kitchen.

"Ewing."

"Go get Gildo."

"Mrs. Rizzo?"

"You get Gildo, *now.*" While she waited, Josie tapped her foot
against a carpet worn past the point of threadbare and imagined the
reels of the tape recorder as they turned, gathering Carmine's doom,
four stories below. The day was drawing closer, her own personal day
of judgment. She could feel the powers gather, a dark army, irre-
sistible, an army of demons eager to claim the spoils of war. To
drown itself in blood.

"Aunt Josie?"

"Yeah. Where they take you, Gildo?"

"I don't know. There's nothin' out the window but trees."

Josie knew the agent would be listening. That's what the FBI did
best. That was why they'd prepared a signal. When she needed her
nephew, she'd be able to bring him to her side. Josie had no illusions
about the witness protection program, no faith in the promise she'd
exacted from Kirkwood and Holtzmann. Sooner or later, they'd have
to erase the dark shadow falling across their moment of triumph. All
she'd bought was time.

"How they treat you?"

Jilly's laughter flowed into her ear. "First thing I got in the car,
Ewing banged me with a taser, one of those electric guns. I don't
know how many volts, but it put me out for a minute. When I
woke up, I had enough chains around me to sink the Staten Island
Ferry."

"Whatta you expect, Gildo? They see a man like you, they wet
their pants."

"And, me, I'm such a sweetheart. I can't understand it." He
laughed again. "They got me stuck in a corner of the house with a
bed, a toilet, a television. It's a hundred percent locked off, plastic

windows that don't open, like in a bank, if you could believe that. They pass my dinner through a food slot."

"You all by yourself? They don't come inside?"

"All by my little lonely self, Aunt Josie."

"That's good," Josie said before remembering Agent Ewing's big ears. "All by yourself, you won't get into no trouble. Remember, you gotta practice bein' a good boy, Gildo. For when they put us in the program."

"At least he's off the street," Karl Holtzmann said.

"We've bought a little time, Karl," Abner Kirkwood responded. "The game has been postponed, not erased from the schedule."

They were walking on the north side of Washington Square Park. To their right, across the street, a row of identical brick town houses glowed a soft red-orange under the spring sun. On their left, dealers selling upscale reefer and powder cocaine worked the area just in front of the monument, a great memorial arch in honor of the first president's inauguration.

Kirkwood waved a hand at the town houses. "Greek Revival," he announced, "built in the 1830s. The finest examples in the city." He stopped walking, put a hand on Holtzmann's arm. "You know anything about the history of New York, Karl?"

Holtzmann sniffed once. "I'm from Minnesota." He ran his fingers over the lapels of his suit. As if the subject was somehow distasteful.

"Once upon a time, we kept the scum penned up, like any other plague." Kirkwood gestured to the dealers. "We locked them into the Five Points, the Tenth Ward, the Lower East Side, let them do whatever they wanted to each other as long as they didn't come out. That's what Theodore Roosevelt meant when he said real law was found at the end of a nightstick, not in a courtroom."

"That day is long gone, Abner." It seemed, to Agent Holtzmann, as good a response as any.

Kirkwood shrugged his shoulders. "The Warren Court's work, of course. They tossed out the loitering laws, said a human being in the United States of America has the right to go anywhere."

Holtzmann winked. "The Supreme Court made a slight mistake. It assumed that every bipedal hominid is human. We know better."

"That's right, Karl." He set off again, strolling from the shade of an ancient catalpa into bright sunlight. "And when you think of Jilly Sappone, you might want to remember what you just said. That way you won't feel so bad when you have to kill him."

"Kill him?" Holtzmann fought an urge to laugh out loud. It was easy for a punk like Abner Kirkwood to talk about murder, but when the time came to splash the upholstery with Jilly's skull and brains, Abner would piss his pants like any other raw recruit on his first battlefield. By then, of course, it would be much too late. "Oh, by all means."

TEN

Moodrow, having thumbtacked a note to his door, was up on the roof when Ginny Gadd made her appearance at six o'clock in the evening. He was sitting in the shadows with his back against the brick tower enclosing the stairwell, this in deference to crazed snipers like the one who'd scared the crap out of him a few days before. There being no skyscrapers on his part of the island, the sun, though dropping in the west, still flooded most of the roof, silhouetting anybody foolish enough to stand around. Neither Moodrow, nor his neighbor and landlord, Manny Ochoa, were foolish.

Manny, as he pulled on a thirty-two-ounce Michelob, was going on and on about the "old days," the glorious Fifties when he'd run with the Crimson Lords. Yes, he admitted (as he had to Moodrow many times in the past), he, like all his buddies, had carried a switchblade. Once, he'd even tried to build a zip gun in the basement, though that particular experiment had literally blown up in his face. But neither he nor his macho pals had robbed old ladies, fired semiautomatic weapons into crowds of schoolchildren, sold poison to their own community. Instead, they'd battled it out with rivals in playgrounds and parks, defending turf and honor, moving on to jobs and families when they grew into full *"hombria."*

"You see what I'm saying here? I was *el echao pa'lante*, the one who went first into the fight, but I was never an *abusador*. I did not smash my mother to the ground for dope money." He spread his arms out. "And now I have all this."

Moodrow grunted his agreement, though he wasn't so sure about "all this." Manny spent his days driving a truck for UPS, his nights working on his building. He did virtually everything, from boiler repairs to mopping the stairwells to evicting drug dealers at the point of a 12 gauge. This worked out well for his tenants, but it meant a life of endless toil for Manny. Still, if Manny was happy with what he'd accomplished in his fifty or so years on the planet, who was Moodrow to criticize?

"One time, you know, ever'body come up to the roof in the summertime." Manny waved again, indicating the tenement rooftops surrounding his building. "You know what I'm sayin', *hombre*?" He tapped Moodrow on the shoulder. "They came up to eat their dinners, to have a few beers, to sleep when it was too hot to sleep in the house. Remember when every roof had a pigeon coop? Huh? Now you look around, you don' see *nada*."

Guinevere Gadd, as if she'd heard Manny's declamation and wanted to issue a personal denial, took that moment to step into view. She nodded to the two men, said, "I got your note," then, no fool herself, stepped into the shadows.

Moodrow hauled himself to his feet. True to his word, he'd spent most of his day sleeping, the insistent ring of the telephone rousing him just after five o'clock. He'd answered to find a very pissed-off Betty Haluka. She and her clients, it seemed, had waited all day for a city attorney who never showed up whereupon she'd asked for a default judgment. The administrative law judge (shorthand, according to Betty, for incompetent clubhouse flunky), had responded by granting the city, without explanation, a six-week postponement. Meanwhile, the tenants lived in hell.

After five minutes of grunting agreement, Moodrow had finally gotten his chance. He told her about Gadd's unexpected arrival, the promise he made, adding, "Don't ask me why, because I don't know."

"If she's feeling as bad as you say," Betty had suggested, "maybe you're just sorry for her."

Maybe he was, but just now, looking into Gadd's eyes, he couldn't find a glimmer of suffering. She seemed buoyant, if not actually confident.

"You ready to get going?" he asked.

"Yeah," she said, "I got something to tell you."

"This I already figured."

They were headed uptown on Avenue C, the windows rolled down to let the heat out, when Gadd finally decided to explain. "I followed Josie Rizzo this afternoon."

Moodrow, though he cringed inwardly, held his peace, deciding to let her get it out before he explained the obvious.

"You gave me the description, right? I mean it's hard to miss a six-foot-tall grandma in a black dress with her eyes pinned to the sidewalk. I tell ya, Moodrow, she never looked up or around, not once. Like she thought she was invisible." Gadd lit a Newport, blew a stream of blue-gray smoke out the window. "Soot for the soot," she observed, before resuming. "Now, mostly, Josie went from shop to shop. A butcher on Elizabeth Street, a bakery on MacDougal, a dry cleaner on Sixth Avenue, a druggist on Eighth . . . right into the West Village where she dropped a small package into a padlocked metal box in a little courtyard on Grove Street." She smiled, leaned toward Moodrow, almost whispered, "Wouldn't you like to know what was in that package? Wouldn't you like to know if it was a tape recording?"

"Tell me you didn't break into that box?" Moodrow, to his surprise, was nearly whispering himself.

"No, not yet." Gadd settled back into the seat. "But it's what we thought, yes? That Josie was ratting on Carmine Stettecase?"

Moodrow pulled up at the Fourteenth Street stoplight, put the car into neutral. "Gadd, do you have any idea what Carmine would do if he found a private eye following his mother-in-law? You know what he'd have to assume? Remember, you're not a cop anymore."

Gadd chose not to answer the question. "There was nobody else around, Moodrow," she insisted. "Not even the feds. Anyway, now that I know what she's doing, I don't have to follow her. The slot on that box was just big enough to handle a tape cassette."

The light changed and Moodrow slid the car back into gear. "So, tell me how this helps you? To know what you already knew? Remember, if you break into that box, it *would* be obstruction of justice. The feds would have a legitimate beef."

"Not if they don't find out." She jabbed the cigarette between her lips. "I know a trick with a nylon stocking that'll open most padlocks within a few seconds."

Moodrow, with no ready response that didn't sound like pure nagging, pushed the car west on Fourteenth Street past Union Square, maneuvering the Chevy around double-parked trucks and cars turning in the intersections. He let the traffic, just heavy enough to require his attention, absorb him until he finally caught up with the commuters a few blocks from the Lincoln Tunnel on Tenth Avenue. Stopped dead, he turned to Gadd, asked, "Exactly what do you—or *we*—hope to accomplish by knowing the content of that—or any other—tape recording? Assuming what Josie put in that box *is* a tape."

"I like the scenario we laid out this morning." Gadd tossed the cigarette butt out the window. "Josie wants her nephew out of jail, the board turns him down, Josie goes to the feds, the feds spring Jilly. It fits the facts, right? But that's the past and what we didn't do was project the chain into the future." She turned to him, her face dead serious. "Jilly kills a child before the feds have their case wrapped up. He becomes public enemy number one, but that doesn't mean Josie doesn't love him anymore. No, what she does is put the squeeze on the FBI. She forces them to protect her nephew. Which they are doing even as we speak."

Gadd waited a moment, then, when Moodrow didn't reply, continued on. "The house where Jilly and his partner were living? The cops found nearly seven thousand dollars taped behind the bureau. Plus, the closets were full of clothes. I ask you, Moodrow, how come Sappone, if he's broke, if he doesn't have a change of underwear, hasn't done something really stupid? You think he just vanished? Maybe committed suicide by jumping off the George Washington Bridge?"

"It's only been a few days." Moodrow, looking for a way around the cars projecting back across the intersection from the mouth of the tunnel, pushed the Chevy as far to the right as possible. When he'd cleared Forty-second Street, gotten himself moving uptown again, he suddenly admitted that she might easily be right about the feds and Jilly Sappone. He asked himself what he would do if, in the middle of an important case, he was faced with a demonstrably insane informant.

Chain up the prick in some basement, he said to himself. Close the case and leave him to the rats.

Fifteen minutes later, the car safely parked in a lot on Seventy-eighth Street, Moodrow and Gadd walked east toward Broadway. It was a beautiful evening, still warm enough for shirtsleeves. The sun, dropping fast, projected a steady blast of cool golden light along the crosstown streets, exploding in shop windows, the windshields of parked cars, even the eyeglasses of strolling pedestrians.

Broadway, running north–south, was, by contrast, locked into shadow. Nevertheless, the sidewalks were crowded; the citizens of the Upper West Side, with money to spend, were out in force. They gathered in cafés and restaurants on both sides of the avenue, drifted through a hundred small shops, buying everything from baby clothes to hand-dipped chocolate. At Eightieth Street, the windows of an enormous Barnes & Nobles superstore displayed the latest Rush Limbaugh tome next to the latest unauthorized biography of Malcolm X.

"New York ecumenical." Moodrow announced. "Next thing they'll be selling Cardinal O'Connor's collected sermons at pro-abortion rallies."

"If there's a buyer, there's always gonna be a seller," Gadd replied, the display of cynicism being, in her own mind, strictly obligatory. "Say, I don't want to play the party pooper here—and I'm not sayin' it's not a beautiful night for a walk through the neighborhood—but would telling me what we're gonna do actually tear you apart?"

"Hell, Gadd, if I knew what we were gonna do, I would've told you long before now."

"You gotta do better than that, Moodrow." Gadd stopped in her tracks. "Else I'll definitely have to shoot you."

Moodrow watched her reflection in the window of a shop specializing in leather clothing. The name of the shop, Skins and Things, floated just above her bushy hair, its gold letters curling around her skull like a halo.

"We need help." Moodrow turned to face her. "Going from bar to bar, from the dry cleaner to the liquor store . . . hell, it'd take forever." He jerked his chin to indicate the scene in front of them. "I lived my whole life in New York, but this I never saw until about ten years ago."

Gadd looked down the block, nodded thoughtfully. "You're talkin' about the panhandlers, the homeless, right?"

It was too early for the fear of crime (in this neighborhood, any-way) to make its appearance. That would come after eleven o'clock, when most of the spring celebrants were home preparing for another workday. For now, at 7:30, the only thing between the citizenry and a perfect May evening were homeless beggars, black and white, who shook their Styrofoam coffee cups, whispered their entreaties: *Spare change, spare change. Help me out, man. Help me.*

Most seemed robust, young men in their thirties wearing raggedy trousers, ripped sneakers, as if they'd been drawn from central cast-ing. A few were clearly disturbed, mumbling or shouting or crying as they made their halting way along the sidewalk. A still smaller num-ber sat on the pavement, backs against the wall, knees drawn up into their chests, displaying signs lettered on torn pieces of cardboard: HELP ME PLEASE/I HAVE AIDS/HELP ME.

"You think they'd be willing to look for Sappone?" Gadd shook her head. "Wrong question. Do you think they'd be *able* to look?"

"Not that guy." Moodrow pointed to a bearded young man, maybe twenty-five years old, stumbling over parked cars in the gut-ter. He was shouting, "I'm in the soup, I'm in the soup." Over and over again.

"No, not him," Gadd agreed.

"See, I'm not gonna ask them about Sappone. What I think is that Sappone's holed up somewhere, that he's got his partner run-ning errands. That would be the smart way to play it, since it's mostly been Sappone's face on the TV screen."

They walked half a block north, past a cheese store and a gourmet coffee shop before they were approached. Moodrow evaluated the panhandler in the usual cop fashion, doing it quickly, automatically. Black, six feet, maybe one-sixty-five; medium complexion, bushy hair, face narrow, small-featured; two-inch scar on the left eyebrow.

"Can ya help me out, bro?" The man kept his cup away from Gadd, his eyes on the pavement.

Moodrow reached into his trouser pocket, slipped a single off the roll he'd put there a few hours earlier, dropped it in the cup. The panhandler looked at the bill for a moment, then raised his eyes to meet Moodrow's for the first time.

"I'm lookin' for somebody," Moodrow said before the man could begin to thank him.

"Right, I see." The man stepped back, nodded thoughtfully. He pulled the cup into his waist, shielded it with his free hand.

"What's your name?"

"That dollar," the man replied evenly, "it's real nice and all, but it don't buy you my name." He hesitated. "You too old to be a cop."

"You got that right. I'm not a cop, which means I don't want something for nothing. Anybody spots this guy and gives me a call, it's worth a hundred bucks."

Gadd stepped forward. "That's *if* we find him. Bullshit phone calls will be handled with all due belligerence."

The man nodded, extended his hand. "My name's Dwight. What's this dude look like?"

Moodrow handed over Jackson-Davis Wescott's mug shot. He wanted to keep things as simple as possible.

"The peculiar thing about this guy, he's about thirty-five and he's got white hair and freckles. Not gray hair, but white. Platinum blonde, like Madonna."

"Sounds like Alabama white trash."

"Mississippi."

"Can I keep this?" He smiled for the first time.

Moodrow shook his head. "I can't take a chance. The posters end up on the street, my man is liable to stumble across one, know somebody's looking for him."

Dwight gave the mug shot back to Moodrow. "I take it this ain't an exclusive you're givin' me."

"The race goes to the swift, Dwight," Gadd responded, shoving a business card into the man's outstretched hand. "But we're a hundred percent sure he's living somewhere on the Upper West Side. And you can't miss him," she added. "If you're walking around with your eyes open, there's no way you can miss him."

The essential message delivered, Moodrow and Gadd simply

walked away, leaving Dwight to stare at the phone number on the card. They were in for a long evening and both knew it. There were hundreds of beggars to speak to, dozens of blocks to walk, not only on Broadway, but on Columbus and Amsterdam Avenues as well. It would take days to cover the whole area.

Gadd started to say something about Moodrow's grand strategy being a long shot, then realized they had no other line of approach, not unless they found another Carlo Sappone.

"Whatta ya say to this, Moodrow. Whatta ya say we kidnap Josie Rizzo, beat it out of her."

"I'd say you've been watching too much television."

"You didn't say that about Carlo."

"Carmine would have to kill you, Gadd. He might want to give you a reward, especially if she never came back, but what he'd do is protect the family honor."

"Not if Josie didn't tell him."

A few minutes later, they decided to separate. Moodrow crossed the street, then turned north and began to work. He and Gadd kept each other in sight, a mutual protectiveness that was entirely unnecessary. Nobody refused the dollar, nobody refused to look at Wescott's photo, nobody refused a business card. A hundred dollars was clearly more money than any of these men had seen in a long time.

When they reached Ninety-sixth Street, the somewhat arbitrary northern boundary of the Upper West Side, Moodrow recrossed the street to meet his partner.

"Gets old in a hurry," he observed.

"No doubt about it." Gadd lit a cigarette, then checked her watch. It was nearly ten o'clock. "If we hurry, we can get down to Lincoln Center before the concerts let out." She looked up at him. "You doin' okay?"

Moodrow shrugged. "We have to walk in that direction to pick up the car. I'll see how I'm feeling when we get to Seventy-eighth Street."

They didn't get two blocks before an elderly black man limped over to them. He was wearing a knit cap and a heavy, hooded parka. The wool cap had come partially unraveled, revealing a bald, leathery scalp.

"Sir, please." He was polite, but firm. "My name is Archer McNabb, sir. I was wonderin' could I speak to you."

"Fire away," Gadd said. She looked at her watch. "But make it fast. The fat lady is singing down in Lincoln Center even as we speak."

The man looked at her for a moment, then chuckled. "That's a joke," he said. "But, see, reason I'm stoppin' y'all is because I heard you're searchin' after the boy with the white hair. That right?"

Moodrow took the mug shot out of his jacket pocket and handed it over. Archer McNabb looked at it for a moment, then passed it back.

"I understand y'all are payin' a hundred dollars to find the boy. That right?"

"Yeah." Moodrow, looking into the man's eyes, knew he'd found Jackson-Davis Wescott. He'd found him and it wasn't going to do either him or Ginny Gadd the slightest bit of good.

"Ain't no *conditions*, right? Jus' find him and you pay up."

"You know where he is?" Gadd asked.

"Yes, ma'am," he replied. "But see, thing about it, I ain't exactly sure you're gonna give me no money."

"I understand your problem," Gadd agreed. "My problem is that you could be bullshitting here, trying to run a scam. Seeing as we're the ones with the money . . ."

Archer's eyes dropped. He chewed on his lower lip for a moment, then sighed. "I guess if you gon' cheat me, there ain't nothin' I can do about it." He paused as if reconsidering his own conclusion. "But you did say no conditions?"

"Where is he, McNabb?" Moodrow pulled out his folding money, counted off five twenties.

"Boy's in the morgue, sir. Cops found him in that park by the river. I was up there collectin' bottles and I seen it all. It was that boy in the pitcha, sure as shit."

ELEVEN

After a quick phone call to Jim Tilley at the Seventh Precinct, Moodrow passed the hundred to a now-beaming Archer McNabb, then led his partner to the parking garage on Seventy-eighth Street where they picked up Moodrow's Chevrolet. They walked in silence, drove in silence, each locked into a personal chain of consequences flowing from Archer McNabb's revelations. It wasn't until Moodrow had parked the car in front of the triple-X bookstore below Gadd's office that either chose to reveal the nature of those consequences.

Gadd began the conversation by dancing away from the issue. She gestured at the trucks, everything from eighteen-wheelers to minivans, and the workers unloading them. Her Sixth Avenue office was in the middle of New York's wholesale florist district and, like the Gansevoort meat packing district to the south and the Hunts Point produce market in the Bronx, boomed at night when everybody else had gone home.

"The pickups begin after the delivery trucks leave. Altogether, it goes on until six or seven o'clock in the morning." Gadd took a pack of Newports out of her purse, fiddled with the box for a few minutes, then put it back. "You ever hear of white noise?"

Moodrow dredged up a rueful smile. Yes, he'd *heard* of white noise. He wasn't so ancient that he'd lost touch altogether. Meanwhile, he had no idea what it was or what it was supposed to do.

"White Noise," he finally declared, "is the name of a neo-Nazi rock group. Operates out of Illinois. They're on tour even as we speak, playing the hot spots of East Germany." Then he remembered that there was no longer an *East* Germany and quickly changed the subject. "We could still go back to the West Side tomorrow, show Sappone's mug shot around, maybe get lucky."

Gadd shook her head. "For all the above-named reasons, Moodrow. The ones you spelled out a couple of hours ago when you explained why we were showing Wescott's picture instead of Sappone's." She rolled down the window, took a deep breath. The air was faintly damp, though still warm.

"I won't argue the point," Moodrow replied. "Tomorrow morning, when the story breaks, everybody in the neighborhood's gonna be looking for Jilly. If he killed his partner, he must have had a way out of there."

"Still, we were *right* about Sappone living on the Upper West Side." Gadd fished out her Newports again. This time she took a cigarette and lit it up.

"Yeah, there's that." Moodrow pinched the bridge of his nose between thumb and forefinger. Events were running out of control; they were moving under their own power. He had the sudden conviction that he and Gadd (yes, he admitted to himself, *he* and Gadd) were going to spend the next week or so trying to catch up. As a cop, he'd been inside the scenario many times. Feeling like a UN observer trapped in a war zone.

"I ever mention I play the horses?"

Moodrow turned and smiled. "Not that I remember," he said, adding, "and I've got an unholy memory."

"Well, I'm good at it. Very good."

"Does that mean you win?"

"The vig is too high." She waved the idea away with a sweep of her cigarette. "The track takes seventeen percent off the top. It's hard to overcome." After a moment, she shifted her weight so that she was facing him. "I'm gonna go out there tomorrow afternoon, sit in the sun, think about what I want to do with Jilly Sappone. You wanna come, you can always find me on the third floor of the clubhouse. I hang out near the head of the stretch."

"You're not looking for a lift?" Belmont Racetrack was just inside the Nassau County border of Queens.

"I do the racing form on the train." She grinned. "What can I say? I'm superstitious. Wouldn't mind a ride home, though." Gadd slid down in the seat, pushed her feet up against the firewall. "Tell me about Carmine Stettecase. I mean if Carmine's in the middle of all this, maybe I should know a little more about him. Before I do something terminal."

Moodrow took a second to organize his thoughts. Trying to remember what he's already told her, separate it from what he'd told Betty. Finally, he nodded and began. "Carmine is a made guy, has been for a long time, forty years at least. Where does he fit in the mob scheme of things? Well, he's got his own gang and they pretty much run prostitution, bookmaking and loan-sharking on the Lower East Side. Add in the occasional hijacking, the odd drug deal and you have a pretty good picture. I made him for eight murders before I stopped counting. Meanwhile, I couldn't touch him, not working out of the precinct."

"That eat you up?"

"Not really." Moodrow slid the front seat back, stretched out his legs. "In the job you learn to live with the possible. If you're smart." He looked through the window for a moment, watched an enormous tractor-trailer back into a space at the curb. "Wanna hear a funny story?"

Gadd took a deep drag, then tossed her cigarette out the window. "Desperately."

"Carmine's the most paranoid criminal I ever met, lives in his own brownstone on Tenth Street. That's where he does most of his business and word on the street is that nobody gets in except his lieutenants and his family. Carmine's only son, Tommy—he's some kind of computer freak, doesn't have anything to do with Carmine's business—has an apartment in the building, him and his wife, Mary. Josie Rizzo, Mary's mother, lives there too. But that's it. There's no maids, no cooks, nobody else.

"Now, I gotta admit that, so far, Carmine's strategy is working. After all, he's been on the street for forty years. But that doesn't mean he hasn't paid a price. Gadd, you could put Carmine's life on the Oprah Winfrey Show, call it, 'The Dysfunctional Crime Family.' Most of the people in that house hate each other."

Moodrow twisted the key in the ignition, shut the engine down. "I'll give you an example. Maybe eight or nine years ago, Tommy got busted in a vice raid on an S&M club in Chelsea. The cops had reporters along for the ride and somebody got a shot of Tommaso Stettecase trussed up like a turkey. Wearing a fucking *diaper*. Carmine, naturally, went nuts; he's been sitting on the kid ever since."

"And Tommy is supposed to be the next Don? He's Carmine's *only* son?" Gadd's grin seemed to open her face, giving Moodrow a glimpse of something beneath, an underlying satisfaction.

Moodrow shook his head. "I already told you, Tommy's not in the business."

"Then why does he live in the house?"

"Why do people who hate each other stay married for fifty years?" Moodrow flipped up the palm of his right hand. "Tommy's wife, Mary, is some kind of recluse. She hasn't been seen outside the house in five years."

"What about Carmine's wife? She alive?"

"Yeah, her name's Rosa. She and Carmine get along pretty well. Carmine runs a club in Soho and his wife goes there with him a couple of times a week."

"And Josie Rizzo? What does she do?"

"Josie does all the shopping, most of the cooking and cleaning. Remember, it's a big house, five stories, and Carmine won't have servants."

"It sounds like he's got a slave."

"In that case, Josie's middle name must be Spartacus."

"Yoo-hoo, Agent Ewing, sir, do you by any chance know how to play gin rummy?" Jilly Sappone looked out through the narrow iron bars of the door separating his quarters from the rest of the house. He was stoned, of course, had been since his first, straining bowel movement. Fishing the balloons out of the bowl, now that, he admitted to himself, was an ugly job. Too bad old Jackson-Davis hadn't been around to do it.

Ewing dropped the newspaper onto his lap. "They found your partner," he said through clenched teeth.

"My partner?"

"Jackson-Davis Wescott. You proud of that?"

"Not as proud as I am of teaching little Theresa to fly." Sappone watched the blood rise into the young agent's face. Ewing reminded him of all those whiter-than-white screws in all those upstate prisons. "C'mon, Agent Ewing, whatta ya say to a few hands of gin rummy? You don't gotta open the fuckin' door. We'll play through the slot."

"Go screw yourself."

"Well, if that's the way you feel . . ." Sappone turned on the small television in his cell. He was pretty sure Ewing wouldn't kill him no matter what he said, not until after the feds had enough to bust Carmine. But once that was done, once Carmine was taken into custody, the boyish Agent Ewing was gonna pull out his nine millimeter, put a round in Jilly Sappone's skull, bury him out in the woods. That's why Jilly Sappone was in this house instead of a prison, why Agent Ewing was all by his lonesome, why the crew-cut moron passed meals through the slot instead of inviting Jilly Sappone to sit at the table.

Unfortunately for Agent Ewing (and whoever was running him), the FBI didn't know shit about secure facilities. Or maybe his little cell was never meant to serve as a real prison. Maybe it was meant for rats who were safer with the feds than they were on the street. Either way, Jilly Sappone, after spending fourteen years in the worst dungeons New York State had to offer, would have only two problems getting out. The first was Agent Bob Ewing and the second was the automatic he kept within easy reach.

Jilly turned up the volume. He wasn't really interested in the sitcom on the screen, but he wanted to move around without being heard. There was a lot of work to be done: a weapon (or weapons) to be fashioned, a strategy (or strategies) to be devised. Pleasant work, but work nonetheless.

His task, a surveillance more than anything else, was interrupted ten minutes later by the telephone.

"Yeah."

Ewing's exasperated tone left doubt about who was on the other end on the line. Sappone, looking at the back of the agent's crew-cut head, actually felt a moment of sympathy. The poor schmuck was trapped, just like his prisoner.

"It's your aunt."

"Great." Jilly waited for Ewing to put the phone on the small platform in the door slot, then stepped forward and picked up the receiver. "Is this my dearly beloved Aunt Josefina?" No question, he was feeling *very* good.

"Sit tight," Josie responded. "And don't make no trouble."

"They got me in a cell, Aunt Josie. What am I supposed to do?"

"Read a book," she shouted. "Improve your mind."

It was just before midnight and Stanley Moodrow, his car safely parked in the Thirteenth Street lot, was making his way down Avenue B toward his apartment. He was moving quickly, his eyes jumping from shadow to shadow. Pedestrians moving toward him were automatically evaluated, as were the occupants of the few cars moving along the street. As he turned east on Fourth Street, he saw a man in front of his building. The man, still a hundred yards away, was wearing a light sport jacket over a pair of dark trousers and Moodrow immediately registered him as nonthreatening. It took a few more strides until he realized the man had to be a reporter.

On one level, Moodrow wasn't surprised. He'd been expecting some kind of a confrontation, had already prepared the response Betty had suggested, the one about the police *and* his client asking him to keep his mouth shut. Yet, despite his preparations, a sudden rage boiled up inside him. His face contorted, his eyes narrowing until the only thing he could see was the reporter in his path. His hands rose, then balled into fists as he widened his stride before breaking into an all-out run.

He was fifty feet away when the man turned and fled. The action, though it seemed entirely reasonable ten seconds later, confused him at first. The reporter was supposed to hold his ground, whip out pen and notebook, start blasting away. Meanwhile, he, Moodrow, was doubled over, gasping for oxygen like a gaffed fish.

No fool like an old fool, he finally told himself. As if that explained it.

Just about the time Moodrow decided to charge into battle,
Ginny Gadd, alone in the small room that served as her apartment,
punched out the number of a former lover turned friend, a man
named Barry Lowenthal. She'd met Barry a year before at a Computer Expo in Denver; they'd shared a drink, then dinner, then met
again in New York before ending up in bed. Barry, the first man she'd
made love to after the breakup of her marriage, had been tender and
considerate.

Two encounters later, after a pleasant lunch in a midtown restaurant, he'd casually mentioned the fact that he'd been involved in the
bondage-and-discipline scene for more than a decade, that he had
always been the master, that he enjoyed nothing more than the sight
of a bound, helpless (though always consenting) woman.

"It's not sadism," he'd hastened to explain. "Not hot wax or caning. It's about *avoiding* pain. Avoiding it through absolute obedience."

Gadd, though she was a great believer in the principle of consenting adults getting their jollies any way they chose, felt all sexual interest drain away. She never dated Barry again, though they
occasionally used each other professionally. Barry had access to the
Internet system through his job at a downtown brokerage house.

"Lowenthal."

"It's Ginny Gadd, Barry. I didn't wake you, did I?"

"No, what's up?"

"I have a favor to ask."

"Tell me you want to be chained to a rack."

"Afraid not, but I might be willing to chain *you* to a rack. In case
you decide to swing both ways."

Barry laughed. "Not this week."

"Well, a girl can always dream." Gadd paused for a moment, then
launched into it. "I have a guy I want to contact and I can't approach him directly. A business matter, not personal. He's computer

literate and he was once busted at an S&M club. From what I understand, there are BBSs that specialize in kinky sex."

A BBS was a bulletin board system.

"That's true, but most of them are private. They have nothing to do with the Internet."

"I understand that, Barry, but my problem is that I don't have any easy way to locate the systems and I don't have a lot of time, either. I was hoping you were . . ." She paused, smiled to herself. "I was hoping you were involved."

"Ginny, I know people who are too afraid to hit the clubs. They live on those boards. The only problem, for you, is that nobody, and I mean *nobody*, gives a full name. Subscribers are known by their handles. Like truck drivers on their CB radios."

Gadd sighed. "I was afraid of that."

"You say this guy was busted in a New York Club?"

"Yeah, I don't actually know which one. It didn't seem important at the time and I forgot to ask."

"What's his name?"

"Tommaso. Tommaso Stettecase."

"Tommaso the Timid? Ginny, the man is a fucking legend."

TWELVE

Josie Rizzo knew exactly why Carmine Stettecase was in such a good mood. The Chinaman, On Luk Sun, had finally set a date: May 18, exactly five days hence.

"The boat sailed yesterday, boys, and it ain't stoppin' nowhere till it gets to New York. Praise the fuckin' Lord."

There still being a number of details to work out, the celebration had been short-lived, but Carmine, the cloud above his head finally beginning to dissolve, had remained buoyant throughout the meeting. That buoyancy, apparently, had continued afterward, because Josie, as she descended the stairs after listening to the tape, found a grinning Carmine standing between herself and the front door.

"Hey, Josie, come into my office for a minute. I wanna talk to ya."

Josie found it almost funny. When Carmine spun around, the blubber covering his body did an extra quarter turn before it settled down with a final quiver. Meanwhile, there being no way to dodge whatever Carmine had in mind, she dutifully followed him into his office.

"Whatta ya want, Carmine? I gotta make a lotta stops today."

They were standing nearly face-to-face on the polished hardwood floor. Carmine detested wall-to-wall carpeting. The feds could put a bug underneath his carpet and Tommy might not be able to find it. At least, that's what Tommy had told him.

"What I been thinking here, Josie, is that I gotta start bein' more security conscious." A wolfish smirk creased his flabby cheeks. "I mean I got people comin' and goin' like it was Grand Central Station. It ain't only you, Josie. Tommy, Mary, Rosa . . . they could be doin' some kinda bullshit and I wouldn't know. The last couple of weeks, I could barely sleep for thinkin' about it."

Josie, though she knew Carmine's pause was meant to give her a chance to respond, held her peace.

"Okay, so what I was figurin' was that I'd give everybody a quick strip search. Like for my peace of mind. I mean how could anyone object, being as it's for the good of the family?" The forefinger and pinky of his right hand, extended toward her, swung up and down like vertical metronomes. "Now, look, Josie, I don't wan'cha to think I got no dirty thoughts in my head about lookin' up ya pussy or nothin'. That's why I decided we need a witness that I ain't forcin' ya to do somethin' sexual. Hey, Vinnie, c'mon in here."

Vincenzo Trentacosta, his giggling mouth hidden behind hairy knuckles, stepped into the room. Carmine, at the sight, started laughing himself. He made a gesture toward Josie's crotch and she jumped back into Vinnie. Vinnie put his arm around her chest, squeezing her breasts beneath his forearm. Then he let go and she spun around him toward the door.

"Josie, where ya goin'?" Carmine shouted after her. "I bought a new roll of film for the Polaroid."

Out on the street, Josie breathed a sigh of relief. Carmine had only been kidding, another grievance to be added to the years of abuse, a nourishing breakfast for the ghoul that lived inside her heart. Meanwhile, she had the tape in the pocket of her dress. If he'd found it, she'd already be dead, but that wouldn't be the worst thing. No, the worst thing was that if she was dead, Carmine would be off the FBI's hook.

These thoughts continued to occupy Josie Rizzo two hours later when she turned onto Grove Street, stopped in a small courtyard, deposited the tape in a locked metal box. She looked neither right nor left, though whether from habit or from a refusal to acknowledge danger, Ginny Gadd couldn't tell. Gadd was sitting across the street and twenty yards to the west in a rented car, nodding to herself as she watched Josie stride off down the block.

Gadd waited another half hour before making her move, until she was certain the box wasn't being monitored. Then she stepped out of the car, walked over to the box, glanced quickly over both shoulders. Grove Street, a mere two blocks long and completely residential, was quiet, without a pedestrian in sight.

Using her body as a shield, Gadd tied a short length of nylon stocking to the base of the padlock and pulled the stocking toward her, exerting a firm, steady pressure. Then she withdrew a small wooden mallet from her purse and struck the shackle. When the lock failed to open, she increased the pressure slightly and struck again.

"Practice makes perfect," she muttered.

A moment later, she was back in the car, fitting the microcassette into a high-speed dubbing deck. Ten minutes later, the original back in the relocked box, she was on her way back to the car-rental agency.

Moodrow waited until after breakfast to give Betty a call. He wasn't looking forward to relating the prior evening's adventure, and not because he was embarrassed by the evident failure of his strategy. No, what worried him was the near certainty that Betty would ask what he and Gadd were going to do next.

The truth (which he didn't want to admit, not out loud and not to Betty) was that Stanley Moodrow wouldn't be making that decision. Gadd, her other significant option being withdrawal in the face of the enemy, was going to move on the FBI's drop box. He knew it, because that's what he'd have done. Ten years ago when he'd been a rushing fool instead of a fearful angel.

"Hello?"

"It's me, Betty."

"Stanley, did you have a good night?"

Moodrow shook his head. She hadn't wasted any time. But then she probably didn't know what had happened to Jackson-Davis.

"You read the paper this morning?" he asked.

"Not yet."

"Yeah, well you're most likely gonna see Wescott's picture on the front page. They found him dead in Riverside Park."

"Do you think Jilly killed him?"

"Yeah, killed him and took off for parts unknown."

"Maybe it was Carmine."

Moodrow paused to think it over. "It's not impossible," he admitted. "But if I had to put my money down, I'd bet that Carmine's never heard of Jackson-Davis Wescott." He paused again. "You off to court?"

"In a few minutes. Look, I had an idea last night, but I don't think it'll help. Not if Sappone's left the Upper West Side."

"You found a way to run him down?" Moodrow, throughout his entire NYPD career, had accepted help from any source. Had accepted it gratefully.

"Ask yourself this question, Stanley. How did Jilly Sappone, who's been a very busy boy since the day of his release, find an apartment in Manhattan? Remember, the house on Long Island was waiting for him when he got out."

"Somebody had to find the place," Moodrow said promptly. "And that . . ."

"And that somebody," Betty finished the sentence for him, "had to be Josie Rizzo. You remember DHCR from Jackson Heights?"

"The Department of Housing and Community Renewal. That's a state agency."

"True, but they've got computerized information on every rent-stabilized apartment in New York City, including the names of the leaseholders. Suppose Josie Rizzo had to use her own name because it was on the check she wrote. That would mean she's in DHCR's computer."

"You're forgetting one thing, Betty. Even if you've got it right, Josie rented the apartment less than a week ago. We're talking about a state bureaucracy here. It'll probably be months before they update their records."

"Not necessarily. I called Leonora this morning, asked her to check it out. She called back a few minutes ago, told me that many of the larger management companies are linked to DHCR's computer via modem. They enter information as they process the application."

"That's amazing." He wasn't kidding, the concept of an efficient state agency being entirely foreign to him. "I assume you told Leonora to run a search."

"Would I do that without talking to you first?"

"In a heartbeat."

"Bye, Stanley. Have a nice day."

On his way out to Belmont Park, Stanley Moodrow experienced a small miracle. The temperature at one o'clock in the afternoon when he locked his apartment door and headed off to get his car was ninety-two degrees, the first real day of summer. Moodrow, from long experience behind the wheel of a patrol car, had come to call this annual event Radiator Boilover Day. Traditionally, all the jerks who'd used the cold winter as an excuse to neglect their clogged or leaking radiators would now pay the price, as would everybody else driving on the roads they used. Add to that a torturous route (the Williamsburg Bridge to the BQE to the LIE to the Cross Island Parkway), a dozen construction sites, and his own Chevrolet's barely functioning air conditioner. . . .

The trip, though Moodrow shouldered the burden manfully, promised to be very, very unpleasant, a two-hour, twenty-mile odyssey characterized by sweaty armpits, blaring horns, furious drivers. The reality, on the other hand, once he'd cleared the Delancey Street construction site and swept up onto the Williamsburg Bridge, was that his speedometer didn't drop below 55 until he reached the traffic light a block from the Belmont parking lot. The reality was a New York miracle.

Ten minutes later, the blessing still fresh, Moodrow stepped off the escalator onto the third floor of Belmont Park's long grandstand. Moodrow had never liked the track, had always considered the racetrack image promoted by the media, ten thousand screaming fans cheering on their favorites, to be so much bullshit. The truth about horse racing wasn't to be found in the twenty seconds it took the animals to run the length of the stretch, but in the half hour between races when the excitement dropped away like a shed skin and the gamblers gathered in small packs, whispering back and forth, their

gray mood exactly matching the concrete walls and naked super-
structure of the surrounding architecture.

Depression, he thought, is what it's all about. A crop of degenerate gamblers counting their losses.

Then he caught sight of Ginny Gadd standing beneath the tote
board. She was wearing a red, scoop-necked top over a white T-shirt,
bluejeans, and white sneakers. Her hair was swept up and back, as
usual. A folded racing form dangled from one hand.

She was exchanging notes with a much older man, a man almost
as old as Moodrow. The conversation was subdued, both nodding
agreement from time to time. Moodrow, as he watched from a distance, was taken by Gadd's obvious intensity, by her abundant, vi-
brant youth. For a moment, he felt a conscious desire to steal it from
her, as if her energy was an accessory, like a purse or a necklace. Then
she saw him, said good-bye to her companion, and walked over.

"We've got a situation here," she announced. "Let's get outside
before the race goes off."

Moodrow, with no choice, followed her to a pair of empty seats in
the open grandstand. The outer dirt track, newly sprinkled with water, gleamed dully in the sunlight, while the grass of the inner turf
tracks was intensely green. At the far end of the oval, several horses,
led by handlers, pranced their way into the starting gate. Moodrow
started to say something to Gadd, but she was staring out through a
small pair of binoculars, oblivious to his presence.

The starting gate banged open a few minutes later and the horses
burst out, a confusion of brown muscular flesh and vivid jockey silks
that, for a brief moment, seemed to Moodrow like parts of a single
organism. Then a jet-black horse, his jockey whipping furiously,
charged to the front, establishing a four-length margin before the
pack reached the quarter pole. The black held that margin into the
turn, then opened up as they came through the stretch. By the time
he reached the finish line, he was eight lengths in front.

Moodrow waited until Gadd put the binoculars down, then
asked, "Did you bet him?"

Gadd blinked several times, as if waiting for the question to penetrate. "No, no. I didn't bet the race." She continued to stare up at

him for a minute. "We've got a scraped rail here. I wasn't expecting it, but it's an opportunity I can't ignore."

"I'm gonna have to ask you a question, Gadd. If you don't wanna answer me, it's alright. What's a 'scraped rail'?"

Gadd smiled mischievously. "How much do you know about the racetrack?"

"I place bets; I watch races; I tear up tickets."

"That's what I figured." She glanced down at the racing form, then placed it on the empty seat next to her. "The track down there, it looks like so much flat dirt, right?"

"Right."

"Actually, the track is banked, from the outside to the inside, so the dirt tends to slide in toward the rail. Now, every night, after the horses go home, the groundskeepers groom the track. Mostly, they're trying to keep it uniform, but sometimes they make it too deep or too shallow along the inside. If it's too deep, horses that run to the front or run close to the rail almost never win. Naturally, that reverses itself when the rail is scraped."

"And today the rail is scraped."

Gadd nodded. "As thin as I've ever seen it. That pig who won the last race, the four horse? He always runs to the front, that's his style. Meanwhile, he hasn't held up past a half mile in his last six times out." She fumbled in the large purse dangling from her shoulder. "Anyway, I've got something you don't wanna hear."

Moodrow stared at the small tape recorder and shook his head. "You actually went and did it," he said.

"Relax, nobody saw me. The original's back in the box and the box is locked. There's no way they can know I was in there. The fibbies won't even suspect." She hesitated for a moment. "I listened to the tape on the way out here, but I can't separate the voices. I think there's some kind of a deal going down, but . . ." She handed Moodrow the recorder, then picked up the racing form. After a moment, she dropped the paper on her lap and gave him a searching look.

"Those questions you asked me yesterday? About what I wanted?" She waited for Moodrow to nod. "I have to know why,

Moodrow. Maybe I'm not quite as crazy as I was a couple of days ago. Maybe I'm a little calmer. But I want to know—I *have* to know— what they traded Theresa for, what they got in return for her life. And what I'm gonna do is get in there, right in the middle of the deal, see what happens. If you don't wanna come with me, I won't hold it against you."

Moodrow grimaced. "Enough with the heartfelt confessions. Lemme listen to this while you figure out who I should bet."

Three races went by, two run on the inner grass track, before Gadd tapped Moodrow on the shoulder, then led him inside to a small television monitor suspended from a steel girder.

"I'm gonna watch the exacta flashes," she announced. "We might have a bet here."

"You don't wanna know what was on the tape?"

"It'll wait," she announced, turning to the monitor. Ten minutes later, she led Moodrow away from the other bettors. "Look," she said, I'm gonna put a couple of hundred into the race. You wanna come in with me?"

"I don't have that kind of money. Not in my pocket."

"Put in whatever you want. We'll split later."

Moodrow pulled a twenty out of his wallet and handed it over. "I know that's chump change for a big-time bettor like you, Gadd, but would you mind telling me who we're betting?"

Gadd took a second to think it over, then smiled. "We're betting the two horse and here's why," she announced. "He hasn't won in three months; he comes out of a betting stable; he's demonstrated early speed every time he ran well; he took a lot of money on the third exacta flash; the other pigs in the race'd look better in Alpo cans."

Fifteen minutes later, with Moodrow cheering his head off, the two horse, Satan's Brother, blasted out of the starting gate, drew clear in the first eighth, finally won by a head after nearly collapsing in the stretch.

"Christ, Gadd, he almost blew it." Moodrow shook his head. "Eighteen-to-one and he almost blew it."

"Not really. I had him up and down in the exactas. If he finished second, we'd have been okay." She took out a cigarette and lit it, her first since Moodrow's arrival. "What's gonna hurt us is that he came in with the favorite. That and the stable sunk a bundle into the exactas."

Sure enough, when the race became official and the exacta price, six dollars more than a straight win bet, flashed on the tote board, the crowd hissed and booed for a moment before drifting away from the finish line.

"Business as usual," Gadd announced. "Meanwhile, I've got it twenty times."

Moodrow took a minute to do the numbers. "Eight hundred and fifty-six dollars?"

"And you're in for ten percent." Gadd stood up and stretched. "Whatta ya say we cash the tickets, Moodrow, get the hell out of here, talk about that tape?

THIRTEEN

"You think we can finally get down to business?"

They were sitting in a booth in Moreno's, a small, neighborhood bar on First Avenue near Eleventh Street, sipping at frosted mugs of Budweiser. Moodrow, busy with an eight-ounce cheeseburger, mumbled a reply, then bit off another chunk of his sandwich.

"How 'bout repeating that, Moodrow. *After* you swallow."

Moodrow chewed for a moment, then drained his glass. "I've been stuffing my face ever since I came out of the hospital." He signaled the bartender, raised his empty glass.

"So, you're saying it's not genetic."

Moodrow wiped his lips. "Definitely not, Gadd. In fact, up to this point in my life, folks have always considered me a dainty eater."

They'd driven from the track to the Lower East Side in absolute silence, a condition made inevitable when Moodrow had tossed the keys over to Gadd in the parking lot, then fallen asleep on the backseat. Gadd had threaded her way through the late-afternoon traffic without resentment, but now that her partner was awake, she found herself running out of patience.

"Let's get on with it," she said. Her voice was even, almost resigned, a fact she knew wouldn't escape Moodrow's notice.

"Gadd, you won close to eight hundred dollars this afternoon. Doesn't that make you happy?"

"I suppose so." Gadd sipped at her beer, then added, "Tell you the truth, I almost forgot about it." She carefully set the mug on the

258

table. "And it's funny, Moodrow, because finding the rail like that was kind of miraculous. It only happens a few times at every meet and I don't go out every day. You think I have other things on my mind?"

The bartender, a burly middle-aged man who knew Moodrow well enough to call him by his last name, strolled across the room and set two mugs of beer on the table. He dropped Moodrow's empty on his tray, added Gadd's half-finished mug, then walked back to the bar.

"How did he know I didn't want something else?" Gadd asked. "Like maybe a boilermaker."

Moodrow shook his head. "Dave's pissed because I didn't fetch my own beer. He's got a thing about being a waitress. *His* words, Gadd, not mine. Anyway, about the tape."

"Yes, the tape."

"When they were all talking at the same time, I couldn't make anything out. Maybe the feds have a way to separate the voices, but, for me, they might have been speaking Russian."

"What about the rest of it? Did you recognize anybody?"

"Only Carmine. In fact, it was Carmine doing most of the talking." He crossed his legs, leaned against the back of the booth. "There's a deal going down, a drug deal, probably heroin. The drugs are coming in by boat and the smuggler is Chinese."

"That's all?"

"One more thing, the actual date, May 18, five days from today." Moodrow tapped a finger on the table. His voice, when he spoke again, was gentle. "You get in the middle, Gadd, most likely you're gonna get crushed. I watched you at the track. You could have bet every race, the scraped rail was a perfect excuse, but you didn't. Instead you waited, calculated the odds, made the right move at the right time."

Gadd nodded, took a deep breath and let it out. "My father was a degenerate gambler, bet every race, every sport, day after day, year after year." She hesitated for a moment, finally adding, "It was hard on the family."

The jukebox came on suddenly, Ella Fitzgerald doing "How High the Moon." Moodrow and Gadd listened for a moment, then leaned closer.

"This deal, it's why they let Sappone out. Carmine, his lieutenants, his customers, a Chinese smuggler, a pile of dope . . ."

"Makes for a nice photo-op, right? A real career maker." Gadd raised her glass, waited for Moodrow to follow suit, then drank. "Credit where credit is due."

Moodrow started to speak, then changed his mind. He, like Gadd, had no trouble imagining a gaggle of honking prosecutors, politicians, and FBI silks posturing in front of a table piled high with guns and dope. It wasn't the kind of picture that made foot soldiers happy, and Moodrow, throughout his entire career, had never been more than an infantryman battling in the trenches.

"I sent Tommaso electronic mail," Gadd said. "Via a Long Island bulletin board system." She looked up at Moodrow, noting his evident confusion. "Nothing elaborate, just a get-acquainted note."

Moodrow shook his head. "Does this have something to do with what I told you last night?"

"Everything," Gadd admitted. "After I went upstairs, I kept thinking about his obsession, how he wanted to be tied up, humiliated. That's not something you just stop doing, no matter who your father is."

"Speak for yourself, Gadd. Me, I stopped wearing diapers ten years ago. About the time my sexual drive went south."

"In that case you ought to have a foot fetish by now."

It was Gadd's turn to look around for the bartender, raise her mug in the air. When she caught his eye and received a grudging nod, she came back to Moodrow.

"I figured our boy would do what any good computer freak would do under the same circumstances. I figured he'd look for his jollies in cyberspace."

"Cyberspace? Jesus, Gadd, didn't your momma teach you to respect your elders?"

"Forget I said that." Gadd lit a cigarette, waved it like an eraser over a blackboard. "You know what computer bulletin board systems are?"

"Frankly, no."

"Great." She threw him a disgusted look. "Mostly, BBSs are nothing more than personal computers with a few modems attached. Individuals post information on the boards, messages, software, like that. Sometimes, two or more participants get on at the same time and have a conversation." She leaned back, waited for the bartender to set her beer down. Her eyes never left Moodrow's. "Actually," she finally conceded, "it's more complicated, but that's all you need to know."

Moodrow nodded, accepting the reality of the generations. "These bulletin boards, they're all sexually oriented?"

That brought a smile. "They're on every subject known to man. For a few thousand dollars, you could set one up yourself."

"*You* could." Moodrow spun the heavy glass mug between his fingers. "Me, I couldn't stand the excitement." He drank, set the mug down. "Meanwhile, tell me the whole story. Although I'm not sure I can stand up to that excitement, either."

"It's not really too complicated. I have a friend, makes his living on computers, who's also into bondage and discipline. What he tells me is that, in addition to visiting the clubs in Chelsea, he fools around on various bulletin boards. My buddy knew all about Tommaso getting busted. Apparently, Carmine's reaction has passed into official B&D folklore. By the way, Tommaso's handle on the boards is Tommaso the Timid."

"Not Tommy Timid?"

"That's the interesting part, Moodrow. A lot of the sexual freaks who work out on bulletin boards are deep in the closet. They don't want *anybody* to know who they are. Tommaso, on the other hand, is begging to be discovered."

Moodrow smiled. "I take it you left some kind of a message for him on one of these bulletin boards." He waited for her nod, then said, "Before you show it to me—and you *will* show it to me— lemme tell you what I set up with Betty." He quickly outlined DHCR and Betty's strategy, adding, "It's a long shot, Gadd, but we'll see what happens. I should know one way or the other by tomorrow afternoon."

"Does this mean you're finally in?"

Moodrow wanted to pass the question off with a cynical comment, but her dead-serious expression made humor the least likely of all the possibilities.

"I'll answer that question when you answer this one: in for *what?*"

Moodrow's response being eminently reasonable, Gadd shrugged once, then rummaged in her purse, finally withdrawing a folded sheet of paper. "Knowing what a dirty old man you are," she declared, "I figured you'd wanna see this." She started to hand the paper over, then pulled it back, acknowledging his frown with a satisfied smile. "But first, let me tell you about the bulletin board itself. It's called The Slave School and it's operated by a dominatrix named Ingrid."

"Ingrid?" Moodrow interrupted. "Why not Brunnhilde?"

Gadd nodded agreement. "Believe it, Moodrow, subtlety is not their strong point. The graphics feature chained men in latex masks, women with Arnold Schwarzenegger biceps. Lots of degrading oral sex. That's why I wrote the message like I did. What I wanna do is draw Tommaso out of his shell and I'm not gonna do that if I sound like everybody else on the board."

She tossed the paper across the table and Moodrow, who had some familiarity with nasty letters, unfolded the single page carefully, then put on his reading glasses.

Tommaso: I do not speak of leather, chains, latex, or the whip. No more than a sculptor speaks of chisel and hammer. I speak of the perfect serenity that flows from perfect obedience. Grace is not to be found in the masturbatory fantasies of the amateur, but in the minute-to-minute, day-to-day obedience of the true slave. Let discipline burn away the layers of disobedience. Let discipline dissolve the unruly will. Let absolute obedience, ruthlessly imposed from without, lead to serenity, ruthlessly imposed from within.

Amazing Grace

"Nice work, Gadd. Very tasteful." Moodrow waved the letter. "But how do you know it'll work?"

"I don't," Gadd admitted. "No more than I know what really motivates jerks who like to be whipped." She leaned forward and tapped the back of Moodrow's hand. "Truth, Moodrow, I don't have any idea why I want to contact Tommaso, what I'll do if he takes the bait."

Moodrow looked down at her fingers. He was feeling slightly drunk, ready to lie down again. "If we get nowhere, if a week goes by and Carmine is arrested, Sappone taken off the street, are you gonna be able to deal with it?"

Gadd looked at him steadily for a moment, her face relaxed, features smooth. Finally, she allowed herself a thin smile. "Are you?" she asked.

Moodrow, as he walked east on Fourth Street toward his own apartment, half expected to find another reporter sitting on the stoop in front of his building. Instead, he found Agent Karl Holtzmann (with two *n*s) sitting in a Ford sedan. Moodrow pulled himself up short, checked for a surge of anger the way he might check for wounds after a shoot-out, found himself calm if not actually amused.

"Wait right there," Holtzmann called. He pushed the door open, stepped onto the hot asphalt.

"Jesus," Moodrow said, "I'm glad you shouted. I would'a never noticed you if you hadn't."

Holtzmann took his time crossing the street. His gait was stiff, his back ramrod straight, his arms nearly motionless at his side. He didn't stop until he and Moodrow were an arm's length apart.

"We need to talk, mister. You don't understand what you're doing."

"Does that mean you're gonna tell me?"

The agent, despite his macho posturing, was a head shorter and a hundred pounds lighter than Moodrow, a fact not lost on either man.

"Do we have to do this out here on the street?"

"Yes, we do, Karl."

Holtzmann flinched at the sound of his name, then drew himself up. "I'm going to appeal to your conscience, Moodrow. You were a cop for thirty-five years, a detective for thirty. Try to imagine your own reaction if someone from the outside thrust themselves into the middle of your investigation."

"*Thrust* themselves? Gimme a fucking break."

Moodrow, who'd been watching for tails, was almost certain that he hadn't been followed. He wasn't sure about Ginny Gadd, though. Despite her reassurances earlier in the afternoon, it was quite possible, given her lack of experience, that her theft of the tape had been observed. It would depend on how many agents were available to Holtzmann.

"This warning is your 'break,' Moodrow. The next step is obstruction of justice."

"For doing exactly what?"

"For exactly obstructing justice." Holtzmann's tight, prim mouth drew up at the corners. "We're going to prosecute. Remember, you're nothing more than a private citizen. You no longer carry a badge. If you get in our way, you'll be crushed, like any other civilian."

The two men stood silently for a moment, until Moodrow decided it was time to go upstairs, lie down, catch a quick nap before Betty came over.

"Ya know something, Karl? It seems to me like it's you feds obstructing justice. I mean considering that half the goddamned NYPD's looking for Jilly Sappone and you're protecting him." Moodrow noted Holtzmann's left eye jerk slightly. The man tried to cover it by looking over his shoulder, but it was much too late. "Letting him out of prison," he continued, "now that was a judgment call. Sure, the prison shrinks said Jilly was crazy and violent, but that didn't mean he was gonna go out and kill a child. Not for sure. But now that the child is *actually* dead, *actually* buried, the excuses won't wash. Not with the media. Not with, say, Mike Wallace on *60 Minutes*." Moodrow slapped his forehead. "Jesus, they'll be like sharks at a feeding frenzy. Especially if your bosses in Washington don't know what you're doing."

Holtzmann, instead of showing fear, drew up his shoulders and bunched his fists. He was accustomed to command, simply couldn't play the role of the beggar even though it was obviously required. Still, he wasn't so angry that he seriously considered an attack on the giant in front of him.

"You can't go to the media," he sputtered, the words ringing hollow even in his own ears.

"What are you gonna do, kill me?" Moodrow stepped back onto his stoop, waited for a response. "Tell ya what, Holtzmann with two *ns*," he finally said, "why don't you go back to your keepers, try to come up with a strategy in line with our relative positions. I might be willing to bend a little here. For, say, a real wet blow job."

FOURTEEN

When Moodrow awakened, he was literally without breath. His chest and lungs refused to expand, refused to follow the demands of his panicky brain. He sat straight up, his torso jerking to attention like a spring-loaded knife blade. The 3 AM darkness confused him, left him suspended, without time or place. He heard Betty, saw her kneeling in front of him, but neither recognized her nor understood the words she shouted in his face. Finally, in desperation, he sipped at the air through pursed lips, continuing doggedly until his chest finally opened and he began to gasp like a half-drowned swimmer dragged up through a ragged surf.

"Stanley, wake up. Wake up."

Betty was punching him in the chest. Her face was contorted, her mouth forming a nearly perfect circle around her small even teeth. Moodrow stared at her for a moment, then pulled her into his arms.

"Jesus," he hissed. "I couldn't breathe."

"You scared the crap out of me."

Moodrow continued to gulp air, as if afraid that any pause in the rhythm would return him to paralysis.

"I was dreaming," he announced, "about . . . that night. Sort of."

Betty sat back on her heels, pushed an unruly lock of hair out of her eyes. "You want to tell me about it?" She watched him get up and walk to the window. He was wearing his usual sleeping outfit, a pair of boxer shorts and a T-shirt. The T-shirt, soaked with sweat, was pasted to the broad muscles of his back.

"It's already vague." He turned to face her. "Jilly Sappone was there, standing up high, like on the edge of a roof or a mountain, holding that white blanket with . . . with something inside it. He was staring at me, laughing, and I didn't know what to do. I tried to plead with him, but it only made him angry. He said, 'You stupid son of a bitch, it's just a fucking *package*.' "

"It'll fade, Stanley." She felt the cliché even as she mouthed it. Nevertheless, she repeated herself. "Given time, it'll fade."

"Yeah, that's the worst of it. Time will heal the wound. Heal it by reducing Theresa Kalkadonis to an official FBI statistic. By dropping me, Ann Kalkadonis, Ginny Gadd, and Jilly Sappone into our graves. It's already turned the trick for Jackson-Davis Wescott."

Abner Kirkwood and Karl Holtzmann stood nearly hip to hip beneath an oversize umbrella. They were in Battery Park, peering out through a steady downpour at the Staten Island Ferry. Silently, as if by agreement, they watched the ship retreat into the gray, slanting rain, Kirkwood thinking it was a perfect movie image, the two of them in their Burberry trench coats discussing the crime of murder.

It was a simple crime, he decided. A single act, done and over with; not like drug dealing with its network of smugglers and middlemen, or the elaborate scams of corporate sharks.

Finally, he said, "The ex-cop was completely defiant?" One more nail in Jilly Sappone's coffin as far as Abner Kirkwood was concerned.

"Accused me . . . No, he accused *us*, Abner. Accused us of protecting Sappone. Threatened to go to the media."

"Well, he's right, Karl. We *are* protecting Jilly Sappone." Kirkwood took the agent's arm, pulled him in a little closer. "But we had a couple of breaks last night. Things may not be as bad as they look. At least the heat's off."

The last remark needed no explanation. In the early morning hours, somebody had firebombed a low-end nursing home in the Castle Hill section of the Bronx. Eleven different camera crews, including CNN's, had gotten the whole thing, moaning survivors hustled into blocky EMS ambulances, body bags taking a more leisurely voyage into the back of a morgue wagon. The death count, at eight o'clock in the morning, stood at ten and was expected to rise, nine of the victims being Puerto Rican or black. Best of all, the arsonist was still at large and there were serious questions about the nursing home itself. The sprinklers, it seemed, despite a recent Fire Department inspection, had failed to work.

"I spoke to the Suffolk County District Attorney last night," Kirkwood went on. "Man named Robert Cortese."

Holtzmann snorted, rolled his eyes. "Not another one."

"Another what?"

"Another guinea is what. When you're up to your ass in alligators, you don't call in a crocodile."

Kirkwood thought of his childhood buddies. Without exception, they'd been Italian, Jewish, or Irish. "I'm gonna let that one go, Karl, because it's irrelevant here. The call was pro forma." He watched the rain splash onto the dull gray surface of the Hudson River, wished he was somewhere else, maybe a mile north in that ugly frame house New Yorkers called City Hall. Having breakfast with old Rudy. "Anyway, Cortese told me some very interesting things. First, they finally traced the house Jilly was living in to Carlo Sappone. We already knew that, of course, and Carlo has no connection to the Agency, so it's not a problem for us."

"Always expected them to find Carlo in there somewhere," Holtzmann said. "Had to happen."

"Cortese told me a very interesting story. On the morning after the incident, Carlo Sappone was found in a Catholic shrine called Our Lady of Long Island. He was chained to a tree, Karl." Kirkwood raised his hand. "Don't interrupt. We've been asking ourselves how Gadd and Moodrow found Jilly Sappone's house and now we know. Unfortunately, by the time the Suffolk cops put it together, Carlo had moved out of his own home. They're looking for him, naturally, but I doubt that he'll testify against Moodrow, who must have been the muscle, even if they find him. Stanley Moodrow and Guinevere Gadd don't know that, of course, and I want you to use it against them. Tell them you know where Carlo's holed up, that you might be willing to protect Carlo if he testifies."

Holtzmann waited until he was sure his boss was finished. "Got the picture," he finally said.

"Good. Now tell me about Ewing."

"He's coming along, Abner. Hates Jilly Sappone."

"Have you spoken to him?"

"Not yet. Not until we're sure. Ewing has his suspicions, naturally. One man to guard a dangerous prisoner." Holtzmann shook his head. "Definite procedural violation."

In the silence that followed the agent's last remark, the wind picked up, first driving the rain beneath Kirkwood's umbrella, then flipping the umbrella inside out. Kirkwood, instantly soaked, turned back toward the Bureau car parked fifty yards away, but Holtzmann grabbed his arm, spinning him around.

"Don't tell him anything, Abner."

"Pardon?" Kirkwood's drenched suit had cost nearly a thousand dollars and he was having a hard time driving that particular fact out of his mind.

"Don't speak to Bob Ewing," Holtzmann said patiently. A steady stream of water ran along his nose and down over the corners of his mouth. "When the time comes, one or both of us will drive out there and handle Mister Sappone. Let Agent Bob deal with it after the fact."

The more Jilly Sappone evaluated his prison, the more convinced he became that it was never designed to be a prison. First thing, it had real furniture, not slabs of iron or steel bolted into a concrete floor, and an air conditioner set into the wall. Furniture could be broken up, the pieces shaped into weapons, which was why Agent Ewing stayed on his side of the bars. Second thing, the windows had some kind of bullet-proof plastic instead of glass, but the plastic was set into ordinary wood frames and not into the walls. It was designed for protection, not confinement. Give him five minutes alone and he'd be out in the shrubbery. Third, and best, there were no walls around the walls. Once you got out of that little apartment, you were gone.

There was still the steel door, of course, the door between his cell and the rest of the house. Jilly figured the door most likely made Agent Ewing feel safe, that's what it was there for. Meanwhile, the door was gonna be Agent Ewing's immediate cause of death.

The phone rang just as he was about to get off his stoned-lazy ass and go to work. Jilly stepped over to the door and watched Agent Ewing emerge from the kitchen, pick up the receiver, say, "Hello."

"That for me?" Jilly called. "Is that my loved one?"

Ewing responded by carrying the telephone across the room. He dropped it on the shelf, then turned away.

"You don't gotta hurry, Agent Ewing," Jilly called merrily. "I'll wait until you get the earphones on." He watched Ewing until the kitchen door closed behind the agent, then picked up the receiver.

"Yeah."

"Jilly, how you doin'?"

"Great, Aunt Josie. Considering they got me back in prison."

"No complaints. You don't know what it's like to suffer."

Jilly groaned. If he didn't shut her up, she'd run through every goddamned thing Carmine ever did to her, finish with her fucking *jetatura*.

"I'm not complaining," he said quickly. "Agent Ewing takes good care of me. Every night, after I shut the lights off, he tucks me into bed. Sometimes, Aunt Josie, sometimes he stays under the covers for a long, long time."

Josie grunted. "Hey, *strunza*, stop with the games," she ordered. "You gonna stay four more days. Then we go in the program. I'm gonna make 'em send us to Hawaii."

She hung up before Jilly could say good-bye. A minute later, Ewing crossed the room.

"Hey, look, Agent Ewing, I was only kiddin' around," Jilly said. He was still holding the telephone. "I mean about you tuckin' me in at night. You're much too chickenshit to open that door."

"Put the telephone down." Ewing's jaw was clenched. His lips barely moved.

Jilly dropped the phone, raised a hand to his mouth. "Jesus Christ, he *is* tough."

As Ewing picked up the phone with his right hand, he touched

the tight network of steel bars with his left. The gesture was habit-
ual, the agent doing it each time he approached the door. Jilly,
though he noted the touch with great satisfaction, kept his eyes focused on Ewing's. When the time came, he was going to rely on that
hand.

Meanwhile, he had work to do. Not much work, but work
nonetheless. He strode into his bathroom, squeezed a dab of toothpaste onto his finger, stepped onto the rim of the toilet, covered the
lens of the pinhole camera behind the wall. Then, ignoring Agent
Ewing's shout, he walked into the larger room and did the same
thing to a second camera, this one concealed in a clock.

"What do you think you're doing? What, you goddamned son of
a bitch?"

"Sticks and stones, Agent Ewing." Jilly stepped up to the barred
door.

"I want you to clean those cameras."

"Why? So you can see me naked? Hey, Agent Ewing, you wanna
see me naked, you don't have to peep through a camera. Come inside with me." Sappone licked his lips, blew Ewing a kiss. "I wanna
make you my sweet honey, Agent Ewing. I wanna run my fingers
through that crew cut, lick the sweat off the back of your neck, push
your head down where it belongs."

Without warning, Jilly slammed the heel of his hand into the bars
on the door. The sudden movement, the sharp crack as the door rattled on its hinges, sent Agent Ewing stumbling backward. He stared
at Jilly Sappone as if seeing him for the first time.

"My sweet honey," Sappone screamed. He wrapped his fingers
around the bars, yanked at them until the veins in his throat stood
out like swollen blue worms. All the while screaming, "My sweet
honey. My sweet, sweet, sweet fucking honey."

"I don't want to do a goddamned thing," Moodrow told Betty
over breakfast. "Even if I could think of *what* to do, I wouldn't
wanna do it. And I can't think of anything, Betty." He shook his head
decisively, as if determined to convince himself. "Personally captur-
ing Jilly Sappone, even if I could bring it off, would be nothing more

than an ego trip. You could believe me when I say I'm not exaggerating here."

The bell in the lobby sounded before Betty could frame a response. Three minutes later, Leonora Higgins walked into the room and stripped off her dripping raincoat.

"I ran Josie Rizzo's name through the DHCR computer," she said, accepting a cup of coffee. "But before I give you the result, I need to know exactly what you plan to do."

Moodrow groaned, nearly dropped the coffeepot.

"About what?"

"About Theresa Kalkadonis." Leonora was blunt, as always.

"If you were in my position," he said after a moment, "what would you do?"

"Nothing, Stanley, because there's nothing to be done."

Leonora was wearing a navy blue suit over a white blouse. Moodrow recognized the outfit as her courtroom costume, her take-no-prisoners uniform. He smiled, trying to disarm her.

"My point exactly."

"In that case, Stanley," Leonora tapped the edge of the table with a crimson fingernail, "maybe I should call Jim Tilley, hand the information over to the police."

Moodrow plopped himself down into a chair on the opposite side of the table. He ran his fingers through his close-cropped hair, then dropped his hand to his lap. "I was hoping you wouldn't get a hit," he said.

"That doesn't answer the question." She leaned forward, glanced at Betty. "Look, I got a call yesterday from D.E. Brecker, the DA's personal aide. He wasn't angry, Stanley, didn't order me around. No, what he did was suggest, since you and I are known to be friends, that I advise you of the fact that you're interfering with an ongoing Major Cases' investigation."

"How?" Moodrow kept the question simple. Not that he had any real hope of a simple answer.

"Brecker didn't tell me that."

"Why am I not surprised? Look, I had a visit from the FBI last night. You remember Agent Holtzmann with two *ns*? Well, Agent Holtzmann with two *ns* told me the same thing you're telling me now. Meanwhile, I'd bet my left hand against a quarter the scumbag's protecting Jilly Sappone."

"I wouldn't take the bet, Stanley. Mainly, because I don't need an extra left hand." Leonora's mouth opened into a warm, genuine smile. She recited an address, 618 West Ninetieth Street, then added, "You guys see the paper today? Watch the news?"

"No," Betty replied, "we just got up."

"It must be nice to be part of the leisure crowd." Leonora tossed the *New York Post* across the table. "Big fire in the Bronx last night. Enough bodies to draw the vultures away from Jilly Sappone, drive the investigation back to page twenty-three. Whatta you bet, come tomorrow, it's not in the paper at all?"

Moodrow hesitated for a fraction of a second. "That leaves the feds in the clear. If the press isn't looking, they can do whatever they want."

"Not quite, Stanley." Betty opened the refrigerator, took out three navel oranges, began to cut them into quarters. "Even if the vultures go somewhere else for their daily dose of carrion, there's still you and Ginny Gadd to worry about. You guys would be the only remaining witnesses."

FIFTEEN

Gadd began to complain before she was inside Moodrow's door. "I hope you had a better morning than I did," she announced as she pulled off her Gore-Tex jacket and shook it out in the hallway. "Because mine has been an absolute nightmare. Jesus, I hate the rain. I hate the rain and I hate the FBI." She stopped suddenly, dropped her jacket into Moodrow's waiting hand. "I think I've found out what it's like to be a criminal. At least, part of it. Swear to God, Moodrow, I wanted to shoot that fed in the worst way."

Moodrow stepped aside to let her pass into the apartment, then hung her jacket on a hook attached to his closet door. "Why didn't you?"

"Fear of incarceration," she answered promptly. "Hi, Betty. You're just the person I'm looking for."

The two women exchanged a quick hug, then Gadd took off for the bathroom. Betty, after a quick shake of her head, poured out three mugs of coffee, while Moodrow, who found that he couldn't stop grinning, set milk, sugar, and a plate of oozing jelly doughnuts on the kitchen table. When Gadd reappeared a few minutes later, she bit into a doughnut, sipped at the steaming coffee, then wiped her mouth with a paper napkin. She was about to have a second go at the doughnut when Moodrow cleared his throat.

"That was a grand entrance," he declared. "But it needs a punch line."

Gadd held the doughnut in front of her mouth long enough to

declare, "Well, the shit's hit the fan, now. Agent Holtzmann caught me staking out the tape box." Then she bit into the doughnut, chewed thoughtfully for a moment. "Actually, 'caught' may not be the right word. I think the bastard was following me."

"And you didn't spot him?"

"It was raining, Moodrow, raining hard." She waved the question away. "And maybe he was only making a pickup. Maybe I'm being too paranoid. Either way, that tape I copied yesterday is the first, last, and only."

"Did he accuse you directly?" Betty asked. Her sharp black eyes were glittering. "Of stealing the tape?"

"Yes."

Gadd shook her head. "Holtzmann didn't mention the tape at all, though he had to know what I was doing. Instead, he asked me about an old friend of ours, Carlo Sappone."

"Well, the chickens are coming home." Betty folded her hands and laid them on the table. "Did he threaten you?"

"Absolutely. The man was anything but subtle. He told me that if I didn't lay off, he'd offer to protect Carlo in return for his testimony."

"Protect Carlo from whom?" Betty asked.

"He didn't actually say, but I'm assuming Carmine Stettecase." Gadd looked over at Moodrow. "I don't think it matters all that much."

"You're right. It doesn't." Betty took a breath. "What did you tell him, Ginny? How did you respond?" Her calm tone masked a lawyer's concern for an unpredictable client.

"I told him if he didn't take a hike, I'd get my partner to slap him around."

Moodrow started to laugh, then caught a glimpse of Betty's stern expression and covered his mouth with his hand.

"Maybe I'll do that," he mused. "Take his badge and his gun and shove them up his ass." He looked directly into Betty's eyes. "Because this prick, this Holtzmann with two *ns*, is getting me more and more pissed off as time goes on."

"Stanley, look . . ."

"I don't *want* to look, Betty. This mutt is responsible for getting

Sappone out of prison. I know he's protecting Sappone even as we speak. Now, he threatens to put me and Gadd in jail for the crime of trying to save a child's life. I swear to Christ, if I didn't know better, I'd say this is one dog that needs a serious beating."

Gadd raised her mug. "I'll drink to that."

After a brief hesitation, Betty raised her own mug and drank. "Just keep one thing in mind, boys and girls, needing and receiving are two different sides of the coin. The risks, here, are genuine." She waited long enough for the message to sink in, then continued. "Now, Ginny, what did you *really* tell the agent?"

"I said, 'Message received,' then walked away. Call it a Mexican standoff."

Moodrow shook his head. "He was bluffing you, Gadd. If Holtzmann had Carlo in his pocket, he would have dragged you down to FBI headquarters, made a big production out of it. What I think is that he's scared, really scared. Remember, he could have waited for you to go into the box, then arrested you."

"Why didn't he?" Betty asked.

"Because," Gadd declared, "we, meaning Moodrow and myself, are holding all the cards. Maybe a week from now, the day after they takes Carmine, it'll be different." She turned to Moodrow. "We get a hit on that housing computer?"

"As a matter of fact," Moodrow announced, "they, meaning Betty and an ex–FBI agent named Leonora Higgins, did. An apartment on West Ninetieth Street leased to Ms. Josefina Rizzo."

Gadd jerked up straight. "Then why are we sitting around with jelly on our chins?"

"Because there's no rush," Moodrow declared. "Jilly Sappone's not there. He *couldn't* be."

"You're sure about that?"

Moodrow giggled. "Not so sure that I plan to go unarmed," he admitted.

It took Moodrow and Gadd more than an hour to cover the five miles between Moodrow's Lower East Side apartment and West Ninetieth Street. The Chevrolet, slow to start under the best of conditions, had gone through its own battery and most of a nearby Pontiac's before it finally coughed its way to life. A grateful Moodrow had given the lot attendant, Walberto, a ten-dollar bill, then run head-on into an FDR Drive packed with traffic. By that time, both he and Gadd had taken the hint. New York, a city of endless frustration under the best of circumstances, was about to snatch another piece of their collective adrenals.

"Think of it as a test." Moodrow had gestured at the surrounding traffic. "All these people trapped behind their windshield wipers. Peering out through the grease smears."

"A test of what?"

"Well, when I was in Catholic School the nuns used to tell us that calamity and suffering, especially when they happen to good people, are God's way of testing the faithful." He paused to flip on the heater, turn it to defrost in an effort to clear the foggy windows. "See, what I was thinking was maybe there's a junior-apprentice god in charge of New York. Maybe the frustration is a way of testing our worthiness to live here. I mean, let's face it, Gadd, everybody wants to take a bite out of the Big Apple. The only problem is that most of the time it's the Big Apple taking a bite out of us. You can't tell me it doesn't need theological justification."

In an effort to let the heat out, Gadd rolled down her window slightly, thereby letting in the rain. "Fine," she said, adjusting the hood of her jacket to cover the side of her face, "but what I need to know is how you *pass* the test?"

Moodrow slapped the steering wheel as a Federal Express delivery van cut in front of him. "You pass by taking the bullshit." He turned to her. "I'm serious, Gadd. If you stay, you pass."

They were on Forty-second Street, inching their way crosstown along with much of the FDR Drive traffic, making a few car lengths on each green light. The rain drummed on the roof and steamed on the hood of their car, raising a filmy gray curtain between their little capsule and all the capsules around them. The office towers lining both sides of Forty-second Street rose into the mist, their rooflines disappearing altogether. Even the textured, salmon pink brick of the old GE Building loomed cold and gray, its sharp edges indistinct, reduced to simple, overwhelming mass.

Once they passed Lexington Avenue, Moodrow, knowing there were no left turns between Lexington and Ninth Avenue on the west side, cut into the left lane with every intention of staying put. As traffic strategies go, it was decent enough. Or it would have been if the cabbies weren't jammed up in front of Grand Central Station and the Hyatt Hotel, forcing every other vehicle, including the buses, to pull off the same maneuver.

"You see that guy?" Gadd pointed to a thoroughly enraged, thoroughly soaked traffic agent. He was waving a soggy ticket book at an indifferent cabdriver.

"Yeah, I see him."

"That's how you survive in New York."

"By screaming and shouting?"

"No, by seeing how bad off the other guy is."

Moodrow nodded agreement, muttered, "Thank God for the homeless."

The traffic didn't break up until they turned north on Tenth Avenue, some forty minutes later. It was only then, when the pressure had lifted, that Moodrow introduced a topic of conversation sure to be painful.

"What I wanna do," he said evenly, "is throw back whatever we find up there to Jim Tilley and Leonora Higgins, let them run it back to the detectives and the DA's office."

His statement produced the expected explosion. Gadd turned to him, her eyes narrowed, nostrils flared. "You telling me you wanna cover your ass?"

"It's partly that."

"Partly?"

"Yeah, and it's partly the fact that I was a cop for thirty-five years. The job's not the enemy here."

"Is there any other *partly*?" Her voice was sharp, her sarcasm more than evident. "Before I rip the ears off your skull."

Moodrow looked at her for a minute, a smile playing at the edges of his mouth. He tried to remember the last time he'd liked someone as much as he liked Ginny Gadd, finally decided that only Jim Tilley could wear those shoes.

"There may come a time," he patiently explained, "when we need the job for some favor. It's gonna be a lot easier to get that favor if the cops are in our debt." He held up a finger. "Think about this: If Sappone isn't there, what we're giving them costs us exactly nothing. Meanwhile, if we step aside, don't try to take credit, it's a gold star for the dicks assigned to the case. One thing cops do is pay off on their markers."

Gadd nodded reluctant agreement. "Yeah," she admitted, "that part of it is true enough. But if we find something in the apartment, something that leads to Jilly Sappone, all bets are off. I want Sappone for myself."

Moodrow let it go at that. The traffic was moving quickly now, vehicles darting left and right like kids in a lunchtime playground. Just ahead, on the east side of the avenue, Lincoln Center, its milky stonework dulled by the continuing rain, showed its rear end to a low-rise housing project across the street, the juxtaposition defining the essential New York dichotomy.

"Time to get ready," he muttered.

"Say that again?"

"I don't think there's one chance in a thousand that Sappone's in that apartment. Meanwhile, if I was squeezing any harder, the edges of my asshole'd weld themselves together."

Gadd looked at him for a moment before replying. "Yeah, I hear ya, Moodrow." She took her S&W out of her purse, checked the cylinder, then slid it beneath her jacket. " 'Be prepared,' right."

"That's exactly what I had in mind." Moodrow shifted his weight to one side and withdrew a small automatic from his coat pocket. The butt, trigger guard, and most of the barrel were covered with surgical tape. "Look," he said, "if we do run into Sappone, there's a chance . . ." He took a breath, started over. "We're not gonna have a lotta time to think it out. It could be we'll misinterpret Sappone's motives, do something stupid. If that should happen, I'm gonna put this piece on the floor next to his hand, give the cops an excuse to cut us some slack. Or maybe a lawyer an excuse to give to a jury."

Ten minutes later, Moodrow and Gadd were parked in front of the Monroe, a small, decrepit hotel, directly across the street from the ancient tenement that housed Jilly Sappone's apartment. The Monroe, like a number of similar hotels on the northern end of the Upper West Side, was an SRO, a designation that allowed the city to pack it with homeless men. SRO stood for single room occupancy, a term which, some years before, had replaced the word "flophouse."

Moodrow shut the engine down, put the key in his pocket. He was about to say something to Gadd, something about not knowing what to do next, when a security guard, tattered umbrella in hand, came out of the hotel and tapped at Gadd's window.

"This here is a hotel loading zone," he said after Gadd rolled down the window. "Y'all ain't supposed to park here." He squatted down, stared at Moodrow's chiseled-stone expression for a few seconds, then added, "Unless y'all are cops."

"We're sorta like cops," Gadd replied, "like the Monroe is sorta like a hotel." She smiled brightly and held up a ten-dollar bill. "Being as there's a bad element on this block, I was hoping you could watch the car for a little while. That and help us out with some information."

The guard took the ten, put it in his shirt pocket, said, "Now I'm lookin' after the car."

Gadd came up with another ten, watched it go the way of the first. "That building across the street, they got a super in there?"

"Yeah, Polack name of Gregory. Lives in the basement. You hurry, you can catch him sober. The boy's a friend of mine and I know he don't drink much before noon."

"That's nice to hear. You think you might wanna do your friend a favor, knock on his door, get him to come out to the car? I say it's a favor, because we're gonna take care of him."

The guard thought it over for a minute, then shook his head. "I ain't sposed to leave the hotel. My boss wouldn't like it. Probly give me hell."

"Yeah, but when was the last time your boss paid you twenty bucks for ten minutes work?"

"There is that, now," the man admitted. "There is that."

Once he'd made up his mind, the security guard wasted no time. He trotted across the street, pulled open the apparently unlocked door, and disappeared inside. A few minutes later, he emerged with a short, squat balding man in tow. The man, lacking umbrella and coat, jumped into the backseat without any preliminary conversation.

"You're Gregory?" Moodrow turned in the seat, extending his hand. "My name's Moodrow."

"Name is Gregory," the man admitted, giving Moodrow's hand a cautious shake.

"We're interested in a pair of tenants, Gregory. You think you could help us out?" Moodrow held up a twenty, but didn't offer it.

"That is depending on who is tenants. Gregory does not tell tales on his friends."

Moodrow looked at Gadd, tried to warn her with his eyes. In his experience, white immigrants, especially those from Eastern Europe, hated to be questioned by female cops.

"Fair enough, Gregory. I wouldn't rat on my friends either." He finally passed over the twenty. "The two men I'm looking for live in Apartment 3C. They moved into the building a short time ago."

"Gone, now." The super, a triumphant gleam rising into his tiny, ice blue eyes, pocketed the twenty. "I have not seen them. . . ." He ticked the days off on the fingers of his left hand. "Three days I have not seen them. This morning when I mop hall, no sound is in the apartment."

"Are they coming back?"

Gregory shrugged. "Rent is paid, but they no tell me nothing."

"I guess they wouldn't," Moodrow admitted.

"Tenants talk to super about leaky faucets, not traveling plans." He started to open the door, then jerked to a stop when Moodrow held up another bill, this one a fifty. "One more thing I can do for you?" he asked.

"You got a key for that apartment?"

Gregory's mouth said, "For this I lose job," but his eyes never left the greenback in Moodrow's hand.

"Fifteen minutes, Gregory. We're not gonna take anything. We just wanna have a look around. If you want, you can stay with us the whole time."

"You no take nothing?"

"Nothing."

"What happen if tenants come back?"

"Well, Gregory, if that should happen, I advise you to locate the nearest closet and get your ass inside."

SIXTEEN

"Flats are furnished," Gregory explained as he led the way up to Jilly Sappone's third-floor apartment. "Tenants are mostly students from University of Columbia. This is why I remember new tenants even if I see only them one time when they are moving in. I think students these are not; these are trouble. Then they are not showing themselves after the moving, but I hear TV set made very, very loud when I sweep. *Sesame Street* and the Barney dinosaur." He stopped, turned, patted his chest proudly. "Every single day I sweep floors. Twice times each week is mopping."

Though the paint on the walls was faded, the finish on the wooden banister chipped and darkened by sweat, the stairs were clean, the hallways free of graffiti. Moodrow, who felt some comment was in order, nodded thoughtfully, said, "Sounds like you own the place."

The super responded with a sad shake of the head. "Some time," he announced before turning away, "it will be."

They resumed their journey in silence. Moodrow, as they trudged upward, felt his gut tighten, the sensation familiar though not terribly pronounced. Like any other cop, he'd prowled tenement stairways and project hallways on a daily basis. No matter how benign his mission, he'd always felt like an intruder, like the natives might well decide to drive him off.

He turned to Gadd, started to remind her to be careful, but she'd already taken the S&W from her holster. As he watched, she slipped it into her jacket before tossing him a smile and a small shrug.

"Boy Scouts," she muttered.

"Yeah, Be Prepared." He unbuttoned his trench coat, freed his own revolver, was about to dump it into his pocket when Gregory stopped again.

"Door is open," he announced. "Very strange. Tenants must to be returned."

Moodrow, even as the hairs on the back of his neck rose to full alert, covered Gregory's mouth with his left hand and literally pulled the man down the stairs and out of sight. Gadd, .38 in hand, kept her eyes on the open door as she backed her way down. When all three were out of sight on the second-floor landing, Moodrow spoke directly to the super.

"Gregory," he whispered, "it's time for you to go back to your apartment and call the cops."

The super looked up at Moodrow through pleading, hangdog eyes. "Please," he said, "my building." His gaze traveled to the revolver in Gadd's hand. "No to hurt my building please."

Gadd shook her head. "Forget the goddamned building. Call 911, tell 'em you've got a burglary in progress."

Gregory took a hesitant step, paused momentarily, then, his mind apparently made up, took the stairs two at a time. Gadd waited until he was out of sight before turning to Moodrow.

"It's not Sappone," she announced. "The lock's been jimmied."

"You're sure about that?"

"The frame's splintered." She was about to add, *didn't you notice?*, then changed her mind. "Maybe the FBI beat us to the punch."

"And maybe Sappone lost his key."

Gadd smiled. "One way to find out, Moodrow." Her back pressed to the wall, she began to climb the stairs, pausing momentarily when they were high enough to see the apartment. As advertised, the door frame had been severely damaged.

From that point on, they did it by the book. Moodrow, pistol extended, covered Gadd's quick, quiet move to within a foot of the doorway, then Gadd returned the favor. She kept the two-inch barrel of her .38 trained on a small circle in which she imagined Sappone's head might appear, while Moodrow half ran down the hallway and into the apartment. Once inside, Moodrow stepped to his right and let his eyes follow the sights on his ancient S&W as they swept the room. Gadd followed an instant later, dropping into a shooter's crouch as her revolver exactly and deliberately reversed the path of her partner's.

Their first reaction, so immediate it seemed almost collective, was anger. The figure wrestling with a television set bolted to a wooden table at the far end of the room could not be Jilly Sappone. Male or female (viewed from behind, neither Moodrow nor Gadd was entirely sure), the tangled filthy hair, black T-shirt, torn greasy pants, and ulcerated feet proclaimed the glories of terminal drug addiction. Sappone, or so it seemed to both of them, had escaped once again.

"What the *fuck* do you think you're doing?"

Gadd's shout was cop-tough. Moodrow, standing a few feet away, nodded once, then whispered, "Still got the knack," out of the corner of his mouth.

"Fear'll do that to you," Gadd returned. "Jog your memory."

Then the mutt turned far enough to show himself male, muttering, "What, what, what, what." Seemingly out of nowhere, a long, heavy-bladed hunting knife appeared in his trailing hand.

Moodrow looked into the man's swollen eyes, noting the red veins, as sharply defined as those of a movie vampire, and the wildly dilated pupils. No hope, he said to himself. I'm looking at a crack junkie who's been awake for days. He's not gonna just assume the position. Not without encouragement. Meanwhile, the cops are on the way and my partner's about to blow him into his next incarnation.

A series of individual facts jumped, one after another, into Moodrow's consciousness. He and Gadd had no badges, no right to detain or make an arrest, no right to be in Sappone's apartment, no right to be pointing their weapons at the creep on the other side of the room. Pulling the trigger, even if attacked, wouldn't change any of the above, wouldn't change them even a little bit, while actually provoking an attack (by, for instance, refusing the legal obligation to retreat) might be construed by a gung-ho prosecutor as out-and-out murder.

Moodrow took a deep breath, then stepped between his partner and the killer he couldn't kill. The man hissed like a trapped rat, then retreated to the wall.

"I'll cut you, motherfucker. I swear it; I'll cut your fucking head off." He pushed the knife farther out in front of him, held it with a shaking hand. The bunched ropey muscle in his neck jerked like a second pulse.

"For Christ's sake, Moodrow, get out of the way." Gadd's voice was choked, almost desperate.

Moodrow took another step forward. "If you shoot me, Gadd," he muttered, more to himself than to his partner, "I'm not gonna forget it." He grabbed a dining room chair with his right hand and swung it with all his strength in a shoulder-high arc. Fortunately, the chair was made of wood and not metal; the glue binding the legs and stretchers was dry and cracked. It splintered on contact, yet still retained enough force to drive a spectral-thin crack junkie into the wall, to severely lacerate the back of his scalp and the bridge of his nose while breaking every bone in his left wrist.

Jane Lublin, the detective, third grade, who took Moodrow's and Gadd's statements, was not unsympathetic. Sure, she explained to Moodrow, the perp was a lowlife sleazeball crack junkie. No doubt about it. And, also true, Moodrow's thirty-five years on the job entitled him to a certain measure of respect. Still, she didn't see how she could finish her paperwork unless somebody told her what they were doing in that apartment.

"See, it's like this," she insisted, "my boss, Lieutenant O'Bannion, is a real tight ass. 'Dot 'em and cross 'em'—that's what he said when the brass sent him up here to whip us into shape after the scandals last year." She leaned across the desk, spoke directly to Ginny Gadd. "I'm sure you can understand my position, Ms. Gadd. Even if I was to let you walk, it wouldn't do you any good because I'd just have to go out and find you again. Meanwhile, the lou would fry my ass. Now, if you want a lawyer . . ."

Neither Moodrow nor Gadd wanted a lawyer. No, what they wanted to do was get the bullshit over with. Unfortunately, Gadd's mention of Jilly Sappone's name produced the opposite result. They were consigned to a bench at the back of the squad room, told to remain there for the duration.

"You try to take a hike," Lublin explained, "I'm gonna put the both of you in cuffs and subject you to a strip search. You think I'm kidding, make your move."

Three hours and a dozen sympathetic shrugs later, a still-cheerful Detective Lublin escorted them to Lieutenant O'Bannion's office.

"I dare not cross this threshold." She pushed the door open, glanced inside, then flinched. "I didn't know you were so popular. Good luck."

Moodrow stepped aside to let his partner go first. "Tell me something, Gadd," he whispered as she went by, "would you be really pissed if I offered to testify against you in a court of law?"

Gadd stepped inside the room without responding. She took a quick look around before focusing on the uniformed officer seated behind the desk. The small office, a cubicle, really, matched her expectations nicely. The furniture was old and clean, the floor tiles faded and polished. Neatly arranged files covered every inch of the desktop. Various department directives, memos from above, surrounded a worn duty chart, a frame within a frame.

The room, she decided, neatly fit the personality Jane Lublin had ascribed to Lieutenant O'Bannion. It demonstrated a deeply held need to make order out of chaos, to jam the twenty-five thousand half-crazy cops who worked the streets into a mold designed by middle-aged deputy chiefs who never left their offices at One Police Plaza. Unfortunately, one of those same middle-aged, big-house silks, this one a full inspector, was sitting in Lieutenant O'Bannion's chair, his head tilted slightly back, his eyes focused somewhere above her head.

"Moodrow." The officer spoke without looking down.

"Inspector Cohen."

Gadd watched Moodrow cross the room and take the inspector's extended hand. For a second, she was sure he was going to kiss it, but then he turned slightly and she noted that his expression was wary.

"This is Inspector Cohen," he said, apparently assuming the inspector would know her name.

Gadd nodded, received an answering nod in return. The fact that Cohen and Moodrow knew each other meant that their options were about to be sharply defined. Settling back, she told herself to keep her big mouth shut, to let the scene develop.

The conversation began with a chat. Moodrow asked if the inspector had recently heard from somebody named Allen Epstein. Cohen replied that he'd visited Tampa in March, that Epstein and his wife were "hale and hearty." Epstein apparently had taken up the game of golf and was on the links three times a week. His unnamed wife, referred to as "the missus," drove a van for Meals-on-Wheels. It was, Cohen finally pronounced, "a retirement to envy."

An obligatory moment of silence was officially ended when Inspector Cohen cleared his throat and dropped his eyes to Moodrow's.

"You can't accuse me of not having respect, Moodrow. We came on the job within a couple of years of each other, stayed on the job when others fell away. I both understand and appreciate your term of service." He paused long enough to force a nod from Moodrow, then said, "And you, Moodrow, cannot claim ignorance of the job and how it works. I'm not going to ask you how you discovered the apartment, because I don't want to know, but, once discovered, you were obligated to hand the information over to the detectives working the case."

Cohen's voice was warm and soothing, the tone of a patient father instructing a wayward child, but the expression on his face remained fixed, as if he was posing for a formal portrait.

"Again, out of respect, let me tell you that we've assigned the task of finding Jilly Sappone to a ten-man unit working out of Major Cases. This in addition to showing his face at every roll call in all five boroughs. Obviously, we've failed to capture him, but that doesn't mean we aren't trying." Cohen took out an unfiltered Chesterfield, tapped it on the desktop before lighting it, then looked at Moodrow expectantly.

"Tell me something, Inspector," Moodrow said. "You think the FBI's protecting Jilly Sappone? Maybe in return for Josie Rizzo's cooperation in their investigation of Carmine Stettecase?"

"I really hope so," Cohen mused. "If it should ever come out . . ."

He chuckled manfully. "But I don't want to know it for a fact. Co-conspiracy plays no part in my career strategy." He flicked his ashes onto Lieutenant O'Bannion's desk, then fired off the salvo he'd come to deliver. "There are people out there who think I should arrest you, that you're indictable. And not only the FBI. I'm getting pressure from the mayor's office, too." His voice dropped a full octave as he leaned across the desk. "Believe me, it's not something I want to do. But it's not something I *won't* do, either." He straightened up, puffed contentedly on his cigarette. "You might want to know the task force ran down that car rented by Jilly Sappone, found it in a long-term parking garage on Ninety-sixth Street. Found an arsenal in the trunk as well. Even as we speak, the garage is under a twenty-four-hour stakeout. Sappone's apartment too, of course."

Cohen stood abruptly. He looked at Gadd for the first time. "Congratulations, Ms. Gadd, for getting to the parking garage first. The attendant, by the way, remembered you well. Something about your ears drew his attention." He crossed the room, opened the door, stepped through, then turned. "Do yourself a favor, Moodrow. Find some quiet bar, have a few drinks, ask yourself exactly what you're doing here. Me, I've examined your position closely and I can't see an upside anywhere."

SEVENTEEN

By the time Ginny Gadd reached her apartment-office, two hours and that "few drinks" later, she was ready to agree. Not that she was driven by fear. Inspector Cohen's threats meant less than nothing to her. After all, it wasn't like she was still a cop and at the mercy of the job. As a private citizen, she had rights. Like any other criminal.

That was the essential message she'd conveyed to Moodrow over her first Bloody Mary. He'd nodded wisely, then, concession by concession, forced her to admit they had no place to go, that the investigation was over, brought down by circumstances beyond their control. The job had Sappone's car and apartment under surveillance, she couldn't get back into the tape box, the deal was going down in less than seventy-two hours.

"Maybe," she'd suggested, "we should visit Holtzmann, threaten to warn Carmine. Maybe we can trade our silence for Jilly Sappone."

"And exactly what," Moodrow, the rim of his glass suspended just in front of his mouth, had replied, "would we do with him?"

"Administer a good caning. Before we throw him out the window."

Moodrow had managed a smile, then drained his glass. "I'm feeling pretty good, almost back to normal. Now I wanna put it behind me." He'd raised his eyes to meet hers. "Everything, Gadd, including Theresa. I'm an old fart and I need my rocking chair."

Gadd, surprised, had sipped at her Bloody Mary, taken a moment to chew on the small chunks of horseradish. "Which rocking chair, Moodrow," she'd finally asked, "the one you broke over that mutt's

289

head?" When he didn't respond immediately, she'd added, "Kind of mean-spirited for a senior, don't you think?"

"Actually, I was afraid you were gonna shoot him."

"And there's nothing the matter with your eyesight, either."

The conversation had jumped from topic to topic after that, from Moodrow's early days in the job, to computer investigation, to Moodrow's relationship with Betty, and Gadd's current lack of attachment. It had continued to jump during the short ride to Gadd's office on Sixth Avenue as each, there being no compelling reason for them to meet again, tried to frame a proper good-bye.

But the proper good-bye, whatever it was meant to be, was rendered meaningless by the scene in front of the porno shop below Gadd's office. Bishop Peter McLoughlin, a bullhorn to his lips, was leading several hundred of the faithful in prayer while a squad of bored cops lounged against blue police barricades and stared blankly at the forest of placards in front of them. On the opposite side of the avenue, several network camera crews, looking as bored as the cops, clustered around large vans and dreamed of police riots, bloody nuns, overturned cruisers. As it was, they'd be lucky to get fifteen seconds of airtime.

Moodrow, stymied by the traffic, pulled over to the curb a block away from the action. Gadd opened the door, then turned to face her soon-to-be ex-partner. "Moodrow," she said, "you were raised Catholic, right?"

"Yeah."

"Is the priest at the beginning or the end of that rosary he's holding?"

"He's just getting started."

She nodded, sighed, then stepped out of the car. "Whatta ya say, when they take Sappone, we get together for a drink?"

"Sounds good to me."

Gadd tapped the roof of the Chevy, then turned away. As she marched up the street, listening to the chant of the crowd, a wave of depression so purely physical it threatened to root her feet to the sidewalk rushed through her body to center itself in her heart. It wasn't the first time she'd been there and on some level she knew it would pass. Like a toothache or a broken arm.

She had to detour into the street to avoid the crowd, then duck between police barricades before she reached the safety of the stairwell leading to her office. The crowd booed and hissed as she approached the padlocked and shuttered bookstore, then cheered when she entered an adjoining door. As if their presence had directed her footsteps.

Enough with the self-pity, she told herself. It's time for a shower. A shower and a shave.

The light on her answering machine was blinking steadily, a fact she noted, but ignored. Across the room, the monitor on her ancient IBM, which was never shut down, glowed a pale, luminescent green. Gadd ignored the monitor, too, though she knew she'd finish her evening sitting in front of that screen, pounding away at the keyboard. Maybe she'd work up an invoice for the Haven Foundation, see if they'd like to pay for her failure. Or take a trip on the Internet, see if it was possible to be lonely in cyberspace.

She undressed quickly, tossing her clothes on the overstuffed chair in her bedroom, then stepped into the bathroom, turned on the light, and stared at her reflection in the mirror. Wondering why it always came to this, why every failure in a woman's life eventually worked its way down to physical attraction. She'd failed to save Theresa Kalkadonis, failed to capture Jilly Sappone, failed at her marriage, failed in her career. Now she had wrinkles at the corners of her eyes, frown lines at the corners of her mouth, ears like demitasse cups stood on edge.

And (of course and most especially) her breasts had surrendered another inch to the force of gravity.

"Fuck you," she said, stepping into the tiny shower stall and turning on the hot-water tap. The stream that hit her was lukewarm, the building's owner, Pietro Marizi, having, as usual, shut down the hot water when he closed his porno shop. Gadd's use of her office as a residence was a technical violation of the building code, an excuse for Marizi to pretend his tenant went home every night. By eleven, the water would be actually cold.

Gadd lathered herself carefully and thoroughly, covering herself, from her forehead to her toes with a lotion-fortified soap from the Body Shop, then slowly rinsed. Her hands moved across her skin automatically, leaving her mind free to ponder old losses, the pattern itself more ritual than thought. Her father came first. God, how she'd loved him, blindly defending him when he gambled away the rent money, the food money, looted the checking account for the twentieth time. Her reward, bestowed when she was ten years old, had been to arrive home from school one afternoon to find him gone, run out not only on his family, but also on a loan shark named Joe Alonzo who fully expected the family to honor its obligations.

Louise Gadd was still paying off fifteen years later, the year her daughter graduated from the police academy and canceled the debt with a single visit to Joe Alonzo's "office" in a Woodhaven diner. Instead of a weekly interest payment, Ginny had brought her badge and her gun and a pure determination that Joe Alonzo, ever the realist, had no difficulty recognizing.

"Let's call the debt paid off." He'd waved his hands magnanimously. "Let's say everybody did the right thing but your old man."

Unfortunately, Louise Gadd had long ago retreated into bitter resentment, had become a carping, supercritical hag and was happy to remain that way. To hang with her pals, Hazel and Martha, proclaiming the inevitability of pain and suffering, to verbalize a perpetual disdain that lay a hair's breadth from outright hatred. Now, six years later, she and her daughter rarely spoke.

Gadd quickly washed and conditioned her hair, then soaped her legs and began to shave. Summer's arrival, a time of shorts and bathing suits, being imminent, she went at it carefully, working from her ankles to her knees before rinsing off and stepping out of the shower. This time she avoided the mirror while she toweled off, only glancing at it for a moment when she brushed out her short hair.

As she left the bathroom, Gadd briefly considered the possibility of going out, hitting a few meat-market East Side bars, maybe getting lucky. But that would mean at least fifteen minutes in front of the mirror, an effort beyond her current abilities. And degrading enough, in the long run, to have consequences of its own.

She remained in her tiny bedroom long enough to pull on a pair of drawstring cotton pants and a green sweatshirt, to jam her feet into faded, corduroy slippers, then nearly ran into her office, closing the door behind her. Her bedroom/apartment, her home, with its two-burner stove, its tiny sink and refrigerator, its one chair and narrow single bed, was almost as depressing as the mirror in the bathroom. More evidence of failure, of loss. More emotional garbage for the self-pity landfill.

The light on her phone machine beckoned seductively. Work was what she needed, a remedy as solidly established in her personal mythology as chicken soup. She pressed the button, leaned over the desk to grab pen and pad. Her jaw dropped open when Patricia Kalkadonis's voice, distorted by the small speaker, declared that she and her mother were leaving New York on the following afternoon, that they might or might not return after her father was captured, that her mother would like to see Ginny Gadd and Stanley Moodrow before she left.

"Shit." Gadd jabbed a finger at the reset button, then repeated herself. "Shit." She debated calling Moodrow for a moment, finally deciding to catch him in the morning, let him have a decent night's sleep.

She walked over to her IBM, dropped down in an armless swivel chair, stared at the lit screen. The letter she'd written to Tommaso stared back as if it had been waiting for her gaze. As if her computer was alive, a patient beast eager to prove its worth.

Whatta ya think, Gadd? she asked herself. Wanna check and see if the fish took the bait?

On the one hand, she couldn't see how seducing Tommaso could lead to Jilly Sappone. At best, it would be a path to Carmine Stettecase in whom she had zero interest and who was a couple of days away from permanent incarceration in any event. On the other hand, she was facing a very long evening and the software she'd need, Procomm, was already booted.

Five minutes later, Gadd, having identified herself, was inside the Slave School. Sure enough, Tommaso the Timid had posted a message for Amazing Grace. Gadd scanned it quickly, found the usual crap. Yes, Tommaso the Timid had long ago realized that he lacked a true commitment, that he'd been in the closet too long, that he was going to make his move very soon, that he was prepared to make a special offering to the right master.

How, Gadd wondered, is it possible to get off on this bullshit?

Sure, being tied up (or tying someone else up) has its erotic side. No doubt about it. But this crap is so damned mediocre, so lacking in imagination, it's like watching a troupe of octogenarians do an orgy scene.

She got up, walked over to the front window, listened to the crowd outside. Funny how Bishop McLoughlin stood while most of his parishioners knelt on the filthy sidewalk. As if his actual presence rendered a show of piety unnecessary.

Hail Mary, full of grace, the Lord is with thee.

Gadd shook her head, then returned to her computer, erased Tommaso's message, and began to type her own into the machine.

> *I see you in a lace-trimmed gingham apron, your back and buttocks exposed to the corrective lash. I see you kneeling at the base of my halogen lamp, polishing out the last bit of tarnish. I see a trickle of blood on the back of your shaved right leg, a large drop of blood behind your knee. I see you in my living room, holding a drink-filled tray while your inferiors achieve sexual satisfaction. I see the years passing, your gradual acceptance of the fact that you will never, never be worthy. I see you, one cold January night when a frigid wind rattles the French doors leading to my balcony, finally crawling beneath the quilt to warm my feet against your back.*
> YOU WILL NEVER HAVE ANOTHER CHANCE!
> *Amazing Grace*

EIGHTEEN

Carmine Stettecase couldn't help it. When he was nervous, he ate. That's how it had always been and that's how it was going to remain. He'd fought it when he was younger, fought the urge and lost so many times he'd finally surrendered altogether, let the pounds and the inches accumulate, kept his mouth full, his jaws working.

This time it was the money that set him off, actually touching all those stacked hundreds, three million dollars' worth of stacked hundreds, now resting behind him in a trunk on the floor of his office. Never mind the fact that nobody in their right mind would try to rip him off, that only his closest lieutenants knew he had the money, that his house was an actual fortress, that two of his boys sat outside in a Buick sedan. If something went wrong (if On Luk Sun was preparing a little surprise in that warehouse), the investors would expect him to make good. Meanwhile, he'd be dead broke.

Slowly, his fingers calm and deliberate, he peeled the silver foil away from a Perugina chocolate, then set it on his tongue without soiling his fingers. A little fear on the inside was useful, made you take precautions. But fear on the outside? Men like Guido Palanzo, who sat on the other side of Carmine's desk, lived on fear, sucked it in like crack junkies on the pipe.

"So, whatta ya think, Guido?" Carmine ground the chocolate between his back teeth, crunched the little nuts inside, let the mass drop onto the tip of his tongue. Guido, he knew, was surprised to be talking business in the office instead of the kitchen. That was okay.

Once Guido found out what Carmine wanted, he wouldn't be thinking about where he was sitting when he got his orders.

"About the job?" Guido Palanzo, short and jockey thin, perched on the edge of the chair like an eager squirrel.

"Yeah, the job." Carmine took another wrapped chocolate from the box. "First, the job."

"What could I say?" He stared at Carmine, his perpetually drooping eyelids nearly covering a pair of shiny-black irises. "Everything looks good."

"That's it? That's your fucking counsel?"

Palanzo drew back, clearly offended. "Carmine," he said, "We been talkin' about it for the last two hours. In the kitchen, remember?"

Carmine leaned back, dropped the unwrapped chocolate on his tongue, tossed the foil into the wastebasket. "I wanna hear ya sum it up," he mumbled. "In the kitchen, nobody summed it up."

"Whatever you say, Carmine." Guido held up a thick hand covered with curly gray hair and began to tick the items off on his fingers. "First, the Chink comes highly recommended. Second, we got the money together. Third, our people are ready to go. Fourth, we got enough guns to start a war." He dropped his hand to his lap. "Carmine, how could it be better?"

"Yeah, yeah, yeah." Carmine swallowed hard, then took a sip of water before snatching another Perugina out of the box. "Anyways, I got somethin' else I wanna talk about." He watched Palanzo's shoulders drop slightly, his neck inch forward. "I gotta make a hit on somebody and I want ya to set it up for the day after the deal. Get me a shooter with balls, Guido, somebody from the outside who knows how to keep his mouth shut."

"No problem, Carmine. I'll pull somebody out of Newark. They got a lotta shooters in Newark." Guido's head bobbed once. "Yeah, no problem," he repeated. "Who's the lucky target?"

"The target, my good buddy, is a piece of shit I been tryin' to get outta my life for twenty goddamned years." He spit the last part out, the emotion surprising him. "The target is Josie *fucking* Rizzo. I want the crazy bitch should disappear forever."

Guido Palanzo recoiled slightly, the jerk purely reflexive. According to official mobster mythology, family members were noncombatants. Like Mafia bosses were wise old men with cotton-stuffed cheeks. Then he actually pictured Josie Rizzo with the barrel of an assassin's .22 pressed behind her right ear.

"Awright, Carmine," he said, "I'll call Frankie Fish tonight, let him pick the shooter." He paused momentarily, then repeated, "I hear they got good shooters in Newark."

"I don't care who ya give it to, Guido. Just set it up before we do the deal. And pay for it in advance. I don't want nothing should go wrong." He looked at his watch. "Meanwhile, I got work to do. On your way out, tell my son I wanna see him."

Ten minutes and the remaining chocolates later, Tommy Stettecase walked into the room. He glanced once at the locked trunk behind Carmine's desk and half smiled before sitting down. "You takin' a trip, pop?" he asked.

It took Carmine a minute to understand his son's comment, to remember that when it came to the family business, Tommy was an outsider.

"Yeah," he finally said, "that's just what I wanna talk about." Nodding to himself, he opened a lower desk drawer, removed a can of honey-roasted almonds and peeled back the lid. "Look, Tommy, I got some news I think ya oughta know, but which I want ya to keep under your hat for the time being. Me and your mom, we're probly gonna retire, like real, real soon. I'm too old to be doin' what I'm doin' to make a living." He popped a handful of nuts into his mouth, waited patiently for his son's comment.

"I think that's great, pop." Tommy looked down at his hands for a minute. "But what's that have to with the trunk?"

Carmine ran his fingers across his naked scalp. "We're leavin' is what it is, Tommy. No way could we stay here in the middle of the action. Me and your mom are gonna sell the house, go live in Europe." He chewed relentlessly as he spoke, letting the words drop, one after another, like the lash of a whip. "Coupla months from now, ya gotta be gone. You and Mary."

"And Mama-Josie," Tommy interrupted. "Unless you plan to take her with you."

"What I'm gonna do," Carmine persisted, "is set ya up with

twenty large. If ya should need more, ya can write me." He dug into the can of almonds. "Cause what it is, Tommy, is me and your mom decided that you're a big boy now. It's time ya were out on your own."

Josie Rizzo set the phone on the table next to her bed and smiled. Agent Ewing, faithful as a trained dog, had just informed her that she would no longer be able to contact her nephew. He'd expressed regret, explained that he was following orders, but his voice had been tinged with barely repressed derision. Josie had responded with the proper indignation, had roundly cursed the agent, threatened to withhold the tape she held in her hands. On the inside, however, where it really counted, she felt a rising satisfaction, a peace unknown since the time before her brother was murdered. The spirit, her *jetatura*, had popped out of her soul like a squeezed grape deserting its skin. It was now hovering just above Carmine's bloated frame.

Gildo would have to take care of himself. He knew the schedule, knew what would happen to him if he didn't get out. Besides, Gildo had done everything he was supposed to do already. Annunziata Kalkadonis would never be free of him. Every spring, for the rest of her life, she'd think of her child, of her ex-husband, of what she'd done to bring down his wrath.

Josie Rizzo closed her eyes, remembering Gildo's description of Carol Pierce after Jackson-Davis was through with her. "Lemme put it like this," he'd said. "The doc won't need a scalpel to get to the bitch's vital organs. All he gotta do is pick 'em off the carpet."

With a shake of her head, Josie reminded herself that a decision had to be made. Should she deliver the tape or destroy it? If Carmine found her with the tape, if he pulled out of the deal, she'd lose everything. On the other hand, if Holtzmann didn't get his package, he might panic, try to contact her. She'd listened to the tape, knew there was nothing important on it, nothing the FBI didn't already know.

Footsteps sounded on the stairway three floors below her own and Josie quickly shoved the tape into the pocket of her dress. Despite recognizing Tommaso's quick tread, despite having heard him descend a few moments before, her heart pounded in her chest.

No more, she decided. No more tapes. If the FBI won't let me speak to Gildo, it's because they don't need Josie Rizzo *or* the tapes.

Quickly, before she could change her mind, Josie ripped the tape out of the spool, crushed it in her hands, dumped it beneath a pile of corn husks on the bottom of her kitchen garbage. Then she stepped over to the sink and quickly rinsed her hands. Downstairs, the steel door at the front of the house squeaked open, then clanged shut. That would be Carmine, heading out to meet the Chinaman.

Snatching a towel, Josie half ran to the window in her living room and pulled the drapes aside. Carmine, as expected, was ducking into the back of his Lincoln town car. Totally unaware that, five floors above, Josie Rizzo, her chin raised high, nodded her satisfaction at the dark, voracious creature that followed him.

"Here, pussy. Heeeeeeere, pussy-pussy. Come to daddy, you cocksucker."

Agent Bob Ewing, as he prepared Jilly Sappone's breakfast, shook his head in amazement, told himself not to lose his temper, that Sappone would be gone soon, this amazingly repulsive assignment over and done with. Twenty-four hours, a single day, that was all that remained of what he'd come to consider a sentence.

"Hey, Agent Bob, you got a daughter somewhere, little kid maybe catching the school bus even as we fucking speak? One day I'm gonna track that kid down, see if she can fly. That was Theresa's problem, Agent Bob. I mean, how was it *my* fault if she couldn't fly? Ya can't expect a busy man like me to pay attention to every little detail."

Ewing snatched a bowl of ham cubes, onions, and peppers. He spread them over the omelet cooking on the stove, then gave the pan a quick shake to prevent the eggs from sticking. It was a little after eleven o'clock in the morning and he'd already had a phone call from his boss. Holtzmann had listened to his complaints, clucked sympathetically from time to time.

"We'll be coming for Mister Sappone tomorrow, Bob," he'd finally interrupted. "Jilly's going to be taken into custody, charged with kidnapping and murder. The US Attorney will push for the death penalty and he'll get it. What jury could find redeeming value in Jilly Sappone?"

The question had been strictly rhetorical and Holtzmann had rung off a few minutes later without answering the deeper question. When Ewing had first been assigned directly to Holtzmann and this particular investigation, he'd been overjoyed. No question about it, Carmine Stettecase and his dope had career-making potential. Of course, he hadn't known anything about Jilly Sappone or the deal Abner Kirkwood had cut with Josie Rizzo, but his ignorance was all to the good. The only important thing was to be standing in front of that table, the one piled high with guns and dope, when the video cameras began to roll.

Ewing lifted the omelet pan, flipped the half-cooked omelet back on itself, laid the pan on the glowing burner.

"Hey, pussy, I'm holding it in my hand. Right now. I'm holding my dick in my hand and I'm thinking about your wife. She's blond, right, a perfect blond wife for a corn-fed pig on his way up. She's blond and she's hot and you're out here all alone with me."

Ewing slid the omelet onto a plate, then poured out a glass of orange juice and a cup of coffee. He put cup, glass, and plate on a tray, added a plastic fork, took a deep breath. This was the worst of it, the look of triumph in Sappone's eyes when Agent Bob Ewing played the servant. When he straightened up or ran the vacuum or fetched the telephone. As if Jilly Sappone really believed the Justice Department would put him in the witness protection program.

Maybe, Ewing thought, as he picked up the tray and stepped out of the kitchen, I'll let him skip his next meal. And the next and the next.

"Hi, sweetie-peetie."

Ewing glanced up, felt distinctly relieved to find Jilly Sappone with his pants zipped. He placed the tray in the door slot, leaned briefly against the interlaced bars, finally stepped away.

"Tell ya what, Agent Piggy." Sappone put the edge of the plate against his lower lip and pushed a third of the omelet into his mouth. "I got an idea we could both live with. After I get outta here, whatta ya say we *swap* wives. Cause it looks to me like you could use a little ethnic pussy, a little guinea girl with olive oil between her legs. Somethin' to give that whitebread face a little character. And me, I ain't had no pink-pussied blond bitch since before I went to prison. Be a lotta fun to make her beg."

Ewing, propelled by the torrent of abuse, backed halfway across the room. Sappone had been going at it for the better part of two days, as if something or someone had triggered a switch in his brain. Going on and on and on, the hatred clearly visible in the twisted sneer, the flared nostrils. The cumulative effect was almost physically painful.

"One more day," Ewing said. His hand dropped to the waist of his trousers, to an empty holster. Then he remembered that his nine-millimeter Glock was in the kitchen where it belonged. Ewing wondered if the procedure had been designed to prevent agents from executing prisoners in custody.

"Say what, sweetie-pie?" Jilly's smirk remained firmly plastered to his face. "Are they sending new troops to the front? Is my honey being relieved?"

Ewing took a step forward. "Wrong guess, scumbag." He held up a shaking finger. "You think you're going into the witness protection program, you and that crazy bitch? Well, here's your fate, Jilly Sappone. You're going to spend the next ten years in the worst prison the federal system has to offer while you appeal your death sentence. After that, it'll be up to God."

Jilly Sappone's face relaxed for the first time. The information— the timing—was interesting enough; it fit into his personal schedule nicely. But, all along, he'd simply assumed that Ewing would be the triggerman. Now Ewing was babbling about arrest and trial, which wasn't gonna happen. No way could they let Jilly Sappone talk to a lawyer, have access to the media. Still, if Ewing really believed it, if he thought he had no reason to fear Jilly Sappone . . .

Well, credit where credit was due, Jilly finally decided, Agent Bob *was* right about one thing. Another day was all it would take.

NINETEEN

Stanley Moodrow awoke to the faint odor of his lover on the sheets and pillowcase next to where he slept and the much stronger smell of brewing coffee drifting in from the kitchen. He rolled onto his back without opening his eyes, let the pure pleasure of having nothing to do run through his body. Lazy was the proper word for the way he felt, as limp and relaxed as Betty's crumpled nightgown at the foot of the bed. For the moment, he wanted nothing more in life than to lie right where he was.

"Stanley, you awake?"

Moodrow reluctantly opened his eyes. "Yeah." He stole a glance at the clock on the night table: 9:47. "It's late," he announced, pleased with himself. On most days, he was up before seven.

"How are you feeling?"

"Great." He touched the back of his head, found the remains of the wound dry, pronounced himself healed. Sitting up, he reached out to Betty and gently pulled her down next to him. "I feel like I'm getting this behind me."

Betty glanced at his lap. "Looks to me like you're getting something in front of you as well."

"Purely reflexive, my dear, by-product of a good dream and a desperate need to urinate."

Twenty minutes later, shaved and showered, he sat at the kitchen table, a steaming coffee mug in his hand. The odor of toasting bagels filled the room.

"A good morning for smells," he announced.

"Pardon?"

"Nothing." He drained half the mug, then got up to stand behind Betty who continued to chop away at a bunch of scallions. "Whatta ya say we take the ferry to Ellis Island, hang out with the tourists?"

Ellis Island, processing center for tens of millions of immigrants, had been a museum for nearly a decade. Moodrow have been determined to pay a visit ever since reading an article in the *Daily News* bemoaning the fact that more Japanese toured the exhibits than native New Yorkers, that the ratio of all tourists to New Yorkers was fifty-to-one. This despite the fact that six million people in the Greater New York area had ancestors who'd come through Ellis Island.

"I've never been there," Betty said. "My grandparents—my mother's parents—landed on the Island in 1916." She slid the chopped scallions into a small bowl with the edge of the knife, turned and set the bowl on the table, shut off the oven. "My *bubbe* told me she nearly got sent back. She had an eye infection and the doctors initially told her she'd be refused admission to America. Can you imagine, Stanley? You can see the Statue of Liberty from Ellis Island. She told me she stared at it for two days. Until the doctors decided to let her in."

Moodrow opened the oven and began to carefully slide the toasted bagels onto a plate. "Your grandmother ever say why they changed their minds?"

"She never asked." Betty set glasses and a quart of orange juice on the table, then sat down. "The family came from a place where Jews didn't question authority, at least not openly."

The phone rang just as Moodrow finished spreading a layer of cream cheese on a sliced onion bagel. "If that's Gadd," he announced, "I'm gonna be very pissed." He sprinkled a few scallions over the cream cheese, then carried the bagel to the phone.

"Yeah."

"A little abrupt this morning, aren't we?"

"How did I know it was you?" He sensed her hesitation, that his hostility had taken her off guard, and was instantly apologetic. The progression surprised him. "Tell me you're calling because the cops've taken Jilly and you want that drink we talked about last night."

"No such luck." She hesitated briefly. "Look, yesterday, when I got home, I found a message on my answering machine from Patricia Kalkadonis. She and her mom are leaving New York, leaving *tonight*, Moodrow. They want to see us before they go."

Moodrow started to say, *Tell 'em I died*, then checked himself. "No matter what I do," he finally declared, "I can't seem to shake this case."

"Hey, Moodrow, look at the bright side. Once Ann takes off, it really will be over." She paused long enough to clear her throat. "Meanwhile, it's time to pay the piper."

An hour later and several miles to the north, Abner Kirkwood and Karl Holtzmann strolled beside the fountain outside the complex of white marble buildings that make up Lincoln Center for the Performing Arts. They'd gravitated to the fountain because of the noise, the rush of the waters, instinctively protecting themselves against eavesdroppers. This despite the fact that neither believed himself to be under surveillance.

Kirkwood, more aware than his companion, put their collective paranoia down to a guilty conscience. After all, they *were* talking about murder. "You speak to Ewing?"

"An hour ago. He's beside himself, Abner. Sappone's been riding him pretty hard." Holtzmann laughed, shook his head. "The way we set it up, Bob's as much a prisoner as Jilly Sappone."

"Just make sure he doesn't try to do something about it, Karl. Make sure he doesn't open that door."

"I told him we'd be taking Sappone off his hands in twenty-four hours. He'll last that long." Holtzmann stopped abruptly. "What I think we ought to do is drive Sappone into New Jersey, leave his body where it'll be found. With a little encouragement, the media are nearly certain to lay it on Carmine Stettecase's doorstep." He took Kirkwood by the arm and resumed walking. "In the long run, if we time our leaks properly, it'll add to the publicity, keep the case alive between the arrest and the trial."

As they spoke, the sun finally cleared the high-rise condos to the east of Lincoln Center. Pouring onto the plaza from a cloudless sky, it seemed to penetrate the stone on which they walked, adding a buoyancy to their steps. Kirkwood glanced up at the enormous arched windows lining the southern face of the Metropolitan Opera. The windows were dark now, the building open only to workers, but at night, lit from inside by glowing chandeliers, they framed knots of well-dressed patrons as they strolled toward the inner hall, forming a promenade worthy of an Ivory-Merchant film.

"I assume you want me to go with you tomorrow?" he finally said.

Holtzmann stopped again. "There can't be any deniability here, Abner." He ran his fingers over the lapels of his gray, double-breasted jacket. " 'Universal participation protects universally.' " A smile lit his face. "Must say," he admitted, "I like the sound of that."

"Yeah, very nice. Look, I'll be there with you, but I don't think I can pull the trigger." He hesitated, tried and failed to smile. "I've been considering alternatives, Karl. For instance, why can't we arrest Sappone? You know, just take him into custody and let the chips fall where they may? Or bring him back to New York and release him? With Ann Kalkadonis gone and Carmine in jail, with Sappone's apartment and car under surveillance, he won't last a day on the streets."

Holtzmann, who'd seen it coming, fought a sneer. He'd served three tours in Vietnam, most of it in command of battle-scarred grunts. Kirkwood, on the other hand, at least according to his FBI package, had spent the war years at Rutgers University, angling for a National Guard slot until a high lottery number had freed him altogether.

"We can't have him killing anybody else, can we? Or telling his story on *Donahue*?" Holtzmann's eyes narrowed slightly. "Don't worry, Abner. When the time comes, I'll be glad to handle Jilly Sappone. More than glad." He allowed himself a warm smile. "Now for something more pleasant. I've worked out a plan to eliminate the last variable in the equation. That's what I asked you here to talk about."

As Moodrow, a step ahead of Ginny Gadd, approached the door leading into the Kalkadonis apartment, he felt a hesitation that bordered on paralysis. The last few days had done a lot to heal his wounds, both physical and psychological. But time had not (and *could* not) change the facts; time hadn't relieved him of responsibility, only made his ultimate responsibility easier to accept. Until now.

"It's not gonna get any better, Moodrow." Gadd stepped around him to knock on the door. "Not until after it's done."

A moment later, Patricia Kalkadonis opened the door, then moved aside, nodding to each of them as they passed. Moodrow returned the nod as he walked into the living room to find Ann Kalkadonis, the bruises on her face and neck reduced to a few muddy patches, sitting on the couch. A uniformed cop stood in the center of the room. He watched Moodrow and Gadd enter, then turned and strolled into the kitchen without saying a word.

"Ann?" Moodrow raised his head far enough to meet her steady gaze. He had a little speech all prepared, but found he couldn't open his mouth.

"Thanks for coming." She indicated the two clubs chairs at either end of the couch. "Please, sit down."

Moodrow nodded, then took the chair farthest away from where he stood. He looked over at Gadd as she sat, watched her cross her legs at the knee, drop her hands to her lap. A momentary resentment flooded his consciousness, but then he remembered that she'd been an innocent bystander, a witness and not the perpetrator. She had a right to relax.

"I don't know if it will do any good." Ann Kalkadonis looked directly at Moodrow. "But I want to tell you that never, not for one moment, have I held you responsible for what Jilly did to Theresa." Her voice was steady, if not actually strong, filled with clear determination, the voice of a survivor. "I'm angry, you understand, but not at you."

Patricia strode into the room carrying a packed suitcase. She laid it next to several others, then returned to the rear bedrooms. Ann waited for her to leave, before resuming.

"I've had questions all along. How did he get out? Why wasn't I notified beforehand?" She took a deep breath, glanced from Moodrow to Gadd. "Where is he now? Why has he been quiet? For the first two days after Theresa was killed, I kept expecting Jilly to come through the front door. That's his nature and he can't help it. So, where is he?"

"I don't know, Ann." Moodrow inched forward until he was sitting on the edge of the chair. "We've been looking for him, me and Gadd, but we've run into a dead end." He quickly outlined their efforts, including their discovery of the apartment and the car. "I'm glad you're leaving," he concluded, "because the cops found an arsenal in the trunk of that car Jilly rented. He wouldn't have put it there if he didn't expect to come back. If he didn't have his next move planned out."

Ann nodded. "Do you think Carmine Stettecase might have . . .?"

"Anything's possible. But if Carmine whacked Jilly, he wouldn't hide the body. Carmine'd want everybody to know."

"So I'm to be left with my questions unanswered? A poor, helpless woman whose rantings are tolerated in the name of her loss?" She hesitated momentarily, then smiled. "As you might've heard, I'm involved in a lawsuit with Con Edison over the death of my husband. Well, I've decided to settle and use the money to get some answers. I'll be working through a lawyer, mostly, using the Freedom of Information Act." Her voice tightened down, her eyes narrowing as well. "This morning, I gave an interview to a *Newsday* reporter named Marcia Hammond. Once Jilly is taken, I intend to appear on every talk show that'll have me. My lawyer's negotiating with a production company that wants to make one of those terrible fact-based network movies out of my life story."

Moodrow held up his right hand as if warding off an attack. He knew what was coming next and didn't want any part of it; he felt like a spectator at his own funeral.

"My attorney has investigators of his own, of course, a midtown firm he uses regularly, but I told him I wanted to continue with the two of you. That was presumptuous, I know, but . . ."

"Tell me something, Ann," Gadd interrupted, "what happened to the FBI?"

"They left several days ago."

"Just like that? Just took off?" Gadd looked over at Moodrow, but failed to catch his eye.

"They didn't think Jilly would try to contact me." Ann Kalkadonis rubbed the side of her face with the fingertips of her left hand. "Once Theresa was gone."

"That figures. And the cop in the kitchen?"

"He hasn't asked to stay in the apartment, but Detective Gorman told me the police would keep the building under surveillance."

"That's great, just great." Gadd glanced at Moodrow again, noting the tight jaw and closed fists. "Look, I don't wanna get into the details, but we have reason to believe the situation's gonna resolve itself real soon. Like the day after tomorrow. If Jilly doesn't make an appearance by then, he's not gonna make an appearance at all. So, what about you give us a key, let us stay in the apartment? That way, if Jilly decides to pay a visit, he won't lack for company."

As Moodrow walked the mile and a half back to his Fourth Street apartment, his mood went from bitter anger to even more bitter resignation. He'd confronted Gadd, of course, as the two left Ann's building, demanding to know how she could speak for him.

"Or maybe," he'd concluded, his hand on his hips, "when you said the word 'we,' you were speaking as a member of the royal fucking family."

Gadd had simply turned away. "Look, I wanna go over to my apartment, put a few things together, get back before Ann takes off. That doesn't leave me a lotta time." She's stalked off a few steps, then turned. "What could I have done?" she asked, "make it seem like I was gonna cut you out? We're talkin' about a paying client here. And a private investigator who lives in an office above a pornographic book store."

"You could've just backed off, let the game play itself out." His response had sounded lame, even to his own ears.

"I don't see it. Not while there's still a chance." A smile lightened her face. "C'mon, Moodrow, it'll be fun. I'm gonna bring my laptop and a modem, see if Tommaso's left me another message. I didn't mention it, but we exchanged electronic mail last night. Tell ya the truth, it's the closest I've come to a genuine romance in the last year."

And that had been that. Ginny Gadd had stalked off down the

street, leaving Moodrow to his own thoughts, thoughts that ran from the pleasure of watching Holtzmann with two *ns* squirm in the public spotlight to the stark reality of the blue wall of silence. Breaking the code was unthinkable, as was letting the hated fibbies off the hook. Meanwhile, out of nowhere, he was tired again, ready for bed.

By the time he reached Avenue A and Fourth Street, two blocks from home, Moodrow was ready to once again acknowledge the possibility that Jilly Sappone would return to his wife's apartment. It wasn't going to happen, of course. Even if he somehow got free of his keepers, Sappone would go for his stashed weapons, maybe try to get back into that uptown apartment. The cops would be waiting, as they'd be waiting in front of Ann's building. Given any sort of excuse, they'd shoot him down like the rabid dog he was.

Unfortunately, that wasn't the bottom line, not even close. No, for Stanley Moodrow, all the probabilities were rendered meaningless by the simple fact that if Sappone actually got through, if he somehow did to Ginny Gadd what he'd done to Carol Pierce, Stanley Moodrow would not be able to live with the results. And the only serious question, given that admission, was whether or not he had enough clean underwear for an extended stay.

The question, still unanswered, was rendered meaningless a few minutes later as Moodrow crossed Avenue B and started to walk into the block. The FBI came at him from both ends of the street, a dozen agents in three cars, waving their automatics like cowboys, demanding that he lie flat on his face, like any other criminal. Moodrow, as he dropped slowly to his knees, found himself strangely calm, as if he'd been on this end of an arrest many times before. He noted the level of force, pronounced it overwhelming, finally decided that he approved of the operation, that it was just what he, if he was in Holtzmann's place, would do.

TWENTY

Betty Haluka didn't begin to panic until after the eleven o'clock news. Up until that point, she'd been able to convince herself that Moodrow's visit to Ann Kalkadonis had uncovered some new piece of information, that perhaps Moodrow was sitting on a stakeout, unable to leave the car. She'd phoned Ginny Gadd, of course, and Ann Kalkadonis, but there'd been no answer at either place, though Gadd did have an apparently defective answering machine which disconnected immediately after the beep. Betty wasn't upset by the lack of response—Ann had wanted to see Moodrow because she was leaving the city and Gadd was with Moodrow now, pursuing whatever they'd decided to pursue. It was that simple.

Then the news came on, a litany of the day's violence recited alternately by the coanchors, Sue Simmons and Matt Lauer. There was a murder on Ninety-fifth Street, another in a Lexington Avenue subway car, a ten-year-old wounded in a Brownsville drive-by, a pair of lice-infested toddlers found wandering in a reputed crack house. Finally, after a commercial break, Matt Lauer introduced a long piece on the still-unsolved nursing-home fire, then mentioned New York's other unsolved crime, the execution of Theresa Kalkadonis. Jilly Sappone's mug shot, silent and unyielding, propelled Betty from her chair to the telephone.

She tried Ann Kalkadonis and Ginny Gadd again, with the same result, then Leonora Higgins. Leonora's phone rang four times before her answering machine picked up and Leonora's disembodied voice urged her to leave a message. Betty, feeling just as disembodied, briefly explained the situation before hanging up. She was rummaging in the closet, looking for Moodrow's phone directory, when the telephone rang back in the kitchen.

Betty, always optimistic, charged across the room, grabbed the receiver and half shouted, "Stanley, where the hell have you been?"

But the voice on the other end of the line wasn't that of her lover.

"It's not Stanley, it's me, Artie, calling from Los Angeles. Long distance." His tone was crisp and efficient, as if arranging an appointment with a client. "You were supposed to call me tonight. I've been waiting."

Betty groaned. "Artie, I'm sorry. I've got some problems out here and I just forgot. How's Marilyn?"

"The same, but the hospital wants to throw her out."

"Into the street?"

"Very funny."

"Artie, I don't . . ." She stopped, decided to push one of his many buttons. "This is long distance, Artie," she said, "it's costing a fortune."

"You're right." His voice dropped a half octave, became conspiratorial. "What they say is she's not getting better. I'm talking about the doctors. She's not getting better and the insurance won't pay for the hospital beyond the end of the week. What I've gotta do, they say, is arrange for long-term care which means a nursing home. Betty, it's $6,000 a month and they want I should pay every penny out of my own pocket. How will I do this? Marilyn's breathing is good now, her insides are working. It could take years before . . ."

Artie paused, maybe expecting a response, but Betty didn't intend to prolong the conversation. Not when Artie lived in a two-million-dollar house.

"You could always bring Marilyn home," she finally said. "And take care of her yourself."

That stopped Artie cold. "Betty," he said, after a series of false starts, "I have to make a living."

"I understand, Artie. What I'll do is call you next week, see if there's any change. When Marilyn's settled, I'll come out to Los Angeles. In the meanwhile, you keep your chin up."

Artie hung up without another word and Betty, still angry, began to leaf through the phone book. Then she remembered Jim Tilley.

"Damn," she said to herself as she dialed his number. "You must've taken an extra dose of stupid pills this morning. Where is your goddamned brain?"

As if to confirm her self-judgment, Tilley answered on the second ring. After listening patiently while she detailed everything she knew and everything she feared, he spoke with no trace of anxiety in his voice.

"Stanley had identification, Betty. That means if he was in the hospital, you'd know it, because somebody from the cashier's office would've called for his insurance ID number. Those people don't fool around." He hesitated briefly, then continued when she didn't challenge his assertion. Or his weak attempt at humor. "He might've been arrested, although I can't believe they wouldn't let him make a phone call. What I'll do is see if he's in the computer. Remember, it's not like the old days when they could bounce you from precinct to precinct, one step ahead of your lawyer. Now, you go into the computer when you're booked and the computer tracks you through the system."

"And if he's . . ." She couldn't bring herself to say the word.

"Dead, Betty?"

"Yes, or lying somewhere hurt."

"Look, when he left, he was heading for the Kalkadonises' apartment and he was planning to come right back when he was finished. That means whatever happened to him, happened between here and there. This is Manhattan we're talking about, with tens of thousands of people walking around. You can forget about him lying in some alley."

"Make me feel better, Jim. Tell me why he can't be . . . the other."

"Because I would've heard about it. The Kalkadonis apartment is in the One-Three. Half the cops in the house know Stanley. Plus, if a cop went down, even a retired cop, it would've made the news. But what I'll do is call the ME's office. I've got friends there, so it won't be a problem."

Betty felt the muscles in her neck and shoulders relax, her breathing open up. Jim was right. The odds against Moodrow being in some terrible trouble were huge.

"Look, Betty," Jim continued, "when I spoke to Stanley this morning, he told me the feds were on his back. I can't help you with that, but Leonora used to be an agent. Have you tried her?"

"I left a message on her machine." She carried the phone over to the stove and turned on the burner under the tea kettle. It was going to be a long night, but she was now ready for it. She was going to handle it step-by-step, piece it together as if Stanley Moodrow was a client.

"Look, Jim, will you call me as soon as you know anything? I don't care if it's four o'clock in the morning."

"As soon as I know anything for sure."

Despite Jim's assurances, Betty called every hospital below Fifty-seventh Street, spending most of the next two hours on hold. Wasted calls to Ann Kalkadonis, Ginny Gadd, and Leonora Higgins followed. By the time she finished, it was almost two o'clock in the morning.

She found a blanket in the hall closet, wrapped herself in it, and lay down, fully dressed, on the couch. Her body craved sleep, but her mind was jumping from thought to thought like a flamenco dancer on a bed of hot coals. It was after three before she finally drifted into a troubled sleep in which Marilyn's broken body became Theresa Kalkadonis lying by the side of a road, in which a small body bag swelled like an inflatable boat, until there was only one person big enough to fill it.

The ringing telephone yanked her awake half an hour later. For a minute, Betty didn't know where she was and she fought her way out of the blanket, convinced it was a shroud. Then she shook her head clear, half staggering across the room to grab the receiver. It was Jim Tilley, calling to say that Moodrow was definitely not in custody and even more definitely not in the morgue.

"So, it's good news and bad," Jim concluded. "We know where he's not, but not where he is. What I'm gonna do is take a couple of days off, make myself available until he shows his face. I'll be over as soon as I get a few hours' sleep."

Betty, after hanging up, glanced at the clock. It was almost four o'clock and she was wide awake. Resigned to her fate, she went into the kitchen, shoveled a few scoops of coffee into the basket of

Moodrow's percolator, then added water and set the percolator on the stove. She was about to light the burner when the phone rang again.

"It's Leonora. I just got in."

Under other circumstances, she and Betty might have spent an hour discussing why she was coming home at four in the morning, who he was, and the exact nature of his intentions. Now, she settled for, "I'm glad you called."

"Your message didn't get into specifics. . . ."

"He's gone, Leonora, that's the only damn specific I've got."

When Jilly Sappone awakened at first light on the following morning, he swung his legs over the edge of the bed and sat up without exhibiting any sign of his inner excitement. His movements were quick, but deliberate, as if he'd planned every muscular contraction, every breath, every beat of his heart. This was it, the seventh game of the World Series, the final act in the Jilly Sappone story; he wanted to drain every last drop of glory.

He listened, briefly, to the light buzz of Agent Bob's snoring as it drifted down from an upstairs bedroom. Then he pulled on his trousers, walked quietly into the bathroom and opened the mirrored door to the medicine chest. Again he stopped, again he listened, again he heard only the natural sounds of the house, the hum of the refrigerator, the ticking of the wall clock in the living room, the groaning of the bedsprings as Ewing tossed in his sleep. Satisfied, he quickly wrapped the mirror in a heavy towel, then flushed the toilet, turned on the water in the sink and shattered the glass with the heel of his hand.

Catching the edges of the towel between his fingers, he pulled it away from the frame without allowing a single shard of glass to fall to the tiled floor. Then he shut off the water in the sink and carried the package, handling it as if it held his own beating heart, through his bedroom and over to the wall next to the air conditioner before laying it gently on the carpet. Finally, he unplugged the air conditioner, chose a long, narrow shard of glass, and began to saw through the cord where it entered the machine.

When Jilly had the entire cord in his hand, he stopped again. Ewing's snores had grown louder, the familiar sounds of water running in the sink and toilet apparently lulling him into a deeper sleep. As Jilly listened, one ear cocked toward the empty stairs, he felt an odd mixture of anticipation and regret. Curiously (to himself, at least) he found that he had nothing against Agent Bob Ewing, felt no inner rage, either at the fact of his imprisonment or the double-cross Ewing had admitted to a day before. Instead, he experienced a profound inner calm, as if his hands were being guided. As if he'd rehearsed it all a thousand times before and was simply following a memorized script.

Yet, at the same time, he was looking forward to the next day of his life as if it was Christmas morning and he was four years old and his father was still alive. Jilly Sappone had only two memories of his father. The first was of his father bursting into his room on Christmas day, a child's football helmet jammed onto his head. The second was a confused jumble of sunlight on broken glass, a two-inch patch of hairy scalp, dripping knots of pink tissue on his face, chest, and lap, his own blood running down into the collar of his starched white shirt.

Carefully, so as not to cut himself, Jilly stripped the insulation from the last few inches of the cord, exposing the inner wires, then knelt just to the side of the door leading to the outer room and wrapped the wires around the steel bar closest to the floor. Finally, he carried the glass-filled towel back into the bathroom and laid it gently on the floor of the shower.

Back in the outer room, he slid the mattress and the bedclothes to the floor, exposing the bed's steel frame and its platform of small springs. Noise didn't matter now, it was time for Agent Bob to rise and fry, but Jilly paused anyway. He took a deep breath and held it for a moment, then let it slowly wash over his tongue and lips. Ewing continued to snore away and Jilly wondered, briefly, if the agent was locked into a happy dream, if he was holding onto a woman, caressing her breasts with the tip of his tongue. If he was so lost in his dream that he wouldn't wake up at all.

Time to find out, Jilly decided. With a grunt, he hoisted the bed frame up onto his right shoulder, ran forward several steps, and slammed it into the Plexiglas window. Then he began to scream.

"What, what, what?" Bob Ewing snatched his gun off the night table and leaped out of bed. Sappone's insane rant, a series of choked obscenities surrounded by a high-pitched wail, seemed to fill the room. Then a second crash shook the small house and Ewing's confusion was instantly replaced by a mixture of rage and panic. Sappone could not be allowed to escape; Sappone could not be allowed to live.

Ewing took the stairs two at a time. He could see Jilly Sappone through the bars, see him raise the bed frame, slam it into the window, then raise it again.

"Put it down, you bastard." Ewing pulled the trigger, sent a round into the ceiling, then dropped the sights onto Sappone's chest and pulled the trigger again. The slug hit the bars and deflected into the base of a lamp. Sappone froze briefly, then tossed the bed frame onto the floor and jumped out of sight against the wall next to the barred door.

"Come on out, Sappone. Come out so I can kill you." Ewing's panic, now that he could see the window still intact, dropped away, leaving only rage to guide his actions. Sappone had been torturing him for days, just as he'd tortured Theresa Kalkadonis, just as he'd tortured his partner and so many others before that. He had no right to live.

"Where you gonna hide, Jilly?" Ewing crossed the room quickly, reminding himself that the steel bars on the door were only an inch apart, that Sappone could not reach through, with his hands or with a weapon. "Where you gonna hide, Jilly," he repeated. "There's no place to hide."

Sappone responded with another drawn-out scream and Ewing, momentarily stunned, paused in mid-step. Then Sappone, his choked, phlegmy voice nearly unintelligible, began to curse him.

"You ain't got the balls, you fucking faggot. You ain't got the balls to kill me. That's why your boss put you here. Because he knew you were too chickenshit to do what's in your heart." Sappone slammed the side of his fist into the door, then dropped to his knees and snatched the plug off the floor. "Too chickenshit to pay the price."

With his head slightly forward, Jilly could see a few feet beyond the interlaced bars. Agent Bob was standing in the dim light, one foot off the ground. He was shouting something, most likely another threat, but the words were lost on Jilly who was listening to a familiar melody as it sounded faintly in his consciousness. He couldn't put his finger on it, couldn't put a name to the tune, but it compelled all his attention until Ewing stepped forward and pressed the fingers of his left hand against the steel mesh.

"Sympathy for the Devil," Jilly muttered as he jammed the plug into the wall.

The resulting crack, as sharp as a bolt of lightning, was as purely satisfying to Jilly Sappone as the rush of heroin through his bloodstream. The sight of Agent Bob, jerking like a landed fish, was even better. Jilly wanted to stay right where he was. He wanted to savor the moment, to suck it into his memory, but he knew he had work to do. With a sigh of regret, he picked up the bed frame and began to heave it against the Plexiglas window.

It took longer than he expected, a full seven minutes before the window popped out and he climbed into the yard. The grass was cold and wet against his bare feet as he trotted around the side of the house and came in through the unlocked front door. Agent Bob had stopped twitching, but he was still lying on the carpet, moaning softly with his eyes closed. Sappone stared for a minute, then picked up Ewing's nine-millimeter Glock.

"You think it'll work, Agent Bob?" he said. "I mean I never seen an electrocuted gun before." Smiling, he put the barrel of the gun against Ewing's head. "Nothing to say, huh? Well, I gotta find out anyway. Being as your boss is gonna pay me a visit and I don't wanna be caught unprepared."

TWENTY-ONE

Karl Holtzmann felt himself to be every inch the commander in chief. Never mind the jerk, Abner Kirkwood, sitting off by himself on the edge of the little stage. There wasn't a single man in the room, not from the FBI or the DEA, who didn't know Karl Holtzmann was in charge. It was something even the locals could understand.

There was no way to maintain it beyond the actual bust, of course. That was why he had to savor the next twenty-four hours, why it was so important. Once the bad guys were in custody, the politicians would simply assume the glory. Karl Holtzmann would be expected to stand off to the right or the left, a few feet behind Abner Kirkwood and Rudolph Giuliani and Commissioner Bratton and whoever else had the juice to put himself at stage center. If he was lucky, *real* lucky, one of the reporters would ask a question the politicians couldn't answer and he would be summoned to the microphone, allowed to bark out a short answer, then returned to his cage.

"Gentlemen," he said, quickly adding, "and ladies" with a nod of his head and a warm smile. "This is an aerial photo of the target area." He snapped on the laser pointer almost hidden in his fist, dropped the little red dot on a narrow rectangle in the center of the photograph. "And this is Ground Zero. I realize that most of you haven't had a chance to familiarize yourselves with the terrain, so take a minute to study the photo before we get into the specifics."

Holtzmann pressed the pointer's switch and the red line seemed to withdraw into the hard plastic case. He stepped away from the easel, took a deep breath, let it run out through his nose. Kirkwood had stood up and was approaching. The poor man looked as if he'd had a very bad night. His eyes were shot through with jagged streaks of red and underscored by heavy, gray pouches. No stranger, looking at the two of them, would believe Abner Kirkwood to be Karl Holtzmann's superior.

"Yes, Abner?" He allowed his voice to betray just the slightest touch of annoyance.

"I've been thinking, Karl. Maybe we should wait on our boy in New Jersey. Wait until after . . ."

Holtzmann shook his head. Like all good officers, the foot soldiers under his command came first. "Bob Ewing's served us well, Abner. We can't, in good conscience, leave him to baby-sit while we steal the glory." He kept the reprimand gentle, but let his eyes go hard. "And afterward, of course, we'll be very busy. What with the paperwork and the news conference."

Kirkwood started to answer, then looked down at his hands for a moment before meeting the agent's stare. "It's fuckin' wrong, Karl. What we're gonna do is fuckin' wrong even if we get away with it." Too late, he realized that his speech had returned to its Bronx roots, that he'd lost control, that Karl Holtzmann knew it.

"Unless you've written your resignation," Holtzmann said, a triumphant grin raising the corners of his mouth past the tip of his nose, "I really suggest you sit down." He ran his fingertips along the lapels of his jacket. "And allow the troops to prepare for combat."

Carmine Stettecase scooped a forkful of Josie Rizzo's soufflé into his mouth and swallowed without chewing. With a deep sigh, he sliced off another piece and repeated the process. He was in his glory, now, and he knew it. The way the numbers broke down, after paying off the investors and taking care of his boys, he'd be sitting on thirty kilos of the purest China White in the good old USA. The dope would take a full step, then be sold in quarter pounds to a cadre of dealers up and down the east coast who'd step on it again before passing it on to a thousand neighborhood retailers. By the time it was all done, by the time a half million addicts were blasting it into their veins, Carmine Stettecase would be packing a very full suitcase for his trip to the old country. Meanwhile, he was so nervous he couldn't stop eating, not for a second.

"Listen up," he mumbled, ladling fruit salad into his bowl, "I'm gonna make a last-minute change." He dropped a spoonful of fruit onto his tongue, let the taste of slightly overripe papaya wash through his mouth. "What I'm after here is a little more security." He swallowed quickly, then glanced at Vinnie Trentacosta. Vinnie was looking down at his plate, as if the sight of a feeding Carmine Stette-case was too gruesome to contemplate. "Let's put cellular phones in all three vans, stay in contact from the time we leave. Instead of the decoys goin' to the garage, we'll have 'em check for tails, then circle up to White Plains Road by the subway yard. If the Chink decides to pull any shit, I'll have ten shooters a few blocks away."

By the time Peggy McDonald answered her telephone, a little af-ter nine o'clock, Leonora Higgins was eager to press her point home. She'd passed the prior three hours telling herself, over and over, that Peggy McDonald was in her debt, that a marker was a marker at every level of law enforcement. Even if the favor had been given freely. Even if testifying for Peggy McDonald had been a matter of principle.

And that, Leonora admitted to herself, was exactly what it *had* been. Peggy, an agent for less than a year, was being harassed by her direct superior, a middle-aged ex-marine named Bertrand Pendleton. The harassment included frequent grabs at Peggy's flesh, front and rear, usually accompanied by a nasty comment, a short bark of a laugh, and a quick wink to anybody else in the room. At first, Peggy McDonald, seeing the dreams of a lifetime impaled on one man's in-different ego, had been devastated. Then she'd gotten a lawyer.

Potential witnesses had begun to melt away even before the suit was actually filed. By the time McDonald's lawyer was ready to take depositions, only two remained, one of them Leonora Higgins. At considerable risk to her own career, she'd backed her graphic descrip-tions of Pendleton's behavior with notes from a detailed journal.

The end result—Peggy McDonald still an agent ten years later, Bertrand Pendleton retired to southern Arizona—was deeply satisfying. It should, Leonora knew, if virtue was truly its own reward, be enough. Meanwhile, Stanley had to be found and Peggy McDonald was going to have to break a few rules and that was the end of that.

Ten minutes later, after listening to a series of excuses, Leonora finally got herself to say the magic words: "You owe me."

"Please, Leonora . . ."

"Don't bullshit me, Peg. We both know there are only six cells for male prisoners in the entire building and they're all on the seventh floor. How hard could it be to go up there and look for a six-foot-six-inch senior citizen? I just need to know if he's being held."

"What if they've bused him over to the MCC?" The Metropolitan Correctional Center, a few blocks away, held federal prisoners awaiting trial.

"Then you won't find him at headquarters." Leonora paused long enough to frame her next statement carefully. "Look, Peggy, I'd much rather have you refuse me than lie to me."

It was McDonald's turn to hesitate. "If I do this," she finally said, "we're even, right? It's over and done with?"

"Well, it'd help if I knew whether or not he's been formally charged. And if he's had a nice breakfast."

Stanley Moodrow was sitting on the edge of his bunk, furiously writing in a small pad balanced on his knee, when Karl Holtzmann approached his cell. He glanced up at the agent, then returned to his writing.

"I don't mean to be rude, Agent Holtzmann with two *n*s, but I'm just finishing up here. I'll be with you in a minute."

Holtzmann turned on his heel, ready to explode at the corrections officer who'd given pad and pencil to a federal prisoner. He was halfway across the room before he remembered that after confiscating Moodrow's weapon on the street, his agents had been instructed to leave the prisoner alone. Apparently, they'd taken the instructions literally.

Once again, he spun on his heel, this time marching up to the cell bars.

"What do you think you're doing?" he asked.

"I'm writing a letter."

"A letter?"

"Yeah. I got inspired by my partner. Of course, she writes on a computer and I still gotta do it by hand, but it comes to the same thing."

Holtzmann ran his fingers over the lapels of his jacket, took a deep breath, told himself to calm down. Even if he confiscated the letter, there was nothing to stop Moodrow from writing it again once he was released.

"The letter, Moodrow," he said calmly, "who's it for?"

"Ann Landers." Moodrow tore off several sheets of paper. "You wanna see?"

Dear Ann,

I have always prided myself about the fact that in my life I have been a politically correct person. I learned to say black instead of Negro, then African-American instead of black. I learned to say Ms. instead of Mrs. or Miss; hearing impaired instead of deaf; Native American instead of Indian; morally challenged instead of psychopath. Believe me, Ann, I have really, really tried.

But now things have just gone too darn far. The other day a professor friend of mine told me about the new conduct code at Antioch College in which a boy has to ask his girlfriend for permission to do every little thing they're gonna do. For instance, the boy will say, "May I kiss you," and the girl will say, "Yes." Then the boy will say, "May I kiss you on the mouth," and the girl will say, "Yes." Then the boy will say, "May I put my tongue in your mouth," and the girl will say, "Yes."

Well, Ann, you can see how this is fine for young folks who have a lot of energy and plan to do somethin' real simple, but me and my sweetheart, we have reached an age where we need to save ourselves for the genuine article. You see, we are the both of us cross-dressers and by the time we have worked our way from, "May I wear the blue, edible panties," to "May I wear your Tower of Power green boxer shorts," watchin' David Letterman is startin' to look mighty good. In fact the last time we tried it, I never even got to Joan's adorable red rhinestone pumps. We stopped at, "May I wear your sweat-soaked leather chaps," and went right to sleep.

Ann, I tell you before God Almighty that I never thought I'd see the day when I turned my back on my ideals, but this afternoon when Joan came walking out of my closet wearing those dirty jeans and that oil-soaked sweatshirt and those mud-caked Knapp work boots, I near-about went crazy with desire. Then I done every damn thing I could think of without never once askin' permission first.

Now I am sitting here at my desk writing this letter and I have to say my conscience is far from clean. In fact, I feel like a child who has wandered into a deep, dark forest. Because, Ann, I know that tonight I'm gonna sneak into my sweetheart's closet and try on that no-nonsense, double-breasted business suit she bought at Lord & Taylor the other day. And when I come out, I'm sure gonna be hopin' Joan don't ask permission to do what comes unnatural.

Signed: He Used To Be A Good Soldier.

Holtzmann, enraged by Moodrow's cool attitude, crumpled the pages in his fist, then tossed them back into Moodrow's cage. "I want you to listen to me for a minute." He stepped up to the bars of the cell. "Your partner is still out there somewhere. If she does anything to interfere with this operation, the both of you will be placed under arrest. At present, you have not been charged with a crime and it's my intention to release you when it's safe to do so, but . . ." He sucked in a deep breath, drew himself up to his full height. "The charges," he announced, "may well be kidnapping and extortion."

Moodrow stood up and took a step toward the agent. "Why don't you dump the 'good cop' bullshit and tell me what the fuck you want?"

"I want you to tell me where she is, Moodrow. This is not rocket science." Holtzmann flicked a finger in the general direction of the crumpled pages on the floor of the cell. "Even for a lunatic."

To his credit, Moodrow never considered betraying his partner. This despite the fact that a clear vision of Jilly Sappone getting into that apartment, of what he'd do to Ginny Gadd and how long it would take him to do it, tore through his mind like acid through a paper towel. Instead, Moodrow's left hand snaked between the bars to grab Karl Holtzmann's face.

"Karl, you ready for the real deal?" He bore down with all his strength. "Because the real deal goes like this: If anything happens to my partner as a result of your putting me in this cage, I'm gonna kill you with my bare hands. And I'm gonna be wearing my grand-mother's wedding dress when I do it."

TWENTY-TWO

Karl Holtzmann, as he piloted a Bureau Ford along I–80 in central New Jersey some three hours later, continued to feel the imprint of Stanley Moodrow's fingertips on both cheekbones. It was as if the ex-cop was still holding onto his face. As if he intended never to let go.

Violated. That was the word that kept popping into the agent's mind no matter how firmly he tried to keep it out. He didn't like the word because he associated it with rape victims and rape victims were all women. *Helpless* women.

"Are you listening to me, Karl?"

Holtzmann studiously ignored the man who sat on the passenger side of the Ford's bench seat. He wanted to deal with Moodrow, get the ex-cop out of the way, before he considered Abner Kirkwood's insistence that they take Jilly Sappone into custody. Unfortunately, he couldn't manufacture a realistic course of action that wasn't dominated by negative consequences. And he couldn't put Moodrow out of his mind, either.

A part of him insisted that Moodrow be arrested and charged with obstruction of justice, that even if Moodrow managed to beat the charge, he'd be tied in knots for as long as it took, and out the money for a lawyer who knew the federal system. It would be revenge of a sort, and enough until (and unless) Carlo Sappone turned up. But Karl Holtzmann would need the cooperation of a US attorney to make it really painful and that, considering Abner Kirkwood's current state of mind, seemed very unlikely.

Another part of him, this one peeking in from time to time like a toddler from behind a piece of furniture, whispered, *Catch him on the street and kick his fucking ass.*

Well, Karl Holtzmann wasn't about to play macho man with an ex-cop who outweighed him by a hundred pounds and had the kind of grip generally associated with the Terminator.

"Karl?"

Holtzmann ran the fingertips of his right hand along the rim of the steering wheel. "Moodrow corroborates Jilly Sappone," he whispered.

"Say that again."

"Moodrow is being held without charge; Sappone is being held without charge. The facts of their incarceration lend credence to the rumor that Sappone was paroled at our request." Holtzmann glanced at his companion. Kirkwood had his arms folded across his chest and his jaws were clamped together. "Sappone is certain to claim he was held against his will. How do we explain it?"

"If we're forced to, by a judge, we say Jilly Sappone offered to inform, that he voluntarily submitted to a debriefing and we persisted until we realized that he had nothing to offer."

Holtzmann managed a short, contemptuous laugh. The bureau had already inserted Sappone's name into its list of the most-wanted criminals in America. Meanwhile, one of the bureau's senior agents had taken Sappone into custody without either informing his superiors or filling out a single page of the required paperwork.

"You know, Abner, when an informant agrees to talk without a lawyer present, it's customary to have him sign a release. In case the voluntary nature of that agreement is called into question at some later date. Nor did we generate any of the other paperwork relating to the detention of criminal informants. That was because we had no options. We couldn't very well admit that we were protecting Jilly Sappone. To do so would be tantamount to admitting that we freed him in the first place. No, we used up our options—*all* of our options—when we agreed to Josefina Rizzo's terms."

"I don't care. I won't step across that line, Karl. I won't become the enemy." Kirkwood unfolded his arms, looked at his clenched fists as if he'd never seen them before, finally dropped them onto his knees. "It's murder, Karl. I must've been crazy to even think about it."

Karl Holtzmann nodded thoughtfully. Just before the start of his third tour in Vietnam, he'd been assigned to an Operation Phoenix interrogation team. For the next thirteen months, his whole life had been about murder.

"It's *not* murder. An execution is not a murder." He savored the lie for a moment before continuing. "But that's neither here nor there, because the thing of it, Abner, is that I'm going to kill Gildo Sappone within sixty seconds of our arrival. And if I sense, even for a minute, that you'll betray me, I'm going to kill you, too."

As he slid the Ford onto the Route 517 exit ramp, Karl Holtzmann began to hum tunelessly. A genuine smile, the first in weeks, brightened his face. It was funny how it all came flooding back, the games they'd played with those tough little dinks, how tough those tough little dinks actually were. Even the spooks admired them.

Holtzmann's first two years in-country had prepared him for the work, had covered him with enough blood and fear to make that third year the best year of his life. And what he should have done, when he again found himself on American soil, was take the spooks' best offer. He should have made himself a part of their meaningless battles in order to avail himself of their tactics. Instead, he'd gone to law school, joined the FBI, wrapped himself so deeply in the Constitution that it was now squeezing his life away like a python around the chest of a geriatric monkey.

"Cat got your tongue, Abner?" He dug the knife in, gave it a twist. Wanting to gauge Kirkwood's response, see if he was ready to accept reality the way the dinks accepted it when you offered to scoop out their eyeballs. When Kirkwood didn't respond, he drummed his fingers on the steering wheel impatiently. "In all the years, Abner, I've never taken a dime. There was opportunity, of course. Occasions when I knew I could fill my hands without running any risk of apprehension. But I refrained and now, as I approach retirement, I find that my wife and I will have to depend on my pension. I'm not complaining, really, because the plan is generous enough to see us through our declining years. As long as we have it."

"You're doing this for your pension?"

Kirkwood's voice dripped contempt, and Holtzmann willed himself not to react.

"And yours too, of course."

"Well, I can't stop you. That's obvious enough. I'm not armed." Kirkwood looked down at his hands. Now that he knew it was going to happen, he felt much better. Like a child released from a promise.

Holtzmann turned the Ford onto a two-lane blacktop road and headed north along the western edge of Allamuchy Mountain State Park. A dense mix of hardwoods and stringy red pine, relieved only by the occasional, isolated house, lined both sides of the road.

"It was your idea, Abner," Holtzmann finally said. "Do you remember that?"

"What?"

"We were strolling through Washington Square Park and you were going on about Greek Revival houses. I was proud of you then, Abner, though I didn't say so at the time." Holtzmann took his pipe off the car seat and put it, unlit, into his mouth. "Perhaps I should have made my feelings plain, but I didn't. I took you at your word."

Kirkwood popped his seat belt and let it slide over his chest as Holtzmann turned the Ford onto a hard-packed dirt road. Thirty feet ahead, a padlocked steel bar mounted on hinges set into concrete pillars blocked the way. Holtzmann brought the car to a stop and Kirkwood opened his door.

"It's murder, Karl. I didn't see it at the time, but I do now." He stepped out of the car and fished in his pocket for the key to the padlock. "And that's the way a jury would see it, too."

He unlocked the bar, swung it to the side, waited until Holtzmann drove past. Then he pushed the bar into place and got back in the car to find Holtzmann with a large automatic, probably a .45, in his hand.

"Took it from our lab," he announced, "a long time ago. The techs had it for a week. Couldn't bring up a serial number. We'll leave it with Jilly." Smiling, he laid the gun on the seat between himself and Kirkwood. "In time, it'll fade, Abner. Believe me, that's the way it works. When Sappone's body is found next to an untraceable murder weapon, the media will call it a mob hit, then forget about it. In time, your conscience will do the same."

The road wound for two hundred yards beneath interlaced branches of oak and maple. Dense brush lined the soft shoulders on either side. Holtzmann drove slowly, avoiding the occasional pothole and the deeper ruts. The setting was perfect, as isolated as a hermit's cave. The house and clearing, when he finally emerged, seemed almost exotic, a gingerbread cottage in a fairy tale.

Holtzmann pulled up behind Ewing's car, a Ford nearly identical to the one he drove, and shut down the engine. He tapped the horn twice and waited for Ewing to step onto the porch, give them an all-clear. Despite his self-proclaimed bravado, he wanted to get it done as quickly as possible, which was why his attention was so focused on the little porch in front of the door that he failed to see Jilly Sappone until Jilly was fifteen feet away. Still, he might have had a chance. If he hadn't shut off the ignition, he could have jammed his head against the post between the front and backseats, slammed the car into gear, hoped Sappone's bullets found their way into Abner Kirkwood's body. As it was, he reached for the .45 on the seat, tried to jack a round into the chamber, to turn and fire in the space of a heartbeat.

Abner Kirkwood didn't see Jilly's approach at all. His attention was focused on his own fears, his own rising excitement. He was vaguely aware of the agent's hand dropping to the seat, but the implications of the move didn't register until after Jilly Sappone fired a round directly into Karl Holtzmann's skull and the agent collapsed against him. Kirkwood's first thought, in the last moment of his life, was that the odor filling the car was the odor of blood. Then he realized that his bladder had let go and that he was sitting in a puddle of his own urine and that was the way he was going to die.

"Hi, sweetie."

Kirkwood managed to swivel his head a few inches. Sappone, automatic in hand, was leaning into the window, the grin on his face belying the hatred in his eyes.

"I tried to save you," Kirkwood whispered.

Sappone's eyebrows shot up, but the smile held firm. "Shit, man," he said, "that was real white of you. Now here's your fucking reward."

● ● ●

It was almost dark by the time Ginny Gadd admitted to herself that Stanley Moodrow had called it quits, that he'd meant what he said and he wasn't coming back. She was sitting in the Kalkadonises' apartment, in the living room, half watching a repeat *Seinfeld* episode. Wondering what she could do to fend off the inevitable. What she could do that she hadn't already done.

What you could do, she told herself, is pack your bag, catch a cab back to the office, get on with your life. You're not obliged to be here on a fool's errand. Nobody's gonna care; nobody's even gonna know.

Instead of following her own advice, she went to her computer, already set up on the dining-room table, and dialed into the Slave School bulletin board. Sure enough, Tommaso had left a message announcing that his life had been reduced to a single ambition. He wanted to clean her bathroom with the silk lining of his best dinner jacket.

Gadd scrolled through the message quickly. She could feel Moodrow's derision as if he was in the room looking over her shoulder and this time she could muster no defense. Tommaso, best case, led to Carmine Stettecase, not Jilly Sappone, and Carmine was about to go down for the count, taking any connection between himself and Josie Rizzo to prison. Answering Tommaso was a clear waste of time.

But wasting time was exactly what she'd been doing for the last six hours, what she wanted to keep on doing as long as possible. Tommaso's message stared up at her, white letters on a luminous azure background. Maybe if she stared at it long enough Tommaso's obsession would offer some clue to her own behavior.

She got up, sat down, got up again. An approaching helicopter, so loud it might have been skimming the rooftops, droned closer, its throaty roar a seeming complement to the relentless *Seinfeld* laugh track. Gadd felt a sudden rising anger, an urge to snatch her computer off the table, to fling it through the open window as if its memory was her own. Her hands were on the keyboard, the small laptop several inches above the table, when she stopped herself. A cold shudder rolled up her spine and into her neck.

Turning on her heel, she walked into the tiny kitchen, opened the refrigerator, drank directly from a quart of orange juice. Then she went back to the computer and informed Tommaso Stettecase that his presumption could not go unpunished, that he was not worthy of her toilet bowl, that he had blown his one and only chance. Then, without resolving the obvious contradiction, she signed off, unplugged the modem, plugged Ann's phone back into the wall, dialed her mother's number.

After the usual perfunctory *How are you*, Louise Gadd launched into a precise recitation of her best friend's latest failures. Hazel Benton had met a new man, had thrown herself at him, was being treated badly, did not have the strength of character to toss him out on his butt.

"Purcell's five years younger and good-looking. What would he want with an old prune like Hazel?" Louise Gadd's voice dropped a full octave. "Last week she paid his telephone bill. Does that give you a hint? The other day he calls up at five o'clock in the morning, blind drunk, wants to know if he can drop by. So what does Hazel do? She takes a shower. In *case* he should want sex, which he doesn't. No, Purcell wants breakfast and coffee before he goes to work. And she *cooks* it for him. Bacon and eggs, hash browns, toast, the works. I'm telling you, Guinevere, the woman has no self-respect. She's pathetic, a loser, a . . ."

The harangue went on and on. New charges were added to the old, then the old recited anew. Gadd took it as long as she could, before interrupting. She saw the sharp acid tone, as well as the actual words, as pure therapy. Louise Gadd was everything Guinevere Gadd didn't want to be, a negative role model that could be consulted for the price of a phone call.

"Mom, I just phoned to see how you were."

"We haven't even talked about me yet. So how could you know?"

"Well I can see you haven't lost your fighting spirit and that's what I'm gonna have to settle for. I'm in the middle of a job."

"You call what you do a *job*?"

"Bye, ma."

Gadd hung up and smiled. She was ready now, ready for what she had to do if she was going to stay in Ann Kalkadonis's apartment. Without hesitating, she strode across the living room and into the hallway leading to the bedrooms. The first door she opened led to the master bedroom, the second revealed walls covered with a mix of rock and movie posters, the third opened into the room of a very young child. Gadd was prepared for the stuffed animal, a lumpy, tired cat with a missing ear. The bright covers of a half dozen children's books lying on top of the small pink dresser caused her no surprise, nor did the wallpaper with its dancing Disney characters or the Little Mermaid poster hanging by the window. She was prepared for all of that, but not for the neat white blanket covering the bed. Her eyes jammed shut and her head jerked back as if avoiding a punch.

Look, she commanded herself. For once in your life, open your chickenshit eyes and see what you have to see.

Despite the *chickenshit*, Gadd didn't comply until a small white coffin flickered on the backs of her closed eyelids. The image jerked her to full, wide-eyed attention. Then she stood there, one hand resting lightly on the door, and let the full force of Theresa's short life rush into her heart.

TWENTY-THREE

The last thing a near-exhausted Carmine Stettecase expected to find as he entered his darkened study at a quarter to five on the morning of his personal liberation was his nerdy son, Tommaso, pursuing a little liberation of his own. Yet there he was, a shadow within a shadow, strapping Carmine's three-million-dollar trunk onto a chrome luggage carrier.

"Tommaso?"

"Don't move, Pop."

Carmine squinted, tried to peer through the darkness. He couldn't really see the gun in Tommaso's raised hand, but he decided to stop anyway. Carmine, having spent a good deal of his life on the right side of a weapon, had a great respect for firearms.

"Can I turn on the light, Tommy? So's we could talk about what you're doin' here?"

"Okay, Pop. Just shut the door."

At first, Carmine could do no more than blink, then his eyes adjusted to the light and he saw that Tommaso did indeed have a gun clutched in his bony hand, a big, fat revolver, probably a .44. Worse yet, Tommaso's bony hand was shaking uncontrollably and the hammer was cocked.

"C'mon, Tommy, take it easy. You could see I'm not strapped." Carmine's gray silk pajamas encased his body like a sausage skin because of all the pre-deal eating. They were definitely tight enough to eliminate the possibility of any concealed weapon larger than a hat pin.

"Stand over against the wall, pop, while I finish." Tommaso waited for his father to comply, then put the revolver on Carmine's desk. Though he hadn't held a gun in twenty years, Tommaso knew the report of a large-caliber pistol would bring his mother running and he didn't want to kill his mother.

"This okay, Tommy?" Carmine, over his initial shock, fought a rising anger. There was a time in his life when he'd have taken the pistol away from Tommy, taken it away and rammed it between his son's narrow cheeks. Unfortunately, that time was twenty years and a hundred pounds ago. "You know you can't get away with this. I've got two guys watching the house. Whatta ya think they're gonna do if they see you walk out with that trunk? I mean it's five o'clock in the morning, Tommy. That's a hard time to sneak."

"I told them to go home." Tommaso pulled the carrier's straps tight around the trunk, then hooked them into the crossbar. "Last night after you went to sleep. I told them you said they should go home and get some rest before the big day."

Carmine's jaw dropped. "What do *you* know about the big day?"

"I know everything, pop. When, where, who, how . . . everything."

"You bugged me, you cocksucker." Carmine, overwhelmed, took a step forward. He was ready to go to war until his son picked up the revolver. Then he stopped, began to tremble, raised a single accusing finger. "How could you do that to your father?"

Tommaso shrugged, put the revolver back on the desk. "I just wanted to be there." He tilted the luggage carrier back, then recentered the strap. "It was so easy, pop. I waited until you and mom were out, then wired a transmitter into the base of the chandelier." Rising to his full height, he turned to face his father. "But I never meant to do you any harm until you kicked me out. That wasn't right, pop. All these years you been keepin' me in the house and now you wanna dump me." Tommy let the carrier down and folded his arms across his chest. "It's just not right."

Carmine, unable to come up with a counterargument, shifted his weight nervously and wished with all his might for an oven-warmed cheese Danish. There was no way he could let that trunk walk out the door with his son and he didn't want to die on an empty stomach.

"Tell me something, Tommy." Carmine tried to keep his voice gentle, let the force of his argument drive the message home. "Where the fuck are you gonna go? You ain't hardly been out of the house in years."

Tommaso shook his head. After all this time, his father still didn't get it. Alone, locked into his little room with the door shut and the drapes pulled tight across the window, he could travel at the speed of light. Computers into computers into computers, an entire world connected by tiny fibers. He had friends everywhere.

"I guess I'll have to try to get along the best way I can, pop."

"And Mary? Your *wife*. What about Mary?"

Tommaso smiled softly. Being rid of Mary was the best part. "Mary has her mom," he said, as if the naked fact had some practical application. "Look, I gotta get goin'. I rented a car and it's parked illegal. If I don't get a move on, I'm definitely gonna get a ticket."

Carmine tried to muster a next step that wasn't suicide and didn't sound like begging. Unable to do so, he decided to beg.

"Tommy, please," he whispered, "that's not my money."

"I know that," Tommy interrupted. He tilted the carrier back and gave a little push. The wheels turned reluctantly, with the heavy trunk threatening to slide off at any moment. "Damn it," he said, as he let the carrier drop with a little thump and began to retighten the straps.

"But you don't know why you can't take it. Understand? You don't know *why*." Carmine wet his lips. His hands began to weave in front his face. "You can't take it because I can't pay it back and the people I got it from . . . Tommy, they'll have to kill me."

"I don't see it that way, pop." Satisfied, Tommy picked up the gun and pointed it at his father. His hands were much steadier now. For the first time in his life, he wasn't afraid. "See, all those investors want is dope. Which you can still get from On Luk. You just can't *pay* for it."

Carmine's hands stopped moving while he thought it over. At first glance, it sounded like a way out that wasn't either suicide or begging. It sounded like a way to buy enough time to run down his son, exact a little cold, Sicilian revenge.

"You sayin' I should rip the Chink off?"

"I been thinkin' about it for a couple of days and I don't see what else you could do. Unless you manage to find me in the next eight hours." Tommaso waved the revolver in a little circle. "Turn away from me, pop."

"Tommy . . ."

"Please, I don't wanna kill you."

Carmine sighed and turned. Facing the wall, he fought a nearly overwhelming desire to spin around. He could feel his son approaching and he didn't want to know what was going to happen next. Now that he had a way out, it didn't matter.

Tommaso, smiling at his father's apparent resignation, pulled a stun gun from his pocket as he walked across the room. The catalog he'd bought it from (available, of course, through CompuServe and Prodigy) had promised that its 40,000 volts would override an attacker's nervous system, removing voluntary muscle activity for as long as fifteen minutes. Even allowing for the manufacturer's (not to mention the retailer's) inevitable exaggeration, that would be more than long enough.

Though she was awake and dressed at five o'clock, Josie Rizzo was totally unaware of the quiet rip-off taking place three floors below. She did hear the front door squeak open, then clank shut, but she didn't get up out of her chair, walk over to the window as she would have as little as twenty-four hours before. These people, she'd decided, as if they'd been reduced to the status of neighbors, the people downstairs, were no longer part of her life. And that included her daughter, Mary. Maybe, if the family could afford it, they'd continue to live together after Carmine went to jail. Maybe she'd stay here as well. But she had shed them, now and forever, and she felt as light as the dust that floated through her open window.

That didn't mean, however, that she was entirely at peace. There was still the matter of her nephew, Gildo. If the FBI had him, if he hadn't managed to get loose, it would definitely cast a shadow across the festivities to come. Not much of a shadow, to be sure, but the image of Ann Kalkadonis alive and walking the same streets as Josie Rizzo didn't sit well. Ann had been punished, no doubt about it, but

Ann was the greatest of the betrayers. If she hadn't brought those bloody clothes into the precinct, hadn't sold out the husband she'd sworn to love, honor, and obey, the cops would've seen through Carmine's bullshit and Gildo would not have gone to prison. It was really that simple.

Meanwhile, there was nothing Josie Rizzo could do but stay in the apartment, wait for the phone to ring. By the time it did, more than two hours later, she'd gone through six cups of coffee, been to the bathroom four times, and was very, very pissed.

"Why you take so long, huh?" All in all, she considered the greeting to be restrained.

"How did you know it was me?" Jilly's voice was calm, almost somber.

"Who else gonna call me at seven-thirty?" Actually, there was nobody else to call her at any time.

"It could have been a wrong number."

Josie snorted contemptuously. "Enough with the nonsense. You get out okay?"

"Yeah, no problem."

"You know what you gotta do today?"

"Let's drop the fucking interrogation, all right? I'm not in the mood for it." This most likely being the last day of his life, Jilly figured he was entitled to a little respect.

"I wanna hear if you got a plan. And stop with the language."

"Look, Aunt Josie, I ain't got the time for this."

"When your father got bumped off, who took you in?"

"Aw, for Christ's sake . . ."

"Maybe there were people lined up around the block. Huh? Begging to raise you. Maybe . . ."

"I'm gonna hang up."

". . . somebody else got you out of jail, somebody I don't know, a stranger." Josie listened to her nephew's sigh. The soft hiss brought a smile to her face. Gildo was a good boy, a loyal boy. He'd do what was right; he always did.

"All right, Aunt Josie, I got a plan. By tonight, I'll be out of the country." Jilly shook his head. Escape, for Jilly Sappone, was about as likely as having the angels blow their trumpets as he marched into heaven. The charade was strictly for the pigs if they happened to be listening. And for Josie Rizzo, who'd devised it, then bludgeoned him verbally until he'd agreed to play his part.

The situation was funny enough to get him laughing into the telephone. Here he was, a man who went off at the slightest provocation, a man who went off with *no* provocation, a man the doctors claimed would never be able to control himself. Yet his Aunt Josie could berate him for hours at a time and all he did was hang his head, beg her forgiveness like a puppy dog after a beating. It was crazy, but it was true. It had always been true.

"What's funny?" Josie voice was heavy with suspicion. "You got a woman there?"

Jilly flinched. He'd sent the whore back to her dope-dealing pimp less than a minute before making the call. The whore was why he hadn't called last night.

"Nothin', Aunt Josie. Nothin's funny."

Now that it was time to say good-bye, Jilly could feel his heart thumping in his chest. He took a deep breath, wondering if maybe he should do exactly what he'd said, just hang the phone up and get into the wind. That wasn't going to happen, of course, because a promise made to Josie Rizzo simply could not be broken, but he could still wonder. As long as he didn't do it out loud.

"I gotta go," he finally said. "Before somebody comes lookin' for me."

"Yeah," Josie answered matter-of-factly. "Okay. You go do what you gotta do. And don't fool around."

Betty Haluka, as she threw a pearl gray pantsuit over a sparkling white blouse, added a pair of small turquoise earrings and a necklace of matching stones on a silver chain, told herself to please slow down. She'd been trying (and failing) to send herself the same message ever since Leonora Higgins's second call. That had come three hours before, just after six o'clock in the morning and its essential message, that Stanley Moodrow was sitting, all by himself, in a cell on the seventh floor of the FBI headquarters building on Worth Street, should have been enough to alleviate her fears.

Unless, she told herself immediately after hanging up, they decide to charge him, book him, and ship him over to the Metropolitan Correctional Center in the middle of the night. Unless they decide to let him spend the night with a couple of dozen cop-hating drug dealers, teach him a lesson about power relationships.

The nature of that lesson, as drawn•by her imagination, had been horrific enough to get her up and pacing. She simply couldn't shake the urge to grab a coat, charge into FBI headquarters as if she was leading a cavalry charge, demand the immediate release of her lover and client. Joan of Arc brandishing the Constitution in lieu of a sword.

"Don't go down there, Betty," Leonora had patiently advised when Betty called her back. "You'll never get past the lobby. Remember, Stanley hasn't been charged. That means nobody *you* can reach will even know he's there. Tomorrow morning I'll try to call Holtzmann. If he won't speak to me, I'll go to the US attorney. If that doesn't work, I know a deputy attorney general in DC. . . ."

"Leonora?" Betty had interrupted, her imagination already running away with itself. "What if they take him over to the MCC?"

"That's a definite possibility—I won't deny it—but what I think is there's more chance of his being charged and transferred if you try to call their bluff."

Leonora's "trapped rat" scenario had been enough to keep Betty in Moodrow's apartment until Leonora's third call, but it hadn't gotten her a night's sleep. By the time the phone rang, a little after nine o'clock in the morning, she was on her fourth cup of coffee.

"I found somebody you can talk to," Leonora had announced. "An agent named Marsha Millstein in the Division of Public Relations."

Betty had failed to keep the disappointment out of her voice. "Leonora, that's like talking to a very polite statue. Stonewalling is what they do. Hell, it's *all* they do."

"I won't argue the point, but it's a place to start. Right now, I can't reach Holtzmann or anyone close to him." Her voice had dropped to a whisper. "Look, there's something big happening over there and I can't get a handle on it."

"Bigger than arresting Carmine Stettecase with a couple hundred kilos of heroin?"

"Maybe that's it, but I keep sensing fear, not anticipation. Like something's gone wrong and they don't know how to fix it. Anyway, I called the MCC from my office a few minutes ago and Stanley's not there."

"Or so they claim."

Leonora had paused briefly, looking for a polite way to frame the essential message. When she couldn't find one, she opted for frank and to the point. "Don't go in there with an attitude. Be Stanley's attorney, not his lover. Remember, they've been holding him for less than forty-eight hours. It might be irregular, but it's not a technical violation of his rights, not in the federal system. Try to make Agent Millstein understand that releasing Stanley is in the Bureau's best interest."

"In the Bureau's best interest," Betty repeated as she locked the door and made her way down to the street. She said it again as she walked into the Metropolitan Correctional Center and presented her credentials.

"Pardon me?" The corrections officer seated behind the low counter, a middle-aged white man with a sagging gut and deep blue-gray pouches beneath a pair of tiny ice blue eyes, seemed utterly bored. "Were you talkin' to me?"

"I'm here to see my client, Stanley Moodrow." Betty laid her identification on the counter, watched him pick it up, examine it like an entomologist trying to identify an unfamiliar insect, then pass it back. "You wanna spell out that name?"

"The first or the last?"

"The last." His expression didn't change, didn't even flicker.

"M-O-O-D-R-O-W." Betty glanced at the man's nameplate. "Officer McTaggert."

"No such."

It was Betty's turn to say, "Pardon me?"

"No such." McTaggert swiveled the monitor 180 degrees. "Look for yourself. He ain't here."

"I spoke to him last night." Betty wondered, briefly, if lying fit the general heading of "in the Bureau's best interest."

"Maybe he got bailed out. You want me to check?"

"I want you to be sure he's not here right now."

"I'm already sure."

"In that case, so am I. And thank you for your cheerful assistance."

It took Betty less than ten minutes to walk the few blocks to FBI headquarters in the Federal Building on Worth Street. Inside, she received a visitor's badge marked with her name and her ultimate destination, the FBI's Public Relations Division on the thirty-fourth floor. The lobby was crowded with men and women heading off to dozens of federal bureaucracies, some as workers and some as supplicants. Betty, as she waited for an elevator, made a conscious effort to see herself as the latter. And not as an avenging angel.

In the Bureau's best interest, she said to herself. The Constitution will just have to fend for itself.

Moodrow was still eating his breakfast (cold cereal, cold juice, cold coffee) when two beefy corrections officers approached his cell, ordered him out, then walked him down the hall to a tiny interview room. Without explanation, they put him inside, leaving him to sit in a chair bolted to the green tile floor while they stood guard outside. Moodrow noted the mustard yellow walls, the metal table, the dirty white ceiling, and nodded to himself. While the room didn't have the cachet of the Canary Cage in the old Seventh Precinct, it did reek of squirming, sweating mutts and the sharply focused men who pursued them. Apparently, interrogation was a facet of law enforcement the feds hadn't managed to sanitize.

Twenty minutes later, he stood and walked over to a small mirror set into the door, stared at his reflection, wondered if his guards were just outside looking back at him. When the COs ordered him out of the cell, Moodrow had anticipated only two possibilities: Holtzmann was either going to charge him or let him go. After all, what question could Holtzmann ask in an interview room that couldn't be asked in Moodrow's cell? And why, it being a few hours before the big bust, would Holtzmann be thinking about Stanley Moodrow at all?

Neither question was answered by the sudden appearance of a very tall, very elegant young man. At least as tall as Moodrow and rail thin, his black, summer-weight suit draped his bony frame perfectly, dropping in an unbroken line from his shoulders to the tops of his polished wingtips. Moodrow stared at the suit for a moment, relishing his own resentment, then raised his eyes to look into the man's face. The man's features were uniformly strong, the bones of his face prominent. He returned Moodrow's contemptuous gaze frankly, but without apparent aggression.

"Cooper," the man said. "Justice Department." His voice carried vague traces of a southern drawl.

Moodrow thought about it for a moment, then said, "Justice Department, huh? That's an unusual last name, but I guess it's not impossible. I once knew a guy named Bureau. He spelled it with two *ns*."

Cooper's expression didn't change. "Why don't we sit down?" he said after a long pause.

"Why don't you . . ." Moodrow bit off the rest of the message. Something was very wrong and he wasn't going to find out what it was by playing the tough guy. "Why don't we run through that one more time," he said as he dropped into the chair. "Your full name and full title."

"My name is Cooper. Buford Cooper. From the state of Mississippi."

He smiled for the first time, a quick, broad flash of gleaming white teeth. Moodrow read the grin as supremely confident, the grin of a doctor treating a disease from which he, himself, was immune.

"And the title?"

"I'm what they call a Special Counsel." He crossed his legs and took out a pack of Viceroys. "You smoke?" When Moodrow shook his head, he added, "Mind if I do?"

"Knock yourself out."

Cooper shook out a smoke and lit it with a slender gold lighter. The lighter, Moodrow noted before it disappeared into Cooper's trouser pocket, was neither flashy nor cheap.

"I'm Special Counsel to the Attorney General of the United States of America." He blew out a stream of smoke. "Has a nice ring to it, don't you think?"

"A wonderful ring," Moodrow agreed. "Now why don't you tell me what you want."

Cooper stared at Moodrow for a moment, then took a deep breath and smiled again. "I want to know why you're here," he said. "No matter how stupid that sounds."

A vague uneasiness flitted through Moodrow's consciousness like a bat through an underground cave. "You saying you haven't asked the man who brought me?"

"And who might that be?"

Moodrow shook his head slowly. "Don't try to play the interrogator," he said evenly. "You don't have the experience to bring it off." That brought a flush to Cooper's tanned cheeks. "If you're gonna answer every question by asking another one, I want my lawyer."

"That would be Ms. Haluka. She's in the building even as we speak. Inflicting psychological damage on a PR person."

Moodrow giggled his appreciation. "One for you," he admitted.

"One for me, yes." Cooper put the cigarette into his mouth, let it rest on his lips for a moment before inhaling. "Let me put it simply," he said. "I was in Manhattan on Justice Department business when I got a call from DC asking me to check on the status of an ex-cop being detained without charge by the FBI. Just to check, mind you, not to actually do anything about it. Now I can't find a single agent who admits to knowing anything about Stanley Moodrow beyond the bare fact that he's actually here."

Moodrow leaned forward, placed his palms flat on the table. "And Karl Holtzmann?" He closed his eyes in anticipation of the blow sure to follow. "What does Karl Holtzmann say?"

"Karl Holtzmann is missing. Along with US Attorney Abner Kirkwood and Agent Bob Ewing." Cooper tapped his ash onto the floor. "Would you know anything about that?"

It was the worst possible scenario. Ginny Gadd alone in that apartment; Stanley Moodrow in a cell, unable to even warn her; Jilly Sappone on the loose. Repressing a groan, Moodrow stared at his clenched fists. "You have to let me the fuck out of here." He raised his head, glared at Buford Cooper as if contemplating an all-out attack.

"That's not an answer to my question."

Moodrow slammed his fist into the table. "Give me one good reason why I should bail you out? You arrested me without probable cause, detained me without charge, denied me the right to make a phone call or consult an attorney. . . ."

"*I* didn't do any of that." Cooper, who hadn't flinched in the face of Moodrow's tirade, dropped his cigarette on the floor and slowly ground it out with the heel of his shoe. "Until a couple of hours ago, I didn't even know you existed."

"What're you lookin' for, Cooper, tea and sympathy?"

"I'm looking for a little help."

"You still haven't given me a reason why I should give a shit about you." He leaned back, took a deep breath, readied himself for the actual bargaining. "Or the Justice Department or the Federal Bureau of Incompetence."

"Perhaps," Cooper smiled again, "because giving a shit might go a long way toward getting you out of here." He took a white handkerchief from the breast pocket of his jacket and gently wiped his mouth. "Within, say, the next few hours."

Jilly Sappone squatted, then sat on the gritty, tarred rooftop. Frowning, he leaned against the narrow ledge, took a sandwich bag from the pocket of Agent Bob's forest green windbreaker, and stared at the small pile of dope at the bottom. For some reason, ever since his good-bye phone call to Aunt Josie, he couldn't do anything without thinking it was the last time he was gonna do it. The last shower, the last shave, the last piss, the last bacon, eggs, toast, coffee. It was stupid, really, because he didn't have to die. Captured, yeah; he was definitely gonna be captured. Even if he somehow got into that apartment, did the deed, got away, Jilly Sappone had nowhere to hide. But that didn't mean he'd be killed, not unless he decided to put a round in his own head, let a big piece of lead chase the small one already down there, and he hadn't made that decision. Not yet.

Nevertheless, as he dug his pinky into the heroin, scooped out a little heap, pushed it up into his nose, he heard himself say, *the last snort*. As clearly as if he'd spoken out loud.

The day was warm and the sun, directly overhead, poured down on the rooftop. Jilly could feel hot tar beneath his buttocks, knew he'd carry some of it with him when he finally got his act in gear. He didn't mind, didn't think Ann would mind, either. This being the last time and all.

He tilted his head back, closed his eyes, let the sun heat his face while the heroin worked its way through his body. Twenty minutes later, when he began to pull himself together, he was still sitting against the wall, though his chin had dropped down to his chest and he was snoring softly.

"The last nod," Jilly said without opening his eyes. Laughter bubbled over his tongue and lips, seemed to dribble out of his mouth, the sound wet and ugly even to himself. Christ, he thought, I *gotta* get moving.

But he didn't move, not until he heard the door to the roof squeal on its hinges. Then, as if someone had thrown a switch, his eyes were open, the automatic in his hand, his brain on full alert.

"Don' shoo me, bro. Don' shoo me."

Jilly stared at the man in the doorway for a moment before dismissing him as a junkie looking for a place to fix or something to rip off. No surprise in a building like this. "You got business with me?" he asked.

"No way." The man took a step forward, his eyes riveted to the barrel of the gun. "I don't even know nobody's up here." He opened his clenched fist to reveal several bags of dope. "I gotta get off, bro. I'm sick."

Jilly flicked the automatic in the general direction of Second Avenue, said, "Take it somewhere else," watched the junkie half trot across the rooftops. When the man was several roofs away, Jilly dragged himself to his knees and turned around to peer over the low concrete parapet at a twenty-story apartment building across the street. The building, of white brick and studded with balconies, was solidly middle class and fronted Third Avenue at the corner of Twenty-seventh Street. Another, almost identical structure, faced it from the west side of the avenue. From each of these buildings, a string of five-story brick tenements radiated east and west along Twenty-seventh Street like the tendrils of a spreading cancer.

There was dope in virtually every building, even in those where the landlord bothered to repair the broken locks and mailboxes. Some, like the one Jilly had used to get to the roof, were almost entirely given over to the trade. At least half the twenty apartments, though unrented, served as shooting galleries, crack dens, or both. Four or five others were occupied by prostitutes who worked the lower end of Lexington Avenue a block to the west. The remainder housed working families whose economic survival depended on low rent.

Jilly, like every other committed druggie, had an infallible nose for dope. When he'd first smelled it out, on the day he'd been released from prison, he'd immediately filed the information away for later use. Then he'd ripped off Patsy Gullo's heroin and almost forgotten about Twenty-seventh Street. Almost.

As his head began to clear, Jilly focused his attention more sharply. With his eyes raised a few inches above the low wall, he could see the south side and back of his ex-wife's building, as well as two cops parked in a brown Caprice on the west side of Third Avenue. The cops were making no effort to conceal themselves, sitting there with the windows open, elbows hanging out, as if their view of the front door guaranteed Ann Kalkadonis's safety.

Jilly, of course, had never expected to go through the lobby. He was interested in a narrow strip of concrete running along the back of the building to a service entrance in the basement. If he approached this ramp from the north side of Twenty-seventh Street, the cops wouldn't be able to see him or the door at the bottom. At least not the cops parked on Third Avenue. Thinking it over on the trip from his motel room, Jilly had figured that windowless steel door would be his biggest problem. If it was locked, which it usually was, he'd have to stand around, make himself a perfect target while he waited until somebody opened it from the inside.

Jilly put his palms on the ledge, pushed himself up a little higher, and laughed out loud. "My lucky day," he said, then quickly amended the statement. "My *last* lucky day."

Somebody had tied the wide-open basement door to a faucet on the wall of the building, that somebody undoubtedly being a representative of B&A Moving and Storage whose truck was parked at the curb. As Jilly watched, smiling to himself, two burly men came through the opening, one after the other, each pushing a dolly loaded with household furniture.

Once Jilly started moving, his body decided to wake up, get with the program. By the time he reached the second floor he was taking the steps two at a time. He paused in the hallway for a moment, inhaling the stink of piss and mold as if it was an aphrodisiac, then came out of the building, took a right without glancing at the cops, and began to walk east toward Second Avenue. Halfway down the block, he crossed the street and headed back the way he'd come. His right hand, despite the need to appear as natural as possible, remained by his waist, ready to dip beneath Agent Bob's jacket. There was always the chance that the cops or the feds had another team out there, one he hadn't spotted. If that was the case, he was determined to bust a few caps before he packed it in.

As he approached the moving truck, Jilly kept his eyes focused on the fat man standing inside, half expecting him to turn, weapon in hand, shout, "Police, motherfucker. Keep your hands where I can see 'em." But the man continued to pack a mix of furniture and taped brown boxes into the front of the truck, ignoring him altogether. The same was true of the two cursing workers struggling to pass an enormous leather couch through the basement door.

"It don't fuckin' go, man," the taller of the two said as Jilly slipped past. "We're gonna have to take it out the fucking front."

"I'm not gonna put it back in that elevator," the second man replied. "And I'm not walkin' it up them stairs, neither."

They continued to argue, ignoring Jilly who stopped a few feet away to consider his next move. He was standing at one end of a wide corridor running the full length of the building. A series of doors on either side led to the boiler and compactor rooms, various storage areas, the building's communal laundry, the super's little office, and the elevators. Jilly had been this way on his first visit, but he'd come through fast, looking for those elevators and nothing else. Now he needed to get his bearings.

"Could I help you?" A short, broad-shouldered man wearing a blue cotton uniform stepped out of a room twenty feet away. He was standing in the middle of the hallway, feet wide apart, a fuck-you sneer plastered to his face. "You a tenant?"

"I'm lookin' for the super." Jilly forced himself to smile. He could feel the molten core at the base of his personality begin to bubble upward, knew that if he didn't close the furnace door, it would own him.

"Whatta ya want him for?"

"I'm a salesman. You know, janitorial supplies, like that."

"We got somebody."

"Are you the super?" Jilly's hand was already moving toward his waist.

"Uh-uh." The man held his smirk for a moment longer, then relented. "Last door on the left."

"Thank you." Jilly, momentarily disappointed, consoled himself by deciding to retrace his steps when he finished with his wife, pay the man a last visit. Then, smiling, he squeezed past his interrogator and walked down the hall to the super's office where he found an elderly black man, telephone in hand, sitting behind a battered wooden desk that seemed to fill the tiny room. The man was tall and wiry-strong, with a prominent forehead made even more prominent by a raised scar that ran over his left eye like a second eyebrow. He glanced up as Jilly entered, then returned to his conversation.

"I'll have someone up after lunch, Ms. Carozzo. I don't have nobody right now. Remember, this here's the third time you plugged that drain in the last two weeks." He rolled his eyes, muttered an occasional "yeah" as he listened, finally said, "Ya'll wanna blame the plumbing, that's fine with me, but last time we took a tube of Crest outta the trap. You tole me your little boy done flushed it down there." He paused again, listened briefly, then ran his fingers through his snow white hair. "After lunch, Ms. Carozzo. First thing."

Jilly, fighting an urge to lick his lips in anticipation, glanced at a nameplate lying on the super's desk. Originally of white letters on a black background, it was now so gray and dirty that it took him a moment to read the words, *Leuten Kitt*.

"You lookin' at the name right? My mama called me Leuten because my father was in the army. Leuten is short for lieutenant."

"No shit?"

"If I'm lyin', I'm dyin'." He flashed Jilly a friendly smile. "Now what could I do you for on this fine, fine morning?"

"You could answer a simple question."

"I'm listenin'."

Slowly, as if reaching for his business card (which he was, in a way) Jilly slid a hand beneath his jacket, pulled Agent Bob's automatic, pressed it against the tip of Leuten Kitt's nose. "The question of the hour," he said, "is do you wanna live or do you wanna die?" He cocked the hammer by way of driving his point home, then quickly added, "Don't be shy now. Because you ain't got the time to think it over."

"What I need to know," Moodrow said as he plucked a jelly doughnut from a greasy paper sack and bit into it, "is why, you being a politician, the FBI would give you the time of day?" He popped the lid on a container of coffee and sipped at the steaming liquid. "Any more than a New York cop would give the time of day to a deputy mayor." A half hour had gone by since Special Counsel Cooper's unexpected appearance and Moodrow still wasn't sure what the man wanted to hear.

Buford Cooper toyed with the crease on his trousers for a moment, then raised a pair of lazy blue eyes to meet Moodrow's unwavering stare. "Well, they won't," he admitted. "Give me the time of day, I mean."

"Then how'd you get to me?"

"I took advantage of the chaos." Cooper stood up, pulled off his jacket, folded it carefully before laying it on the table. "With the commander in chief among the missing . . . Well, let's just say none of the ranking officers wanted to tell me an outright lie. Not when I already knew you were here." He walked to the far wall, faced it as if looking out a window. When he spoke again, his tone was almost wistful. "We've been under pressure since the day we took office. One scandal after another, most of them pure bullshit. I suppose we can deal with another political crisis—we've certainly had enough practice—but it would be nice to see it coming."

"Pardon me if I don't cry in my coffee." Moodrow had always reserved a special position on his mutt list for professional politicians. "Tell me how you plan to get me out of here. Being as you have no direct authority over the FBI." Determined to maintain an external calm, he resisted the urge to turn and face Cooper. Instead, he finished his doughnut in a single, gargantuan bite, then, one at a time, licked his fingers clean.

Cooper replied without hesitation. "Assuming that I'm satisfied with your story, I plan to simply *walk* you out." He strolled back to his chair, sat down, shook a Viceroy out of a half-empty pack. "There's no paperwork on you, none at all. Theoretically, even as we speak, you're not here."

Moodrow contemplated the bag of doughnuts for a moment, wanting to reach in, mask his anxiety by stuffing his mouth. Instead, he rolled up the edges of the bag and pushed his coffee away. "You a lawyer?" he asked.

"Of course." Cooper followed the admission with a faint smile.

"Then you can understand me when I say I've got a very circumstantial case here. One that couldn't be proven beyond a reasonable doubt in a court of law. At least, not by me." He waited until Cooper nodded his understanding, then continued. "You aware of the narcotics bust that's supposed to go down today?"

"Assume I don't know anything," Cooper replied. "Because I don't." He lit his cigarette and leaned back in the chair.

"In that case, we're gonna have to back up a little." Now that he'd made the basic decision, Moodrow wanted to tell the story completely—knowing that if he didn't, Cooper, despite the buddy-buddy manner, would have him going over the details for the next twelve hours. He began with Jilly Sappone's father and the injury to Jilly, worked his way through Josie Rizzo and her daughter's marriage, Carmine Stettecase's problems with Jilly, and the frame-up that sent Jilly to prison.

"The board turned Jilly down when he came up for parole," he concluded, "then reversed itself when Karl Holtzmann, or maybe his boss, intervened because Josie Rizzo was supplying the FBI with information on Carmine Stettecase and a huge dope deal Carmine was setting up."

Cooper started to speak, then changed his mind. He signaled Moodrow to continue with a languid wave of his cigarette.

"What I've told you so far, that's the good news." Moodrow picked up the bag of doughnuts, weighed it in his palm for a moment, then returned it to the table with a little sigh. "On the day he got out of prison, Jilly Sappone teamed up with a former cell mate, Jackson-Davis Wescott. They kidnapped a child on the first day, then committed at least three murders together, one of which I personally witnessed. A few days ago, Wescott turned up in Riverside Park with a knife in his ribs and Jilly Sappone disappeared. I'm saying that Karl Holtzmann and Robert Ewing and the US attorney you mentioned decided to protect Jilly Sappone, at least until after they took Carmine down. I'm saying something went wrong and now Jilly Sappone's on the loose."

The silence that followed was entirely obligatory and both men knew it. Cooper, his eyes nearly closed, puffed on his cigarette as if he didn't have a care in the world. Moodrow, watching him, knew the question to come and was busy preparing an answer that would satisfy Buford Cooper without exposing Stanley Moodrow or Ginny Gadd to the possibility of criminal prosecution.

"You haven't told me," Cooper finally said, "your part in . . ." He spread his hands, smiled again. "In all *this*."

Moodrow tapped the metal tabletop with the side of his fist. "I'm a licensed private investigator and I was hired, for obvious reasons, by the mother of the kidnapped child. The story I just told you was pieced together in the course of my investigation. Holtzmann was afraid I'd go public before he arrested Carmine Stettecase, so he decided to put me in a cell for the duration, to stash me like he stashed Jilly Sappone." Moodrow began to fumble with the bag of doughnuts. Now that he'd clearly stated his case, he felt entitled to a reward. "Tell me," he asked, "what are you going to say when the bodies turn up?"

Cooper ignored the question. "I'm hearing an awful lot of speculation here," he said.

Moodrow shrugged, mumbled, "Time will tell," and swallowed hard.

"I suppose it will." Cooper sat up in his chair. He glanced at his watch, shook his head, muttered, "Welcome to hell," as he rose to his feet. "I'm going to ask you to sign a release before I let you go."

"A release?"

"Basically stating that you were here of your own free will, that you do not now and will not in the future hold the FBI or any individual employed by the FBI responsible for your incarceration."

"That would be a lie."

"True, but it would at least take care of one of the several dozen problems we're going to have to address when . . . when the bodies turn up."

Moodrow stood and leaned across the table. Unable to control his joy, he giggled in Buford Cooper's face, then quickly apologized. "What could I say, Cooper? I guess I'm just an emotional guy. Now, where the fuck do I sign?"

What Leuten Kitt said, with his mouth, was, "Yessuh, I wants to live," but what he said to himself was, *Another white man with a gun.*

Leuten Kitt knew quite a bit about white men with guns, having spent virtually all of his third decade at Angola State Prison in the great state of Louisiana. There were no gray stone walls at Angola, just swamps and forests and lots of shotgun-toting white men. Of course, all that was twenty-seven years ago and he'd put his life together since then—come up north, gotten married, raised a family—but the lessons he'd learned in those nine years were never far away.

"You know who I am, nigger?"

"Nossir." That was one of the most important lessons. *Yessir, Nossir* and bide your time.

"Get up and come around the desk."

Kitt rose slowly, careful to keep his hands in sight. He walked over to Jilly Sappone, turned his back, submitted to a thorough frisk.

"You ready for the deal, Sambo?"

"Yessir. Ready for anythin' y'all say."

"I'm goin' up to 14D. You know who lives there?"

"Yessir."

"Turn around and look at me."

"Yessir."

"Who lives there?"

"In 14D?"

"You play the dumb nigger with me, you're gonna be the dumb, *dead* nigger."

"Kalkadonis family lives there. In 14D." Leuten didn't need to look into Sappone's eyes to see the fire stoked at the back of the man's brain. Jilly's voice was enough to convince Leuten Kitt that death was right around the corner.

"And who am I?"

"You . . ." The way Leuten saw it, he had a big, big problem. The Kalkadonis family had pulled out and the apartment was empty and Jilly Sappone didn't seem like the kind of man who could deal with disappointment. "You the man took the baby."

"Very good." Sappone stepped back. "Now what's gonna happen here is we're goin' up to that apartment and you're gonna get me inside. You with me so far."

"Yessir."

"So, how ya gonna get me in?"

"With my keys."

"Wrong answer, monkey. Try again." When Kitt didn't respond, Jilly continued. "If I was gonna use the keys, why the fuck would I need you to come upstairs? I could just kill your black ass right here and now." He raised the gun several inches, forcing Kitt to look into the barrel. "So, let's try it again. How you gonna get me in?"

Leuten stared at the weapon for a moment, then moved his eyes a few inches to the left. He could still remember the first time he'd looked into the barrel of a guard's shotgun, still feel the sudden hot rush of urine through the hairs on his thigh. "I gots to tell 'em somethin'. Make 'em open the door."

"And who says you people can't learn?"

When it became obvious that Sappone expected a reply, Leuten said, "Ain't nobody says that."

"Nobody except everybody." Instead of laughing, Sappone grunted. "Now, *what* are you gonna tell 'em?"

"Tell 'em there's somethin' wrong and I gotta get inside."

Jilly, his expression fixed, stepped forward and cracked Leuten Kitt in the mouth. He listened to the echo for a moment, savored the obvious pain in Kitt's eyes, then said, "I don't wanna hear the fuckin' stall. Understand me?"

"Yessir." Leuten fought the urge to touch his face, see if his teeth were still there. "Yessir, here's what I tell 'em. I say, 'Ma'am, we done got a leak in the bathroom ceiling downstairs and I need to come inside, check the pipes. Won't take but a minute.' "

Sappone nodded. His eyes were blazing now, his mouth twisted. Once those locks were thrown, even if a cop answered, he was definitely gonna get inside. Shoot through the door and keep on shooting until it was over, one way or the other.

He took off Agent Bob's windbreaker, folded it in half, then draped it over the hand holding the gun. "You got grandkids?"

"Yessir."

"Then remember what I'm tellin' ya here." He stepped back to let Kitt pass in front of him. "If you're thinkin' about how you're gonna make a break soon as we leave this room, think again. You get more than two feet away from me, them brats are gonna have to grow up without a grampa."

With nothing more to be said, Leuten took a tentative step forward.

"Ain't you forgettin' somethin'?"

Jilly voice stopped him as if he'd run into a wall. "Sir?"

"The keys, nigger, the fuckin' keys. In case they're not home."

Forgetting the keys being Leuten's only strategy, he cursed Sappone inwardly. "Yeah, you right," he said. "They in the drawer." He walked back to the desk, careful to keep his hands in sight, and removed an enormous ring of keys. Without being asked, he flipped through the ring until he found the pair for the Kalkadonis apartment. Then he walked past Jilly Sappone and out into the hall.

"Straight to the elevators. No stops, no conversation."

Leuten, as he walked down the corridor, was hoping to find the small room that housed the building's three elevators completely empty. Sooner or later, the way he read the situation, he was going to have to make his move and the elevator seemed as good a place as any. If Sappone sent him in first, he could step to the side, press the button that closed the doors, maybe . . .

The sound of a child's voice cut through Leuten's speculations with the finality of a meat cleaver. *Vroooom, vroooom, vrooooooooom.* A moment later, he glanced through the open doorway to find his worst fears confirmed. A short, heavy woman pulling a shopping cart filled with carefully folded laundry was jabbing her rigid forefinger into the elevator call button while a young boy on a tricycle whizzed back and forth just behind her legs.

"Afternoon' Miss Green."

The woman turned and smiled. "Good afternoon, Leuten." She glanced at Jilly Sappone, then back at the super, then down at the ground.

"Kinda hot today." Leuten moved a few inches to the left. He could feel Sappone tense up and was trying for enough room to swing an elbow in case the man decided that Myrna Green had recognized his famous face, that the only remedy was blood and bullets.

"Well, summer's here." Myrna Green smiled up at Jilly Sappone. "Are you moving in?" she asked.

Leuten Kitt heard Jilly Sappone release the breath he'd been holding and figured it was gonna be okay, at least for now. Then Jilly said, "I'm thinkin' about it," and the elevator arrived. Leuten stepped inside and pressed the button that held the doors open.

"All aboard," he said, his voice as cheerful as he could make it.

Myrna Green tugged the shopping cart into the elevator. "C'mon, Tommy," she called to her son. "And take it easy."

Tommy responded by crashing his trike into the elevator's rear wall, producing a hollow boom that he apparently found hilarious.

"How many times do I have to tell you about that?"

Leuten pressed the buttons for the third and fourteenth floors. He could see Jilly Sappone's face now. The man's eyes were blank, unfocused, the eyes of a lizard waiting for a meal to happen by. They stayed that way until the doors opened on the third floor and Myrna Green stepped into the corridor.

"Let's go, Tommy."

When Tommy showed no inclination to leave the elevator, Leuten again pressed the button that held the doors open. Sappone was looking straight at him, the lizard with a fly in sight.

"I said *now*, Tommy. Or you can forget *Animaniacs*."

With a final whoop, Tommy backed his tricycle in a half circle, then flew out the door, spun around the shopping cart, and headed off down the hall.

"Ever since his father and I divorced . . . I don't know. I think I've lost control." Myrna Green tossed Jilly a last, sidelong glance. "Good luck with the apartment," she said. When he didn't respond she turned to Leuten Kitt. "You have a good afternoon, Leuten."

Leuten released the button, called, "You too, Miss Green," through the closing doors.

"You done good, nigger." Jilly Sappone moved to the far corner of the elevator. "No shit, man. You saved the bitch's life. The kid's, too. Now it's time for you to save your own."

"Yessir," Leuten replied automatically. Not wanting to be shot down like a dog, he still intended to make some kind of a move. Only now he was pretty sure that he and the dog were gonna end up in the same place, move or not.

"Because, say I get what I want, I'm gonna let ya slide. You hear me?"

"Yessir." What Leuten heard was the lust in Jilly Sappone's voice, the lust for blood. He'd heard that call many a time down at Angola. The cry of an animal that liked to hurt.

The elevator came to a halt and the doors slid open. Jilly Sappone tossed the jacket over his shoulder, exposing the automatic in his hand. "Take a look down that hallway," he said. "Tell me exactly what you see."

As Leuten moved into the doorway, he felt Sappone come up behind him, hook a finger in his belt. "I don't see nothin'," he said, quickly adding, "but a empty hall with doors."

"That's good. That's very good." Sappone pressed his knuckle into the base of Leuten's spine. "Because I'm real, real hot for this and if you fuck it up for me I'm gonna . . ."

"Yessir, I gets the message and I'm goin' do just what y'all say to do and nothin' else. Soon as y'all tell me what it is."

"I want you to go straight to that apartment, 14D. I want you to stand in front of the peephole, ring the bell, let 'em know it's Uncle Sambo and not Jilly Sappone standing in the hall. I want you to get that fucking door open any way you have to." Sappone paused momentarily, then said, "This is my last time, man." Like the statement explained everything Leuten needed to know.

As Leuten Kitt followed Sappone's directions exactly, walking down the hall at a steady pace, stopping directly in front of 14D, pressing then releasing the bell, a plan began to form in his mind. Ann Kalkadonis had called him the morning before and told him she was leaving New York. Later in the day, he'd seen Ann and her daughter, both carrying luggage, go out through the lobby. That meant the apartment was going to be empty and Sappone was going to be very disappointed, like a kid without a Christmas present, a kid with a gun. What he, Leuten Kitt, had to do was convince Sappone that if just hung around for a while, his wife and his daughter would come back.

Without waiting to be asked, Leuten again rang the bell, this time holding it down for several seconds. Then he let off, cocked his ear to the door and pressed it again. "Don't seem to be nobody home," he said, trying the words out as a kind of experiment before pounding on the door with his fist. "I seen 'em goin' out, Mrs. Kalkadonis and her daughter, round ten o'clock. Figured they'd be back by now."

"Shut the fuck up," Jilly whispered. His head swiveled back and forth, checking the hall, then he began to back away from the door, stopping midway between his wife's apartment and the apartment to the north.

Leuten meekly followed. Figuring that he and Sappone were going to be together for quite a while, that all he'd bought was time.

"Whyn't you tell me this shit before?" Jilly's eyes were on fire. The gun trembled slightly in his hand. "If you're tryin' to play some dumb spook game . . ."

"I jus' figger they be back." He paused, started to raise his eyes to meet Jilly's, then remembered and yanked them down to Sappone's chest. "See, what I'm sayin' is they was pullin' one of them carts. You know, like they was goin' to the supermarket." He was shifting his weight from foot to foot, aware of it, but unable to stop himself. A little voice inside his head was calling *mama, mama, mama* from what seemed like a great distance. Working around and through his thoughts with a will of its own.

"What about the cops? Where are the goddamned cops?"

Leuten, caught unawares, took a second to think it over before replying. "Well, they out in front. I seen 'em this mornin' when I was fixin' the stoop." He shrugged, his shoulders so tight it felt like he was pulling them up out of the mud. "As for inside the house . . . well, like I don't live there or nothin', but I ain't seen no cops around the apartment in some time." He paused again. "If they was in there, why wouldn't they be answerin' the door?"

Jilly's pent-up breath whooshed out of his chest for the second time. His eyes closed for a moment, then popped wide open. "I want you to ring the bell again. If nobody comes, use the keys." He raised the gun a few inches. "Push the door open, but don't move a fucking inch until I tell you. Remember, if there's somebody waitin' in there, if it's a trap, you're gonna go first."

Leuten didn't bother to say, "Yessir." He walked over to the door, feeling for the keys as he went, and gave the bell a short, sharp jab. A few seconds later, he opened the two locks and pushed the door back to reveal a narrow hallway.

"Say somethin'." Jilly stepped forward, taking Leuten's shirt in his free hand.

"Maintenance," Leuten called. "Anybody inside?"

When there was no reply, Jilly shoved Leuten through the doorway. "Keep callin', keep movin'. We're gonna look in every room, every closet. Startin' with this one in the hall. You're gonna open the door, move the clothes around, make sure nobody's hidin' inside." He ground the barrel of the automatic into Leuten Kitt's scalp, drawing a trickle of blood in the process. "Let's move."

"Maintenance. Maintenance."

Leuten kept repeating the word as he walked to the hall closet, opened the door, leaned inside, rummaged through the coats and jackets. Sappone was draped all over him, a second skin, and both of them were entirely focused on the dark shadows inside the closet. That was why, Leuten figured later on, neither one of them heard Guinevere Gadd come up behind them.

"You feel that, Jilly Sappone? You feel it?" Gadd's voice froze both men. "That's my .38 pushed into the base of your skull, with the barrel angled up at 45 degrees. You move and you're fucking dead."

What Leuten Kitt figured was that *he* was the one who was dead. And he wasn't encouraged when Jilly Sappone snarled, "I'll kill the nigger. I ain't kiddin'. You don't back off, I'll kill the nigger right this minute."

Gadd's answer only made it worse. "So what am I supposed to do now, Jilly, arrange for a helicopter and five or six million bucks in untraceable bills? You wanna shoot him, go ahead. I'm not a cop and the man doesn't mean shit to me." She made a half-strangled sound that Leuten took for a laugh, then said, "I beat the shit out of your Aunt Josie this morning."

Leuten didn't waste any time trying to figure out what that meant. He grabbed at Sappone's gun with his right hand, managing to get it away from his head a second before it went off, then slid his left hand behind his own buttocks and into Sappone's groin. Then he squeezed, yanked, and prayed.

A few seconds later, when Leuten found the courage to open his eyes, Jilly Sappone had stopped screaming.

"You could let go of his balls now," Gadd said. "He's unconscious and I wanna put cuffs on him before he wakes up."

Leuten, panting like a rescued swimmer, pushed Sappone into the hallway, noting the blood running from the man's head with some satisfaction. "I didn't hear you hit him."

Gadd knelt on Sappone's back and quickly handcuffed him. "Christ," she said, looking up at Leuten Kitt, "I been waiting a long time for this."

"I don't mean to change the subject, lady, but what you said before, about me not meaning shit to you? That mighta got me killed." Leuten, much to his surprise, was holding Sappone's automatic in his right fist, holding it by the barrel. He stared at the gun for a moment, then reversed it in his hand.

"The way I see it," Gadd replied evenly, "you're alive and Sappone is on the floor wearing handcuffs. You oughta be grateful." She got up and closed the front door. "I'm gonna go in the kitchen, look around for some tape. You think you can keep the beast subdued?"

"Lady, you're crazy."

"That's not an answer."

"The man's in handcuffs." Leuten felt some of the tension run out of him as he spoke the words. Yes, the man *was* in handcuffs, the man who wanted to kill Leuten Kitt, the man who did kill Theresa Kalkadonis. Leuten had six children and nine grandchildren and loved every one of them. His initial relief at finding himself alive began to dissipate. What rushed in to take its place was pure rage. He dropped the barrel of the gun to a spot just in front of Sappone's left ear, his attention so focused he might have been staring through a telephoto lens.

"Don't do it." Gadd's tone was matter-of-fact, like she didn't care all that much one way or the other.

"Gimme a reason."

"Because I've got something better in mind. Or, at least, slower." She touched Kitt's arm. "You gotta trust me here."

"Two minutes ago you told this scumbag to blow me away. Now you want me to trust you?"

"At least you know I'm honest."

She was gone before Leuten could respond, leaving him to care for Jilly, who'd begun to moan and shift his weight.

"Just stay down there, motherfucker," Leuten said after a moment. "Else I'll turn that crazy bitch loose on y'all."

"What crazy bitch?"

Leuten turned to find Gadd standing right behind him. She was holding a ball of twine in her hand, offering it to him like it was an apple. "You wanna stop sneakin' up on people?"

"I'll give it some thought." She pressed the twine into his hand. "Do me a favor and tie him up, starting from his ankles. For what I got planned, he can't be moving around."

Leuten was about to tell her to do it herself, then changed his mind. Looking into her eyes, he could see a mix of fear and anger and, behind both, a childish pleasure. Like she and Leuten were about to play a trick on the grown-ups.

"How tight you want the boy?" He dropped to one knee, looped a strand of twine around Sappone's ankle, tied the loose end back onto the roll.

"Tight enough so he shouldn't even *think* about moving. I want the fucker helpless." Gadd let the revolver drop to her side. "Yeah," she half whispered, "completely helpless."

Leuten took his time about it, drawing each loop tight before starting another revolution, letting the individual loops overlap slightly. "How you come to get behind us like that?" he asked. "Seemed like you come outta nowhere."

"I was in the stairwell, with the door cracked open a couple of inches, when you came out of the elevator. I saw you all the way."

"But you not a cop?"

"Uh-uh." Gadd sighed impatiently. "My name is Guinevere Gadd and I'm a private investigator working for Ann Kalkadonis. I made arrangements to stay on after she left. Just in case Jilly showed up, which he did. There's no mystery to it." She sighed again. "Could we hurry this up?"

"We could if you'd hold his feet off the ground so's I could slide the cord under him without stoppin' every time."

Gadd complied without hesitation, dropping to her knees. "Yeah," she admitted, "I should've thought of that myself."

"Now, lemme see if I got this right. You been sittin' on them stairs ever since Mrs. Kalkadonis and her daughter took off. That'd be yesterday, 'round two o'clock." He was up to Sappone's chest now, working quickly.

"Actually," Gadd confessed, "I was out there having a cigarette. After Ann took off, I went through the house looking for an ashtray and I couldn't find one." She shrugged and grinned. "People get nuts, you smoke in the house without permission. They buy extra life insurance, mail checks to the American Cancer Society, assault the smoker. I just had this picture of my client returning to a house filled with cigarette smoke. . . ." Gadd stopped abruptly. She watched Leuten Kitt tie off the twine just below the tops of Jilly's shoulders, decided that Jilly looked like a bug trying to work its way out of a cocoon. "I wanted to get away from the apartment. I wanted to get away and I wanted to watch it at the same time. You know what I mean?"

"What I know is I hope you cleaned up after yourself." Leuten stood and stretched. "What y'all plan to do with him?"

"I plan to throw him out the window. The one by the couch. I already oiled it up, just in case."

Gadd began to slap Sappone's face, the slaps soft, but persistent. After a moment, Sappone's eyes opened, then closed, then opened again. He looked directly at Gadd, who was kneeling beside him, her face only a couple of feet from his own, then twisted around to stare up at Leuten. At first, he appeared to be puzzled, as if there was something he'd forgotten, something important. Then he looked down at his body.

"What the fuck is this?" he whispered.

"This is hell, Jilly," Gadd replied without hesitation. "And I wanna be the first to offer you an official welcome."

When Sappone responded by thrashing like a landed fish, Gadd kicked him lightly in the groin, watched him try to double over, try to bring his hands up, try and fail to protect himself in any way. "Still tender, eh? I always heard they were like that, though I wouldn't know from actual experience." She waited for Jilly's eyes to come up, until she could look down into the fire, match it with her own. Then she got up and trotted off, returning a minute later with a small, white blanket.

"You recognize this blanket, Jilly?" she asked. "You ever seen one like it before?"

Sappone's mouth worked silently, his eyes looking like they were about to explode. Gadd stared down at him, her expression cold and clinical, like a scientist examining a white rat in a laboratory. "I got this blanket from the Medical Examiner's office," she said, the lie coming easily. "It's the one you wrapped around Theresa Kalkadonis before you threw her to her death. I think it's only fitting that I tie it around your neck before I throw you to your own death."

"Who the fuck *are* you?"

"Well, I'm tempted to say, Your worst nightmare. Only it's been used too many times. So let's try . . . Lorena Bobbitt on a real bad hair day." Gadd dropped to one knee, put the center of the blanket against the top of Sappone's head, began to work the edges around his shoulders. When he tried to bite her hand, she unholstered her .38 and tapped him lightly on the forehead. That stopped him long enough to get the blanket tied off beneath his jaw with the last piece of twine.

"Man looks halfway between a Halloween ghost and the Mummy." Leuten was standing with his back to the wall. He knew he was only a spectator here, that whatever he'd brought to the party had been overwhelmed by Guinevere Gadd and the baggage she carried. Not that he minded. Gadd was doing just fine without him. "Now what?" he asked.

Gadd stood up, took a minute to admire her handiwork. "It's like Christmas. You know, when you were a kid and you didn't want it to be over." She squatted down, grabbed the collar of Jilly's shirt, and gave him an experimental tug. "I think I'm gonna need some help here."

"He gotta go feet first." Leuten stepped forward and took Sappone's left ankle in both hands. "The way you got him tied, his feet are the only things left to grab hold of."

Sappone didn't really begin to struggle until his head bumped over the wooden saddle between the dining area and the living room. Then, as if someone had thrown a switch, he started to jerk uncontrollably. Gadd, though she recognized the involuntary nature of his convulsions, responded to the delay by kicking him several times.

"The man appears like he's speakin' in tongues," Leuten said. "You think he's havin' a blessed conversion?"

Gadd listened for a moment, catching the nouns *bitch, cunt, pig, whore* surrounded by the usual modifier, *fucking.* "I think he's having something between an epileptic fit and a temper tantrum." When he abruptly lost consciousness, she said, "Make it a fit," then grabbed his ankle and went back to work.

It took them another five minutes to get Jilly Sappone draped over the windowsill with his feet hanging outside. He was moaning softly and Gadd wasn't sure he was awake. "Hey, Sappone," she called, "you with us?" Crouching, she wrapped her arms around his shoulders, tilted him slightly, felt his torso begin to slide through. That brought a deeper moan, followed by a single word.

"Please." Sappone drew it out, his voice rising through the octaves like an air-raid siren in an old war movie.

"Almost done." Gadd let her weight settle back down. She looked at Leuten Kitt, started to smile, then saw Moodrow step into the room. "I don't think you're gonna need that," she said, nodding at the gun in his hand.

"Doesn't look like it," Moodrow admitted with a shrug. "Congratulations."

Leuten, hearing a voice behind him, jumped straight into the air, his body making a half turn before he touched down again. "Jesus Christ," he shouted.

"Stanley Moodrow, actually," Moodrow said without looking away from Ginny Gadd. "And this is Betty Haluka. She's an officer of the court."

Betty stepped out of the hallway and into the living room. She took a second to register the scene, her eyes moving from Leuten to Gadd to the open window. "I take it that's Jilly Sappone hiding under the blanket," she finally said. When Gadd failed to reply, she added, "Self-defense is gonna be a toughie here."

"How'd you get in this apartment?" Leuten demanded.

"I used the keys somebody left in the locks." Moodrow let his shoulders drop as he holstered his weapon. He was looking directly into Gadd's eyes, reading the essential message. "You think we could talk this over? I mean, being as you're gonna be the one doing the time, I wouldn't mind seeing how far Jilly can bounce, but . . ."

He took a step forward, trying to will himself into a dead run, but she was much too fast for him. Gadd came out of her crouch, heaving Sappone up and through the window before Moodrow got halfway across the room. Then the two of them, Gadd and Moodrow, their eyes still locked, shared the terror in Jilly's scream until it was abruptly cut off when he crashed into a redwood table set out on Sid and Myra Kupferman's balcony ten feet below.

TWENTY-FOUR

Moodrow and Betty, having spent the night in Moodrow's Lower East Side apartment after hours of questioning by city detectives, were preparing breakfast when Ginny Gadd rang the bell at nine o'clock on the following morning. Moodrow was chopping onions and peppers for an omelet while Betty flipped bacon slices in an ancient, cast-iron skillet. A thirteen-inch portable television sat on the kitchen table, tuned to CBS and a special report on what the media were alternately dubbing a tragedy or a fiasco as reporters struggled to make sense of the bloodbath that'd taken place in the north Bronx on the prior afternoon. This despite the visual aid supplied by a camera crew assigned by the networks to video the operation at the request of US Attorney Abner Kirkwood, a request made the day before he disappeared.

"Good morning," Gadd said when Moodrow opened the door, "I just thought I'd come over, let you know what I was doing." She grinned. "*Before* I actually go ahead and do it."

Moodrow nodded, the wheels already beginning to turn. What she ought to be doing—and what wouldn't be worth mentioning—was trying to ease her way out of the lunacy that'd taken place in Ann Kalkadonis's apartment. Jilly Sappone had survived the fall, his injuries limited to a dislocated shoulder, a pair of severely swollen testicles, and an attitude that bordered on genuine psychosis. For now, the cops, happy to have him, weren't making too much of a fuss. For now.

"C'mon in," he said, "have some breakfast. We're watching the video."

He didn't bother to specify which video and Gadd didn't ask. Instead, she handed him a copy of the *Daily News*, said, "Check out the headline," as she walked into the kitchen and greeted Betty.

" 'BRONX BLOODBATH.' " Moodrow read the words aloud as he followed Gadd. " 'Botched bust leads to butchery.' " He tossed the paper on the table, went back to his vegetables. "How do you like your omelets, hard or runny?"

Gadd was about to suggest a middle ground of some kind when the face of George Johnson appeared on the screen. Johnson, his deep, gravelly voice instantly recognizable after twenty years in the television news business, had a reputation for never smiling on the air. Today his long, bony face seemed especially grave as he informed his audience that the death toll had risen to sixteen, including four New York City cops and two innocent bystanders, one of them a child.

"For the next half hour," he intoned, "we will go through the videotape, a frame at a time if need be, in an effort to reconstruct the actual sequence of events."

Moodrow, with a sigh, picked up the cutting board and carried it to the kitchen table. Cops were dead and he was going to have to watch, feeling somehow responsible, as all cops do whenever a cop goes down. Gadd was already seated. She looked at him for a moment, then turned back to the television as the video began to run.

On the screen, a gray van, a Ford Econoline, entered what appeared to be a deserted street. It moved slowly for a hundred yards or so, until somebody in the control room stopped the tape.

"That van, that gray van, was carrying more than two hundred kilos of pure Asian heroin." Johnson's voice-over carried a near perfect mix of excitement and concern. "It was registered to a company called the Ching Hua Trading Corporation. Ching Hua Trading is owned by a man named On Luk Sun who was eventually captured inside the van. Mr. Sun is a trade representative for mainland China with offices in Beijing and New York."

The van began to move again, proceeding another fifty feet before a second van pulled out of a parking space blocking the way. At the same time, a third van entered the street from behind and screeched to a halt a few feet from the gray van's back door. Within seconds, men were pouring out into the streets, firing on the gray van with a mix of assault rifles and 12-gauge shotguns.

"Okay, let's stop it right here. These two vehicles, this red van and this blue van, held soldiers from the Carmine Stettecase crime family. This man—can we zoom in, Brian?—is Carmine Stettecase himself. He and his boys were there to steal the heroin, a fact unknown to the NYPD, the FBI, and the DEA, all of whom were represented on the scene, all of whom expected a common drug deal. Unfortunately for Mr. Stettecase, the gray van was heavily armored. The men you see falling in the street were hit by ricocheting rounds from their own weapons."

As the video began to roll again, Moodrow started to rise, coming halfway out of the seat before settling back down. He shook his head, muttered, "What a mess, what a fucking mess." A dozen men and women, city cops, poured from doorways up and down the street, responding automatically to the sound of gunfire while the leaderless feds (and their team of rooftop sharpshooters) held back. At the same time, the door to a brick warehouse in the middle of the block opened and On Luk's remaining troops charged into the street, firing as they came. Stettecase's soldiers (Carmine was dead by this time), seeing themselves surrounded, first tried to get to their vans. When that failed, they began to shoot at the cops who were already being fired on by On Luk's men. Then somebody opened up from the roof and, within seconds, the scene descended into utter chaos. It stayed that way for several minutes, until the video camera took a direct hit and the screen went black.

"There are questions here." Johnson's face reappeared. He was hunched forward, leaning over his desk. "Questions that demand answers. Last night, the bodies of three men, FBI Special Agent in Charge Karl Holtzmann, United States Attorney Abner Kirkwood, and Special Agent Robert Ewing, were discovered near an isolated house in western New Jersey. Karl Holtzmann was supposed to command the federal team." Johnson paused, took a deep breath, turned into a camera positioned to his left. "Yesterday afternoon, a fugitive named Gildo Sappone was captured by a private investigator in

Manhattan. Sappone had known connections to the Stettecase crime family." The camera moved in until Johnson's head filled the screen. "Did Gildo Sappone, as rumors suggest, have something to do with the New Jersey killings? What effect did Karl Holtzmann's absence have on the Bronx disaster, and who, if anybody, was in charge? Was the FBI protecting Gildo Sappone, the man who kidnapped, then murdered, Theresa Kalkadonis? After a brief commercial break, we'll be joined in our studios by three experts. . . ."

Moodrow shut off the television. "Enough is enough," he said. When neither Gadd nor Betty disagreed, he rose and carried the cutting board to a counter between the sink and the stove. "I think I've lost my appetite," he announced.

"You're not blaming yourself?" Betty turned on the light under a second skillet. "You've got a bad habit of doing that." She dropped a chunk of butter into the pan, watched it begin to melt.

"No, no, it's something else." He began to chop at the onions and peppers on the cutting board, then stopped abruptly and looked over at Gadd. "You listen to that tape again?"

"Of course." A quick grin opened Gadd's face. Moodrow had expected her to do what he would have done under the same circumstances. In a way, it was the ultimate compliment, one she'd never gotten from any of her NYPD partners. Or from her husband. "And you're right. Not only is there no mention of a rip-off, at one point somebody—I think it was Carmine, but I'm still not sure who's who—says they've got all the money together."

Moodrow went back to his chopping. "It *had* to say that," he called over his shoulder. "Otherwise, the feds would've been prepared for what actually went down." Finished, he laid the knife on the counter. Betty was stirring a bowl of scrambled eggs into the skillet and the hiss and crackle of the cool, yellow liquid hitting the hot pan held his attention for a moment. "So, who got the money?" he finally asked.

"Tommaso the Timid," Gadd replied. "Who else?"

Josie Rizzo stood in front of her daughter's bedroom closet, sliding hangers from left to right as she examined the wardrobe inside.

Mary was sitting on the edge of the bed, her eyes glued to the television set, watching Carmine go down for the fourth time in the last twenty minutes. "Carmine's dead," she whispered.

"How many times you gonna say the same thing?" Josie had never been happier. She had to admit it, had to admit that, for as long as the spirit possessed her, she hadn't been happy at all. "So, whatta you think?" Turning, she held a white, long-sleeved dress against her chest. "Is it the real me?" When Mary didn't respond, Josie put the dress back in the closet. The basic decision she'd made—to never again wear a black dress—didn't offer a clue to what she actually *should* wear.

Mary, interrupted by her mother in the act of dressing, had on a pair of beige panties and nothing else. She was looking down at her breasts, a bewildered expression clouding her face. "Tommy's gone, too, mama."

"Whatta you sayin'?" Josie, a sky blue suit draped over her right arm, stared at herself in the mirror on the closet door.

"Tommy's gone, too," Mary dutifully repeated.

Josie took a moment to process the information, trying to decide if it meant anything. "How you know he's gone?"

"I watched him, mama. The night before last. I pretended I was asleep, but I saw him pack his things into a trunk. It was five o'clock in the morning."

Suspicious, Josie crossed the room and looked into her son-in-law's closet. "It's fulla clothes," she said, dismissing Tommaso from her thoughts.

"He only took a few things."

Ignoring the statement, Josie went back to her daughter's wardrobe, rummaging from outfit to outfit until she discovered a blazing red dress with a flaring skirt and a matching bolero jacket. Pressing it to her waist and the base of her throat, she again turned to her daughter.

"Whatta you think?"

The ensemble looked hideously youthful against Josie Rizzo's sixty-year-old form, but Mary, if she noticed at all, didn't bother to comment. "Mama," she said, "you're three inches taller than me. And fifteen pounds lighter. You can't wear my clothes."

"I gotta do what I gotta do. We'll pin it." Josie's fingers played with the buttons at the top of her cotton nightgown. She wanted to try on the dress, but it'd been more than thirty years since she'd been naked in front of another human being and she hadn't cared for it even then. "I'm gonna take the dress upstairs, try it on. You go find a safety pin."

Mary watched her mother stride across the room and open the door. "Mama," she called.

"Yeah?" Josie stood with her back to her daughter.

"You're holding your head up."

Josie snorted her contempt for the weak thing on the bed. "A girl's gotta do what a girl's gotta do," she said.

"I don't know what that means, mama. I just thought you might have a sore neck."

"I think we need to talk about this tape." Betty slid the edge of a metal spatula under the half-cooked eggs in the pan, dropped in the onions and peppers, flipped the omelet back on itself. "Specifically, about why, in light of the fact that its mere possession is a felony, the tape hasn't been destroyed."

"I'm saving it for *Hard Copy*," Gadd replied. "Whatta you think, Betty, could I get enough for the tape to make it worth spending a couple of years in a federal prison?"

"Is that what you wanna do?" Moodrow set three mugs on the table, then went back for plates, silverware, and napkins.

"No," Gadd replied evenly, "it's not what I *want* to do. What I want to do is go on the classy shows, *Today, Oprah, Donahue*, but they don't pay their guests. I think it has something to do with journalistic integrity." She looked at Moodrow long enough to be sure he wasn't going to offer any help, then went on with what she'd come to say. "I'm twenty-nine, divorced, and living behind an office located above a porn shop." She stopped again, this time to let Betty shovel a third of the omelet and several slices of bacon onto her plate while Moodrow filled her mug. "Many thanks," she said.

"You're welcome." Moodrow filled Betty's mug, then turned to his own. "You were talking about pornography."

Gadd flushed to her ears. "Look, Moodrow, it's easy for a guy with a fat pension and money in the bank to play at being high and mighty. When you went into the job, you were what? Twenty? Twenty-one?"

"Twenty," Moodrow admitted.

"And you've had a steady paycheck all these years, right? Medical insurance, dental, disability. . . ." She waited for his grudging nod before continuing. "Well, I've gotta put it together all by myself, and I can't afford your ethical standards." Drawing a deep breath, she forced herself to settle down. "Look, it's real simple. Fate, for once, has taken a kindly turn and I've got a chance to get the sort of publicity that'll put me in a real office. Not to mention a real apartment with a real kitchen. I didn't ask for it, but now that the opportunity's out there, I'd be a complete jerk if I didn't take advantage." She snatched a forkful of the omelet, held it up to her mouth. "After all, a girl's gotta eat."

Betty raised her coffee mug. "I'll drink to that."

Moodrow started to lift his mug, then set it down on the table. "I'm not gonna drink to an attack on the job. I can't . . ."

"But that's the beauty of it," Gadd announced. Her eyes were wide open, showing white above and below the dark iris. "I'm gonna put all the blame on the feds, say the job got screwed, which, if you remember, it did. That's gonna be one of my main themes."

Moodrow finally raised his mug. "Sounds like you got it covered," he said before drinking. "In fact, it seems like you had it covered before you got here." Pausing, he allowed himself the ghost of a smile. "Unless you expect me to go on *Oprah*, back you up."

Gadd shook her head. "No, the impossible is not on my agenda." She cut through a slice of bacon with the edge of her fork, put it in her mouth, chewed thoughtfully. "I need money," she said after swallowing. "Before I go public. I need a real office, with furniture and filing cabinets and a phone system that'll accept more than one call at a time." Stopping abruptly, she leaned over the table and jabbed her fork in Moodrow's direction. "Face it, Moodrow, sooner or later, Leuten Kitt is gonna talk to the media. He's gonna tell 'em what happened in that apartment. Then, whether I like it or not, they're gonna come to me for the story."

"Okay." Moodrow waved her to a halt. "I understand what you wanna do and I'm not putting you down for it. So why don't we get to the bottom line? What's all this have to do with me?"

"What makes you think it has anything to do with you?" Gadd endured Moodrow's tombstone expression for a few seconds before laughing out loud. "All right, so you got me pinned. But my motives are not as ulterior as you think."

"Well, just how ulterior *are* they?"

Gadd toyed with the food on her plate, stirring it for a moment with the edge of the fork. She was looking for a way to put the essential message that wouldn't have her blushing. Finally, she decided to just get it out there and live with the red ears. "I want us to become partners." Gadd felt the heat rise from her throat to her scalp, tried not to imagine what she must look like to Moodrow. "The idea is for you to put up ten thousand dollars, five thousand of which is a loan to me and which I eventually pay back. Eventually." She raised her head, looked him in the eye. "The money isn't the only thing, Moodrow. I lack street experience and I know it. I also know that I can't afford to fuck up while I'm learning. Do I have to point out the obvious?"

Moodrow shook his head. "No, you're right, but the thing of it is . . ."

"Just let me finish, okay. I can go out there and get money from one of the tabloids. *The Star, The Enquirer, Hard Copy* . . . somebody's gonna be willing to come up with ten grand, maybe a lot more if I can get them bidding against each other. I don't want that. It's demeaning." She gave Betty an imploring look. "Do you understand what I'm saying here, Betty?"

"Yeah, I do." Betty's smile was so warm it threatened to curdle the half-and-half.

"How about you, Moodrow?" Gadd turned to face him. "Do you understand?"

"Yeah, but I'll have to think about it." Without warning, he burst into a giggle. "I've been a cheap motherfucker for so long," he admitted, "I don't know if I could hold my hand steady long enough to write the check." He laid his fork on his plate, pushed the plate toward the center of the table. "There's a third way, of course. But I don't know if you wanna hear about it."

"Does that mean I don't *have* to?"

Moodrow grinned. "You could always find Tommaso. He's got three million that doesn't belong to him."

"I don't have to find him, Moodrow." Gadd shoved her chair back and crossed her legs. "Because I already know where he is." She glanced at her watch. "We've got an appointment in exactly one hour and fifty-five minutes."

"You're telling me he hasn't left town?"

"Uh-uh. Yesterday, maybe an hour before Jilly made his appearance, I picked up a message from Tommaso. He wrote that he was booked on a midnight flight to South America and he wanted me to come out to his motel and humiliate him before he left." She held up a finger, cocked her head to one side. "I didn't call him, didn't think he had anything to do with Jilly or Carmine. The only reason I sent him E-mail was because I was bored. But, last night, after I saw the video, I got him on the phone and talked him into changing his reservations."

Moodrow rapped a knuckle on the tabletop. "Gadd, you tell me what you told Tommaso, word for word, and I'll sign the check right now."

"Not a prayer." Gadd's solemn head shake was softened considerably by the lopsided grin on her face. "We're talking privileged information here. *Client* confidentiality. So to speak."

"What's it like out, huh?" Josie gathered the sides of the dress and pinched them in tight. "You always watchin' the television. Is it gonna rain?" Releasing the material with her right hand, she took a safety pin out of her mouth and pinned up the left side of the garment.

"Al Roker said it was gonna be sunny and cooler." Mary was back on the edge of the bed, staring at her mother. Trying to figure it out.

"Al Roker," Josie sneered. "Like he was your boyfriend."

"Please, mama, he's black. And he's fat."

Josie turned to her daughter. "Looks okay, right?" The red dress, meant to fall to mid calf, was riding just above her knees.

"Mama, you didn't even shave your legs. And you're wearing black sneakers."

"Nobody gonna mind." She turned her back to her daughter. "Here, zip me up."

Mary got the zipper midway between her mother's shoulder blades before before she surrendered to nature and went for another safety pin. "You're too big around the chest."

Josie didn't respond. She was looking at her flattened breasts in the mirror. Amazed at how perfectly round they were, like a pair of large, shallow bowls.

"Why can't I talk to you?" Mary said. She was standing behind her mother, pinning the zipper. "We have to talk."

"Why?" Josie, as she slipped into the bolero jacket, was genuinely puzzled.

"We have to decide what we're gonna do." Mary sat down on the bed. "And what about Gildo? He's in jail."

"Gildo!" Josie sucked her upper lip into her mouth. Ann's survival was the fly in the ointment, there was no getting away from it, but Carmine's death more than made up for Gildo's failure. There was no getting away from that, either. "Gildo gotta take care of himself."

"He could get the death penalty. From the feds."

"So whatta ya wanna do, break him out?" Josie walked across the room and yanked her black leather bag off a chair by the door. "Gildo's a man," she said, fully expecting her daughter to understand.

"Mama, when are you coming back?"

Josie stopped in the doorway, but didn't turn around. She started to speak, then changed her mind, crossing the living room to the front door, fumbling with the locks for a minute before charging down the stairs. When she found the door to Carmine's duplex on the ground floor open, she realized, for the first time, that Rose Stettecase was in mourning. Josie looked at the women gathered in the foyer, all of whom were staring back at her. She recognized several faces, the wives of Carmine's *paisons*, and looked around for their husbands before recalling that their husbands were either dead or in custody. As were the husbands of *all* the women in the room.

Well, that was too bad. Josie had nothing against any of these women, not even Rose. If there'd been another way . . .

She turned away from them, opened the front door, and stepped onto the sidewalk. A light breeze curled against her legs, the sensation odd enough to make her look down for a moment. Then she straightened, pushing out her flattened breasts, lifting her chin into the air until she was looking at the world along the length of her nose.

Moodrow was actually grateful for the traffic on the Long Island Expressway. He was inching forward, almost literally, a mile or so from Woodhaven Boulevard, trying to force his emotions to follow the car's example. Eventually he'd come down, find a low to match the high inspired by the events of the prior day, but for right now he was still flying. He felt powerful, confident, like he could do anything he wanted to do. Like he could snap his fingers and the wall of hot metal surrounding his Chevrolet would disappear.

Meanwhile, assuming Tommaso was actually sitting on Carmine's buy money, there was every reason to believe he was armed. And if he'd stolen the money from Carmine, he was crazy as well. The problem, for Moodrow, was what *kind* of crazy.

"I got lucky out there."

Moodrow glanced across the seat. Gadd was wearing Betty's black leather coat. Its soft luster neatly matched the black eye shadow and dark lipstick on her face. "Say that again?"

"Yesterday, when Jilly showed up, I was out in the stairwell. You know, having a cigarette." Laughing softly, she pulled out a half-empty pack of Newports. "Speaking of which, I appear to be a nicotine junkie. Again." She cracked the window, let in a stream of warm air. "Suppose I was in that apartment," she said, "instead of on the stairs. I would've heard Jilly coming, because I kept the chain on whenever I was inside, but I would've had to shoot *through* Leuten Kitt to get to Jilly. I don't know if I could've done it."

"What's the difference? Whether you tell Sappone to shoot Kitt or threaten to shoot him yourself, it's the same bluff."

"The difference is that . . ." Gadd flicked her ash out the window, then looked over at Moodrow. "The difference is that I would've had to look into his eyes. Leuten's, I mean. I would've had to look into his eyes while I threatened to kill him."

Moodrow eased the car onto the exit ramp and stepped on the accelerator. "Actually," he declared, "if Jilly had found the chain on, he'd have smelled out the trap and killed Leuten in the hallway. So I guess you were lucky twice." He stopped for the light at the end of the ramp. "Or twice as lucky."

They rode for several miles in silence, heading south toward the airport and Tommaso's motel, the First Flight, on Rockaway Boulevard. Moodrow, his mind back to the problem at hand, was trying to decide whether Gadd should talk her way inside, see if Tommaso was armed before they made their move. He didn't like the idea of Gadd in the room by herself, even for a few seconds, but if they kicked in the door as soon as Tommaso cracked it open and he had a gun in his hand . . . The biggest problem was they had no right to be there. Tommaso, unlike Jilly Sappone, was just another citizen. How would they explain a public shoot-out? What, for instance, would they say if Tommaso *didn't* have Carmine's missing millions? If an innocent bystander took a round?

He was about to voice his misgivings, when Gadd said, "Do you think it's done now? Is it over?"

"Ya know, Gadd, you're being very inscrutable this morning. I don't have any idea what you're talkin' about."

"Yeah, you do."

Moodrow shrugged. "Okay, so I do. What of it?" She was talking about Theresa Kalkadonis, the sum total of what they'd done for and to her.

"I was asking if we were through it. Now that Sappone's facing the death sentence."

"Look . . ." What Moodrow wanted to do, in the worst way, was change the subject, talk about Tommaso the Timid, decide on a basic strategy. And if Ginny Gadd hadn't actually been there, if she hadn't jumped out of the car, run up to the still form by the side of the road, changing the subject was exactly what he would have done. But the way he saw it now, she'd paid for *his* mistake; she was still paying. "If it was over," he finally said, "you wouldn't be talking about it."

Gadd tossed her cigarette out the window. "You've got a point," she admitted. "But it feels different now." She looked up at Moodrow, the exotic makeup belying her sincerity. "I feel like I'm ready to live with it."

"As if you had a choice." Moodrow ran his fingers through his close-cropped hair. "As for me, it isn't the first time I fucked up, just the first time I witnessed the consequences, so . . . Look, Gadd, the thing of it is that I don't plan to jump off a bridge, and I'm not having nightmares, and I'm giving serious thought to your business proposition."

Gadd smiled, touched Moodrow's arm. "That's good enough for me," she said. "Now, about Tommaso, the first thing is no guns. If I think he's armed, I'm gonna back away, let the cops handle it."

Moodrow banged the steering wheel with the palm of his hand. "Jesus," he said, "I wish you'd stop reading my mind."

Fifteen minutes later, Gadd was knocking softly on the door of Unit 14 at the First Flight Motor Inn. There was no peephole, but she was certain she saw the drapes rustle a moment before the door swung back.

"If you dare to address me," she said as she squared her shoulders and stepped into the room, "you'll pay with your flesh." Her eyes dropped to Tommaso's hands, finding them empty, then jumped to his face, registering his bald head, receding chin, and happy smirk at a glance. "Moodrow," she called over her shoulder, "c'mon in."

Tommaso stopped grinning when Moodrow strode through the door, spun him around, and thoroughly frisked him. "Are you a cop?" he asked.

"Worse," Moodrow replied evenly. He stood behind Tommaso, one hand on the man's back, pinning him to the wall.

"Let's see," Gadd said, "what have we here?" She walked directly to the closet and dragged out a large trunk. "Christ, it's not even locked."

Moodrow looked over, saw the money and the revolver lying on top of it. He wondered, briefly, what he'd do if it wasn't mob money and therefore a death sentence for anyone possessing it. "Son of a bitch," he said, "you really went and did it." He spun Tommaso around. "You have any idea how many people died because you stole that money?"

Tommaso replied by licking his lips. "Are you gonna give me the third degree?" he asked.

"What about the cops, the ones who died on that street? Do they matter? What about your father?" Moodrow, who'd been no more than curious when he'd begun the questions, felt a rush of anger so intense he literally trembled from head to toe.

"Don't hurt him."

Moodrow turned at the sound of Gadd's voice. He looked at her as if she'd just stepped out of one of the cheap prints on the wall. "I'm not gonna hurt him," he finally said. "No, I've got something better in mind. You like to play games?"

Once they got down to it, the production didn't take all that long to stage. They worked in silence, nodding to each other from time to time, until Moodrow finally picked up the phone.

"That's an awful lot of money." Gadd gestured toward the bed.

"True." Moodrow paused to admire their handiwork. Tommaso's hands and feet were cuffed to the head and footboards. He was naked except for a white bath towel that'd been drawn through his legs and pinned like a diaper. The money, all of it, was spread over his body like a blanket. "You wanna take it? Maybe retire to the Caribbean, see how fast you can spend the loot?"

"Uh-uh. For the reason we talked about on the way over here." Gadd worked her tongue over her teeth. "Plus, it's blood money. There's blood all over it."

Moodrow grunted assent as he punched the number of the central desk at One Police Plaza into the phone, then worked himself from switchboard to switchboard until he got Inspector Cohen on the line.

"Yeah, Inspector, I'm fine. How 'bout yourself?" He paused to listen for a moment, then nodded. "And Ginny Gadd's fine, too. In fact, she's right here next to me and she wants to speak to you. If you've got the time." Moodrow passed the phone to his partner, said, "Break a leg."

"Inspector, how are you?" Gadd looked over at Tommaso. He was staring back at her, his look sorrowful and joyous at the same time, an expression she'd never seen before and which she would have thought impossible a moment before. "Look, I've got a present for you, a three-million-dollar present to be exact." She stopped abruptly. "That's right, Inspector. The money is—I mean, *was*— Carmine Stettecase's. And now it's gonna be yours. Yours and the job's, of course." Gadd, smiling softly, again paused to listen. "Actually," she finally said, "there's nothing we really want. Right *now*. As for the future . . . well, I guess we're just gonna have to rely on your personal integrity. That's why I'm calling you, instead of a sleazebag reporter."

Josie Rizzo plowed through lower Manhattan like a supercharged reaper through a field of corn. Once she got started, she found she couldn't stop, couldn't slow down long enough to enjoy the dumb-founded expressions until all her customary stops were made. She hit Patti Barbano's Mulberry Street *salumeria* first, striding up to the counter, spinning on her left heel, marching back out the door with-out saying a word. Then Ira's dairy on Houston Street, Tony's *pastic-ceria* on LaGuardia Place, working west, then north, then east again, demanding they view her in all her glory.

It didn't matter if they thought her mad, if they failed to catch so much as a glimmer of what she felt. Life, for them, was measured out in loaves of bread, pounds of fish; their opinions meant nothing. No, what was important was that they see and remember. Josie Rizzo was nothing, a mere woman, matriarch by default of a family on the decline, but she'd brought down Carmine Stettecase and all his sol-diers. She'd destroyed a kingdom.

By the time she came out of Chu Wen's Chinese laundry on Tenth and University some two hours later, Josie was fully satisfied, yet disappointed at the same time. The thought of returning to her shabby apartment in Carmine's brownstone was yanking her chin down into her chest, turning her nose to the sidewalk. Still, there was nowhere else to go. And maybe that was where she belonged, anyway, in that house with all the widows. Maybe this brief moment was all she was entitled to.

"Mama?"

Josie, shocked, stared up through her eyelashes at her daughter, Mary. "Whatta you doin' outside? You don't go outside."

"I'm on my way to see Gildo," Mary explained. "Somebody has to get him a lawyer, see if he's okay."

"Maybe that husband you got. . . ."

"Tommaso's gone. I already told you that."

Sensing a trace of pity in Mary's voice, Josie peered up through her lashes, saw the same trace in her daughter's eyes and wondered at Mary's ignorance. For a moment, she was convinced that none of them, not one of the widows, really understood, but then she saw the two men walking toward her from Fifth Avenue and she knew that wasn't true. They were big men, wearing identical blue jogging outfits, and they were staring straight at her as they came. Not with the amazement of strolling pedestrians, but with the dead, unblinking focus of true predators.

"*I* did it," she shouted at her daughter. "Everything. Gildo worked for *me*."

"Gildo needs help, mama." Mary's tone was soothing, but insistent. "We need money to hire a lawyer." She groaned. "And I don't even know where Tommaso kept the checkbook."

The two men were being paced by a long black sedan. Josie noted the Jersey plates and slowly lifted her head. "Save yourself," she said to Mary. "Forget about Gildo."

"How can you say that after all these years?" Mary's lips curled into a stubborn pout. "And why won't you help me?"

The taller of the two men lifted his jacket and yanked at the small automatic tucked behind his waistband an instant before the second man did the same. Josie put her hands on her hips, lifted her chin proudly. She held the pose for a few seconds, then, without warning, slammed her palms into her daughter's chest, knocking Mary to the ground.

"This ain't for you," she said.